Praise for Lyn Cote and her novels

"*Finally Home*, by Lyn Cote, has series written
all over it…With reunions, romance and floods,
there's never a dull moment. This is possibly
Ms. Cote's best yet for Love Inspired."
—*Romantic Times BOOKreviews*

"*Finally Found*, by Lyn Cote, blends strong
writing with an interesting cast to create an
entertaining, memorable story."
—*Romantic Times BOOKreviews*

"Lyn Cote's lively romance engages the reader."
—*Romantic Times BOOKreviews* on
The Preacher's Daughter

"*Loving Constance* is a superb example of
compelling fiction from a master storyteller."
—*Romantic Times BOOKreviews*

LYN COTE
Finally Home

Finally Found

Steeple
Hill®

Published by Steeple Hill Books™

STEEPLE HILL BOOKS

Steeple Hill®

Recycling programs for this product may not exist in your area.

ISBN-13: 978-0-373-65132-0

FINALLY HOME AND FINALLY FOUND

FINALLY HOME
Copyright © 2001 by Lyn Cote

FINALLY FOUND
Copyright © 2002 by Lyn Cote

www.SteepleHill.com

Printed in U.S.A.

CONTENTS

Books by Lyn Cote

Love Inspired

Never Alone
New Man in Town
Hope's Garden
*Finally Home
*Finally Found
The Preacher's Daughter
**His Saving Grace
**Testing His Patience
**Loving Constance
Blessed Bouquets
  "Wed by a Prayer"

*Bountiful Blessings
**Sisters of the Heart

Love Inspired Suspense

*Dangerous Season
*Dangerous Game
*Dangerous Secrets

*Harbor Intrigue

Love Inspired Historical

Her Captain's Heart

LYN COTE

Lyn now lives in Wisconsin with her husband, her real-life hero. They raised a son and daughter together. Lyn has spent her adult life as a schoolteacher, a full-time mom and now a writer. Lyn's favorite food is watermelon. Realizing that this delicacy is only available one season out of the year, Lyn's friends keep up a constant flow of "watermelon" gifts—candles, wood carvings, pillows, cloth bags, candy and on and on. Lyn also enjoys crocheting and knitting, watching *Wheel of Fortune* and doing lunch with friends. By the way, Lyn's last name is pronounced "Coty."

Lyn enjoys hearing from readers, who can contact her at P.O. Box 864, Woodruff, WI 54568 or by e-mail at l.cote@juno.com.

FINALLY HOME

Forgive us our trespasses, as we forgive those
who trespass against us.
—*The Lord's Prayer*

With love to my sweet sister, Carole; with thanks to Pat Birkett-Roby, my friend and the Prairie Cook, who inspired Hannah's career.
And thanks to Cousin Jane, who remembered party games I'd forgotten!

Prologue

"That can't be our sister!" Doree shut her large blue eyes, then opened them again.

Spring turned gracefully in her seat at the restaurant table to view the woman who'd just entered. "Oh, my, what has Hannah done?"

"Thank you for that characteristic understatement." Doree continued to gawk. "Aliens must have sent an impostor in Hannah's place. She's wearing lime green!"

"Designer lime green," Spring added.

"You would notice that."

"*Anyone* could see that," Spring answered without offense.

Hannah Kirkland strode toward the table across a thick teal carpet. Both her sisters looked just as she had pictured them. Spring in a blue linen suit of impeccable cut. And in spite of the first-class restaurant setting, Doree in jeans and a UW Madison red-and-white

Badger T-shirt. With a confidence she didn't feel, Hannah sat down, straightened the hem on the short skirt of her new linen suit, then checked the neckline of its ivory silk blouse. She tossed her head, letting her fifty-dollar haircut swing, then settle into its new, sophisticated style.

Only then did she speak. "Doree, I heard every word you said. When are you going to learn to lower your voice? Now close your lips. You look like a largemouth bass."

"Well," the redoubtable Doree replied, "do you know what you look like?"

Spring touched Doree's arm. "Hannah looks like an attractive young woman, just as she always has."

Grateful to Spring for her kindness, Hannah blinked back tears. She'd known exactly how both her sisters would react. No surprises. Spring, tactful. Doree, outspoken. But something in Spring's gaze caught Hannah's eye. Was Spring worried?

"How are you, dear?" Spring asked in her soft, caring voice.

"I am better than I was." Hannah lifted her chin.

Both Spring and Doree stared at her.

"What does that mean?" Doree asked. "What gives, dear sweet Honey? I thought you'd still be wearing your sensible bun and dove gray suit or maybe black for mourning dear Edward."

"Stop right now." Spring glared at Doree.

Hannah sighed. "It's all right, Spring. Our little sister is just being her brash self." She'd taken great pains with her appearance today, and her haircut, makeup and trendy clothing rivaled Spring's ever polished style. It all made Hannah feel as though she were masquerading as someone else. But after breaking up with her fiancé this spring, she had needed to take some positive action or give in to despair. Something she wouldn't do!

"Doree was raised to be polite and kind," Spring said sternly.

Hannah sat more comfortably in her seat, trying to relax. At the end after months of doubt, breaking the engagement had almost been a relief. More and more, she'd discovered Edward wasn't the caring man she'd imagined him to be. In fact, she'd begun to suspect she'd created her own perception of him, which had nothing to do with the opinionated man she'd discovered under her nose. "It's all right. I've been through a lot in the last few months, but the pain was less than I thought it would be. Really."

Spring nodded, then pushed her long golden hair over her shoulder. With arms folded skeptically, Doree watched them both.

Hannah noted an edge to Spring's voice. She'd have to get a private word with her, but now she decided was the time to implement another change. "One thing, though, I'd really like to leave my nickname, Honey, behind me. Would you please call me Hannah from now on?"

Doree and Spring exchanged startled glances. The waiter came to take their drink order, then left them.

Before Doree could put in any more provocative

remarks, Hannah spoke up. "Lunch is on me today." She opened the large gold-embossed menu. "I'm ordering lobster." From behind the tall impressive menu, she couldn't see, but she sensed her sisters' surprise.

"Works for me." Doree put her unopened menu on the array of silver and china. "Make that two. A poor college student like me has a hard time remembering what any shellfish tastes like, much less lobster. I can taste the drawn butter already. Yum."

A moment passed while Spring perused the menu. Hannah let the soothing atmosphere of the luxurious restaurant—the murmur of voices, the clink of ice and the occasional chuckle—work on her, relax her. The waiter returned with their iced teas.

Hannah smiled at him. "Two lobster luncheons with baked potatoes. Double butter and sour cream for my younger sister. Spring?"

Spring closed her menu. "The Caesar salad please."

"Large?" The waiter held his pen poised.

"No, small."

The waiter accepted the three menus and hurried away.

Hannah was splurging by ordering the lobster. She'd always been the one who had to watch her waistline. Spring seemed able to exist on air, while Doree's metabolism burned calories like a blast furnace.

"Sheesh!" Doree groaned. "Are you ever going to develop an appetite?"

"Probably before you develop adult manners," Spring replied without heat.

Doree leaned forward to continue the tiff.

Hannah held up her hand like a referee. "I invited you here to discuss Mom and Dad, not my wardrobe or Spring's appetite. That's the agenda. Stick to it, Doree, or you'll be paying your own check."

Doree wrinkled her tanned nose. Her short blond hair had been nearly bleached white by the summer sun. "Take it easy. I'll be good. It's just so much fun to get a rise out of you two."

Hannah ignored Doree's flippant comment. Doree had a good heart. With her first year of college under her belt, she'd spent the summer working with children in the Head-Start program here in Milwaukee. But as the baby of the family, Doree wanted it both ways. She insisted she be taken seriously while at times still acting as the family rebel and tease.

Spring fidgeted with the gold chain around her neck. This uncharacteristic sign of nervousness in Spring held Hannah's attention. Hannah discreetly eyed her older sister. Spring, in charge of community relations at Milwaukee's renowned Botanical Gardens, never seemed ill at ease, but she definitely was today.

After taking a deep breath, Spring returned Hannah's gaze, then asked, "Do you know something about Mother and Father we don't?"

This question startled Hannah. "No, their plans and medical conditions are about the same."

"I was afraid you had bad news for us," Doree mumbled in a subdued tone. "I thought Mom's leukemia had started up again." She lowered her gaze to the white linen tablecloth.

Hannah's stomach tightened with guilt. "I'm sorry I worried you," she murmured with real regret. Was this what was concerning Spring?

Spring took a sip of iced tea, then held her glass in front of her mouth as though concealing her expression. "I was worried, too, but I've also been worried about their making this move to Petite Portage, especially now that Dad's heart is giving him trouble."

Hannah nodded. "I have, too."

Doree sat back and challenged them both with a tart smile. "Why? I think this is just what Mom needs. The pressure of being the perfect pastor's wife of a large congregation—"

"Father has been under the same pressure." Spring set her glass down.

"Both of them needed a change." Like setting lids on two simmering pots, Hannah extended a hand palm-down toward each sister. This had always been her role, the middle child, the peacemaker. "But change can be very difficult on people nearing retirement."

"I read an article about that in an applied psych class." Doree nodded with a serious expression. "Moving can really stress people."

"Exactly. So I've decided to go to Petite Portage and help them get settled." Hannah observed her sisters for their reactions.

"Can you get away?" Spring nervously rearranged the salt and pepper shakers, not making eye contact.

Hannah studied Spring. Her beautiful and intelligent sister always kept her own counsel. What else was she keeping under wraps today? "Yes, I can fax in my column from anywhere. And I've already talked to someone who wants to sublet my apartment for the remainder of this year. I called Mom this week. She and Dad are leaving tomorrow. They are going on a few side trips, then they plan to move into a room with a kitchenette at a local motel for a few weeks until their house is done."

"What about your food styling shoots?" Glancing up, Spring asked another practical question. "Don't you have several food photos to do for that special corn oil promotion?"

"I'm going to arrange a few field shoots in Petite Portage, letting the corn oil company advertising team make use of some local color. I thought I could use Mom's new kitchen. Maybe visit a cornfield—"

"Yeah, a little town in central Wisconsin will really jazz things up." Doree smirked.

Fingering her neck chain again, Spring ignored Doree. "When will the new house be done?"

"Their contract specifies three weeks from now, August thirty-first, but Dad mentioned something about delays—"

"Uh-oh." Doree sounded the alarm.

"Exactly." Hannah leaned her elbows on the table.

"Someone needs to make certain our good-natured parents don't get taken advantage of."

Looking more concerned, Spring nodded. "I didn't agree with their signing with such a small builder—"

"That's because you didn't meet Guthrie Thomas!" Doree's face crinkled with amusement. "What a hunk! Blond. Muscles. Wow. He could build something for me any day of the week!"

Both Hannah and Spring frowned at Doree, who chuckled, then shrugged.

"Where will you stay?" Spring probed.

"I asked Dad to reserve me a room at the local motel also," Hannah replied.

"Thank you, Hannah." Spring smiled, and her face relaxed momentarily. "I appreciate your doing this. But if you need help, just call. I'll come right out."

The conversation paused while the waiter brought a basket of hard rolls and filled their glasses. He smiled and proceeded to the next table.

Spring caught Doree's eye, then Hannah's, then glanced down. "I hate to bring up another serious concern, but I think this is the time to discuss it."

Hannah braced herself for more bad news. Now they'd find out what caused Spring's fidgeting.

Still hesitating, Spring rearranged the butter dish and sugar bowl. "With Doree leaving to go back to school in Madison and your going to be with Mother and Father, we may not be together again until Thanksgiving or even Christmas."

"What is it?" Doree picked up a crusty roll and tore it in two.

Spring continued in her soft voice, "Last June after Mother was diagnosed with leukemia, I started reading as much as I could about the disease. I wanted to be able to understand what was happening."

Hannah nodded, encouraging Spring.

"So?" Doree prompted.

Spring sighed. "You remember how the doctor had the three of us tested as possible donors, in case Mother needed a bone marrow transplant?"

"Yeah?" Doree slathered half her roll with butter.

"Didn't it bother you that we were Mother's only known blood relatives?" Finally, Spring made eye contact with both of them.

Doree paused. She dumped the roll on the plate. "Yes, it did."

Hannah nodded. "None of us matched." The pain of that memory squeezed inside her, making her catch a breath. She recognized the same deep distress on the stricken faces of her two sisters. Their mother had needed them, and they'd been helpless!

"What are you driving at?" Doree asked. "Do you think we should try to find Mom's natural parents?"

"So I'm not the only one who thought of starting a search?" Spring asked sounding relieved.

Doree pursued it. "But wouldn't Mom's natural parents be dead by now? I mean, Mom was born in 1945."

Spring shook her head. "That means Mom's only in

her fifties. Her adoptive parents both died early, before they even retired. But her natural parents would probably be in their seventies, and they could still be alive and active."

"But Mother had always refused to look into her past, her adoption," Hannah objected. "She said she'd never wanted to be disloyal to her adoptive parents!" The idea of going against her mother's wishes startled her most. "She was even upset with the doctor when he suggested she should search for blood relatives."

"I realize that, but I think Mother's leukemia makes the difference. What if this period of remission ends a few years from now and what if her leukemia progresses to the point where we need a match? What do we do then?" Spring's gaze lingered on Hannah.

Her elbow on the table, Doree rested her chin on the back of her hand and considered Spring. "You mean, Spring, the perfect daughter, that we should go against our mother's wishes?"

"That is exactly what I mean." Spring pulled her shoulders back, sitting up straighter.

"As I live and breathe." Doree shook her head as if she couldn't believe her ears.

Hannah waved an impatient hand toward her younger sister. This wasn't time for teasing. "You mean without telling Mom or even Dad?"

Spring moved forward in her chair. "Yes. If you are there while they're moving in—"

"Right!" Doree grinned. "You could look for Mom's

adoption papers. See if any names or places were listed."

Hannah frowned. She understood Spring's reasoning, but doing what she asked went against everything they'd been taught by their parents. She gazed at Spring and recognized the same worry and doubt in her eyes. "I don't like going behind Mom's back."

"I wouldn't suggest it, either, under normal circumstances." Spring's voice had thickened with emotion.

"But it's for Mom's good and Dad's," Doree said. "They've been married thirty-five years. Moving is stressful, but not as much as losing a life partner!"

Wishing Doree hadn't voiced those awful words, Hannah stared at her hands. "I will have to take some time to think and pray about this."

Doree piped up. "Hey, I've already started—"

"We'll all pray about it." Spring warned Doree with a pointed look. "But it will be your decision, Hannah. I wouldn't ask you to do something you thought was wrong."

Hannah nodded. She knew Spring was being kind, but the reality of the situation was that she alone would carry the burden of this decision, one that might violate her conscience and could mean life or death to their mother.

Chapter One

Two weeks later, with Dad's hand-drawn map on the seat beside her, Hannah glanced ahead and made a right turn at Humphreys Road. Her parents' future home should be about three-fourths of a mile ahead on the right. After another week of cloudy weather and heavy rain, today had dawned bright and warm.

On her way to Petite Portage, she'd chosen to take the back roads through kelly-green cornfields and sage-green cabbage fields. She'd stopped for lunch at a small hometown restaurant. There, in a lively conversation with the cook, she'd picked up two new recipes, one for preparing wild pheasant and one for wild duck. They'd make great topics in her fall columns.

Now on her way down Humphreys Road, Hannah passed three widely spaced houses, two newer ranch styles and one old farmhouse, then came to a dead end. She stopped, studied the map again, turned around. This time she drove like a snail, keeping her eyes to the left side of road. She found it, a muddy gravel track without a house in progress in sight. She turned in. At its end, she stopped.

Oh, no. Her mind repeated this phrase several times. With a sinking heart, she put her car in "park" and got out. Crows squawked overhead. Beneath her feet, soft ground under grass, then ahead, mud with a path of boards spanning it. A field of mud with truck-tire tracks carved through it in a deep criss-cross pattern, stray hillocks of muddy grass, stacks of lumber under heavy blue plastic tarps. A concrete foundation.

No house.

Just a foundation.

"I'm dreaming this," she whispered in the quiet of the country. "This house is supposed to be complete in eight days."

Things like this take time. Edward's irritating voice echoed in her memory and set her teeth on edge. How many times had she endured hearing Edward say that galling phrase? Over the past three years, she'd put up with too much too long. Never again.

She could imagine all the builder's polite excuses. *Bad weather slowed construction. Building materials shortage. Had trouble getting quality workmen.* Each phrase turned up the heat higher under her simmering temper. "Guthrie Thomas," she growled to the place where her parents' house should have been. "I am not buying any excuses. My parents paid good money and signed a contract in good faith with you. If you couldn't fulfill the contract, you should have released them and let someone else build it."

Edward's disembodied voice interrupted. *But, Honey, things can't always run on your schedule.*

"Shut up, Edward!" Hannah declared. "And don't call me Honey! I'm not sweet, little Honey Kirkland anymore!"

She charged back to her fire-engine-red sport utility vehicle, got in and slammed the door. She started the car, then threw it into reverse. Mud flew up around her tires. At the road's edge, she ground to a halt, cast a hasty glance each way, then shot onto the deserted road. She shoved the gearshift back into "drive" and took off with squealing tires.

The powerful motor under the hood charged her with adrenaline, momentum. Consigned to the unappetizing past, she'd left Edward and her VW bug behind in Milwaukee. The last fourteen months had been the most difficult of her twenty-five years. A broken engagement, then…. "I was a fool, a blind little wimp," she muttered.

With only a sustained pause, she slid by the stop sign at the empty crossroads, then barreled down the two-lane highway into town. She blew past the "Reduced Speed Ahead" sign and didn't slow until she saw the city limits sign, "Petite Portage—Population 2356—Speed Limit 25 M.P.H."

Still pushing the speed limit, she swept through town looking for the small motel where her parents were staying. Within minutes, she slowed on Front Street. Ahead, a red-and-white painted sign announced Hanson's Cozy Motel with a green neon Yes over Vacancy. The motel, a one-story white building with six red doors in a row, also had an attached restaurant, Hanson's Cozy Café.

Hannah had found her parents' temporary home. She rolled to a stop in front of the motel office. She'd barely stopped and exited her vehicle before a large woman in blue polyester stretch pants and a hot pink T-shirt that proclaimed her to be the World's Best Grandma hurried out of the office.

"You must be the Kirkland girl! I'm Mrs. Fink, Lila Fink, the owner. Welcome to Petite! You're just going to love it here! Your parents are great people. I knew it the moment I laid eyes on them!"

The flow of words sloshed over Hannah. She floundered in the sensation of being swept up in a rushing current. She said the first words that came to mind. "But this is Hanson's Cozy Motel."

The large woman shook with laughter. "Sure it is! Would anyone stay at Fink's Cozy Motel?"

Hannah could think of no reply to this, but Lila efficiently produced a plastic-tagged key, then led her to a small room. Hannah assessed the room, and her mood slipped another notch. Obviously Mrs. Fink had decorated the Cozy Motel thirty years ago. Avocado green and gold vinyl reigned supreme. But the off-white paint on the walls gleamed, and the brown shag carpet had been steam-cleaned recently.

Lila pressed a key with a bronze plastic tag printed with a large two into Hannah's hand. "I'll let you get settled. Then we can get to know each other."

"My parents?" Hannah prompted.

"They can't wait to see you. They told me, 'Honey is coming today.'"

"Where are they?" Hannah asked, trying to hold her own against the flow of words.

"They're at the church. They spend most of their days there. I only get to talk to them in the café in the mornings—"

"Where's the church?" Hannah edged toward the door.

"It's easy to find. Everything in Petite is easy to find." Lila chuckled. "Just go back up Front Street and turn right, go about half a mile, you can't miss it. I walk there on nice Sunday mornings—"

Escaping, Hannah smiled, waved and jumped into her car. Back up Front Street, she drove half a block then turned right. She wasn't surprised that her parents spent their days at the church. Good grief! Mrs. Fink rattled on more than Edward's mother, and that woman could talk the hind leg off a horse!

"This isn't happening," Hannah told the steering wheel. She pressed down on the gas pedal.

Instantly, a police siren 'burped' just behind her. A look in her rearview mirror confirmed a police car nearly touched her rear bumper. "Where did he come from? Thin air?" She pulled over.

A tall, lanky police officer who didn't look old enough to shave appeared at her window. "Hi, do you need any help?"

Of all the words she might have imagined this junior office asking, these weren't them. "What?"

He pointed back to where she had turned. "You were driving kind of fast and I didn't recognize your car. I thought you might need help, directions or something." He gazed at her, hope in his eyes.

"Aren't you a little young to be a police officer?" She asked feeling like Alice after she'd passed through the looking glass.

"I'm eighteen and I'm going to go to college this fall in law enforcement. But my dad had to testify in court at the county seat today, so he deputized me to keep an eye on things. It's been pretty boring. Are you sure you don't need—"

"I'm just driving down to the church."

He hung his head like a scolded puppy. "Okay."

"May I leave?"

"Sure. Just wanted to help." Mournful, he took a step back.

She moved the gearshift into drive and headed on. "Good grief!" She had the sensation that she'd driven a bit too far that day. Around the bend maybe?

The white steeple loomed ahead. As she pulled into the small parking lot, she gathered the scattered pieces of her purpose for coming to the church. Mrs. Fink and Officer Peach-fuzz had thrown her a bit off stride, but she wouldn't take excuses. She'd find out from her parents where the builder was and she'd have a talk with him today regardless of what her parents might say. The house should be nearly built by now, not barely begun.

If the builder couldn't deliver on time, she'd do everything she could to persuade her parents to enforce the contract deadline, no excuses. She wasn't going to let any man give her the runaround, as Edward had, ever again.

When she parked and slipped out of the car, the sound of hammer on wood greeted her. Well, something was getting built in Petite today!

Hannah recognized her parents' ten-year-old blue sedan parked beside the quaint one-story classic white prairie chapel. Good. They were here, as reported by Mrs. Fink. Hannah edged around the grassy side of the church, following the noise of the hammering. The squishy, soaked grass underfoot wet her shoes. She tried to ignore it.

Looking skyward, she noted the church's roof had been stripped of shingles. One patch of new plywood looked out of place above the period building, but the majority of the roof looked old and discolored with water damage. What was going on?

She halted, stunned by the man she saw straddling the peak of the roof facing the steeple.

Definitely the most perfect male she'd ever seen in

real life. He wore no shirt. Tanned brown, his chest, shoulders and arms bulged with muscles. Real muscles, not the kind a man got from working out at a gym. His firm legs stretched against the tight blue denim covering them. Heaven in blue jeans.

She watched him lift the billed cap off his head and swipe his forehead with his arm, obviously brushing away the sweat on his brow. Sunlight glinted on golden waves.

Hannah swallowed with difficulty.

The man settled the hat on his head and eased up. Cautiously he balanced himself until he squatted, perfectly poised. Was he going into the steeple?

Feeling her pulse racing, Hannah wished he'd get down from the roof. He was making her nervous. Shouldn't he be wearing a safety harness or something?

A flicker of movement caught her eye. She followed the man's gaze and saw, in the opening at the bottom of the steeple, her father reaching out.

"No! Daddy, don't!" Her shout echoed in the stillness.

The man on the peak lost his balance. He tried to catch himself on a roofing rack. He couldn't.

Hannah shrieked.

Chapter Two

Horrified, she watched the man sliding down the side of the bare roof on his rump. He hit the gutter. It launched him forward.

Hannah screamed and closed her eyes.

He landed with a sickening thud facedown in the nearby grass.

She rushed to his side and knelt. With shaking fingers, she took his wrist to check for a pulse. His heart was still beating, racing, in fact.

"Oh!" Her mother ran toward her. "Is he all right?"

"He's got a pulse." *Thank you, God!*

"Is he breathing?" her father shouted as he came around a corner of the church.

Hannah rested her hand on the man's broad back. No. He wasn't taking breaths. "Call nine one one!"

The strong back under her hand shuddered. The man rolled over. He spit out a wad of grass and sputtered, trying to rid himself of green grass particles in his mouth. Grass clippings stuck to his face and hair. His eyes opened. Grass matted his thick eyelashes.

"Oh, Guthrie!" her mother exclaimed. "You're alive!"

Forcing down her budding hysteria, Hannah turned to her mother and caught her hands. "Sit down and lower your head. You're as white as a sheet!"

Mom obeyed, but she gasped, "You look as white as a ghost yourself. You sit down, too."

Concerned, Hannah turned to her father, who stood about ten feet away trying to catch his breath. "Dad?"

He held up a hand. "Okay… I'm okay. Take care of Guthrie."

Hannah went to her original victim. She'd arrived in Petite and in less than an hour nearly finished off her parents and their builder! This man fit Doree's description to a T. Guthrie Thomas, the hunk, the very man she had intended to tell off!

She knelt by Guthrie again. "You landed in a pile of grass clippings. Do you hurt anywhere?"

He sat up. With his knees bent, his elbows propped on them and his head bowed, he drew in deep breaths. "I just fell off a roof, lady."

"I know. I screamed."

"I heard you."

The vision of him catapulting toward her flashed in her mind. "Why weren't you wearing a safety belt?" she accused.

"Because I wasn't driving a car!" he gasped. "I

wasn't going to do any more work. I was taking another look at the steeple from outside." Stiffly, he pulled out a faded blue bandanna from his pocket, wiped his face and noisily blew his nose. "I've got grass all the way up my nose." He looked into her eyes. "Why did you scream?"

Weakness snaked through her. "I thought my dad was going to get out on the roof."

"I'd never let him do that. He just wanted to give me a hand in."

Hannah sat down and lowered her head.

"Feeling faint?" Guthrie asked.

Embarrassed by the first impression she'd made, she nodded. "I'm so sorry, Mr. Thomas."

"Me, too." Guthrie gave her a lopsided grin.

In the cooler evening, Hannah walked out the hospital emergency room doors with a rumpled, grass-stained Guthrie at her side. The sun had crept into bed for the night. Wispy clouds fluttered across a full moon, making it appear to wink at her.

Pausing, Hannah glanced at the hospital where she'd insisted on taking both her father and Guthrie to be checked out.

"You don't want to leave your parents," Guthrie rumbled sympathetically. Kindness filled his gaze.

She looked at him. "I didn't come to town to give my dad a heart attack."

"You *didn't* give him a heart attack. The doctor just

wants to keep him overnight for observation. Your mom's staying with him. He'll be fine."

The man's rough sympathy did her in. Tears suddenly spilled down one of her cheeks. Just one. *I can't even cry right today!*

"You're not going to cry, are you?" He put his hands out as if she might break apart and he'd be expected to catch the pieces. Evidently feminine tears scared Guthrie more than falling off a roof.

A sob caught in her throat and became a giggle. "Oh, stop it. I refuse to cry." She wiped her moist cheek with her hand. "Let's go." She walked firmly to her red car and stretched out her hand to open the door.

A long arm reached around her. "I'll drive. You look upset."

"*You're* the one who fell off the roof. I'm perfectly capable of driving us home."

"Are you sure?" He hovered beside her.

Overwhelmed with his nearness, she waved toward the other side of the car. "Get in the passenger seat. I'm driving." She unlocked the door and got in. He followed suit. She drove away without another word.

Petite was only an eight-mile drive north of Portage. Good health-care facilities weren't available in every rural community. But fortunately, Petite Portage was close to an excellent medical center in the bigger town of Portage. That had been one of the reasons her parents had felt safe in moving from Milwaukee, which had several excellent hospitals, to Petite Portage. Last year, good health care had become very important to both Mom and Dad.

As she drove through the quiet streets to the highway north, she became more and more aware of the handsome man beside her. The scent of honest perspiration and freshly mowed grass floated in the air. He filled the vehicle, which had seemed so large to her after years of driving her little VW Beetle. "He's certainly big enough," she muttered to herself.

"What?"

Blushing, she turned onto the highway. "Nothing. I'm sorry you had to spend the whole evening being X-rayed and whatever."

"Poked and prodded?" He offered.

"Yes, it couldn't have been pleasant." Hannah thought ruefully that the nurses had been eager to help, however! At one time, three nurses had hovered around Guthrie while only one treated her father. Evidently, the nursing staff had agreed with Doree's assessment— "blonde, muscles, wow!"

He shrugged. "It turned out okay. I'm just bruised and a little stiff. Doc says a few days taking ibuprofen and I'll be fine."

"It's amazing you weren't hurt seriously." Hannah knew God's hand must have broken Guthrie's fall. The doctor had called him the luckiest man in Wisconsin.

"Well, the ground was wet, really soaked, from three days of rain. When Orville Jenkins mowed the lawn, I guess he dumped all the clippings in that pile because he was in a hurry."

"Fortunately." Hannah heaved a ragged sigh. Her emotions had run the gamut today. She felt peculiar, not herself.

"Yeah. You know I wouldn't have let your father come on the roof. I was just getting ready to come back in."

"I know. I believed you the first time. And it's just like my father to want to help someone."

"He's a great guy. We were lucky to get him as our pastor." Guthrie moved his seat back a little farther and stretched his legs in front of him.

She nodded, trying to keep her gaze off his long blue-jeaned legs and on the road. "Have you ever had a day where nothing went the way you planned?"

He snorted. "How about a whole summer? This has been the worst building season I've ever had. All the rain has been a real kick in the head. I got a late start as it is on your parents' contract, but I wasn't able to even pour your parents' foundation till July."

Hannah couldn't help herself. "What were you doing up on the church roof? On such a nice day, I would think you would be working on the house."

Hannah prepared herself to hear a long list of excuses, knowing she couldn't scold him.

"Didn't your parents mention the problem with the church roof?" Guthrie stretched his arms overhead toward the back seat and gave a little growl in the back of his throat.

That little sound shook her up, made her aware of him being so near. Why? "What roof problem?"

He lowered his arms and folded them in front of his chest. "All the rain in June destroyed what was left of the old roof. I've had to strip all the layers of old shingles off. Six layers, one layer too many. Now I've begun replacing sections of the roof itself. I'll also have to replace some of the joists and beams in the church attic and the steeple."

"Can't someone else do that work?" Though the traffic on the road ahead was light, she concentrated intently on her driving. Ignoring the man beside her had become hard work.

"Sure, but the church wanted me to do it. I guess because my family helped build the first roof on the church a hundred years ago."

"And my parents agreed?" *Why am I asking him this? I already know their answer.*

"Of course." Guthrie shifted in his seat, making a subtle swishing sound on the leather.

Of course, her parents would agree. They would never make a fuss. Or put their needs before the church's needs. Hannah stared at the road. Another question slipped through her disobedient lips. "Why didn't you hire more help if you had two jobs to do?"

"Hire someone? I have a few guys that help me out when I need them, but they all have regular day jobs. I don't build enough to keep anyone else busy. I build houses and raise dairy cattle. So I usually only build one or two homes a year."

"I see." The words she'd wanted to say to him earlier

came out. "My parents' contract says this house is to be completed by August thirty-first." She bit her lower lip.

He gave her a lopsided grin. "I just hope I can get the church roof done and your parents' home framed in before snow flies."

His calm tone ignited a spark of temper. "Framed in, not even completed before snow flies? Are my parents supposed to stay at Hanson-Fink's Cozy Motel for four more months? My parents have to be in a house before then!" Shocked at her outbreak, she swallowed. For a moment, she'd forgotten she'd scared this man off a roof.

Evidently, her outburst didn't faze him. "I know. I've told them over and over I'd tear up the contract. They should look into a factory-built home."

Turning off the highway, Hannah glanced at him with disbelief. His golden hair gleamed in the moonlight. "You offered to tear up their contract?"

"Yes, but they wouldn't hear of it."

The next afternoon, Hannah walked out of the hospital beside her parents into afternoon warmth and sunshine. After waiting four hours for one more test to be done, then a doctor to release her father, she felt like the proverbial cat on a hot tin roof. But a guilty, ineffective cat, she thought as they got into her car.

"I see you bought yourself a new car," Dad said.

She focused on the surface topic, pushing down the bubbling confusion inside her. "The old VW bought the farm in July. I thought a sport utility vehicle would be good for winter driving."

"And such a nice bright red," her mother remarked. "You'll be visible in any weather. How long are you going to be able to stay, Honey?"

Hannah swallowed. She couldn't stand to be called that name, not after Edward had used it to belittle her. *Honey, you don't know what you're talking about.* "Mom, Dad, I'd like to ask you a favor. I would really appreciate it if we could do away with Honey."

There was a pause. Then Dad cleared his throat. "You've grown up, been that way a long time. If you want to leave that childhood nickname in the past, no problem. Right, dear?"

"Certainly. I may forget, so please remind me," Mom agreed.

Hannah felt foolish making a point of this, but she needed to draw a line between the old Honey and the new Hannah. Her parents had noticed the clothes she was wearing, a pair of designer chinos in royal blue and a blue-and-white-striped pima cotton T-shirt. But they were too polite to make a big deal about her change into colorful clothing. She suddenly had the impression that they both thought she was a bomb that might explode if handled roughly. It wasn't a comfortable feeling.

"So, Hannah, when do you have to be back in Milwaukee?" her mother asked.

"I don't have to go back. I sublet my apartment for the rest of the lease." Her eyes on the road, Hannah sensed her parents' uneasiness. She knew them so well, she could hear their unspoken questions to each other. *Does this have to do with her breakup with Edward? Is she having some kind of crisis? Does she mean to move in with us? What's going on? How can we help her?*

Tears caught in Hannah's throat. Ever since that dreadful day two months after her breakup with Edward, the day she'd experienced shattering embarrassment, tears came out of nowhere whenever they wanted to. Gripping the steering wheel and refusing to give in, she drove onto the two-lane highway, concentrating on the scenery. But fields of ripe corn and pastures dotted with huge green rolls of drying hay and black-and-white dairy cattle didn't distract her.

The feeling that the three of them were holding hands, like children playing ring-around-a-rosy while circling an untouchable topic, hit Hannah. But she still couldn't broach what had happened *after* she had broken up with Edward. After the endless three-year engagement, just the breakup had been hard enough on her parents. She couldn't tell them the rest. It would break their hearts.

"Then what are your plans?" Dad asked.

"Nothing drastic." *That's already happened to me.* "I plan to help you two move into your new home. I'd like to get acquainted with your new church. Then I might go back to Milwaukee or see if I like the Madison area instead."

Dad cleared his throat. "There's something that we

need to tell you, Hannah." He paused. "Our new home isn't going to be ready on time."

Hannah let out a deep sigh. "I know. I drove by your…foundation yesterday before I came to the church."

Dad breathed what sounded like a sigh of relief. "The wet weather all summer and spring has held Guthrie up."

"Guthrie explained that to me last night when I drove him home." She recalled the pleasant sensation of having Guthrie with her in this car. She gripped the steering wheel tighter. A dreamy feeling affected her as she recalled Guthrie sitting beside her. Obviously being on the rebound made her more susceptible than usual to a handsome man. That could only mean danger to her already mangled heart and pride!

Mom spoke from the back seat. "We think a lot of Guthrie."

Hannah replied in an even tone. "He seems like a nice guy. I mean he doesn't plan on suing me for causing him to fall off the roof yesterday. He didn't really even seem angry with me." He'd been sweet through it all. Some woman had raised one fine son.

"Guthrie Thomas is a special young man," Dad agreed.

Hannah heard the unspoken words. *Not like Edward who never appreciated you.*

"Guthrie mentioned that he was working on the church roof, too," Hannah said. Her parents were right. Guthrie and Edward had nothing in common except making Hannah wait!

Dad finished with, "Yes, the church has sustained water damage. It's really quite serious. Things had been neglected too long. The work couldn't be put off any longer."

Hannah added, "Guthrie told me that he didn't mind if you broke the contract with him."

"Yes, that was very thoughtful," Mom said soothingly.

"He mentioned he thought you should go with the company that makes factory-built homes," Hannah added without much conviction.

"Yes, he told us all about them." Beside her, Dad gazed out the window, looking unperturbed.

Hannah said brightly, but without hope, "So? Which company are you going to go with?"

"Why, none, Hannah. We'll just wait for Guthrie." Mom's placid voice floated forward.

Hannah made one last attempt. "Mom, he really sounded like he wouldn't be upset if you changed your minds."

"But we haven't changed our minds," Dad said as expected.

I don't believe this; then again, I knew just how this would go. "But your house might not be done for months. You don't want to stay at Fink's, I mean Hanson's Cozy Motel through the winter, do you?"

"Why not?" Mom asked, sounding tickled by some unspoken joke.

"Your mother is enjoying a welcome break from entertaining and housekeeping." Dad glanced over his shoulder with a smile in his eyes.

"Yes," Mom agreed, "it's a dream come true. No cleaning. Just making a snack at lunchtime. We even have dish-network TV," her mother added.

"But aren't you feeling crowded in just one room?" Hannah already felt cramped.

But her parents both chuckled.

"It reminds us of our first efficiency apartment where we lived while your father attended the seminary." Then her mother frowned.

Just the word *seminary* had brought the specter of Edward into the car. Edward had refused to juggle working and studying at the seminary with marriage. So stupid little Honey had pushed ahead the wedding date and waited.

"Only this bathroom is larger," Dad said.

Hannah felt the sensation of trying to cross a bog. Every time she tried to move forward, sticky, unstable mud sucked her backward. "I give up. What's so special about waiting for a house Guthrie Thomas builds?"

"When we were deciding whether or not to take this pastorate, we took a long time to think it over," Dad said.

"We wanted this to be where we semiretired, so we had to make the right decision," Mom added.

"I can understand that, but—" Hannah tried once more, against all odds.

"Hon—Hannah," Dad interrupted, "your mother has never complained about the little efficiency apartment we started out in or the old drafty-barn parsonages that we lived in when you children were being born—"

"Garner, I never minded—"

"Ethel, I think our daughter needs to hear this. When a man marries a woman, he longs with all his heart to provide a castle worthy of her. In thirty-five years of marriage, I've never been able to do that." He cleared his throat. "Starting early this year, we spent several months deciding whether or not to take this pastorate. Then we spent a month looking for just the right lot. After that, we looked over hundreds of floor plans until we decided on the one that had everything we wanted. Finally we toured model homes of every kind in the area."

Ethel took over. "We decided on Guthrie Thomas, right in Petite. He does the most beautiful workmanship. Little touches like arched doorways and built-in cabinets, carved moldings. His houses are perfection!"

Garner nodded. "This is probably the last house we will live in before we begin downsizing, when we get too old to keep up a full-size house and yard. That's why I insist that your mother get the house she wants. She's waited long enough. God has promised us a mansion in heaven, and I don't doubt it will be magnificent. But this is *my* last chance to give your mother the house I've always wanted for her, the one she's always deserved. And I won't be denied!"

Hannah loved every single word her father said, but she sighed anyway. It was a beautiful sentiment, but she had to think of something she could do to move matters along. Perfection could take a long time!

Chapter Three

Feeling like a lump of dough with sadly inactive yeast, Hannah lay on her double bed in her harvest gold and avocado green "box" at Fink-Hanson's Cozy Motel. After bringing her parents home, she'd tried to write her column, but had ended up, stretched out on her bed, staring at the ceiling. She'd come to Petite with a simple task, simply to help her parents move into their new home, maybe to hurry the local builder along with the finishing touches.

"Finishing touches," she moaned to the ceiling. At the back of her mind, her conscience reminded her she had to fax her column in before tomorrow. Column? She hadn't even written a word yet, hadn't even thought of a topic! She had never been late for a deadline in her life. Even this didn't stir her to action.

The bedside phone rang. Four rings jingled before Hannah had the energy to pick it up. "Hi."

"Hannah? Is that you?"

"Spring?" Hannah's eyes opened wide.

"Yes, it's me."

"Oh, Spring, it's so good to hear your voice," Hannah said.

"What's the matter?"

Images from yesterday flashed through Hannah's mind, Lila Fink, Captain Peach-fuzz, Guthrie Thomas sliding down the roof. "Oh," Hannah wailed, "I've entered the twilight zone!"

"What?"

Hannah sat up. "Yesterday was a once-in-a-lifetime nightmare! Nothing has gone like I planned!"

Spring had the nerve to chuckle! "Hannah, the busy planner."

"Don't make fun of me!"

"Life isn't a recipe you plan, measure out, then cook. It's time you realized that."

Hannah ran her fingers through her mussed hair. "Don't lecture me either. You're not here on the front line."

"What's the matter? Is the builder a hard nut to crack?"

Hannah pictured again Guthrie wiping grass clippings off his face. Later on the ride home, his grin had made her anger with him melt away. Now she didn't know if she felt like laughing or crying. "The house is just a foundation."

"What!"

"You heard me," Hannah grumbled.

"Why?"

Hannah explained the facts of the situation, then finished, "But the kicker is the builder has told them he would let them out of the contract whenever they want."

"He what? Is he for real?"

"Yes, he meant it." Hannah stood up and walked to the window. The Front Street business district stretched before her, Carlson's Auto Repair, the Kwikee Gas station-convenience store and the Bizzy Bee Beauty Shop.

"Then…what's the problem?"

"Mom and Dad insist they want him to do it anyway!" Hannah had lost all her starch. She slumped into the straight chair at the small desk.

"What are you going to do then?"

Hannah sighed. "I wish I knew." Glancing at the clothes hanging against the wall, she shook her head. She'd brought a designer wardrobe for Petite. Now her new fashionable clothes mocked her.

Spring went on, "Well, if Mother and Father are convinced that this is what they want, there doesn't seem much you can do. Maybe you should just leave. You can always come back and stay with me if you need a place for a few weeks."

"I'm not ready to give up yet, but…"

"Have you done any more thinking about what we talked over at lunch?" Spring's voice became uncertain.

"You mean about finding Mother's adoption papers?" Hannah felt a twinge of fear. *Mother, what should I do? Obey you or do what's best for you?*

"Yes."

"I'm still trying to decide, but what I think right now isn't very important. All Mom and Dad's stuff is in storage. And until they can get into their new home—"

"That's where it will stay." Spring paused. "If you need backup, just call me. I can get away from the Gardens with a day's notice."

"Thanks. But I don't see anything you could do here." Hannah paused, then perked up. "Oh! A thought just occurred to me."

"What?" Spring sounded excited.

"I'll tell you if it works."

"All right. Keep in touch. Love you."

"Love you, too. Bye."

At five that evening, Hannah walked between her parents down the crumbling sidewalk of Front Street, then turned up Church Street. They'd been invited to eat supper with Guthrie's family. Hannah hoped meeting Guthrie with his family wouldn't be awkward. She still felt embarrassed about the roof incident. What must they think of her?

"You'll love Martha, dear," Mom said. "She is so warmhearted."

"A good cook, too." Dad grinned. "Not quite up to your mother's standards, but good."

Hannah listened as her parents teased each other. The thought that had come to her as she'd talked with Spring that afternoon had rolled around in her mind ever since. She didn't think this would work, but she had to try it. She'd talk to Guthrie. He might agree. He might.

"Martha Thomas's daughter's name is Lynda Garrett."

"Yes." Hannah was used to her mother priming her with social details.

"Lynda's children are Amber, Jenna and Hunter. They are six, five and four."

"She's got her hands full! What's her husband's name?"

Dad spoke. "That's the unfortunate part. Lynda's husband deserted them just after Hunter was born."

"How awful!" At least, Edward had figured out he didn't want her before they were married.

"Yes. After that, Martha moved into town to live with her daughter and help out. But Lynda is wonderful. She's earned an associate degree at the community college and has just gotten a job as an executive assistant."

"I'm glad." Hannah concentrated on recalling all the names she'd just heard—Martha, the mom, Lynda, the daughter, Amber, Jenna, and Hunter, the kids. Would she have a chance to talk to Guthrie alone?

They arrived at the Thomas home, a small yellow house, and walked to the front door. A little blond girl in braids and red shorts waited at the door to the large screened-in porch. She squealed, "Grandma, they're here!" She swung the door wide open and launched herself into Garner's waiting arms.

He caught her. "Hi, pumpkin, what's for supper?" He planted a noisy smooch on the little girl's cheek.

Nostalgic longing swirled through Hannah. She remembered when Dad had called her pumpkin and given her noisy kisses. In those days, he had always been able to solve every problem, soothe every fear. Hannah brought herself back to the present. Her parents needed her help now, and she wouldn't fail them.

"Jenna, this is our middle daughter, Hannah." Dad nodded.

"Hi." Two huge brown eyes stared at her.

"Hi." Hannah grinned.

Mom held the door open, and Hannah stepped inside, followed by her parents. A rush of greetings and introductions took place, and soon they all sat on the porch with glasses of iced tea in hand. A second little girl with short, dark hair, Amber, sat in her grandmother's lap while blond Hunter played with a large plastic toy truck on the floor.

Martha, sitting across from Hannah, didn't look anything like Hannah had expected. A slender woman, Martha wore stylish navy slacks and a plaid oxford short-sleeve shirt and pretty leather sandals. Her golden hair, threaded with silver, had been cut in an easy care but attractive style.

"Mrs. Thomas." Hannah took a deep breath. "I want to apologize for yesterday—"

"Call me Martha and don't give that another thought.

Guthrie needs a good shaking up from time to time. You'll meet my daughter soon. Lynda will be here in a few minutes. She called just before she left the office." Martha stroked Amber's back.

"Do you have any other children?" Hannah asked.

"Yes, my oldest, Brandon, is a lawyer in San Francisco."

Hannah nodded politely.

"Will Guthrie be coming to supper?" Mom asked.

Hannah listened for the answer. Would she have to face him in front of his family and be expected to eat?

"Who knows?" Martha grinned as though this were a perennial question. "I always serve dinner at six. Those who show up for it get it fresh. Those who don't…" She finished by lifting one hand, then gave an easy grin.

Garner chuckled as he glanced at his wife. "That's what you should have done."

"If I had," Mom replied with mock severity, "you would never have eaten a fresh meal."

"Guilty as charged." Dad tickled Jenna, who squealed with delight.

Martha looked at Hannah and asked, "I hear you are a food writer?"

"Yes, my Real Food, Healthy Food column appears in twelve papers now across the Midwest."

"Wonderful. I hear you've written two cookbooks already, too."

Blushing, Hannah nodded. "I see you've been

talking to my parents." A door slammed, and the three children suddenly went on alert.

"Guthrie?" Martha called.

Hannah waited for the answer, breathless.

"It's me, Mom!" a feminine voice replied.

"That's Lynda," Martha said.

Hannah didn't know if she was relieved or disappointed.

Within moments, a thin young woman, very much like Martha, stepped onto the porch. Her children mobbed her. She kissed her daughters' heads, then swung Hunter into her arms. "Hello, rug rats!"

A touch of envy stung Hannah. If she and Edward had married right after college like she'd wanted, she could have been a mother by now. *A divorced single mother,* a bitter voice added. Edward had never been eager to become a parent. *That should have warned me off. How could I have been such a fool?*

After greetings and introductions had been accomplished, they all went to their places around a long picnic table on the wraparound porch.

A light tapping on the porch door caught Hannah's attention. She glanced over to see two slender older ladies standing on the top step.

"It's the great-aunties!" Jenna shouted and ran with blond braids flying to let them in.

"Hello!" Martha greeted them. "You're just in time for dinner."

Hannah watched Lynda welcome the two older

women who wore identical pink-flowered dresses, which might have been new in 1965.

Martha looked at Hannah. "These ladies are my late husband's twin aunts, Ida and Edith Thomas."

Hannah exchanged greetings with the women, who reminded her of two of the actresses in a recent production of *Arsenic and Old Lace* she'd seen at a community theater in the spring. These two ladies could easily have played the aging sisters who were quietly poisoning lonely old men. Ida wore her silver hair pulled into a topknot, but soft bangs framed her cheerful face.

Edith's hair had been cut short and curled around her face into gentle waves. Edith was the same height but a bit rounder than her sister.

When everyone was seated, Hannah's father said a brief prayer, then Martha began to pass bowls family-style. The menu was the classic spaghetti with marinara sauce, salad and garlic bread.

Hannah tasted the tangy red sauce, chunky with tomatoes, onion and green pepper. "This is delicious!"

"It's just spaghetti sauce." Martha's cheeks turned pink. "Cooking for a food writer made me nervous, but I decided to go ahead and make the meal I'd planned for your parents."

"That's Mom's own recipe," Lynda said proudly. "She cans it herself."

"I don't wish to contradict you, Lynda," Ida said, "but this is our recipe. We gave it to your mother when she first married dear Randall. May he rest in peace."

"Absolutely," Edith commented.

Martha turned pinker. "Yes, of course, you've given me so many of your excellent recipes."

Martha and her daughter exchanged glances, then they both gave Hannah an uneasy look.

"Do you can a lot of this?" Hannah asked, puzzled. Had the great-aunts given her the recipe or not?

"No, I used to can almost one hundred quarts of tomatoes every summer and freeze bags and bags of sweet corn and green beans. But no more. Now I spend one day canning just tomatoes, then a day making spaghetti sauce and one day for salsa."

Hannah wiped her mouth with her napkin. "Is the salsa also your own recipe?"

This time neither aunt claimed the salsa as their own.

"Yes." Martha finished tying a bib around squirming Hunter's neck.

"I can see and taste that I'll have to get to know you better." Hannah grinned.

"Yes, Martha is a wonderful cook!" Ida and Edith chorused.

Martha glowed with honest pride, then she humbly changed the topic. "I guess Guthrie was unable to get away from work. I'll have to fix a dish for you to take to him, Lynda."

Her pulse sped up, and Hannah raised her hand. "I'll take it out to him."

"Oh, no." Martha objected.

"Please, it's the least I can do for him after scaring

him off the roof yesterday!" *Besides, I have something to discuss with Guthrie.*

Nervous but determined, Hannah parked her fiery red sport utility vehicle on her parents' muddy gravel track. She opened the door and got out to deliver the covered nine-by-thirteen-inch pan Martha had filled with supper. She stepped gingerly on the mud-mired grass, then onto the path of boards toward the building in progress. She hummed "Onward Christian Soldiers" loudly so she wouldn't take Guthrie by surprise a second time.

"I hear you!" Guthrie called cheerfully. "Let me guess—that's your favorite song!"

His easygoing humor tickled her, made her feel alive. "No," she teased, "but do you smell your supper?"

"It's Mom's spaghetti and garlic bread. I'm starving!"

"Then you should have come home!"

Guthrie was shirtless again. Hannah dragged her eyes away from the bronzed picture he made in the golden twilight. Didn't the man know what the sight of him did to her knees?

"Sit with me while I eat?" he invited.

Still keeping her gaze away from the visual feast he offered, she sat on a hard, sharp-edged stack of lumber, leaving a chaste two-foot gap between them. "Okay. Get busy and eat before it's completely cold."

Guthrie used the wet wipes his mother had sent to

clean his large, work-roughened hands. He sat beside her, took the pan onto his lap and bowed his head for grace.

Hannah bowed her head also, praying for guidance in this situation. The crickets of fall were already singing. Warm breezes whispered against her nose and earlobes.

"Amen," Guthrie murmured.

The sound of the word brought tears to Hannah's eyes. *I'm becoming a cry baby. I cry over everything.* Hannah blinked away the moisture. Ever since that day two months after the breakup, when Edward's sister had called to prepare her in case someone mentioned his wedding. She drew in a deep breath and began talking away the blues. "Two days without rain in a row. Think this might be the beginning of a trend?"

"I hope so. This summer has been frustrating."

I've had better summers myself. "I believe you. How much work do you have left on the church roof?" she asked, trying to get the facts she needed.

"I checked things over today. I'm waiting on an order for some joists, beams and wallboard to repair water damage in the attic. After I replace all the damaged roof boards, all I have left to do is replace some of the siding on the steeple, then I can start the shingling."

"Good."

"So today I worked on your parents' house, as you can see." He waved a slab of fragrant garlic bread toward the foundation. He'd been working on floor joists. For one man, he'd accomplished quite a bit in one day. Why did he insist on working a job alone?

Not voicing this concern, she bowed her head as if scolded. "I noticed. Here I was trying to be polite by not bringing this up."

He chuckled.

She looked at him sideways. His golden hair was damp from hard work. A fine layer of sawdust frosted his curls. She nearly reached over to fluff his hair and shake off the pale particles. "I like your family."

"Imagine that. I do, too." He tore off a hunk of the garlic bread.

Trying to come up with some safe newcomer-type subject, she asked, "What is there to do for fun around here?"

"Fun? You want to have fun, Miss Hannah?"

The rich coaxing tone he used made the hair on the back of her neck prickle. "If I decide to hang around."

"I thought you were just here to make sure that your parents got into their house on time." Guthrie twisted saucy spaghetti around his fork.

"That's true." No sense mincing words, then. "Guthrie, you said that you have offered to let my parents out of their contract. Did you mean that?"

He swallowed his swirl of spaghetti. "Yes."

"Then I was wondering if you would take it a step further." Hannah stretched her legs and gazed at the fading sunlight.

"How do you mean that?" Guthrie took a drink from a quart jar of iced tea.

"Would you tell them *you'd* like to break the contract?" She held her breath even though she could almost predict his answer.

He stared at her. "But that would be a lie. I don't want to break the contract."

She hung her head, discouraged. "That's what I expected you to say. In fact, I agree with you."

"Hannah, your parents may be semiretiring, but they are still competent adults. At the very beginning, I explained to them that I work mostly alone with little help. We discussed the possibility of weather causing delays. As of yesterday, they still wanted me to build their home."

She nodded. "I know. You are the builder they want to build their dream house." She hadn't fully realized that before, but she did now.

"Then why do you want them to settle for a factory-built house?" He began twisting his fork again, gathering another tangy mouthful.

She gave him a rueful smile. "I don't, really. I just thought it was important for them to get into their home as soon as possible. They may say they don't mind staying at the Cozy Motel, but it will cease to be a novelty in the next few weeks."

Guthrie nodded.

Leaning backward, she looked at the endless twilight sky—golden bands between slate-blue layers. "My sister called today and laughed at me. Called me Hannah, the planner, and told me I couldn't treat life like a recipe."

"What?"

"Oh, nothing, but…" Mom's leukemia was certainly something. She didn't want to take her mother's return to health for granted. And her sisters' idea of looking for Mom's adoption papers lurked in the back of her mind, lending urgency to the need to get her parents settled. What to do?

Pushing away these concerns, she turned to face him. "I really want to help my parents with this move. They've had health problems crop up in the past year, and I wanted this to go smoothly."

"I can see that."

"I'm not licked yet. I want my parents in their dream house before snow flies and I will find a way."

He shook his head. "Well, be sure to let me know what you come up with. I'll be interested."

"Don't worry. You'll be the first to know."

Sitting with her black laptop in her lap, Hannah rubbed her eyes. The bedside clock read one a.m. She ran the spell-check on her computer, then connected the jack and cord between the computer and phone. She quickly set up the fax information and tapped "Enter."

"Goodbye," she murmured as her column, "Old and New Canning Recipes and Tips," traveled through the phone lines to her newspapers. With a groan, she laid down on her bed. She yawned and whispered a good night prayer….

The blare of a trucker's horn woke her. She sat up. Thin, early sunlight sifted through blinds into her room. The images in the dream she'd awakened from sent a thrill through her. The memories must be an answer to prayer. *Thank you, Lord. Now I know what I can do.*

Chapter Four

Several hours later at nearly ten on another cloudy morning, Hannah swung into the church parking lot and with a quick spin of the wheel parked her red SUV beside Guthrie's sky-blue pickup. Aha! When she'd driven by her parents' lot and found it uninhabited, she'd known she'd find Guthrie here.

Right after breakfast at the Cozy Café, she'd driven to the Farm and Fleet out on the highway and bought heavy-duty overalls and tan work boots. Then she went to her room, tore off the tags and pulled on the stiff denim. Finally, she'd wiggled her cotton-socked toes in the steel-toed boots making sure she had enough toe room.

She was ready. She was set. It was a go!

Saying a quick prayer, she grabbed her red plastic toolbox, climbed out of the vehicle and jogged through the side door leading into the church basement.

Her mother was speaking on the phone in the

church's outer office. No doubt her father sat in the inner office hard at work preparing Sunday's sermon. *I'm doing this for you, Mom and Dad. You need to get settled and the sooner the better.* Mom's remission and her sisters' suggestion that Hannah look for Mom's birth documents nipped at the back of her mind, but Hannah waved and went on. Hammering from above beckoned her irresistibly.

The church was so small it wasn't difficult to find the short flight of tan-painted steps that led her to the main floor, then to the narrow, dark-wood staircase and attic. The pounding became louder with each step. And each step lifted her spirits. Since she'd arrived in Petite, she'd been mired in a bog of disappointment.

Today that had changed! She bubbled inside with happy purpose. Arriving in the attic, she breathed in the welcome scent of fresh-cut wood.

Guthrie's back was to her as he crouched, pounding replacement boards over floor joists. He hadn't heard her approach. She opened her mouth to say something, then paused to watch as he hammered. The muscles of his back rippled under the taut white T-shirt.

No doubt about it. Guthrie Thomas was a master-piece of a man. When God had crafted this carpenter's genes, He'd been extravagantly generous. But God Himself had chosen to be born into a carpenter's family. Maybe He had a soft spot for them.

Guthrie's every move was sure and strong, without hesitation or fumbling. But something, some thought she'd had about Guthrie in her late-night deadline session last evening eluded her now. She creased her forehead, thinking. *Yes!*

"Why aren't you married?" The words popped out of her mouth.

Guthrie shot up and spun around. "Hannah!"

She covered her hot face with her hands. "I'm sorry." After three years of holding back her true feelings so she wouldn't upset Edward, she'd lost control of her tongue. Now words she'd never dreamed of saying aloud would pop out of her mouth. *I hope this goes away—and soon!*

"Why did you sneak up on me like that?" He put down his hammer.

"I know! I'm sorry!" She didn't blame him for being exasperated with her, but she hoped he hadn't heard her question. How embarrassing!

Experience had taught her that whenever a woman mentioned marriage near a man, he thought she was interested in him. If he only knew! Marriage should be the last thing on her mind. Besides, Guthrie could give any leading man competition, and she was just plain old Hannah. But why hadn't he married a high school sweetheart and started a family by now? That was the mystery!

Bending his head under a low rafter, he stepped closer to her. "What can I do for you?"

He must not have caught her question, and he wasn't angry over her startling him again. His calm words and manner showed this. Easygoing Guthrie.

Trying to ease her stress, she shrugged her tense

shoulders to relax them. "Nothing. I mean, I came…."
Her words petered out. How would Guthrie Thomas
take to her idea?

In her rush to get rigged out and in the excitement
of finally coming up with some positive action, she'd
ignored a fluttering in the back of her mind, a touch of
concern over how Guthrie would like her plan.

He paused, eyeing her. "I need to keep at it. More
showers are predicted today, so I gave up the idea of
working on your parents' house. I've started to work
here inside on the attic—"

She decided to say it and get it over with. "Guthrie,
I finally thought of a way to help you get my parents'
house done more quickly."

"Really? How?" He sauntered over to where he'd
been hammering and squatted, his thigh muscles
molding the well-worn denim.

"I'm going to work with you. Be your carpenter's
helper."

He popped up like toast from a toaster. "What!"

She'd snagged his attention, all right. Would he
proceed to opposition next? "Yes, I suppose you didn't
know that I've done construction work."

"You? Construction?" He looked at her as though she
were babbling nonsense.

She nodded. "I went on mission trips to Arkansas
and Haiti."

"Mission trips? What has that got to do with building
your parents' house?"

She anchored one hand on her hip. The other gripped her toolbox. "I helped rebuild a church in Arkansas after a tornado destroyed it. In Haiti, I built small cement-block homes for the poor."

He took a step nearer. "This is not going to be a one-room cement-block—"

She lifted her chin. "I also helped build two Habitat for Humanity homes in Milwaukee."

He stopped and stared at her. "You're serious."

"Very serious. My parents need their house finished, and the sooner the better. The weather has delayed you. You're only one man. One person can only do so much." She waved two fingers in the air. "But two can do twice the work of one."

Looking nonplussed, he measured her with his gaze. "You're not strong enough. I mean, look at you."

His frank stare made her blush, so to hide this she looked at herself. What did he see? She was no ethereal angel like her sister Spring. Anyone could see she was built to work. She said in a determined tone, "They didn't seem to think I was too weak to do a day's work in Arkansas, Haiti and Milwaukee."

Guthrie pushed his hands through his golden hair. "This beats all." He grinned then. "This is really sweet of you, but I can't let you."

Giving him a confused look, she set her toolbox on a nearby sawhorse. "Why not?"

"You're a food writer, not a carpenter. Don't you think that will keep you busy enough?"

He's evading the issue. "Guthrie, I'm perfectly capable of helping you build my parents' house. Why don't you let me worry about whether I have enough time?"

"It's not right." He shoved his hands in his back pockets and looked down.

Imitating him, she shoved her hands in her back pockets and took a step closer to him. "It makes perfect sense, and I'm here to assist you with the church, too."

"No." He shook his head. "It's just not right. I contracted to build your parents' house, and I can't have you working without being paid. But I can't afford to pay—"

"Seeing my parents in their home before Christmas will be my payment."

He sucked in breath. "I don't know if the construction insurance would cover you."

"Guthrie Thomas, you're grabbing at straws." Why did men react like this? Like women couldn't do he-man stuff, pound nails and work a saw? "Now let's get busy." In her stiff new work boots, she picked her way over the exposed floor joists to the sawhorse and opened her small toolbox. She turned to Guthrie expectantly.

"What's that?" He pointed to her red toolbox.

She felt like saying something sassy like, "I'll give you three guesses," but she suppressed it and said with a straight face, "I brought my own hammer and a few other tools. I've gathered a small collection of necessary items. I know how carpenters hate other people using their tools." She pulled out her hammer and hefted it in one hand. "Now let's stop talking and start working. How can I help with this floor?"

Guthrie stared at her as though she'd just spoken in Greek. He didn't move a muscle.

Tossing the hammer from one hand to the other, she walked as close to him as she could. "What job are we doing here today?"

With a decided frown, Guthrie folded his arms over his chest.

With a deceptive smile, Hannah folded her arms over her chest. *I'm not giving in, Guthrie Thomas. I let Edward overrule me for three years. Now you're stuck with me. This church and my parents' house are going to be finished and I'm going to help you.*

The sound of footsteps came from behind her. "Hannah!" her mother said. "I wondered why you were wearing overalls and work boots. You've come to assist Guthrie!"

From behind her mother, Hannah's father chimed in. "What a generous idea, daughter. We can always count on our Hon—our Hannah!"

Guthrie stared forlornly at the light rain trickling down the dirty, grease-smudged front window of Carlson's Auto Body and Repair. The garage was more than fifty years old, steeped in motor oil, dirt and gas fumes.

Under the hood of Guthrie's blue pickup, his lifelong friend Ted Carlson twisted another cleaned spark plug into place. "So could she do the work or not?"

That morning Hannah had expertly measured and

cut the boards for him. They'd put the new floor in the attic in no time at all. But by the time they'd broken for lunch, Guthrie had been ready to explode. He swung around and growled, "That's not the point."

"Well, it's going to be. If she can do the work, it will probably turn out okay." Ted bent over the engine. "If she can't, you're in for it."

Guthrie looped his thumbs in his belt. "I work alone because I like to work alone." In his mind, he heard Hannah's startling question once again. "Why aren't you married?"

"Know what you mean. Feel the same way. But how can you tell her not to help when her parents think it's great? Isn't polite. He's the new preacher. Can't tell him off, or at least you shouldn't."

Guthrie leaned under the raised hood to watch Ted. "Tell me something I don't know." Why had she brought up his not being married, then gone on like she hadn't asked it?

"Well, I'll tell you this. Mr. Kirkland stopped by yesterday to introduce himself." Ted pulled out, then cleaned another spark plug with a metal brush. "Said he'd heard my dad had been a regular church attender till he died two years ago."

"Did he invite you to church?"

"Said he'd be glad to see me back on Sunday mornings. I said I like to sleep in on Sunday mornings. Wondered how he'd take that. Just laughed." Ted twisted the clean plug in.

"He's a good guy." Guthrie made himself concentrate on what Ted was saying. "I liked him right away. He's solid, not a fake."

"Asked me if I'd ever be interested in attending a singles' night at the church." Coming out from under the hood, Ted stared at the toes of his scratched work boots.

"What?"

"Said he was going to start a singles' night in the church basement once a month this fall. Snacks, country music, videos. Everything just casual. Come and spend the evening. Also said he'd like to get up some groups to go to some football games in Madison."

"College games?"

Ted nodded.

Guthrie wondered if these were the preacher's ideas…or Hannah's. "I don't want to hang around with a bunch of kids."

"Said the singles' nights would be for twenty-one and older. No teenyboppers."

Guthrie could see that Ted looked interested, and why not? Their little town had nothing to offer socially after high school for singles. Most of the marrying took place in the year or two after high school graduation. But in the eight years since Guthrie's graduation, those marriages had been breaking up at an unpleasant but steady rate. Just like his sister's had.

Ted and he hadn't followed the general practice. Ted had always been too shy. Had Ted ever guessed why Guthrie hadn't married? He wondered if that had anything to do with his not wanting Hannah Kirkland working beside him. He wasn't lucky in love. He liked Hannah so far. But had she come to town with marriage on her mind?

"Think your sister would be interested in going to a singles' night?" Ted nonchalantly wiped his hands on some gray-blue paper toweling.

"Might. Mom will probably encourage her to."

"Rain's stopping." Ted pointed outside.

Guthrie exhaled with relief. "It's time I got back to the church. I might get some work done on that steeple before supper."

Ted nodded. "See you. Maybe the preacher's daughter will work out."

Guthrie glared at his friend. "I'm not going to cut her any slack. If she wants to work, I'll let her. But I don't think she will be able to hack it."

"She may surprise you."

"*I* may surprise *her.*" He got into his truck and backed out of the garage, feeling as grumpy as a ten-year-old getting socks for Christmas. But not clear on why.

Guthrie found Hannah sitting innocently beside her mother in the church office in the basement. He nodded politely to Mrs. Kirkland. "Ready to do some work, Hannah?"

Looking perky, Hannah saluted him and stood up. "Reporting for duty, sir!"

He refused to be charmed. "Come on then. It's not raining, so I want to try to replace the flashing around the steeple before it starts again."

"Guthrie, you'll use the safety harness, won't you?" Hannah's mother cautioned.

He grinned, accustomed to maternal warnings. "No problem. My mother already reminded me this morning."

"We just don't want any more surprises," Mrs. Kirkland said apologetically.

"Then you might tell your daughter not to scream suddenly while I'm out on the roof." He kept his tone vaguely humorous. After all, Hannah hadn't intentionally scared him off the roof. He didn't want to be rude, but he didn't want Hannah working with him, either!

Hannah grinned. "Don't worry. As long as neither of my parents are on the roof, you won't hear a peep out of me."

He waved Hannah ahead of him. Without further conversation, he followed her as she trudged up the church steps to the attic. He tried to ignore the intriguing feminine swing of the denim blue overalls in front of him. Overalls shouldn't make a woman more attractive. It wasn't right!

In the attic, she turned to face him. "So what can I do to help you?"

"Flashing is the—"

"Is the covering applied wherever there is a joint on a roof. As the house settles, the flashing keeps any joints on the roof covered even if joints separate some. It's usually metal. I'm figuring this church is old enough to have lead instead of aluminum. Am I right?"

The easy flow of information knocked Guthrie for a loop. "Did Habitat for Humanity put you in charge of flashing?"

She grinned. "No, I just like to sound like I know what I'm doing."

Her brash candor teased him, easing the tenseness inside him. He almost smiled, but conquered it. He wouldn't let her push the advantage a pretty woman always had. He went on without emotion. "The old flashing is lead. I need to remove it and replace it with modern aluminum. I'll put on the harness and attach it to the steeple. You can sit up in the steeple opening and hand me out what I need."

"I'm not afraid of heights."

"Neither am I, but I'm the only one who's going out on the roof today." He pinned her with his intense gaze. "That tight area around the steeple won't allow two of us to work out there. You'd just get in my way." *Just like you are, anyway.*

She teased him with another saucy grin. "Whatever you say. You're the boss of this job."

And don't you forget it. He snapped on the brown leather harness. Sitting in the opening on the side of the steeple, he secured his harness rope. He backed out onto the shingleless roof and straddled its damp, slick peak. "Now use the tin snips to cut each piece the same length and hand me out one piece of step flashing at a time."

After he stripped the old flashing, Hannah offered him the first piece of silvery aluminum. He pounded a ninety-degree angle, then tapped and nailed the L-shaped piece snugly into place, bridging the gap where the steeple and roof met. Piece by piece, Guthrie worked away from the steeple opening until he reached the next side of the steeple, forcing Hannah to venture out to perch on the peak to feed the flashing to him.

"Now I don't want you to move from that safe spot. I want your feet inside the steeple," he ordered. He was standing with his feet braced against the roof. The harness around his midsection attached him safely to the steeple so his hands were free to work and his eyes were free to look at Hannah. He tried to ignore the way the breeze tousled and played with her walnut-toned hair.

"I wouldn't have it any other way." She waved a piece of flashing at him, and it made a funny wobbling whistle.

Replying with only a stare, he stonewalled her attempt to lighten the mood. He rarely felt grumpy, but her horning in on his territory had pushed him too far.

She appeared to ignore his dark mood. "I'm going to cut several pieces ahead, and when you get to the point where you're going to be on the side opposite me, I'll load you up before you move to that side away from me."

"Who did you say was the boss here?" He needled her.

"Just obeying orders. You don't want me crawling around to reach you, do you?"

"No!" He slammed a nail in hard.

"Then I'll get busy and cut extra pieces for you. You can tuck them into the front of your tool belt."

While waiting for Hannah to lean around to hand him the next piece of flashing, he gazed at the town below. The rain had left every lawn and tree a stunning green. The clouds had cleared off. The August sun warmed his shoulders, and he hoped it meant tomorrow would be a day he could do more outside work. Without Hannah's help.

Looking at the little yellow house where his mother and sister lived, he watched an unfamiliar battered silver truck drive up and park in front of it. Who was stopping there and why?

He tapped another piece of flashing into place and glanced down. He saw the stranger get out and head toward his sister's front door. Something about the man's build and walk stirred Guthrie's memory. It couldn't be, could it?

Chapter Five

Guthrie's mother handed him the fresh white dish-towel. She sent him one of those pointed looks, those looks mothers give sons when, out of the blue, they volunteer to dry the dishes, kind of her chin down and her eyes peering over her half glasses at him like he was a specimen in a test tube.

"What?" he asked. "What?"

"Nothing. I'm delighted to have help in the kitchen." Mom turned off the hot water and pulled on bright yellow rubber gloves.

"Well, I just thought you...would," he explained with a lame shrug.

She handed him a dripping Mickey Mouse glass warm from the scalding rinse water. "You were strangely quiet at supper tonight."

"Oh?" *Why don't you just tell me about the stranger in the silver truck, Mom? Was it Terri Sue's truck like I thought?* It was driving him nuts. He had to know! He looked back to find her staring at him.

"Guthrie, what is the problem?"

"Nothing's wrong," he fibbed to his mother. Why couldn't he just ask her?

"Then why are you just holding that glass? Why don't you try drying it?"

He caught the amusement in his mother's tone. "I had a kind of…rough day." He rubbed the glass dry, placed Mickey upside down on the cabinet shelf and accepted another.

"I thought you said you got some work done on the attic and roof."

"I had some unwelcome help."

"Grandma! Grandma!" Jenna, her braids flying, ran into the kitchen. "I finally finished my cake."

His mother accepted Jenna's chocolate-crumb-decorated saucer.

"Mommy's going to read us a story." The little girl started to run into the front room, then reversed and rushed back. "I love you, Uncle Guthrie! I'm glad you came to supper tonight! We missed you last night!" For a split second, she wrapped her arms around his knees.

Guthrie's heart clenched, but before he could bend down and hug her, she raced out of the kitchen door, calling, "Don't start without me! I get to pick a story, too!"

He looked at his mother. This time she was the one with a preoccupied expression on her face. What was on her mind? Was it today's mystery visitor? Or something else?

"You're a good man, Guthrie. And you'll do what is right. I know that. I want you to remember that."

He couldn't think how to answer this, so he accepted the glass she was holding and glanced away. He made his voice brisk. "You won't believe this, but Hannah Kirkland worked as my carpenter's helper today."

"Hannah?" Mom scrubbed Hunter's bright blue tippy cup.

"That's what I said. I couldn't stop her."

"You couldn't?" His mother chuckled, then became serious. "I would think you'd welcome some help."

And I thought you'd tell me about the stranger in the silver pickup without my asking. "I like working alone."

"What did she do?" Mom handed him the rinsed plastic cup. "How did she do?"

The second question made him scowl.

"I know that look very well," his mother said in a teasing voice.

"What does that mean?"

"It means you're just like your father. You make up your mind and don't like people messing with your plans."

"What's wrong with that?" He upended the dry tippy-cup on top of one of the Mickey Mouse glasses.

She chuckled. "Life has a way of making a mess of some of our plans. Haven't you noticed? I never intended to be the wife of a stubborn farmer. I was studying to be an art professor. But I'm glad my plans got messed up. Aren't you?"

He scrutinized her. "Why are you talking about marriage all of a sudden?"

"Because I think it's time you thought about it, talked about it, did it."

"You've never said things like that before," he objected.

"I've been waiting patiently for you to do it without me saying anything." She offered him the first piece of pale green stoneware to dry.

Absently circling the plate with the towel, Guthrie tried to think of a reply. Marry? Didn't his mother understand that he intended to be the bachelor uncle? How could he ever take a chance on marrying?

Years ago, when his parents had gotten married, marriage had been for life. Now it seemed to last only as long as it proved convenient. A guy could marry someone and…bam! Have the rug yanked out from under him. Child support, custody—the very words chilled him. If he fathered a child, he wouldn't be able to bear being legally separated from that child. His nieces and nephew had taught him that. But hadn't divorce happened to about everyone he'd grown up with? Even his own beautiful, sweet sister.

His mom opened her mouth. "Guthrie, I—"

"Martha, dear!" A familiar sweet voice called from the screen door.

Guthrie closed his eyes. The great-aunts had arrived to scarf-up all the leftovers, as Amber would say.

"Ida, Edith, come in. Come in." His slim mother,

dressed in faded jeans like the college girl she'd been when she'd married Dad, held open the screen door.

The aunts, wearing outdated dresses they'd probably sewn in the fifties, entered the kitchen. They must still have every dress they'd ever sewn or bought. Aunt Ida proudly held high a jar of sick-looking cucumbers. "We made pickles today."

Mom took the jar. "Oh, thank you. We have some stew left and chocolate cake. I hope you both have room for it."

Though the arrangement had never been discussed, Guthrie knew his mother always cooked extra. In the summer, the aunts dropped by. In the cold weather, Lynda or Guthrie carried food to their door.

The phone rang. Guthrie lifted the receiver. "Hi."

"Guthrie? This is Hannah. I'm sorry. Tomorrow I won't be able to work a full day…."

Aha! I was right! She won't last.

"I'm really kind of excited. I've done my food column for three years now, but I've never done a live cooking demo for TV. The Madison station that does on-the-scene interviews called my agent and asked if I could fill in for a noon cancellation." Her voice bubbled.

"Great!" Saved by a noon cancellation!

She giggled in his ear. The sound made his neck hair feel funny. "You're not off the hook, fella! I'll still be able to help out after the noon show. I mean, after I clean up my cooking mess in the church kitchen."

"Is that where you'll be cooking?"

"Yes, since neither my mother nor I *have* a kitchen, as yet." She paused pointedly.

He felt the little pinch of the scold she'd meant for him. "Okay! Okay!"

"Tell your mom and great-aunts to come to the demo if they want. They'd like a live audience. Dad's going to set up chairs in the basement."

"Will do." The change in plans and the fact that Hannah wouldn't be working with him hit him funny. Why wasn't he happier?

"Okay then. See you tomorrow after lunch!"

"Who was that?" his mother asked.

As Guthrie relayed Hannah's good news and her invitation to his mother and aunts, the image of Hannah sitting in the steeple opening earlier in the day with her short, walnut-colored hair fluttering in the breeze against the blue sky flashed in his mind.

The church basement was alight and a-buzz. Metal poles with racks of lights brightened the drab room. Fortunately, the basement kitchen, if not stylish, was neat and clean. A TV camera's black coils of thick wire snaked around the tan metal folding chairs, set up in four neat rows of ten across. Senior citizens primarily filled the chairs, along with a few mothers holding children on their laps. Sitting beside Martha with Hunter on her lap, Guthrie's great-aunts, wearing matching lavender dresses, circa 1966, sat primly in the front row. They waved at her.

She waved back and smiled. Then she realized she'd been searching the audience for Guthrie's handsome face. *Get real! He's on the roof shingling!*

"Now, Miss Kirkland, we've only got a few minutes to go, then we're on live." The producer of the crew, wearing a headset like some techno-tiara, asked, "Do you have everything ready?"

Hannah glanced at the precise plan she'd typed and nodded. "I've already prepared one casserole and have the ingredients to demonstrate one for the camera."

"Great! We really appreciate your filling in on such short notice." He glanced at his wristwatch. "You have three minutes, forty seconds. So just hit the highlights."

"I will." She took a deep breath.

"Good choice of outfit." He gestured toward her. "The solid red will be a good background to the green beans."

Thank you. I picked it out just for that reason. I saw it on the hanger and thought, Now, that shade of red will be a good background for green beans. She felt a bit slaphappy from nerves. Live TV. That meant no-mistakes-please TV. *Why did I think this would be a good idea?*

"Okay, here we go," the head of the TV crew announced to the audience. "Everyone, clap after I introduce Miss Kirkland and at the end. Otherwise, please stay still. Thank you."

The TV local-assignments reporter, wearing matching gray sport coat and slacks, took his place beside her in the kitchen and looked through the louvered opening into the fellowship hall.

The producer counted down. "Four, three, two, one." He pointed at the reporter.

"Hi, Jim Harue here, in tiny Petite Portage at the historic Petite Community Church. I'd like to introduce Hannah Kirkland who writes the syndicated column Real Food, Healthy Food for newspapers all over the Midwest."

On cue, the audience clapped. The reporter continued, "Ms. Kirkland—"

"Please call me Hannah." She smiled extra wide and felt like a fake.

"Hannah, what are you cooking for us today?"

"Well, Jim, this is the season of bounty. All the carefully tended gardens in central Wisconsin are pouring out tomatoes, zucchini and green beans, which is our topic today. This is the type of vegetable recipe that takes a traditional favorite, green beans with bacon, and gives it a new healthy twist. It's high in calcium and makes a great side dish to any grilled meat. Or it could be the heart of a delicious meal."

"What are the ingredients?"

"I start with six cups of fresh green beans, lightly steamed and drained." She held up a silvery aluminum colander with prepared green beans in it. "One cup of bread crumbs—"

The sound of two feminine voices and footsteps in the audience caught Hannah's attention, but she kept her mind on the recipe. "And four slices of crisp bacon, crumbled. Set these aside—"

"That's not the way this recipe goes," Guthrie's great-aunt Ida insisted. "I've made this for years and years. You don't need bread crumbs for bacon and green beans."

"Absolutely not," her sister Edith agreed. "Mother never made it that way."

The reporter beside Hannah froze, his eyes bugging out.

Hannah wondered if she wore the same expression. Her chest felt pinched. She had a hard time catching a breath.

"Ladies," Hannah said quickly, "I'm making a new recipe. Why don't you—"

"A new recipe? How marvelous!" Ida said.

"Oh, we can't miss that, then." Edith crowded close on one side of Hannah, forcing back the reporter. Ida hovered on the other side.

Hannah trained her eyes on the camera. *Oh, Lord, help me! This could be a disaster. What can I do but go on with the original plan?* "Now I…we will make the sauce."

"Oh, this is wonderful! She's going to make sauce!" Ida crooned around Hannah to Edith.

Edith applauded.

Everyone else applauded along with her. The reporter eased out of camera range.

Don't desert me now! Coward!

Hannah went on adhering to her plan. "Melt one-fourth cup of margarine and stir in one-half cup of chopped onions." She dolloped the premeasured margarine into a nonstick skillet, instantly producing a cheery sizzle. "Sauté them lightly, then stir in—"

"I've never been able to digest onions, Hannah," Ida interrupted. "They make me bilious."

"Oh, that's right," Edith lamented with a sad shake of her silver head. "Can we take out the onions, Hannah?"

"Of course you can." With a wooden spoon, Hannah womanfully stirred the aromatic margarine and onions. "I'm stirring in four tablespoons of flour and two teaspoons of salt—"

"Oh, we'd have to take out the salt. We have high blood pressure, you know." Ida looked apologetic.

"You might use another favorite seasoning or a salt substitute," Hannah ad-libbed. "Then you add plain low-fat yogurt and cottage cheese and a dash of pepper."

The producer held up one finger, the signal that she had one minute to go. Feeling a bit light-headed, she said, "Bring these to a nice bubble, then pour the sauce over the green beans and half the bread crumbs already in a casserole dish. Top with your favorite low-fat cheese, the rest of the bread crumbs and the crumbled bacon. You may substitute turkey for bacon if you wish, or delete the bacon for a vegetarian dish. Microwave for approximately ten minutes, and voilà!" She bumped Ida's arm, but managed to lift the still warm prepared casserole.

"Oh!" Ida and Edith crowed. "It smells delicious!"

The reporter stepped into camera range. "Thanks so much, Hannah." He paused. "And ladies."

The sisters beamed at him.

He continued gazing fixedly at the camera. "The complete recipe is available on our Web site, shown at the bottom of your TV screen, or you may send us a self-addressed stamped envelope for a copy."

Hannah gave another bright smile to the camera. "Don't forget my latest cookbook, *Real Food, Healthy Food,* Volume two. It's available at any bookstore, or order it from my Web site."

The twin great-aunts led the audience in an enthusiastic finale of clapping.

Setting down the casserole with intense relief, Hannah stepped around the sisters to thank the reporter, the producer and the cameraman.

The demo had been a roller-coaster ride from start to finish. The crew said all that was polite but kept glancing sideways at the sisters. Her heart still palpitating in little jerks, Hannah accompanied the men through the church and outside.

Within minutes, the crew and reporter loaded their equipment and got into their white van, which sported a communication dish on its top. As the van drove away, Hannah waved one last time.

The two sisters led the rest of the audience out the front doors of the church. "Oh, that was fun!"

The happy seniors of Petite crowded around Hannah, congratulating her. Hannah nodded, shook hands and tried to put names with faces. Martha waved as she hurried away with Hunter.

Finally, only the sisters remained. "We're going to make that recipe this week and bring it to the potluck on Sunday," Ida said with a decided nod.

"Oh, yes. Of course, we might make a few bitty little changes." Edith giggled, and the sisters walked away still chattering with excitement.

Hannah plopped down on the church steps. Her mother sat beside her. They exchanged glances, which communicated a family motto—never a dull moment.

"A very interesting experience," her mother murmured. "But you handled it well."

They looked at each other again before bursting into laughter.

Evidently the aunts had taken her invitation as a request to be a part of the program. Hannah felt the tension drain out of her. *Well, God, thanks for an interesting experience. Thanks for keeping me humble.*

Nearly an hour later, wearing her brand-new safety harness over a pair of denim overall shorts and a buttery yellow T-shirt, Hannah scooted through the opening in the steeple. "Guthrie! I don't want to startle you again!" she shouted over the noise of his nailing. "Guthrie, I'm coming out!"

His hammering halted. "Hannah, I don't want you out on this roof!"

"Too bad. I'm out on it already!" Straddling the peak, she inched her way around until she faced him. Laughing with her mother over the "live-TV disaster" earlier had brightened her mood. She grinned at him. "I'm an experienced roofer."

"Of course, you are!" he agreed with a sarcastic twist. "But I don't want you up here. It's too dangerous."

"Please, let's just drop this argument, okay? You'll never get the church and house done this year without help. Now, I've got on my safety harness, and it's hooked to the support." She jiggled it at him. "Plus I noticed the scaffold for shingles and the roof jacks you've put in place. I can see you've taken every precaution, and I won't take any chances, I promise!" She pulled on white cotton work gloves. "Now you just stick to your side of the roof, and I'll stick to mine."

"So much for me being the boss of this job!" Guthrie groused.

"I don't mind your deciding what work is to be done and how, but I think we've exhausted the 'sweet little Hannah doesn't know one end of the hammer from the other' routine—thank you very much!"

Guthrie growled at her. "For the record, I'm still against this! And I'm coming over to show you how to do this right. I don't want to waste time and good money ripping off perfectly good shingles!"

"Yes, Guthrie, of course, Guthrie!" She giggled, then let herself down the side of the roof, as if it were the side of a mountain, to the scaffolding that spanned this side of the roof. Yesterday had been gloomy. Today only cottony white clouds blocked the sun.

The bundles of green asphalt shingles had been delivered directly onto the roof. Guthrie appeared on the peak and looked at her. Before he could speak, she said, "Just watch me and see if I do it to suit you!"

He grunted suspiciously.

She ripped open the brown paper covering the nearest bundle and with attention to detail, she trimmed the first shingle, positioned it and nailed it into place. She did another, conscious of the boss's scrutiny. "So, how'd I do?" she challenged him.

"All right." He disappeared to the other side of the roof.

She suppressed another giggle and nailed down the next shingle.

Their two hammers pounded a raucous duet—sometimes counterpoint, sometimes in unison. High above Petite, Hannah experienced a freedom and a lightheartedness she hadn't felt for three long years. Her hands busy, her mind wandered. Looking back on it, being engaged to Edward had been similar to a prison sentence, one she'd given herself. She realized that she'd never really "understood" the real Edward. She'd fallen in love with the life they'd have together as pastor and wife.

Today she didn't feel like the same woman who'd worn Edward's speck of a diamond. That struck her as good, but unnerving. If marrying Edward and being a pastor's wife wasn't what she was intended to be, what was? She'd had a plan for her life, but no more. Coping with this fact felt similar to shingling a roof without any safety harness. It was scary, sweaty-palms scary.

Forcing herself to concentrate on the task at hand, she measured and hammered, staggering the notches of the shingles and overlapping them to insure water resistance. She'd hadn't shingled for over a year. Her straining arm and shoulder muscles would ache in the morning. Oh, yeah!

From her lofty vantage point, she had a view of the little village below, the crisscross of streets and patches of green lawn dotted with leafy trees. Over her shoulder, she stole a glance at Guthrie's mother's backyard where Amber, Jenna and Hunter enjoyed the rare sunny day by climbing and swinging on the bright orange A-frame swing set. Squeals and happy shouts floated on the air, making her grin. Oh, to be as carefree as a child again!

A battered silver pickup drove up the street and parked in front of Martha and Lynda's house. Who was dropping by this late in the afternoon?

"Hey!" Guthrie shouted from the opposite side of the roof. "Carpenter's helper, this is the boss. It's time for a break! Hop to it!"

Hannah chuckled. Guthrie must be coming around if he was teasing her. She climbed to the peak and ducked into the steeple.

Inside, propped against a sawhorse, Guthrie held out a candy bar. "Want one?"

She shook her head. Taking a blue bandanna from her pocket, she wiped her moist forehead. "Don't open that candy bar. I've got something better, a casserole left from my food shoot."

"Is it edible?" he teased.

"Watch it, Guthrie! I'm holding a hammer!" She waved it at him, then dropped it into her open toolbox. "Let's go to the kitchen." She jogged down the steps, and he followed her.

In the kitchen, she opened the white refrigerator, took out the green bean casserole and put it in the microwave. While it rotated and warmed, she pulled paper plates and two forks out of the well-stocked kitchen cupboards.

Guthrie lifted two soft drink cans from the vintage refrigerator and popped both tops for them. The bell on the microwave dinged, and she spooned up a healthy portion for Guthrie and did the same for herself.

"Green beans?" Guthrie looked at his plate.

"Try it. You'll like it." She dug into hers and let the tangy cheese and bacon flavors roll over her tongue. "Mmm."

Guthrie forked up a small bite, chewed, then helped himself to some more. "Good."

"Thank you." Hannah nodded.

"How did the show go today? Did the TV people like it?"

She swallowed quickly before laughter conquered her. Picturing the two great-aunts helping her cook, she vibrated with amusement.

"What's so funny?" He stared at her.

She shook her head, then took a deep breath. "Your great-aunts."

"My aunts? What did they do now?"

Finally Home

She sighed, smiling. "I don't want to insult your family, but what is it with your aunts?"

He exhaled loudly, giving expression to exasperation. "They are eccentric. My mom says they've never really grown up. They're over eighty years old and still act like two young girls."

"I know. But why?"

"Well, they were premature twins back in 1919 and were sickly most of their childhood. They didn't go to school because their mother didn't want them picking up any germs. She taught them at home, and that was pretty much their life until their parents died after World War Two.

"Then my grandfather, their brother, took over and worked the farm with his wife. In the fifties, Grandpa bought his sisters their bungalow in town so they wouldn't have to live with my grandparents or my parents, but they'd still be close enough if they needed help."

"So what you're saying is that they have just lived a sheltered and very dependent life in a small town and that's why they seem to exist in a world, a reality of their own?"

Guthrie shrugged. "I guess so. Exactly what did they do during your live cooking demonstration?"

"They came up and helped me."

Guthrie groaned. "Was my mother there?"

"Yes, but what could she do? She had Hunter in her lap."

"How did you handle it?" he asked.

"Oh, I just ad-libbed my way through it, but the TV reporter and crew looked like they'd just spent time in the twilight zone."

Guthrie swallowed. "It's my fault. The great-aunts were there in the kitchen when you called me last night and heard about the show."

"I invited them, too!" She playfully punched his rock-hard biceps. "Besides, in a town this size, someone would have told them. Don't worry about it. They certainly kept me on my toes, and since I won't be doing any more live TV demos, I don't think we have anything to be worried about."

"Thanks for being so understanding. I wouldn't have wanted them to get their feelings hurt." He smiled at her. A deep, full, irresistible smile.

Funny little squiggly shocks snaked through her arms and legs. Guthrie Thomas smiling at her at close range was obviously too much for her resistance. Fighting his effect on her, she imagined Captain Kirk asking Scotty for the defense shields to be put up. Brushing her unnerving reaction aside, she nonchalantly offered more of the casserole. "Seconds?"

"Please. This is really good. I like the cheese and bacon flavor with the beans."

"You have a discriminating palate, sir." She gave him another generous helping of the creamy white and green casserole. "Why don't you take the rest of this home with you tonight so your family can finish it up? It will just go to waste here."

"Thanks."

"You might be having company tonight for supper."

Guthrie's expression asked a question.

"When I was up on the roof, I saw an older silver-toned truck I didn't recognize pull up to your mother's house."

Guthrie pushed away from the table and hustled toward the hall to the side door.

Hannah stood up. "Guthrie, what's wrong?"

"I'll be back!" Guthrie's farewell was followed by the slamming of the church door.

Whatever did I say to cause that reaction?

Chapter Six

$\sim$

His heart pumping double time, Guthrie bolted out of the church, his anger outracing his feet. When he reached his sister's corner, he caught himself and slowed down. What if this was a false alarm? The person in his sister's house might not be whom he suspected it was at all. But like a waving red flag, the battered pickup sat in plain sight in front of the little yellow house on Church Street.

Taking even breaths, Guthrie walked up the short path and into the house. He paused and closed the door behind him without a sound. If it wasn't the man he dreaded, he'd turn around and go back to the church. Underneath the outside noise of the kids' shouting and squealing, he detected the sound of muted voices in the kitchen. Why were the voices low? That sounded fishy.

He started forward, but his steps slowed—it was like walking up to a ticking package. If the person he thought was in the kitchen actually was in the kitchen, it would upset everything.

In the kitchen doorway, Guthrie stopped.

Mom looked up from where she sat at the table. Her eyes widened.

Guthrie recognized the back of the man's head. The sight sucked the breath right out of him.

The man stood and slowly turned to face him. "Guthrie."

"You." Words roared through Guthrie's head, but only one came out. *"You."*

A ball of fire torched Guthrie's stomach. A red haze clouded his vision. His right fist shot forward.

Billy dodged to the left, then stumbled out of range.

"Guthrie!" his mother exclaimed. "Stop that right now! Beating up your brother-in-law won't help matters."

Gritting his teeth, Guthrie clenched and unclenched his hands. If anyone ever deserved a beating for all he'd done, his sorry excuse for a brother-in-law did!

"Billy has come back to town," Martha said.

"Obviously!" The word burned Guthrie's throat.

Martha went on as though he hadn't spoken. "Billy's cleaned up his life and has come back to shoulder responsibility for his three children."

"They're not his children. They're *our* children. We're raising them with Lynda."

"I truly regret that." Billy spoke in a quiet voice.

Guthrie singed Billy with a glare. "I'm not talking to you. You're not here."

"I am here."

"Not for long." Guthrie was insistent.

"Stop it right now." His mother held up one hand to each man. "Billy left. Billy's back. He's coming again this evening when the kids are in bed to talk to Lynda and see how she wants to handle this."

"How long has he been here?"

The icy words startled Guthrie. He turned to the screen door. Lynda stared in at them. His sister's accusing tone made Guthrie feel guilty—even though he'd done nothing to bring his deadbeat brother-in-law back to Petite.

"How long has he been here?" Lynda repeated coldly.

Billy took a step toward her. "I moved back yesterday. I'm at my mother's. I'd like to talk to you."

Lynda stared him down. "No."

"Mommy!" Hunter called in breathless excitement. "Mommy, look, I'm swinging all by myself!"

Lynda turned. "That's great, Hunter!" She looked at the occupants of the kitchen and said in a frigid tone, "I don't want you upsetting the children. Please leave."

"I'll go for now, Lynda. When you're ready to talk, let me know."

Lynda walked toward her children.

Billy passed Guthrie. He walked out the front door.

Guthrie shivered. Lynda had doused the fire in his gut.

His mother sat, folded her hands in front of her face and wept.

A few minutes later, Guthrie found himself climbing onto the roof from the steeple opening. He'd walked to the church in a daze. Hannah's hammering sounded in his ears and echoed through his body.

Seeing Billy over three years after his desertion, Guthrie felt pounded, battered, and the sound of the hammer intensified this. Suddenly weak in the knees, he sat in the steeple opening. Billy here in town? He couldn't believe it.

"Is that you, Guthrie?" Hannah shouted.

"Yeah," he answered hoarsely.

"You got a call while you were away. Benard's Building Supply called to say they have the zinc strips and the rest of the shingles that were on back order. We can pick them up any time."

The energy had leaked out of Guthrie. He couldn't have raised a hammer if he tried. Going to Benard's would be a good excuse to get away for a while. "Let's go."

"You go. I'll stay and work."

He inhaled. "This is your boss speaking. I won't leave you on this roof alone. Pack up your hammer and nails. You can go home or you can come with me. Your choice."

"All right. I'll come. I want to look at wallpaper and paint. Mom wants me to bring samples back to her."

He heard Hannah's footsteps as she levered herself to the peak of the roof. He was glad she was coming along. Her presence would distract him.

Inside the attic, he undid his worn leather tool belt. She led him down the attic stair-steps and another flight down to the basement office.

"Mom, I am going to Benard's with Guthrie."

Her mother halted her typing at the word processor. "Thank you, dear. You know the paint colors and wall-paper styles I would be interested in."

Hannah gave her mother a kiss on her forehead. "Love you."

"Love you, too."

Hannah led him out to the truck. He automatically opened the door for her, then he got behind the wheel. Guthrie wondered if his mother was still crying at home.

Something was wrong.

Hannah studied Guthrie from the corner of her eye. In just the few days she'd known this man, she'd come to expect his low-key good humor. Earlier, from her high perch, she'd watched him run to his mother's house and seen Lynda drive up and walk to the back door. Within minutes, a stranger had hurried out the front door and into his truck, then driven away. What did it all mean? The cheerful light in Guthrie's eyes had been snuffed. Why?

"Is your mother all right?" she asked tentatively.

"She's fine."

Next possibility. "You needed something at home?"

"No."

Okay, then. "Your sister came home from work early?"

"Yeah."

Last question. "Your mother had a visitor?"

"That's none of your business!" he exploded.

So the stranger was the problem. She looked out the window on her side. "Sorry."

A few moments passed, then Guthrie said, "I'm sorry. I didn't mean to blow up at you." He sounded miserable and grumpy at the same time.

"No, I'm sorry. I'm afraid I'm so used to having people confide in my parents, and sometimes even in me, that I assume too much. I'll try to remember curiosity killed the cat." She kept her gaze on the scenery, giving him space to grapple with whatever this stranger meant to him.

They'd left Petite far behind them. Lush green cornfields and hayfields, verdant pastures like luxuriant green carpet dotted with black and white Holsteins, Wisconsin's favorite dairy cattle, passed her window.

He cleared his throat. "What kind of wallpaper…I mean, what room is your mother planning to wallpaper?"

Hannah recognized his invitation to smooth things over and go on with the day. She offered him a warm smile. "Mom likes wallpaper or a border in almost every room. She had me bring her samples from several stores in Milwaukee, but she's still looking. She loves to decorate, and she loves looking at samples of wallpaper and paint chips."

"Just like my mother. I remember when she decided to strip the wallpaper off our kitchen walls at the farm.

She wanted to paint and hand-stencil a border around the room. She started stripping and ended up taking off nine different layers of wallpaper before she reached the wall itself."

"Nine? How old is your farmhouse?"

"Built in 1909."

"Nearly a hundred years old." She teased him with a grin. "After your mom took off the wallpaper, did the walls cave in?"

"Very funny. No, but she did have something to say about people who wallpaper over wallpaper over wallpaper." He chuckled.

She joined him. The Guthrie she knew was coming back. From the corner of her eye, she watched him drive. Observing this man was pure pleasure. It wasn't just his physical attractiveness. Today his customary peace had been ruffled, but his solid aura of strength and honesty drew her spirit to his. Guthrie Thomas was a man a woman could count on for a direct answer and kindness. Unfortunately, she'd only imagined Edward had those qualities.

She kept up an easy flow of conversation until they parted at the crowded entrance of Benard's. Though still concerned over her new boss's moodiness, she spent several happy minutes picking out wallpaper and border samples and paint chips. The paint manager stood nearby mixing a custom shade of peach for a young red-haired mother who was expecting a child and had a baby boy sitting in her cart, jabbering to passersby.

Hannah waved her pinkie finger at the little guy, which made him squeal with excitement. She selected a paint chip for that same shade of peach, one of her mother's favorite colors. She also picked up the latest do-it-yourself sheets on rag painting and feather painting. Her creative mother might want to try her hand at those.

Smiling, she met Guthrie at the front entrance. She loved the bustle of customers around them, pushing carts top-heavy with area rugs, light bulbs, plant food, paint and much more.

Carrying the long, narrow, silvery zinc strips that would prevent moss from growing on the roof, he led her to the truck. Then he drove them through the lumber yard entrance and loaded the shingles, which had finally come in. He headed the truck toward Petite.

Only a few miles from home, Hannah saw a welcome sign hand-painted on plywood. Farmers' Market Today! She grabbed Guthrie's arm.

He glanced over at her touch. "What?"

"We have to stop at the farmers' market." Her hand still gripped the bottom of his arm, his warm skin within her grasp.

"But you're not cooking. I mean you're living at the motel." He glanced at her hand.

"I'm sorry." She released his arm, abashed at herself. She went on in a steady voice, suppressing the urge to foolishly apologize for her lingering touch. "That doesn't matter. I can't resist a farmers' market. You never know what you might find!"

"Okay, whatever you say." He pulled the truck into an empty spot in the row of trucks and cars, then parked in matted wild grass. Nearby a double row of tables had been set up at the front of a county park with a ball diamond in the distance. Some vendors stood behind tables, some sold from the backs of their pickups. An abundance of sweet corn, zucchini, cabbage, tomatoes and muskmelon in bushel baskets gave the air a sweet scent.

Hannah jumped out of the truck, avoiding mud from yesterday's rain. She gazed at the feast of color, light green, dark green, red-orange and gold. This was her kind of place.

She stopped to admire the sweet corn in the back of an old, rusted red pickup.

"Picked fresh today. Do you want one dozen or two?" the grandmother in blue jeans and a ball cap asked.

"Just a half dozen. I don't have any place to store it." She'd fix it for her parents for lunch tomorrow in the church kitchen.

"Well, if you're feeding Guthrie Thomas, you'll need half a dozen just for him." The woman chuckled and winked at Guthrie, standing behind Hannah.

"Thanks for reminding me!" Hannah snapped open the paper bag the woman had given her and began choosing a dozen plump ears. She stripped the outer husk and punctured a kernel to watch the milky juice spurt out. The white and yellow kernels looked like rows of exotic pearls.

Guthrie nodded at the woman politely. "This is Hannah Kirkland, our new pastor's daughter."

"Oh, hi! I thought I recognized you. I saw you on TV today. Hey, Karen, this is the new pastor's daughter in Petite. You saw her today on the noon show, didn't you?"

For the first time in her career, Hannah found herself mobbed. She definitely wasn't in Milwaukee anymore! Women swarmed around her, each vying for her attention.

"I have your first cookbook. I wish I'd brought it so you could sign it."

"Your recipes helped me lower my husband's cholesterol twenty-nine points!"

"I thought it was so sweet of you to let the Thomas sisters help you on today's show."

"Imagine someone letting Ida and Edith cook with them! You must be a saint!"

From across the way, Lila Fink waved to her.

After speaking to everyone, Hannah thanked them and walked over to her landlady. "Hello, Lila." Hannah felt a bit dizzy after so much attention. "What are you doing here?"

"I'm helping out my sister. She sells fresh eggs and weaves these rugs."

Hannah looked down. "These are beautiful rugs." Hannah stroked the lush warp and weave of the multi-shaded white, buff and gray rugs and shook her head. "Does she make rugs to special order?"

"Sure. Just tell her the size you need."

"Lady! Lady, do you want a kitty?" A little dark-haired girl with a pixie haircut held up a little yellow tabby with a fat baby belly.

"Oh! He's precious!" Hannah took the tiny ball of silky fur in both hands. The kitten mewled until she cradled it close to her face. She'd wanted a cat of her own for years, but Edward hadn't liked cats.

"Do you want them, lady? I got three left, two from one mama cat and one from another one. Their eyes are opened, and they're ready to leave their mamas."

"I'm sorry, honey. But I'm living in Mrs. Fink's motel and I can't have a kitty."

"Sure you can," Lila said. "Cats don't make any mess."

"You mean it?" Hannah felt as giddy as when she was a six-year-old and her father had brought home her first kitten.

"Can you take two more?" the little girl asked plaintively. "We don't need anymore barn cats at our place."

Hannah shook her head, then stopped. "Yes, I'll take one more for my mother." She giggled. "She'll need a new cat for her new house."

"I'll take the last one." Guthrie spoke up. "Amber and Jenna have been asking for one."

"Hey, Guthrie," Lila asked abruptly, "what's your no-account brother-in-law doing back in town?"

Hannah watched Guthrie's tanned face redden. So that's who'd upset him!

"He won't be around for long." The ugly tone

Guthrie used worried her. It revealed the depth of the anger and pain he was experiencing. How must Lynda be suffering? A homecoming should be joyful, not agonizing.

Guthrie accepted the final cat from the little girl, then asked brusquely, "Hannah, did you need anything else?"

Hannah took the hint in his question. "No, that's all. Lila, please tell your sister my mother will be getting in touch with her about ordering some area rugs."

"Okay." Lila glanced apologetically at the tall man standing beside Hannah. "Sorry if I upset you, Guthrie. It was just such a shock to see Billy in town yesterday."

"No problem," Guthrie said in such a way that reiterated that it was a big problem.

Carrying her two kittens, Hannah walked beside him to the truck. The soft gray kitten looked out of place cradled in the crook of his powerful arm. One of her golden kittens still mewed, but the one in Guthrie's arm looked around, trusting, enjoying the ride. Back in the truck, she took charge of the three kittens.

While Guthrie drove, she sat Indian-style, letting them nest in her lap. Their sharp little claws slipped right through her heavy denim shorts. "Ouch!" she scolded them with a giggle in her throat. Murmuring to them, she stroked under their chins, making them purr and arch their necks, begging for more.

The silent man beside her drew her sympathy. But she knew better than to wound him by saying anything.

At this point, even the most kindly meant words might cause pain instead of comfort. *I'm so sorry for you, Guthrie, and your family and for the pain and worry Lynda must be feeling, too! Lord, you know what has gone before and what is happening now. Please be with this family and help the right things happen. Work your miracle of love!*

When he turned into town, Guthrie finally spoke, "I'm sorry. I'm letting my bad mood get me down, and you don't deserve to be ignored like this."

"That's all right. I realized earlier when you took off from the roof so suddenly that something was wrong. Do you want to talk about it?"

He made a sound of disgust. "I just didn't think we'd ever have to deal with him. He took off right after Lynda delivered Hunter prematurely." He paused as though remembering something he didn't want to recall. He shook his head. "It hit everyone hard."

"How awful for your sister, for your family."

"He's done enough damage. I'm not going to let him do any more! Lynda has worked hard to get over the pain and make a life for herself and the kids. I won't let him jeopardize them again."

She touched his arm for the second time that day. "You might not be able to do anything. Since they were legally married, I'm sure he'll be able to get visitation rights, at least." She caught the boldest kitten as it tried to crawl off her lap.

"I'll do something."

She thought he cursed under his breath.

"I'll do something," he repeated.

The Sunday morning sun gilded the tops of the golden oak pews. The small stained glass window high on the wall behind her father glowed with brilliant red, blue and gold. Hannah knew something had upset the people sitting around her, but she couldn't put her finger on the uneasy emotion she sensed.

She sat in the second pew, next to her mother, as she always had in church, and watched her father lead the first Sunday service she'd attended in Petite. The service had begun normally with a prelude and greeting, then a hymn. During the singing of "Bringing in the Sheaves," a disturbed rustle had gone through the congregation.

Hannah had glanced over her shoulder and observed a young man in clean but worn clothing take his seat in a back pew. Her head wasn't the only one that had turned. The rustle was from the craning of necks and heated whispers.

The arrival of the stranger seemed to paralyze the congregation. Everyone, even the children, stilled. Was this man's presence the cause of the tension around her? If Hannah had brought a thermometer into the sanctuary, she knew the temperature in the room would read chilling. Was this Guthrie's brother-in-law?

If she could have glimpsed the Thomas family's reaction she would have had her answer. But they sat several rows behind her, and she couldn't see them unless she stood up and turned completely around. And, of course, she couldn't do that.

Maybe this wasn't Lynda's ex at all. He could be some other member in a small-town feud who'd entered enemy territory.

This was one of the factors that made switching congregations perilous for a new pastor. No matter what the Bible said about loving one another and forgiving, most churches had some person who acted as a lightning rod. Someone who sparked controversy her parents would have to neutralize, or there would be unpleasant conflict within the church.

Hannah bowed her head. *Dear Lord, whatever this man has done or left undone, please don't let this little church fall into conflict. It's so sad, Lord, to see people who should know the most about loving and forgiving begin to squabble and separate themselves from each other. Oh, Lord, please bind up the spirit of discord and take it far from us here. Bless my father and mother, give them the right words to say and the right actions to take. Amen.*

Hannah felt better immediately. She'd done right this time, not stewing, but turning everything straight over to God.

She glanced up. Her father was smiling at her. She smiled back. The service continued. All through the sermon, the stiff uneasiness in the congregation went unabated. Finally, the organ played the closing hymn, "Just As I Am."

Praying for peace with each word, Hannah sang, "Without one plea, but that your blood was shed for me."

Her father stepped forward to give the benediction.

As if on cue, the stranger walked forward down the center aisle runner of worn maroon carpeting and up the two steps to the pulpit. "If you don't mind, pastor, I'd like to say a few words."

A rustle of startled murmurs passed through the congregation.

Hannah held her breath. Would her questions be answered now?

Her father looked surprised, but asked, "What kind of words?"

"An apology."

Hannah stared at the man. *Oh, my, an apology given from a pulpit. That is very rare. Dad, help him.*

Her father nodded and motioned everyone to sit down, then stepped away.

The young man stood beside the wood pulpit with one trembling hand resting on it and looked out over the congregation. "You all know me, except for your new pastor. You know what I've done and that I ran away. I guess you could call me Petite's prodigal son. I've spent the past three years in Chicago living on the streets. Drugs took me there, put me there, kept me there." The man wiped sweat from his forehead.

The congregation sat in total silence, even the children.

Hannah ached for him. He stood alone. The story of

the prodigal son played in her mind. The prodigal had said, "Father, I have sinned against God and against you. I am not fit to be called your son."

"About a year ago in Chicago, I staggered into the Salvation Army near Maxwell Street looking for a meal and a bed for the night. I got more than that. That night for the first time I faced up to what my addiction had done to me, to my family. That night I promised God I'd get off drugs if He would stand with me. Since you know God, you all know what His answer was." The man stood a little straighter.

The deep emotion in his plain words touched Hannah. She blinked away tears.

"I've been clean since that night. I went through a substance abuse program, and I attend AA meetings weekly. I know most of you never wanted to see my face again, but once I came back to my right mind, I knew I had to come back home. I have responsibilities. I have a job in Portage and will be staying with my mother and assuming responsibility for the family I left behind. I hope you will all give me a second chance. But I won't blame you if you don't." The man stepped down and walked to the back of the church.

Hannah glanced around. She wasn't the only one grappling with overwhelming emotion. Everyone looked stunned. She could only think of Guthrie's sister. This man must be Billy.

At the end of the benediction, Dad said the final amen and everyone stood up. Hannah noticed that, as one, everyone refused to look at the stranger. She'd heard the Amish used shunning on members who didn't conform. Evidently this congregation was so shocked they couldn't confront the man. Instead, everyone gathered around Lynda and her family as though trying to protect them. Lynda's face looked frozen, pained.

As Hannah had expected, however, her father made a beeline to the stranger, shook his hand and talked to him for several minutes while everyone else pointedly kept their attention elsewhere. Wasn't anyone going to speak to him? Finally, the stranger walked out of the sanctuary.

Hannah watched him go. *Dear Lord, you've sent Mom and Dad a tough one this time.*

Chapter Seven

The shrill ring of the phone by the bed woke Hannah. In the midnight darkness, she groped for the receiver while trying to bring the bedside clock face, the only circle of light in the room, into focus. "Hello?"

"Gotcha!" Doree's voice giggled in her ear.

"Oh, go to bed." Hannah closed her eyes. "It's after one a.m. Why aren't you asleep?"

"I'm back on campus. Who goes to sleep before two a.m. around here?"

"Do I care? Good—"

"No! Tell me how Mom and Dad are and how the search is going."

"Haven't you talked to Spring?"

"No. I'm talking to you."

Hannah came fully awake. No use trying to go back to sleep. She sat up in bed, arranging her feather pillow behind her, then leaning against it. Fatigue made her whole body feel heavier than normal. Lifting her arm compared to lifting a twenty-pound bag of cement.

"Doree, I thought you'd stop here on your way back to Madison."

"Couldn't. My car died for the last time in Milwaukee and I had to hitch a ride with a few friends. I couldn't ask them to stop. What's up? What was Spring going to tell me?"

Hannah sighed. Doree wouldn't like the answer. "Mom and Dad's house isn't going to be ready on time." The little golden kitten Hannah had adopted woke up from where it slept near her side. It baby-mewed softly as it yawned.

"Oh? How far is it from being finished?"

"They have a foundation." The stark image of her parents' forlorn foundation came to Hannah's mind.

"And?"

"And nothing else." The issue, the unfinished house, had been overshadowed in Hannah's mind by the dramatic return of Lynda's ex. What did wood and cement matter when human hearts remained broken? The worrying thoughts Hannah had finally eluded with sleep rushed back, seizing her dog-tired mind.

Last Sunday evening, Dad had talked to Mom and Hannah about Billy and Lynda, then they had prayed for healing and reconciliation. So far their prayers hadn't moved Lynda. Nearly a week had passed and still she hadn't spoken to Billy. The town of Petite watched, frowned and murmured. Several had called her father,

.though Dad couldn't force Lynda to deal with the issue. Last night, Martha had called Dad and asked him to speak to Lynda. So he had walked over after the children had gone to bed. No luck. She'd politely thanked him for his concern and turned away. But ignoring Billy wouldn't make him go away.

Doree's voice broke in on Hannah's thoughts. "Hey, you're not listening to me. I said, and I quote, 'A foundation, just a foundation! Is this some kind of sick joke?' And are you trying to get out of looking for Mom's adoption papers?"

Hannah's emotions felt worn thin, like the 1970s faded harvest gold sheets on her bed. "Doree, the rain has delayed the house."

"Hey, it hasn't rained that much since June."

"Dad's church's roof needed to be replaced by the same builder." The kitten climbed onto Hannah's lap.

"And, of course, our parents said, 'No problem. We'll wait.' Sheesh!"

"Yes, you've got the picture." Hannah worried her lower lip.

"Darn." Rock music screeched in the background in Doree's dorm. "You can't do a thing about the adoption papers until the house is done. Everything's in storage."

"Too true."

"You're not trying to weasel out then?"

"Weasel out? In Milwaukee, I told you I'd think about it." Hannah's kitten kneaded her gold twill bedspread with its tiny paws, then curled up to go back to sleep, purring.

"So? Did you *think* about it?"

Yes, in between helping Guthrie, writing her column and outlining her next cookbook, she had pondered and prayed about searching for her mother's biological family. She wished she could wipe her mind clean of prodigal fathers, inclement weather and her mother's leukemia. "Quite a bit."

"And?"

"I'm beginning to think you're right." In fact, Hannah had worried before coming to Petite that she might not have a choice.

"I know I'm right."

"Of course, you do, Doree. You always think you're right!"

Doree ignored her. "Oh, I almost forgot! I saw you on TV! I was in the Student Union eating lunch when I looked up at the wall TV and there you were. Hannah, how did you get on TV?"

Hannah wondered at her sister's flightiness. Straight from discussing their mother's illness to the TV show? "My agent had called them several times in the past trying to get a spot when each of my cookbooks came out, but no luck. Then they called her out of the blue. She gave them my number, and they asked me to fill in their local spot on the noon news. I said yes." Hannah yawned.

"Where were you cooking? I thought, 'If that's Mom's new kitchen, I'm going to strangle the builder even if he is a hunk.' How is he, anyway?"

Doree, let me go back to sleep, please. I don't want

to deal with this now. "I was cooking in the church kitchen, and Guthrie is fine."

"*Guthrie* is fine," Doree's voice teased. "My, we're getting friendly with the builder, aren't we?"

"It's a small town." Hannah recalled the day of the live cooking demonstration, and later, Guthrie's preoccupation on their trip to Portage. He must have known then that his ex-brother-in-law was in town.

Hannah pulled her mind back to the conversation at hand. "Besides, I've begun pitching in to help him get the church done so he can get on with our parents' house."

Doree laughed. "Outrageous! I wish I could see you up on the roof with him."

"Yes, yes, anything else?" Hannah asked wearily. "I have to be up and ready at six for breakfast and at the church by seven."

"Oh, yeah, who were those funny old ladies who were on the show with you? I don't remember seeing them on that station before."

Hannah felt uncomfortable with her sister's careless words. Ida and Edith were sweet, just a little vague on facts and if, because of them, she didn't get asked back to that noon show, the world wouldn't end. "Those were Guthrie's maiden great-aunts who live here in town."

"Don't get huffy. They were great! They were hilarious! Kind of like having an old radio comedy team cooking with you."

One corner of Hannah's mouth crinkled up. "It was

funny. Afterwards," she admitted. "During the show when they popped up from the audience, I nearly passed out."

"You mean you didn't plan on them helping? What a hoot!"

"Yes, and on that note, good night, little baby sister." Hannah hung up on a protesting Doree. She said to the receiver, back in its place, "'Little baby sister' serves you right for waking me up in the middle of the night."

With one last pat for her cat, she slid down, glanced at the clock and groaned. Closing her eyes, she tried to relax, tried to empty her mind of all the thoughts she'd been fighting before she finally fell asleep the first time.

Oh, Lord, let your love flow through Petite and change the hearts here. So much pain, so much of the past to be forgiven. Would Lynda give Billy a second chance? Would Guthrie? Did they have a choice?

At six-twenty the next morning, yawning, Hannah walked into Hanson's Cozy Café.

"None of that allowed in here!" Lila called from behind the worn, speckled Formica counter. "You'll have us all yawning. Coffee?"

Nodding, Hannah swallowed another yawn, sat down at the counter and placed her order.

Lila called the order to the cook behind her. "So when do you think Lynda will break down and talk to Billy?"

Shrugging, Hannah tried to think of a polite, nongossipy reply, but drew a blank. Fortunately or unfortunately, Lila didn't seem to need one.

"Well, I feel sorry for his mother, Terri Sue. She not only lost her son when Billy took off, but she hasn't been able to face Lynda. But he's her only son, and those three children are her only grandchildren."

This bit of news stirred Hannah's sympathy. "I haven't met Terri Sue."

"Well, she isn't very sociable since the trouble with her son. She lives about five miles west of town, works in Portage."

"I'm sorry to hear that. I didn't think Lynda would—"

"Oh, Lynda didn't say Terri Sue couldn't see the children. But the way Billy left and all that happened because he left made his mother too ashamed. Martha even called her after the funeral and told her they didn't bear her any grudge. Real Christian of Martha, I say. It was her husband, after all."

Funeral? Martha's husband? Hannah couldn't follow what Lila was saying, but before she could ask, four boisterous truckers came in demanding breakfast. Lila left the counter to take their orders. Soon she placed Hannah's breakfast in front of her, but was too busy to stop and finish their conversation.

Hannah chewed her buttery eggs and crisp bacon and pondered what Billy could have done that had made his mother so ashamed she couldn't face her grandchildren. Terri Sue was another victim in this family tragedy. Would Hannah ever get used to the way families hurt one another? Spring, Doree and she had been so lucky in the family they'd been born into.

But what about their mother? When...*if* Hannah located the adoption papers, would they lead her and her sisters to another sad, painful story? Giving a child up for adoption must have been the result of one. She bet Doree hadn't thought about that. Hannah closed her eyes and pushed this out of her mind. A heart could only carry so much at one time. She forced herself to finish breakfast and waved goodbye to Lila. On the way out of the restaurant, she stopped at a table to chat with Becky, one of the beauticians at the Bizzy Bee whom she'd met at church. She made an appointment with Becky for a trim and left with a wave. Then she headed to the church for a day on the roof.

By the time the sun had climbed high, Hannah had shingled halfway up her side of the dark green roof. She did know how to shingle a roof, but that didn't mean she was fast. She'd only done it a few times before, but she felt she was getting better, more efficient.

Guthrie, on the other side, sounded close to the peak by the timbre of his hammer. It wasn't like they were competing, but Hannah still didn't like it that she was losing.

"I'll be able to come over and help you after I finish three more rows," Guthrie called as if he'd been reading her mind. "In fact, it's time for a break. Meet me in the steeple."

"Good." She pounded one more roofing nail in.

"I've been thinking," Guthrie shouted.

"Wow! What brought that on?" she teased. She'd tried to act as naturally as possible toward Guthrie since church on Sunday. She surmised he must be suffering internal turmoil, but she couldn't do anything to change what had happened years ago or this week. He'd spent most of the week on his dairy feeder cattle farm, harvesting this winter's hay crop while the fields had been blessedly dry.

The time apart had made it awkward to be working alone with him. She'd hoped he would stop by the motel or church office and open up to her father. Didn't Guthrie realize the danger in which his sister's children stood? It made Hannah feel a little sick every time she imagined Amber, Jenna or little Hunter overhearing something they weren't supposed to hear.

Guthrie didn't reply to her teasing question until he appeared at the peak and looked down at her. The sunshine gilded his tanned arms. Hannah swallowed, trying to moisten her suddenly dry mouth.

He settled his hand on his tool belt. "Very funny. I think I've thought of a way to hurry up your parents' house."

"You what!" Energized, she began pulling herself up to meet him.

He repeated his sentence as she climbed.

"Don't keep me in suspense! What's the idea?"

"Well, you know how I suggested to your parents that they go with a factory-built house?"

"Yes?" She reached the peak.

His hands under her arms, Guthrie swung her effortlessly up the last foot onto the peak, then motioned her to precede him into the steeple opening. She ducked inside.

He thumped down after her. "There's another option I hadn't mentioned to them. Instead of doing the stick-built house that I planned for them, I can order a factory shell."

"What's that?" Tugging off her grimy white cotton gloves, she turned to face him. "They didn't want a factory-built house. How is this different?"

"A shell is the outer walls with windows and doors and roof all manufactured and assembled at the factory. They truck the completed walls here and put them up with a crane. The whole exterior can be put together and enclosed in twelve hours. What do you think of that?"

Words failed Hannah. Twelve hours and the house would be up! She couldn't believe it. She couldn't help herself. She threw her arms around his neck and kissed him.

Guthrie's lips parted with surprise. So close to him, she lost herself in the mingled scents of wood, leather, fresh hay and honest perspiration. Her lips tingled, and she shivered. Sensations, warm and exciting, rippled through her. Needing something solid to hold on to, she tightened her hold around his neck. *Oh, my, this is wonderful. I never knew.... Oh, my...*

Then a quicksilver thought flashed her back to reality. *Oh, no, I'm kissing Guthrie Thomas! What must he think of me?* Before she embarrassed herself more, she pulled away.

"That's a wonderful idea! Twelve hours! Do you mean that? My parents will be ecstatic." Words fell out of her mouth as she tried to distract him from the fact that she'd just kissed him.

Ignoring her words, Guthrie tucked her close again, leaned down and kissed her.

His lips immobilized her. *He kissed me back. What's going on?* She couldn't draw breath. "Guthrie," she finally cautioned, quivering.

A shocked expression on his face, he stepped back. "Sorry. Don't know what got into me."

Her face blazed. *And I don't know what got into me! And Edward never kissed me like that! I never knew....* "My fault. I kissed you first. I was just so excited...."

Guthrie pushed his hands through his moist hair. "It's all this about Lynda's... I don't feel like myself. I would never—"

Hannah touched his forearm. Her glance spoke her sympathy. She wanted to say, "Don't let Lynda wait too long. Someone else might tell the children that their father has come back to town. Lynda should be the one." But she couldn't speak. The look in his blue eyes warned her away.

Changing the subject without saying a word, he glanced over her shoulder toward the stairs. "Let's go down and see what your parents think about my idea."

"Great. Let's go." She automatically tugged off her

tool belt and led him down to the church office. The shell could be up in twelve hours. Feeling the first ray of hope in days, she nearly skipped into the office. "Mom, is Dad busy?"

Hannah bent and picked up her kitten from the laundry basket where it snoozed on a frayed white bath towel. Her mom's new cat looked up, blinking sleepily. The little yellow tabby purred in Hannah's ear, then licked her with its tiny sandpaper tongue.

Her mother looked up quizzically and turned to tap on the door behind her. "Garner, can you put your sermon aside for a minute? Hannah and Guthrie want to talk to us."

Dad came out right away. "What about?"

"Guthrie has come up with a great idea," Hannah started, "for speeding up the work on your house."

Immediately her father looked skeptical.

So Hannah stepped aside, motioning toward Guthrie.

Guthrie stood, his weight on his heels. "You know how bad I feel about not being able to get your house done on time? Well, I was thinking the other night that I hadn't told you about a third way to build a house."

"A third way?" Garner asked. "This won't mean a loss of quality?"

"No. You see, it's only the shell." Guthrie rounded his hands together, demonstrating the idea. "I mean, we just order the shell, and it's made at the factory. They truck it in and put it up with a crane—"

"In twelve hours!" Hannah had to interrupt.

Her mother motioned Guthrie to sit down. "Start at the beginning, Guthrie, not the end."

Hannah sat down on the floor to play with the kittens.

Easing into the chair in front of the desk, Guthrie took his time and explained how he'd take the plans to a company in Prairie du Chein and order the custom-made shell, what it would cost and how much time it would save him. "You see, my custom work actually goes into the interior. As it is, I've held off putting down the subfloor for fear of rain damage.

"This way the house would all be enclosed in one day, really. Then I can spend the fall—after haying is done—just working on putting up wallboard, laying flooring and doing the custom work you want done."

"And I'd still help him with that." Hannah grinned so wide it hurt the corners of her jaw. The two kittens with sharp little claws crawled around in her lap, tumbling over each other. Hannah winced as each tiny claw poked her.

"But won't that take away part of your profit?" Dad asked.

"Some. But I figure I'll get yours up and done, and I'll still have time to take on another house and do the same with it, then spend the winter finishing its interior—after yours is done."

"Well, we'll need to talk this over." Her father glanced at her mother.

"Ouchy," Hannah murmured to the kittens. She lifted one in each hand, high above her lap. "I've got to trim your claws, you little sweeties." She set them on the rug.

Her mother nodded. The church phone rang. She answered it, "Petite Community Church, Ethel speaking."

Hannah looked at Guthrie. "I'm thirsty. I've got sun tea ready for us in the refrigerator."

He smiled, something he hadn't done much since Sunday. "There are some advantages to having you as my carpenter's helper."

Her mother said, "She'll be right over." She hung up. "Hannah, that was the vet. She's had a cancellation this afternoon, and if you go right over, she has time to give the kittens their distemper shots."

Catching her kitten, Hannah rose. "Guthrie, I promised Amber that I'd take her along with her kitty, too. I won't be gone long."

"Okay. I'll drink a glass of sun tea and then go back up on the roof." He bent and scooped up her mother's kitten from beside his work boot. The little ball of gray fur looked minuscule in his large capable hand. "Does Lynda know about this?"

"Yes." Hannah accepted the kitten from him. "Mom, call Martha and tell her I'll be picking up Amber and kitty. That will give them a few minutes to round up the cat."

Within ten minutes, she sat beside Amber in her red SUV. Amber held her velvety gray kitten close to her face. "She's so soft."

"I know." Hannah smiled. "What did you name her?"

"I decided to name her Misty because her fur is like the sky when it's misty outside."

"Amber, what a great name!" Hannah praised the child and meant it. "And it's given me the perfect name for mine."

"Really? What are you going to call her?" Amber asked.

"Sunny! Because she's golden like a sunny day!"

"Cool," Amber said. "Misty and Sunny. What did your mama name her cat?"

"She hasn't named him yet. She likes to take her time in picking out a name. So we'll just call him Cat until he has an official name."

"Okay."

From one of the county roads, Hannah turned into the graveled parking lot of the vet. Inside the office, barking and meowing sounded from the back where the hospital part was located. Amber and Hannah sat down on a bench in the designated cat side of the waiting room.

The door to the examining rooms opened, and a young female vet in a white lab coat walked out, followed by a man carrying a Chihuahua. Hannah was paying only scant attention to the vet as she talked to the man about bringing the Chihuahua back for a reexamination.

But Amber popped up, walked over and stared at him. When Hannah recognized who the man was, she froze.

Amber announced, "Damon Kinney says you're my daddy."

Chapter Eight

Oh, no! Hannah's worst fear for Lynda's children was happening to Amber right in front of her eyes. Damon Kinney had seen Billy at church just as Amber had, and evidently Damon's parents had discussed who Billy was in front of Damon. Hannah stared at the child and her father, frantically trying to think what to say to defuse the situation, how to protect the little girl's feelings.

"Yes, I am your daddy," Billy said quietly.

"How come you went away and left us?" Amber asked. "You didn't even come back for Christmas."

Hannah wept inside. *Oh, Amber, I'm so sorry. I wanted to prevent this from happening to you, but I couldn't.*

"I was stupid." Billy gazed into his daughter's eyes. "I didn't know then how lucky I was to have your mom and you kids."

"Does that mean you want us back now?" Amber asked with bright hope in every syllable.

Hannah flinched at the vulnerability of this innocent child. She slid forward on the bench to go to Amber, to rescue her.

"It means I know now that you kids and your mom are priceless gifts from God. And I would like to get to know you and your sister and brother." Billy's voice quivered with emotion.

Hannah held her breath.

"Okay." Amber nodded. "You can. We'd like to get to know you. We want to have a daddy."

Amber's simple words pierced Hannah's heart like needles. How freely Amber forgave the father who'd abandoned her. Oh, for the faith of a child!

Billy handed the Chihuahua to the vet and squatted in front of Amber at eye level. "I think you'll have to talk that over with your mother first, Amber. I'm the one who left. Your mother stayed and took care of you kids, so she has to be the one to decide when I can see you. That's why I haven't come to your house to see the three of you yet." He reached out and touched the kitten in Amber's arms. His hand trembled. "Is this your kitty?"

Amber nodded.

The vet looked at Hannah as if to ask what was going on. Hannah shrugged.

The tiny dog in the vet's arms yipped as though reminding Billy of its existence. Billy rose and retrieved the Chihuahua from the vet. "It was nice seeing you, Amber, and I hope to see you again soon."

Hannah wondered what it felt like to have your child treat you like a stranger.

"Okay. I'll ask Mommy."

"You do that." With a drawn expression, Billy nodded to Hannah and walked out.

Amber came back to her. "That was my daddy."

"I heard him." Hannah yearned to hug Amber close, but she didn't want to add any emotion to this already heart-rending incident. Better for the child if Hannah acted as naturally as possible.

"Why didn't Mommy tell me he came back? Damon Kinney knew."

Hannah had also dreaded this inevitable question. How did children unerringly go straight to the heart of the matter? She thought quickly and came up with a careful answer. "Your daddy told you why. It's up to your mother to decide when you would meet your father again."

"Well, I met him."

"Then you'll have to tell your mother that." Not wishing to be asked any more questions, Hannah stood up. Cradling two squirming kittens in one arm, she took Amber's hand and led her to the vet. "Now let's get our three kittens their shots."

What will Guthrie do when I tell him about this? Oh, Lord, deal with Guthrie and Lynda's wounded hearts.

Back in front of the little yellow house on Church Street, Amber waved goodbye to Hannah, then ran up the short path to her house.

Though weighed down with worry, Hannah smiled

and waved back. Then she drove her red SUV back to the church and parked in the gravel lot there. Climbing out of the truck, she was greeted by the rhythmic sound of Guthrie's hammer above her. Without enthusiasm, she walked back into the church and deposited the gray-striped and golden kittens in the blue laundry basket. They immediately pounced on one another, rolling over and over each other.

The office was deserted. Neither her father or mother were in sight. Maybe they'd gone to the kitchen for a coffee break. She considered trying to find them.

But that was cowardly. The man pounding nails on the roof was the one she needed to talk to. Her father had already tried to make Lynda see reality. Maybe it was time for her to shake Guthrie up. *God, as Paul stood up to Peter, give me the strength to stand up to Guthrie Thomas and move him to talk his sister into dealing with this crisis. Stand by my side and give me the strength of Samson and the wisdom of Solomon. I'll need both.*

With this prayer in her heavy heart, she mounted the stairs, pulled on her tool belt and crawled through the steeple opening. "Guthrie, I'm back!"

"I thought you'd decided to take the rest of the day off. How long does it take to get three kittens vaccinated?" Guthrie had finished his side and had started on hers. About one-quarter remained undone.

His unconcerned tone deepened her regret at having to bring bad tidings. "It took as long as it needed." After

slipping on her work gloves, she hooked her safety
harness and let herself down the side of the roof. Just
over two weeks ago, getting her parents' house done on
time had been the big issue in her mind. Now it paled
in comparison to this family's crisis. She settled at the
other end of the roof from Guthrie.

He finished pounding a nail. "I think we can get this
done if we stay at it the rest of the afternoon."

Hannah tried to think of a gentle way to tell him
what had happened at the vet's. No easy way presented
itself.

She lifted the hammer from her belt, reached for a
shingle, then a nail. She clung to her resolve. God had let
Amber meet her father in front of Hannah. He'd dropped
the hot potato in *her* lap. She couldn't let Amber down.

"Guthrie, we're going to have to talk about..."
Pausing, she positioned the shingle and began pounding
it in, one stroke for each word. "Some... thing...you...
don't...want...to...talk...about."

"I'm not talking about Billy." He continued hammering.

She ignored his stubbornness. "Today when Amber
and I were at the vet, the thing I dreaded the most for
your niece happened right in front of me."

"What did he do!" Guthrie roared. "Did he follow
you there?"

Where had her gentle carpenter gone, the man who
could laugh about being startled off a roof? "He didn't
follow us. He was already there."

Guthrie charged ahead. "Did he get that new vet to call you?"

"Guthrie, stop frothing at the mouth and let me tell you what happened!"

He replied by viciously pounding a nail into place.

Hannah's temper frayed. "You need to listen to me!" She shook her hammer at him. "You don't even know what happened yet."

He glared at her, but closed his lips as if his mouth was stuffed with one-penny nails.

"I didn't notice him at first, but…" She paused for effect and waited for him to let her know he was listening.

After a moment, he said, "But? Go on!"

She took a deep breath, bracing herself. "But Amber noticed him. She walked up to him."

"What? You let her talk to him!"

"I was in shock! I couldn't move. It was like watching a dream, a nightmare. She walked up to him and said, 'Damon Kinney says you're my daddy.'" Hannah turned to Guthrie.

He wouldn't meet her gaze, but stared at the shingles beneath his boots. His anger appeared to have deserted him. "Why would the Kinneys tell their boy about Billy? I don't get it."

Oh, Guthrie, are you being dense on purpose? "Didn't you realize some husband and wife here would talk about Billy and that their children might overhear it and repeat it to Lynda's children? I've been dreading this since Sunday." She positioned another shingle and banged in the first nail.

Guthrie remained silent.

Hannah went on pounding in nails. When the shingle was done, she turned to him. His expression shocked her. "Guthrie!"

His face was twisted with pain.

Seeing his anguish, she wondered if Billy had done more than abandon Lynda. Lila's mention of Guthrie's dad and his funeral came back to her. Billy had done more than desert his family, hadn't he?

Guthrie answered her unspoken question. "You don't know all he did." Emotion clogged his throat.

"What did he do?" Hannah slung her hammer in her belt. Still tethered by the harness, she jumped sideways to him. "Tell me. Please."

He looked away, obviously fighting not to break down. He mastered himself. "Lynda was pregnant with her third, with Hunter. She started to go into premature labor. Billy was out somewhere, doing who knows what."

He turned to her as though appealing for her understanding. "Lynda called me. I drove her to the hospital in Portage. She delivered the baby nearly six weeks early. He was in neonatal intensive care." Guthrie took a deep breath. "We didn't know if he…if Hunter would live, if he would suffer brain damage."

Hannah ached inside for Lynda and her family. "Did Billy finally come?"

"Yes, his mother found him and dragged him to the hospital. He took one look at Hunter, hooked up to all kinds of tubes, and ran out of the hospital."

Hannah didn't know what to say, but she had a feeling she knew what happened next. "He left town then?"

"Yeah, but first he knocked down his own mother when she tried to stop him, took every penny out of Lynda's and his savings account. He took the money Lynda had earned waitressing at Lila's to pay for the delivery. They didn't have insurance. The costs for Hunter's care were astronomical. The hospital forgave some, but I had to take out a second mortgage on our farm in order to pay them."

Guthrie kicked the roof below his right foot. "Now he's back, maybe he's figured how to get money out of Lynda, probably by holding the kids over her. And I won't let that druggy deadbeat around Lynda's children."

Feeling dragged down by his story of pain, Hannah couldn't argue with the cause of his distrust of Billy, but that didn't matter now. That was then, this was now. But she sensed he was holding something back. Right now their plate was full. "You don't want Billy around his children, but you don't have a choice."

"Yes, I do!" He glared at her.

She gripped his shoulder. Through the cotton of his blue T-shirt she felt his strength, his resistance. "Amber wants to know her father. No matter what he's done, a child wants to know, and if possible, to be loved by her father."

"He's just come back to do it to us all over again! He hasn't changed! He's got some scam up his sleeve."

"Even if you're right, it doesn't change what I've just said. Amber knows. Do you hear me?" She moved her face within inches of his. His warm, sweet breath wafted over her face. She remembered the kisses they'd shared that morning. Hard to believe so much could happen in one day. Guthrie drew her, an honest man who was easy to like.

The temptation to touch his cheek, to soothe his pain rocked her. She tried to ignore it. They were still nearly strangers. "If Amber has found out about her father, you know she's told Jenna and Hunter. They'll want to see their father. It's only natural."

"No."

"Do you know what Amber said to Billy? She said, 'We want a daddy.'" She stopped to let this sink in, then she said more kindly, "You've got to talk to Lynda before she gets home tonight, so she will be prepared. How she handles this with the children is crucial. If you're right, Lynda needs to be the rock her children cling to. She has to show them they can count on her. You understand that, don't you?"

"What exactly did he say to Amber?" Guthrie asked in a gruff voice.

Hannah rejoiced at this. He'd finally begun to listen to her and face the immediate problem. "He said that since he was the one who left, Lynda would have to decide when he could see the children."

"I hate this!" Guthrie spat out the words. "Why did God let him come back here?"

Hannah shook her head. *Do I know the mind of God?* "You can hate Billy's return, but you have to take action or things could get worse, much worse for the children."

He stared at her, looking drained of his usual energy.

"The children and their feelings are what are important today. Billy hurt all of you deeply over three years ago. But your pain isn't the focus now. Amber, Jenna and Hunter have already had to deal with being deserted by their father. They shouldn't have to witness their mother fall apart in front of their eyes when their father returns."

Glancing away, he wiped his forehead with a pocket bandanna.

"On Sunday, Billy said he was the prodigal son. Remember in that parable, the older brother wasn't happy to see his baby brother back, either. But the father said, 'Your brother who was dead is now alive. I must rejoice.' If Billy has truly changed—"

"He hasn't."

Impatient, Hannah ordered, "Go."

"What?"

She didn't waste any words. "Go to the parking lot at Lynda's job and wait for her to come out. You have to talk to her, tell her what's happened."

"What will I say?"

His plea touched her. "Just tell her everything. If she still can't deal with seeing Billy with the children, bring her back here. My dad and mom will do everything they can to help her." She shoved his shoulder, urging him up the roof. "Go. I'll keep at this. Go."

Guthrie grimaced, but pulled himself up to the peak and disappeared into the steeple. Within minutes, she heard his blue truck screech out of the church parking lot.

She reached for another shingle. It was good to have something to do. Hammering nails let her release the anger she felt at this wicked world where innocent children suffered for the sins of their parents. "God go with you, Guthrie," she murmured.

Hannah had just started the final row of dark green shingles when she glimpsed Guthrie's truck pull into the parking lot. Lynda's modest beige sedan trailed right behind. Hannah kept working on the roof, but prayed with each stroke of her hammer that God would begin healing this broken family.

Soon, Guthrie ducked out of the steeple, hooked his harness on and let himself down right beside her. "You've got a lot done."

"I pray good with a hammer in my hand." She gave him a tiny smile, just a quirking up of the corners of her mouth. "Or I hammer good while I pray."

"Lynda's talking to your dad now." He sounded detached.

Though longing to hold this tenderhearted man close and comfort him, Hannah merely nodded. "I'm glad you went and spoke to her."

He picked up a shingle and positioned it. "I didn't have a choice."

Hannah recalled the kisses they'd shared, the sensation of his lips on hers. Pushing these dangerous thoughts out of her mind, she concentrated on the work at hand.

They didn't talk any further, but finished the final row together, then hoisted themselves up and into the church. Hannah ran her fingers through her moist hair.

"I wish I could enjoy this moment more. I thought I'd never get this roof done," Guthrie said. He touched her shoulder. "Thanks, you really helped. But you can retire now. The church is done."

She gave him what she hoped was one of those enigmatic smiles she'd read about. "We'll see. My parents haven't agreed to the factory-built shell. You may not know it, but you need me, Guthrie Thomas."

A voice came from below. "Hannah! Hannah!"

Hannah stepped to the top of the stairs. "Mother?"

"Come down! There's a phone call for you! Your father and I are going to take Lynda home now to talk to the children."

"Okay, Mom!" Hannah turned to Guthrie. "That's peculiar. Who would be calling me here?" She undid her tool belt and draped it on the sawhorse. "I'll be back to help you pack up stuff."

"That's all right. I'm exhausted, but I don't know why. You finished the job. I'll just close up the steeple. I'll start tomorrow shutting down this job."

Nodding, Hannah skipped down the steps. At her

mother's desk, she picked up the phone and leaned against the desk. "Hello, this is Hannah Kirkland speaking."

Guthrie trailed after Hannah. The day had sapped his strength, his joy of accomplishment. He would have done anything to spare Lynda this grief. Wrecking things seemed to be Billy's specialty. Lynda was finally on her feet, and the pain from the past had faded. So, of course, Billy came to stir everything up again.

At Hunter's birth, Billy had carved a deep wound into all their hearts. His coming back to town had ripped the scab off. Guthrie wanted to kick him into next week. He struggled with the anger that spurted inside him every time he pictured Billy's face. What had little Amber thought of her father today? How would this affect the children? They deserved better than Billy.

"Oh? Really?" Hannah's voice sounded loud in the quiet office. The kittens in their basket were mewing for her attention and trying to climb out to reach her.

Guthrie glanced at Hannah, then did a double-take. She had the strangest expression on her face. Who was she talking to on the phone?

"I see. That's very interesting," Hannah commented in an odd tone.

Guthrie bent and picked up both kittens from the white terry-cloth towel in the basket. He cradled them on one arm, stroking their tiny heads and listening to their little engines purring.

"I think that will work. You'll let me know the details of the agreement? Very well. Thank you for calling. This is good news. Goodbye." Hannah hung up the phone.

Guthrie waited for her to explain who she'd been talking to. Finally, he prompted, "Well?"

Hannah stared at him. She looked like she'd swallowed something too big for her.

"Did something bad happen?"

"No, I just…this is so funny…you'll never believe it." Hannah stood up and paced in front of the neat reception desk.

"It would help if you just told me." The gray striped kitten pounced on his thumb, nipping at it and pummeling it with his tiny rear paws.

"It was my agent."

"Yeah?"

"The local Madison TV station wants me to do one cooking demo each week for the next three months. A local dairy company called and wanted to be my sponsor. It won't be much as far as money, but I'll get free advertising for my cookbooks and my syndicated articles. They said they thought the Madison paper and several more in central Wisconsin would pick it up after my spots start airing." She sounded like she didn't believe the words she was saying.

"The station told my agent that they had received more mail, more calls and more e-mail over my cooking spot than anything in the last two years." Hannah faced him.

"Wow. That's good, isn't it?"

She nodded, then she giggled and giggled some more. She plumped down into her mother's office chair and roared.

"What?" Guthrie felt his spirits lighten a tiny bit in the face of her laughter. Hannah laughing struck him as irresistible. He felt himself grinning. "What?"

"It's your aunts!" She shook with mirth.

"My aunts?"

Hannah nodded, trying to muffle her laughter. "Everyone loves your aunts!"

Guthrie had a hard time matching up the woman who'd just finished shingling a church roof with the successful cook and writer. Before Hannah had come to Petite, one of the church ladies had mentioned the fact that the pastor's daughter probably wouldn't stay long in their little town, implying that she'd be too good for Petite. The woman had been wrong. Hannah Kirkland could have been stuck on herself, but she wasn't. She was easy to know, good-hearted. He eyed her. And she was pretty—even after a day spent shingling on a roof. Why wasn't she married by now? Were the men in Milwaukee blind, deaf and dumb?

Chapter Nine

Sitting at the small desk in her harvest-gold room at the Cozy Motel, Hannah shut down her laptop computer and rubbed her tired eyes. Late afternoon sunshine glowed through the window curtains. The phone rang. She picked it up.

"Hannah?" Spring asked.

"Yes, I'm here. I got your e-mail and I've been waiting for your call."

"Okay. I've got Doree on the other line already. Let me access her for you, too."

A click. "Hi, the best Midwest cook." Doree's voice sparkled over the phone line.

"Hi." Hannah's fatigue didn't match her younger sister's high spirits.

"Good." Spring took charge. "Tell us what's going on with our parents."

"Well, the house is still at a stand—"

"No! No!" Doree interrupted.

"But," Hannah talked over Doree's words, "I think that may change in the near future. Guthrie's suggested that they agree to a factory-made shell."

"Wonderful," Spring said.

"What's a shell?" Doree asked.

Hannah ignored Doree. It would be good for Doree, teach her not to be such a pest. "Yes, it could be up in twelve hours, then Guthrie and I will finish the inside."

"You and Guthrie? What does that mean?" Doree squealed.

"Hannah," Spring spoke tentatively, "have you decided yet?"

"Will you look into the family records?" Doree urged.

"Hush, Doree. This is Hannah's decision."

Hannah pondered the question one more time. If her mother had a relapse, but still persisted in refusing to pursue her natural relatives, at least, Hannah's conscience would be clear. The fact of Mom's illness settled like a rock over Hannah's lungs. It made her voice come out rough. "We shouldn't leave anything to chance. I'll look for the adoption papers."

"I'm glad that's finally decided," Spring said quietly.

"Great!" Doree exclaimed.

"Thank you, Hannah," Spring said. "How are Mother and Father?"

"They went to Portage for Mom's routine blood check."

"You'll call us if there is any change?"

"You know I would."

"I'm sorry, Hannah. It's just so hard to be far away."

When the three said their good-byes, Hannah sat with the receiver in her hand till the beeping startled her back to reality. The decision had been made. She'd take the first step in finding her mother's natural parents. *Lord, bless this search or end it. I can't see all the way to the end. You must choose.*

After a long afternoon at the computer making some progress on her writing commitments, Hannah faced the fact that she needed to discuss the cooking show with Ida and Edith Thomas. Her agent had the deal signed, sealed and delivered.

She stood and slipped on her sandals. Each day brought the first taping session nearer. Hannah had specified no more live demos to the TV station and had asked Guthrie not to mention the demos to his aunts. She wanted to tell them in her own way, and she couldn't put it off any longer. She'd waited long enough for inspiration on how to approach the eccentric duo. Time to act.

The ladies' humor lay in their spontaneous helpfulness. If Hannah said the wrong thing, she could spoil their natural charm. In effect, she could knock Humpty-Dumpty off the wall and never be able to put the pieces back together again for another amusing cooking demo.

Sighing, she walked into the warm Saturday afternoon and across Front Street to Church. Though the calendar read September, she wore a peach-colored tank top and shorts and enjoyed the heat of the sun on her bare arms and legs. Two little boys pedaled by on bikes. She waved, and they giggled in return. She knocked at the door of the twin sisters' modest white bungalow, but no one was at home.

After only a month in Petite, Hannah didn't need anyone to tell her where they probably had gone. She walked down the quiet block to the little yellow house, which always vibrated with children's voices.

Maybe she'd fare better asking the two ladies in the midst of their family. It would put less pressure on them if it came up in conversation. Following the well-worn path through the overgrown green grass, she heard the sound of children squealing and shouting in the backyard.

She went around the corner of the house and found Lynda, Martha and the aunts sitting on old metal lawn chairs painted a glossy white in the shade of the tall green maples. They were watching the children splash in a blue plastic wading pool.

"Hannah!" Martha waved to her.

"I was in the neighborhood—"

"Hello, dear," Ida greeted her.

"Yes, hello," Edith echoed. "You're always welcome here."

Hannah chuckled as she sat down in the lawn chair where Martha had motioned her. Ida and Edith definitely must have been their mother and father's pets. Wherever the two went, they always felt they were in control.

"Boy, that looks like fun!" Hannah pointed to the

children in colorful swimsuits chasing each other, sliding their feet on the bottom and making the water slosh over the side. Over a week had passed since the day Amber and Hannah had visited the vet and Hannah had received the call from the TV station in Madison. Though her father didn't break the confidentiality of his recent sessions with Billy and Lynda, he let Hannah know that both parties were working toward Billy meeting his children again after his three-year absence.

Martha sighed. "The days of summer will soon be over. Amber's in kindergarten already, and Jenna just began Head Start in Portage three mornings a week."

Ida clucked her tongue. "They grow up so fast."

Edith added, "It was the same with Guthrie's father, then your children, Martha. These precious years go so fast."

Hannah's heart warmed at the love and affection in the faces of the two great-aunts. *So how do I ask them to appear with me in the cooking show? Would they comprehend what I'm telling them? Would they try to take center stage as the "cooks" when their strength lay in the humor they brought to the cooking demo?* Hannah tried to think of a way to bring up the TV station's proposal. "Ida, Edith, there's a question I need to ask you—"

"Hey!" Amber stepped out of the pool and waved to a woman standing hesitantly at the corner of the house. "Hey! You've got my daddy's dog!"

Hannah swiveled and glimpsed a woman dressed like a country and western singer in spangled denim and with a great deal of large blonde hair. The blonde held the Chihuahua Hannah had seen at the vet's office.

Martha stood. "Terri Sue, oh, Terri Sue!" She hurried over to the woman. The little dog yipped.

Hannah recognized the woman's name. This must be Billy's mother. But she seemed too young to be a grandmother. Hannah studied the woman who had been too ashamed to visit her son's wife and children. Hannah's heart rejoiced.

Amber ran after Martha. "Hey! How come you have my daddy's dog?"

Tears in her eyes, Martha turned to Amber. "Dear, this is your daddy's mother."

Wide-eyed and openmouthed, the little girl halted and stared at the woman.

Martha continued, "Amber, this is your grandmother, Terri Sue."

"Hello, Amber." Terri Sue's voice, low and melodic, sounded fearful, yet awed.

Amber leaped into the air. "A new grandma!" The little girl raced to the pool, shouting at the top of her lungs, "We got a new grandma! We got a daddy! Now we got a new grandma! Come on! Come on!"

Hannah felt like clapping.

Jenna and Hunter tumbled out of the pool and nearly collided with Terri Sue as Martha led her toward the lawn chairs. Rising, Lynda hurried to Terri Sue and hugged her.

"Oh, it's so good to see you again!" Ida and Edith

chorused. "We've missed you!" They both slipped dainty hankies from skirt pockets and dabbed at brimming eyes.

"I didn't know if it was too soon…." Terri Sue looked at Lynda's face, her eyes lowered apologetically.

"You've always been welcome," Lynda murmured. "I told you that."

Terri Sue gave a little self-conscious shrug and sat down. "I just couldn't stay away any longer." Her words trembled with three years of longing.

Hannah blinked back tears. Her parents would be thrilled with news of this reunion.

Amber stared at Terri Sue. "Do we got a new grandpa, too?"

"No, dear, no grandpa."

"Did he die like our other grandpa?"

Terri Sue took a deep breath. "No, dear, Billy's daddy left a long time ago."

"You mean like our daddy?" Amber asked.

With a broken expression, Terri nodded.

Hannah ached for the woman.

Hunter leaned against Terri Sue's blue-jeaned leg, soaking it, and asked, "What's your dog's name? We got a cat. Her name is Misty."

Terri Sue touched his soft blond curls. "His name is Taco."

"My name's Hunter!" The little boy bounced with each word. "Can I pet him?"

"Yes, Hunter, just be gentle." Her forehead creased

as Terri Sue gazed at the children as if they might be snatched from her at any moment.

Hannah yearned to say some reassuring word to Terri Sue. *But I'm just a bystander.*

Hunter reached toward the dog. Taco yipped once. Hunter pulled his hand back.

Terri Sue stroked the little dog's sleek, but roly-poly tan body. "Taco, this is Hunter. Hunter won't hurt you." She took the boy's small hand and stroked Taco's back with it.

"Oooo," Hunter breathed. "He's soft, nice. Hi, Taco." Terri Sue smiled.

"Are you really our grandma?" Jenna asked, skepticism in her voice.

"Yes," Martha answered, "she's your father's mother."

"Amber got to see our daddy, but I didn't." Jenna pouted. "When do I get to see him?"

Hannah closed her eyes and said a quick prayer for Billy and Lynda's reconciliation. *I hope for the best, Lord, and trust in your love.*

"Can my daddy come to my school?" Amber asked. "We're drawing special pictures for Open House. Can he come, Mommy? Can he?"

Looking a bit shaky, Lynda inhaled deeply. "Why don't you invite Grandma Terri Sue? Daddy might not be able to come."

"Can you come, Grandma Terri Sue? Please!" Amber begged.

"I'll try," Terri Sue replied in her soft, sultry voice.

"You got a bag on your arm," Jenna told her.

Immediately all three children focused with rapt interest on the colorful paper shopping bag.

Terri Sue put Taco on the grass, then reached into the bag. She paused and looked at Lynda. "I took the liberty of..."

Lynda nodded.

With the bag open at her feet, Terri Sue smiled and drew out three boxed toys—a fashion doll, a creative dough set with bright yellow, green and hot pink dough along with an intriguing collection of shaping forms and a blue toy pickup truck.

Amber shrieked, "It's a Country Western Tammy doll!"

With wide eyes, Jenna asked, "Is the Play-Clay set for me?"

"A truck! Like Uncle Guthrie's!" Hunter danced up and down with excitement.

The children fell onto the toys and ripped open the packages. Then they each took turns hugging Terri Sue and displaying the toys to Martha, the two great-aunts, Lynda and Hannah.

Hannah wished she had a camera to record all the joy in the faces around her.

Then Hunter took his truck into the pool where it plowed through water to the tune of the little boy's expert engine noises. Amber and Jenna retired to the small shaded picnic table to play with the doll and play-clay.

"That was so sweet of you," Ida and Edith crooned.

Terri Sue blinked her richly mascaraed eyes, then dug into her purse for a lavender tissue to blot tears.

"I'm glad you came, Terri Sue. Really." Lynda offered Terri Sue her hand. "I've missed you."

Terri Sue reached out and clung to Lynda's hand. "Oh, honey, I've missed you, too."

"You didn't have to stay away," Martha murmured, sounding close to tears.

Again, Hannah's mind drifted to Lila's monologue. She had mentioned a funeral and Guthrie's father. Billy had done something terrible that had yet to be revealed to Hannah. Had Garner been told everything?

"Billy says you two are going to counseling with the new pastor," Terri Sue said softly and sat back, releasing Lynda.

"Yes. Terri Sue, this is the pastor's daughter, Hannah." Martha made the introduction, apologizing for its tardiness, then stared into the distance as though peering deep into the past.

Terri Sue looked surprised. "Oh, you're the one who did that cooking show."

"Yes." Hannah spoke, glad of the opening this comment gave her. She could say what she'd come for and also lighten everyone's mood. "And I'll be doing it again. The TV station called and wants me to do one a week for the next three months."

"That's so exciting!" Ida and Edith exclaimed. "And to think that we were there to help you the first time!"

"It is exciting!" Hannah agreed. "And I hope you

ladies will come for the show just like you did the last time. You added so much…liveliness to my demo."

The twin octogenarian sisters looked like they would explode with joy. "Well, if you really want us," Ida said with a coy expression.

"I do. Mark your calendar for this coming Wednesday. A crew is going to come to tape a month's worth of spots at the church starting about nine."

"We'll look forward to it!"

Lord, I don't know if this is going to work out. Please be there on Wednesday, too!

Déjà vu described the situation on Wednesday. The same director-producer and cameraman had arrived and set up in the institutional-looking kitchen in the church basement. Almost the same group of retired farmers and wives filled the short rows of folding chairs. Ida and Edith sat in the front row on the aisle. Hannah waved to them. They waved back.

"All right, Ms. Kirkland. Let's get started." The producer motioned to her.

Hannah smiled into the camera. "Good day. I'm Hannah Kirkland. I write the 'Real Food, Healthy Food,' column and cookbooks. I like to take America's favorite foods and give them a healthy new twist—without losing a bit of their wonderful taste! Today, I'm going to give you a new quick bread recipe, a variation on an all-time American favorite, banana bread. Mine is Apple-Banana-Oatmeal Bread. A yummy quick bread to go with Johnson's Dairy cream cheese or butter!"

Hannah held up a bunch of bananas. "Now the best bananas for bread are, of course, the riper ones with brown spots like these. Also fall apples are just coming into the farmers' markets and orchard stores." She gestured toward a peck of red apples on the counter to her far right. "McIntosh or Jonathans are the best for cooking in my opinion. We don't grow bananas here, but no one can beat our apples!"

The church audience applauded.

Hannah set the bananas down and lifted a round blue box of oatmeal. "And we know that oatmeal along with a healthy diet can lower cholesterol. Besides I love oatmeal! It makes a yummy addition to any quick bread."

She looked expectantly at the audience. Now to get her comic relief on camera. "Ida and Hannah, you were so helpful last time. Would you come up and give me a hand today?"

Ida and Edith both smiled sweetly as they apologetically shook their heads.

What! Shock froze Hannah's vocal cords. She struggled to keep a calm mask on her face. "Okay…then," she stammered. Maybe if she continued with the recipe, they'd come up without an invitation. "This recipe, which makes two standard-sized loaves, begins with two cups of mashed ripe bananas—"

"Cut!" The producer approached her. In a low voice, he said, "The two old ladies have *got* to be in this or the dairy company is going to be disappointed. We don't want to disappoint the sponsor, do we?"

"I'm with you all the way," Hannah whispered back passionately. "My dilemma is how to get them up here without spoiling their spontaneity. They've got to come up on their own!"

"I get it. But do they get it? Maybe they don't like to make banana bread."

"Maybe. Maybe not. Just follow me on this, all right? I'll get them up here if I have to pull them bodily into camera range."

The producer gave her a searching look, then nodded and walked out of camera range.

Okay, Lord, I know you're here watching over me. How can I get them up here? I need some inspiration—quick!

In her place behind the kitchen counter, she plastered a broad smile on her miserable face.

"Take it from the top," the producer barked.

Hannah went through the introduction to the recipe again. When she came to the part where she said, "This recipe begins with two cups of mashed ripe bananas," the clear glass bowl that contained the premeasured mashed bananas slipped from her hands and clattered to the counter. The gooey brown bananas shot up and splattered onto Hannah's apron. She zipped off the skins of three more ripe bananas from the bunch she'd displayed and dropped them into another clear glass bowl. When she started to mash the bananas with a potato masher, sharp pain arced through her wrist. "Oh!

Ouch!" Dropping the potato masher, she clutched her wrist. Days of pounding nails must have strained it.

"Oh, dear!" Ida exclaimed.

"Oh, dear!" Edith repeated.

The two ladies hurried forward.

Ida took Hannah's hand and examined her wrist. "Edith, I'll take care of her wrist while you mash those bananas! I don't care what Martha says. It's obvious this girl needs us!"

Edith nodded. While she attacked the bananas, mashing them into pulp, Ida reached into the freezer and brought out a blue cloth freezer pack, which she wrapped around Hannah's wrist. "Edith and I bought these for the church to keep on hand. A person never knows when some mishap will come and a ready ice pack can be a godsend."

"You're right," Hannah said, her heart doing handstands. "I feel better already." She did feel better, now that the aunts were on camera with her. What was a strained wrist, after all?

"The bananas are mashed," Edith announced.

"Excellent." Hannah grinned. *Wonderful! Thank you, Lord! I would never have appealed to their sympathy.* "Well, since I'm incapacitated, I'll have to depend on you two to do the mixing. Now to the bananas, add two apples, chopped." Hannah pointed to the prepared and measured ingredients in glass custard cups and bowls. "In a separate small bowl, add four tablespoons water to the fruit and put it aside."

Ida hovered over Hannah like a doting mother hen while Edith followed Hannah's directions.

Hannah finished, "Finally stir in one-half cup golden raisins."

"Do they have to be golden, Hannah?" Ida asked.

Hannah nearly chuckled. *Yes, Ida, that's what the dairy wants to hear!* "No, I suppose you could use the regular dark raisins. I just think the golden raisins look prettier in slices of the bread."

"Oh, yes," Edith agreed. "Our dear mother always said food should be as appetizing to the eye as to the tongue."

Hannah grinned as wide as her mouth permitted.

"Hannah, I don't want to put myself forward, but could we substitute nuts?" Edith asked. "I do love nutmeats in my fruit breads."

Fantastic comment, Edith. Hannah beamed at her. *You, go, girl!* "Oh, yes, walnuts would be an excellent addition. Well, ladies, shall we take the finished loaf out of the oven?"

"Yes!" Ida cooed.

"If you please, Edith?" Hannah motioned toward the country-blue quilted pot holders, which Edith used to open the oven and lift out the warm loaf.

"Oh, the fragrance of the apples!" Ida exclaimed.

"It's like being in an apple orchard!" Edith agreed.

"Cut! That's a wrap," the producer called with obvious relief.

Thank you, Lord! We made it!

* * *

"Hello, Hannah."

Her pulse gave a little skip as Hannah recognized Guthrie's voice and his evident unhappiness over the phone. They hadn't spoken for many days. He'd been busy haying, and her parents were still deciding whether to go with the factory shell or not. "What is it, Guthrie?"

"How's your arm?"

"Fine. The pain went away right after the tapings."

"Good. Are you free tonight?"

Why would Guthrie Thomas call and ask her that? The man acted like he was inviting her to a dentist appointment. "I'm just reading a new novel."

"Oh, good." He sounded relieved. "I need you to come to Amber's Open House with me."

"What?"

He sucked in a lot of air before answering. "Lynda says I can't come unless you come with me."

"Why?"

"She says if you aren't there, I might do or say something about…Billy that could embarrass her and the kids."

Hannah pondered this. Evidently, Lynda was open to giving her husband a second chance, but Guthrie still hadn't budged. For this reason and many others, she didn't want to be dragged in as Guthrie's chaperone. "Why don't you just ask my parents to go with you?"

"Lynda says our family is already gossip for miles around. If we have to take a pastor with us to the school to keep peace, she'll die of embarrassment."

"But I'm the pastor's daughter." *And I don't want to be a buffer between you and your ex-brother-in-law.*

"She says that's okay. Everybody knows you helped me with the church roof and had the great-aunts on your cooking show."

Hannah tried to follow this convoluted reasoning, but couldn't. She wasn't surprised. In cases like these, reason rarely controlled action. She let out a deeply sincere sigh. "All right. If Lynda wants me there, come and get me."

"I'll leave now." Click.

Trying to remember what her parents had worn to school functions, Hannah shrugged out of her jeans and red-and-white Badgers T-shirt and slipped into one of her new suits—the peach silk with the creamy white silk blouse. She was just slipping on tan dress shoes when Guthrie tapped on her door.

"Guthrie, are you sure you want me—"

"Let's go."

She shook her head. Single-minded. Stubborn.

Within minutes, Guthrie drove into the crowded school parking lot and maneuvered into a spot at the rear. They'd barely exchanged two words. Looking like a man nursing a broken tooth, he came around to help her out of the cab.

Guthrie wore a pair of casual tan twill slacks and a navy knit sport shirt, which stretched over his wide chest and around bulging biceps. An attractive but glum escort for the evening. *Lighten up, Guthrie!*

Twilight glowed around them. Locusts and crickets harmonized in the fall evening. Suddenly she wanted to pull Guthrie away from the school and wander over to the deserted playground. How long had it been since she'd sat in a swing? She imagined sitting on the wooden board while Guthrie pushed her forward. She'd fly skyward, then backward to Guthrie's strong arms. They would leave behind the family tensions and just enjoy being together.

"We really don't have to go if you don't want to," she offered.

"Nothing is going to make me miss this."

Not encouraged, but unwilling to make a fuss, she took his arm. She quickened her pace as he led her through the school door, then to Amber's kindergarten room. The buzz of voices hummed in the hallways, but zoomed in volume when they walked into the classroom.

Admiring the gaily colored room, Hannah glanced around looking for familiar faces. Several people looked more than a little surprised at seeing them. Was it because they'd come together?

Oh, dear, have I caught the interest of the county gossips? I'll have to make sure everyone knows I'm here only as a family friend!

"Hannah! Hannah!" Amber hailed her, the little girl's high-pitched voice cut through all other voices. "Uncle Guthrie, over here! My picture is on this wall!"

Hannah waved, then found it necessary to cling to Guthrie's arm as he nudged his way through the crowded schoolroom.

Evidently, this was a supportive community of extended families. People of all ages, from great-grand-mothers leaning on canes to babes in arms had come to admire the kindergarten members of their families.

Amber was surrounded by every one of her relatives, including her new family, Grandma Terri Sue and Billy. Amber ran the last few steps and grabbed Guthrie's hand and tugged them forward—right up to Billy. "Look, Uncle Guthrie! My daddy came to Open House!"

Feeling like the end of a crack-the-whip game, Hannah swung in front of Guthrie, who gripped her hand almost painfully. She stumbled against Guthrie's broad chest, then steadied herself. "Hello, Billy. It's so nice to meet you. I'm Hannah Kirkland."

Sensing Guthrie fuming behind her like a dormant volcano threatening to erupt, Hannah smiled.

"She's the preacher's daughter, and she writes cook-books!" Amber announced to the universe.

While shaking Billy's hand, Hannah held on to her smile. This was Amber's night, and Hannah didn't want anything to spoil it. A little child's very first school open house should not be marred by family conflict. She gave Guthrie's hand a warning squeeze.

"Is this your picture, Amber?" Hannah indicated a painted length of newsprint hanging in a row with other pictures.

"Yes, we were supposed to draw a picture of our family. See? Here's the two great-aunties and my grandma Martha." Amber pointed out three stick figures, two with gray hair and wearing dresses and one with yellow hair and apparently wearing slacks. "Over here is Jenna and Hunter and me—we're playing on our swing set." Three small stick figures, one with braids, swung on adjoining swings.

"Then, see, I added my new grandma, Terri Sue, my daddy and Mommy." Amber had drawn Terri Sue holding what must be Taco and her father and mother holding hands in the middle of the rest of the family.

"Oh! I forgot!" the little girl exclaimed. She pointed at another couple in the corner of the large piece of paper—a man with yellow hair and large bumps on his stick arms and a woman with short brown hair who was wearing overall shorts. This pair of figures floated above a very pointed green church roof. "And here's you and Uncle Guthrie."

"But, Amber, I'm not a member of your family," Hannah objected, feeling a twitch of nervousness.

"But if you marry Uncle Guthrie, then you'll be my aunt Hannah. Jenna and I want you to be our auntie."

"Yeah!" Hunter piped up from his perch on his father's arm.

Several nearby parents, still strangers to Hannah, chuckled at this. Since Amber talked loud enough to be heard by any aircraft flying overhead, Hannah couldn't hold them guilty of eavesdropping. She cringed with embarrassment. "But, Amber, your uncle and I are just friends."

"But we want you to marry Uncle Guthrie." Jenna spoke as loudly as her sister. "Now that our daddy's came back, Uncle Guthrie can get married."

Hannah didn't like the direction this was leading. She shut her mouth tight and began edging away.

Martha tried to hush the children.

But Amber wasn't taking direction. She put her hand on one hip. "Don't you see? Uncle Guthrie couldn't get married when our daddy was gone because he had to take care of us *like* a daddy. But now we don't need him as our daddy."

Chapter Ten

A few days later, out of the passenger window of Guthrie's truck, Hannah gazed at the gray clouds layered over the slate sky. Her parents had finally agreed to go with the factory-made shell, and she and Guthrie were on their way to order it from the company in Prairie du Chein along the Mississippi River. A sideways glance informed her that this morning's dreary weather matched her companion's mood. His healthy Nordic good looks didn't match the gloom that dragged down the lines of his face.

How she longed to lean close to him, cradle his cheek and comfort him…. But he was unapproachable.

Where had the real Guthrie Thomas gone? Billy's return had flipped a switch somewhere deep inside him. Guthrie the lighthearted but stubborn had given way to Guthrie the angry and wounded. Who could have guessed—except Martha—that this side of Guthrie existed?

As it had over the past few days, the night of Open House came up in Hannah's mind. Poor, sweet little Amber had announced to everyone in hearing distance that she and her brother and sister didn't need Guthrie as a daddy anymore.

The poignant scene had etched itself on Hannah's heart. The sensation of the moment still dogged her. Her blood had drained toward her feet, leaving her clammy and light-headed. Lynda's face had turned a bright red. People had shifted away from them. But Billy had calmly squatted in front of his two daughters. "Amber and Jenna, I know you mean well, but it isn't for you to tell people who to marry or not to marry. That's between Hannah and Guthrie."

Between Hannah and Guthrie.

Right now all that lay between Hannah and Guthrie was a thick buffer of thorny silence. Hannah knew that Guthrie's anger wouldn't get better until it was lanced like an infected wound. But how could she get Guthrie to open up? He'd shut down that evening and hadn't taken any of the hints she offered over the intervening days. In the not-too-distant past, she'd let Edward stonewall her, and it hadn't done either of them any good. Guthrie had to comprehend the damage anger and resentment could do to those he loved and to his own stubborn heart. This could not go on. She wouldn't let it!

Whispering a prayer, she faced Guthrie. "Stop the truck."

"What?" He squealed to a halt, quickly pulling off the road onto the shoulder. "Why?"

She folded her arms over her breast.

"Did you forget something?" When she didn't reply, he demanded, "What? What's wrong?"

Guthrie, listen to yourself! Nothing used to upset you like this.

He fumed at the windshield. "Tell me or I'm driving on."

"Guthrie, I don't think we can go on until you are ready to talk about Billy."

"I'm not talking about Billy." With a glance over his left shoulder, he gunned the truck onto the two-lane highway.

A fleeting flashback brought Edward to mind again. Whenever they'd had a disagreement, he'd iced over like a snow sculpture. To restore peace, she'd had to wheedle and cajole. *I'm not doing that again! Never again!*

This was a perfect opportunity, away from Petite, to get things out in the open. But how could she corner Guthrie? He sat quite literally in the driver's seat.

She stared out as the panorama of late summer Wisconsin ribboned by. Even the clouds that hung overhead like dingy sheets hiding the sun couldn't dim the countryside's simple beauty. Already harvested hay in huge rolls dotted the fields. There were clumps of pine trees and maples gathered in clumps along the roadside. In the highest maples, red-tinged leaves, a harbinger of the inevitable fall, highlighted the rich lingering greens of summer. A blue road sign announced, Wayside, 1/2 Mile on Rt.

Aha! Guthrie couldn't refuse her a pit stop, could he? "I have to stop at the Wayside."

"We'll be in a town in just—"

"I have to stop at the Wayside," she repeated. "It's urgent."

Though still silent, his fuming got louder. But he turned into the Wayside, a grassy, shaded place with picnic tables under shelters, brick facilities and an old-fashioned pump for water.

As soon as he shoved the truck into park, she snatched his keys from the ignition and darted from the vehicle. She didn't stop until she reached a dark green picnic table. She plopped down on the attached bench, her back to the table. There was more than one way to skin a cat or a pigheaded carpenter!

Guthrie stared after her, then stormed out of his truck. When he reached her, he planted his hands on his hips. "What's the bee in your bonnet?"

"You are the bee in my bonnet, Guthrie." She casually crossed her tanned legs and smiled into his stormy face. "We need to talk this out."

"Give me back my keys." He towered over her, a gentle giant in blue jeans.

She shook her head and leaned her elbows on the table. Sitting on Guthrie's wad of keys couldn't be termed comfortable, but she resisted the urge to squirm on the hard bench. She waited.

He took a deep breath. "We have an appointment in Prairie du Chein."

"Then why don't you sit down and we'll get this settled and be on our way."

"Where are my keys?" he demanded through gritted teeth.

"In my shorts."

Leaning down, he reached for her pocket.

She didn't try to stop him. Instead, she gave him an amused smile, the clean scent of his shaving lotion and soap filling her head. "I said in my shorts. Not in the pocket of my shorts."

Taking a step back, he glared at her. "Why are you doing this?"

Her sympathy stirred, she folded her arms. Only deep love for his family and deep pain could have caused such a change in this man. She sighed. "Guthrie, I really like you. You are a great guy. You have a warm heart, and it's as big as Wisconsin. But you are as stubborn as an old mule. Now please spend just a few minutes talking out what's in your mind and heart about Billy coming back into your sister's life. Then I'll gladly give you back the keys."

He turned his back to her.

She waited, praying silently for wisdom. She spoke softly, tenderly. "Guthrie, we're friends. Your well-being is my concern."

Sparrows chirped around them. The din of grass-hoppers created a constant background noise. Trucks sped past with their distinctive charged whine.

Finally, Guthrie slumped down beside her.

She touched his arm. "Let me help you. You've helped me and my parents."

"How have I helped you?" He sounded defeated.

"You let me work with you—even if it starched your shorts," she teased. "You convinced my parents to go with the factory-built shell so they wouldn't have to stay at Lila's for months and months. You really care about *us*."

He folded his arms and stared away from her. "I just don't want him here."

Guthrie's troubled capitulation saddened Hannah. But if any tender shoot of healing was to sprout, someone had to start the spadework in this sweet man's wounded heart. "I'm afraid you'll destroy your relationship with your sister."

"Why can't Lynda see he hasn't changed?" He wouldn't meet her eyes.

"How do you know that? Can you look into his heart?"

"I don't have to."

"Guthrie, you're not listening."

He turned to look into her eyes, his forlorn gaze wrenching her heart. "Why can't I make her see reality?"

Again the urge to stroke his cheek, to put her concern into a comforting touch, zigzagged through her. "Guthrie, you can't…. No one can make another person think or feel something they don't want to. Lynda seems to be accepting the changes she sees in Billy, and she's helping the children adjust. You're going to have to stop pushing your own feelings onto your sister."

"She's falling for a lie."

"If you don't stop this, you'll lose her." Hannah recalled how Edward's inflexibility had pushed her further and further away. Until they had moved so far apart, at last, nothing good that had connected them remained. "That would kill you."

A pause. Then he nodded, but his neck moved like it hadn't been oiled in a while.

"So talk to me," she pleaded. "You told me some of why you don't like Billy. And you're right—what he did was awful. But you've got to get rid of your anger and start at giving him a second chance. I can tell my dad thinks Billy has experienced a true change of heart, and my dad isn't usually fooled."

"People like him don't change." He spoke as though each word had to be dragged up from deep in his soul. "He'll just end up hurting them again."

"Guthrie, with God's help people do change." She pursed her lips, then continued, "I know you want to protect your sister and her children, but you're not God."

"I don't think I'm God."

"You do if you think it's in your power to prevent your sister from being hurt. You can't. If Lynda wants to let Billy begin to act like a father to his children, that's good— even if it poses emotional danger to her and the kids."

"I thought Billy was in the past. I didn't expect to see him again."

Again the memory of Lila's mention of a funeral, of Guthrie's dad nagged her. Did she dare bring this question up now? A glance at Guthrie's bleak expression told her no. "Give him a chance."

"I'll try." Abruptly, Guthrie stood up.

His sudden agreement didn't sound genuine. Was he agreeing just so they could get on to their destination? Or had some little part of him decided to give Billy another chance? She looked up, studying his honest blue eyes, which plainly warred with his clenched jaw. But she could only take Guthrie's word. She wasn't God, either.

"Keys?" He held out his hand.

She rose, and the bunch of keys fell out of the right leg of her pale pink shorts and made a tinny chink on the concrete. Bending, Guthrie snatched them and started across the green grass.

She trotted at his side, or tried to. "I'm glad you're going to give Billy a second chance."

Guthrie jogged toward the truck. "Come on. We're going to be late for our appointment."

"I'm glad you are giving him a second chance because we're double-dating Saturday night."

"What!" he bellowed, swinging back to her.

"Gotcha!" she teased, then went on more seriously, "now remember how we told my mom and dad we'd help with the singles' party at the church this weekend? Well, both your sister and Billy said they'd come, so you need to figure out how you're going to deal with that."

Looking grim, Guthrie stared at her.

"Don't worry." She patted his cheek daringly. "I have faith in you. Besides, we'll all be well chaperoned."

The Twenty-One Plus Night in the neat but beige church basement witnessed the first public reunion between Lynda and Billy. Hannah had agreed to drag Guthrie along to take some of the heat off Lynda and Billy—that is, give Petite something else to talk about.

Hannah hoped this evening would be the first step in reconciling Guthrie to Billy's return. She had done her part to make the evening a success by fixing the refreshments—a new cheese dip with a hint of jalapeños, double fudge brownies and ripe red watermelon chunks.

Her parents had deputized Lynda and Billy to be in charge of entertainment, and they had brought Lynda's portable CD player and a selection of CDs with songs from the fifties and sixties. Good food, classic rock, but bad vibes.

About a dozen young men and women who were casually dressed in shorts and cutoffs and T-shirts and had known each other or known of each other for most of their lives stood around as though they'd never seen each other or the church basement before in their lives. Hannah tried to think of an icebreaker as Lynda whispered to her, "This is awful. What can we do to get everyone to relax?"

"Good evening, everyone!"

All faces turned to the doorway to witness Ida and

Edith, wearing pink-flowered dresses, make their entrance.

Hannah's mouth dropped open. Lynda murmured, "Oh, my." Glancing at Lynda's face, Hannah saw her own shock reflected there.

Billy hurried forward. "Aunt Ida, Aunt Edith, what brings you here tonight?"

"Well, we're over twenty-one and single!" Ida, with a gleam in her eye, announced. "We came to have fun."

"We've looked forward all week to the party!" Edith agreed.

Ida gazed around at the ill-at-ease group of singles. "And look at all of you, just standing around! We didn't think you youngsters would know anything about party games! Young people today just don't know how to have fun."

"No, indeed. And see—we were right!" Edith added. "Now, Billy, you line up all these handsome young men on one side of the room while Ida and I get all the young ladies lined up opposite them."

For a moment, everyone merely stared at the two elderly ladies. Hannah felt their hesitance. Not party games! The twin octogenarian ladies were clearly out of place, but who could hurt their feelings by saying so?

Evidently no one.

Billy started calling each guy's name, and though somewhat reluctant, all the males lined up alongside Guthrie. The females lined up facing the gentlemen.

Having learned more about the eccentric ladies,

Hannah surmised that no one present could think of a way to refuse the two dear old souls. Everyone present remembered Ida and Edith had first diapered them in the church nursery, then given them Sunday school lessons. And who among them could ever forget the ladies who gave out king-size chocolate bars and cheerful greetings at Halloween?

When the two lines had formed, Ida rearranged the males. Hannah tried to figure out why Ida was doing this. When Ida moved Billy to face Lynda, then Guthrie opposite herself, Hannah got it. The two were shamelessly matchmaking!

Edith came behind her sister, dispensing from a brown shopping bag red-and-white-striped plastic drinking straws and hard candies with holes in the middle like life rings. Each female received a drinking straw, each male a straw and a candy.

When the ladies reached the ends of the lines, they turned and beamed. Ida began, "Now, there will be a prize for the couple who can be the first to transfer the candy from the gentleman's straw to the lady's. The straws must be held in your mouths and hands must remain behind your backs, of course, and no talking allowed!"

"Oh, this is going to be such fun!" Edith tittered. "I remember we did this at our sixteenth birthday party."

"Hush," Ida scolded, then continued, "if you drop a candy, you may have up to two more. If you drop more than three, you will be disqualified. Get ready, get set, go!"

The male and female lines stared at each other. Then, folding his arms behind him, Billy put the straw in his mouth, then the candy on his straw, and stepped toward Lynda. Lynda placed her straw between her lips and tried to touch the end of her straw to Billy's.

Guthrie gave a disgruntled snort, but followed suit.

Feeling ridiculous, Hannah clasped her hands behind her back and stepped closer to Guthrie. She thought she recalled doing this at a fourth-grade birthday party. She tried to aim her straw at the end of Guthrie's. But he was too tall. She made noises and exaggeratedly nodded down, directing him to bend his head.

He made negative sounds and flexed his knees a bit so his straw would be level with hers. She leaned forward and tried to touch her straw to his. The candy sailed down his straw. Unaccountably trembling, she tried to hold the connection. The candy slipped between their straws, shattering on the cement floor. Hannah couldn't believe it!

Clucking like a mother hen, Ida hurried over with another candy, which she slipped onto Guthrie's straw. "Try again!"

Hannah and Guthrie did. All around them was the hullabaloo of others making noises around straws in their mouths. Glancing to one side, Hannah glimpsed Ted, the auto repair shop owner, nearly on his knees in front of Becky, the youngest hairstylist from Petite's Bizzy Bee Beauty Shop. Their candy dropped. Ted groaned while Becky burst into giggles.

Guthrie grunted fiercely at Hannah. She gave him her attention and tried to concentrate on the end of his straw. She wished she could say, "Stop bobbing around, Guthrie, and just kneel down. Then I'll kneel and we won't jiggle so." But of course, she couldn't!

Their second candy took its own sweet time rolling down his straw. Just as Hannah thought she had her straw firmly connected to Guthrie's, the candy slipped between them and hit the floor.

Edith stopped, shaking her forefinger at them. "This is your final candy, Guthrie. Look at each other's faces so you can communicate with your eyes and head. You've got to try harder or you'll never win!"

Hannah took the advice and focused on Guthrie's face. She nodded downward, motioning him to kneel. With his straw pointed toward the ceiling to keep from losing their final candy, he slipped slowly to his knees. She followed suit, then bent her head low. He leaned forward. The straw wavered in front of her eyes, then she glanced to his face. She nearly laughed out loud. His concentration was so intense! She stifled her amusement and held very still.

Their final candy inched its way down Guthrie's straw. Hannah, touching her straw to his, held her breath. The candy slowly, tremulously moved from his straw to hers. It slid down and bumped her lips.

"Guthrie and Hannah win!" Edith and Ida crowed. The sisters presented them each with a super-size candy bar. "Now for the spoon-link race!"

This game involved a race between the two lines. Each line was given a spoon tied to a long string. "Now," Ida instructed, "each of you must drop the spoon down your neckline and shake it out the bottom of your pant leg. No hands allowed!"

Edith shook her head and frowned. "I must say, if you ladies had worn dresses, you would have found this much easier. And it's good none of you wore those tight blue jeans! But as it is, everyone, please take off any belts, and you may unbutton your waist buttons. Now the team that connects every member in the line with their string first will win!" She handed one spoon to Hannah and one to Guthrie.

Momentarily, they stared at each other, then Hannah dropped the spoon into her kelly-green T-shirt. The cold metal made her shiver and of course the spoon immediately caught in her décolleté. She jumped up and down to dislodge it. The women of her team shouted encouragement. She glanced at Guthrie and saw he was jumping up and down also, trying to get the spoon to slide past his waistband into his cutoffs. She started giggling and couldn't stop. Finally, after she imitated a woman with ants crawling up her leg, the spoon clattered to the floor below her right shorts leg.

Becky snatched it up and dropped it down her neckline. Hannah shouted encouragement and instructions to her. Becky wiggled, jiggled, twisted and shimmied. Finally, it slid to the floor. Lynda grabbed it and shoved it down her neckline. Watching Lynda's gyrations, Hannah screamed with laughter. Everyone in both lines was laughing.

Hannah gasped for breath, then began cheering as her team won. "Yeah! Yeah!"

Looking forlorn, Ted had the spoon dangling from his shirttail. "Not fair! Not fair!" the guys complained.

Ida and Edith shook their heads at the male team but beamed at the ladies. "Well done! Now for our final game—musical chairs!" The twin aunts bullied the guys into setting up a double row of back-to-back chairs with one less chair than was needed. Then they made Lynda show them how to work the CD player.

So to the sound of lively rock and roll, the singles all trooped around the back-to-back line of chairs, anticipating the inevitable stopping of the music. During the fourth round, Hannah landed on Guthrie's lap instead of the chair. For only a second, she processed the shock of feeling Guthrie's hard thighs beneath her. Blushing, she popped up and complained, "He stole my chair!"

Ida and Edith waved her away from the line of chairs. "No sore losers, Hannah!"

After Hannah's elimination, the competition became cutthroat. Several more competitors landed in laps instead of chairs, and teasing accusations of cheating echoed off the church basement walls.

Finally, it was down to Lynda, Billy and Guthrie. To a rocking golden oldie, the trio stalked around in a circle, their fingers never leaving the backs of the two remaining straight chairs, their gazes never leaving the faces of their competitors.

The music stopped.

Guthrie thumped down onto a chair, but Lynda docked on Billy's lap. Guthrie jumped up, fire in his eyes.

"Wonderful!" a voice called.

Hannah turned to see her father and mother enter.

"Wonderful!" her father repeated. "Everyone looks like they're having a great time!"

But what Guthrie whispered in an undertone to Billy caught Hannah's ear and stabbed her heart. "You can make up to my sister all you want, but don't think I'll ever forget what you did to my father."

Chapter Eleven

The last ones left in the church, Hannah and Guthrie were standing side by side in the church kitchen. The lemon scent of dish detergent floated above the sink. Hannah had planned it that way, though she'd practically had to tie him to her leg to keep him from following Billy and Lynda out the door. She couldn't put off talking to Guthrie about the changes she'd seen in him since Billy's return. Hannah handed Guthrie the final dish to dry and stared at him.

The words he'd whispered to Billy still burned in her ears. Whatever Billy had done to Lynda and Guthrie's father in the past was nothing to what it was doing to Guthrie right now. She didn't know if she was the best person to speak, but she couldn't call herself Guthrie's friend and let this go on. She pulled out the drain stopper and watched as the last of the suds was sucked down the drain.

She turned, took the dried dish from Guthrie's hand and gently pushed him to sit at the small built-in table in the nook of the kitchen. She switched the large overhead light off and sat across from him, only the low light from the nearby stove's range hood illuminating the room. "Guthrie, this has gone on long enough. It's time for you to get rid of the anger and leftover pain that Billy's responsible for. That's the easiest way I can say it. Please tell me everything that happened so you can put it behind you and start being Guthrie again."

He looked stunned, then recovered enough to frown. "I'm still Guthrie," he said in a prickly tone.

"No, you're not. You haven't been the same man since Billy came back to town."

Folding his large hands on the pine table, Guthrie wouldn't meet her eyes.

"Just tell me. I'm your friend. We'll pray about it. Please give it up. Let God start healing your damaged heart." She reached over and slipped her hand between both of his. His rough hands reminded her of what a hardworking, faithful man he was. In the short time she'd known him he had won her respect and liking. "Only God has that healing power. He wants the best for you." *Guthrie, don't fight it anymore.*

He pushed back on his seat and stretched his legs out on each side of hers. He drew in air, then let it out slowly. "You should know the whole story. So you'll understand why he can't be trusted." He made eye contact with her, but only for an instant. "I told you about how Billy stole Lynda's car and the money she'd saved?"

She squeezed his warm hand and nodded.

"My father had cancer…he was dying of it."

Oh, no. What a dreadful combination. "I didn't know that. I just knew that you'd lost him earlier than you had expected." She lay her other hand over his.

Guthrie stared at the wall above her head. "Billy wrecked the car he stole. He was out near our farmhouse. Dad was there with Aunt Ida and Aunt Edith. He'd been too sick to go to the hospital to be with Lynda when she was having Hunter. Billy walked to our farmhouse and hot-wired our old truck."

Hannah closed her eyes and bent her head, the burden of callous sin, not even her own, weighing her down. *How could you, Billy? How could you pile betrayal on top of betrayal?*

"My dad heard the noise and managed to get outside. Aunt Ida said Billy nearly ran my dad down when he tried to stop Billy." Guthrie drew in breath. "I know Dad was already failing, dying, but his last few weeks were made hellish by worry over Lynda…disappointment over how Billy had treated her and the children."

"It multiplied your grief." Hannah tightened her grip on his strong hands.

"It was…awful."

Hannah didn't speak. She waited, giving both of them time to recover from the ordeal of putting Billy's sins into words. She longed to draw Guthrie's hand to her cheek so she could cradle it there, a sign of comfort, sharing.

Finally, she murmured, "But all that is in the past. Your being angry isn't going to spare your father any pain. He's with God, beyond pain. All the tears have been wiped from his eyes. Don't you think he wants you to be happy? And Lynda and the children?"

"Of course, but I just don't trust Billy."

"You have to have faith. Faith is things hoped for. Right now, Guthrie, *you've* become the problem."

"Me?" He looked aghast, disgruntled.

She nodded. "You're upsetting your whole family. I told you before—you can't control anyone's feelings but your own. You can't stop Lynda from wanting to trust her ex-husband again or Billy from hurting his family again *if* he decides to go back to his old ways.

"All you can do is get out of the way, not *create problems* for Lynda and her family. Don't you think Lynda's children will begin to pick up on your animosity toward their father? How will that affect them? Don't you see that?"

Closing his eyes, he leaned his head back, stretching his neck until the top of his head touched the wall behind him. He finally nodded.

A relieved sigh flowed through Hannah. *Dear God, please let this family, this kind man, have a happy ending.*

Then, when she least expected it, Guthrie increased his pressure on her hands and drew them up to his lips.

Her breath caught in her throat as his lips grazed her

knuckles. How could such a powerful man be so tender, so gentle? He stood, pulling her to her feet. Her gaze never left his face as he drew her closer, closer…and bent his head.

She lifted her face to him.

From outside came the scream of a fire engine. The moment was shattered. She and Guthrie froze in place.

"That sounds awfully close." She thought of her parents, Guthrie's nieces and nephews asleep in this village.

"Let's go!" Guthrie, still holding her hand, hurried through the darkened basement, then outside. In the cooler night air, he didn't break stride. Hannah sprinted to keep up with him. Her concentration was directed to the horizon. It flickered with an unnatural light.

Dear God, it's right on Church or Front Street. Please don't let anyone be injured. Protect the men who are fighting the fire. Her litany of prayers for safety kept pace with her legs. Her heart pounded with fear.

Others from the small town joined the race with them. Ahead, the red lights of one, no, two fire engines turned, splashing their alien glare onto the pavement and the deserted houses. At the corner of Front and Church streets, Guthrie stopped.

Hannah bumped against him. She gasped. "It's the café!"

Hanson's Cozy Café disgorged tongues of flame and billows of coal-black smoke. The mounting smoke obscured the motel. "My parents!" She lurched forward.

Guthrie caught her by both arms. "There! There they are!"

She swung around and followed Guthrie's nod. Her parents stood well away from the fire with Lila by their side. "Mom! Dad! The kittens!" Guthrie released her. She hurried to them and threw her arms around them both.

"Oh, Hannah!" her mother wailed. "We were only able to get the kittens and your laptop out! The smoke, the water will damage everything the fire doesn't destroy! All your beautiful new clothes!"

Not able to speak, Hannah squeezed, her arms stretched around both her parents at once. *Safe! They're all safe, even the kittens! Thank you, God!*

Nearby, her eyes awash with tears, Lila kept moaning, "How could this happen? How?"

Firemen shouted to each other. The engines churned, powering the pumps and lighting the scene. Windows in the motel exploded from the heat. Water hissed as it quenched flame.

Finally, the fire surrendered, drenched into extinction. The café had been demolished by water and flame. The motel stood blackened and empty. The odor of burned wood and melted plastic fouled the air.

Hannah shivered in the dark chill of midnight and folded her arms around herself. Though she'd only brought her writing and clothes with her to Petite, she was experiencing a keen sense of loss, disorientation. *I have no place to go.*

In twos and threes, those who'd come to watch began

drifting to their homes. Everyone stopped to say a word to Lila or to hug her. Ida and Edith insisted that Lila come home with them for the night.

Lila tried to refuse.

But Ida insisted. "No, no, Lila, you shouldn't be alone after something like this. We'll make you a cup of hot chamomile tea, then you can sleep in our guest bedroom upstairs."

"Absolutely. You mustn't be alone," Edith agreed. "We are happy to be able to do something for our neighbor."

Hannah watched the two old ladies lead the disheveled and silent Lila away.

Hannah's father spoke. "Well, it's good we left our car parked at the church. I guess we'd better drive to Portage and see about a hotel room."

"No." Guthrie appeared beside her and her parents. "I've got a whole farmhouse to myself."

Hannah stared at him, his words taking her by surprise.

"Oh, no, we couldn't impose," her mother said.

Guthrie shook his head with no-nonsense determination. "I'm not letting you three go to another motel. Now come on. Hannah's SUV and my truck are still parked at the church." He turned to her. "Are you in shape to drive?"

She nodded, too tired, too shocked at this turn of events to object.

"Then you can drive your parents and follow me out to the farm."

Hannah felt unable to form an opposing opinion.

Too much had transpired in too short a time. Mom had made the right choice in the thing she'd salvaged. The laptop with all her writing on it was the one thing Hannah couldn't do without. But what a feeling! She didn't even have a toothbrush to take to Guthrie's! And did she want to stay in Guthrie's house? At the moment, she didn't have the luxury of choice.

A lowing of cattle woke Hannah. For a few seconds, she couldn't remember where she was. Then scenes from the night before, the Twenty-One Plus Night at church and the fire, cascaded through her mind. She closed her eyes, then with a sigh opened them again.

In the dark early morning hours, Guthrie had led her parents and her up to rooms on the second floor. Her parents had taken the room across the hall from her. After they'd gone into their room, Guthrie had murmured that this room had been his sister's, then left her with a pair of his folded cotton pajamas in her hand. She pictured it like a scene in an old black-and-white movie. The two of them, standing close in the dark hallway, the funny feeling of wanting to move into his arms, but knowing she couldn't.

Hannah got out of bed. Holding up the too-long pajama legs like folds of a long skirt, she walked to the old-fashioned double-hung window. Guthrie's dairy feeder cattle wandered, grazing, spread out over the muted green and golden pastures. The faded pink curtain beside her was soft under her fingertips. She bent her head against the wooden window frame.

How would she and her parents adjust to being, in effect, homeless? It was a peculiar feeling. Lila's Cozy Motel hadn't been a five-star hotel, but it had begun to feel like home. What now? Should she go back to Milwaukee and move in with Spring or to Madison and bunk with Doree? Neither appealed at all. Her parents needed her, and the idea of leaving Guthrie behind left her feeling empty.

Guthrie almost kissed you last night, her conscience whispered. *You shouldn't lead him on when you don't intend to fall in love with him.*

"Too late," she murmured with dawning dismay. *How could I help falling in love with Guthrie?*

You just ended a three-year engagement— Her conscience broke off at a tap on her door.

"Hannah, the coffee's ready down in the kitchen."

Guthrie's voice made her spine tingle.

"All right," she called in a voice that didn't sound quite like her own.

She listened to his footsteps shuffle quickly down the wooden steps. Not having any choice, she shrugged out of the oversize pj's and into her fire-scented shorts outfit from last night and quickly made her bed. She knocked at her parents' door, but found the room empty. Were they downstairs or was she all alone in the farmhouse with Guthrie? Phantom butterflies fluttered their gossamer wings in her stomach.

In the kitchen, Guthrie lounged at the table sipping coffee, alone.

"Where are my mom and dad?" she asked, pausing in the doorway.

He motioned her to help herself to the pot of coffee still warming on the old white porcelain stove. A mug decorated with yellow daisies and a spoon had been set out for her on the nicked Formica counter.

Feeling as self-conscious as a new child in a strange school, she made a wide circuit around him.

"They went to Portage hospital to visit one of the volunteer firemen who was burned last night."

His words startled her. She halted her first sip of the hot coffee. "Was he seriously hurt?"

"No, just some second-degree burns on his face and hands. But he's on oxygen until his lungs clear a bit more. He should be home by tomorrow. Your mom said she'd stop and pick up some clothing and toiletries for you. She said she knew you wanted to write today."

Write today? It was the farthest thing from her mind. Hannah sat across from Guthrie and tried not to stare at him. She'd been alone with this man many times over the past weeks, but had never experienced quite the same sensation. She couldn't take her gaze from him. The gold of his corn silk hair, the way it curled around his ears, the squareness of his determined jaw…

She closed her eyes and took a deep breath. *I've just ended an engagement. I'm vulnerable.* Rebound bait, Doree had called her in a recent phone call. *And I've spent a lot of time with this man. These are just feelings, and they will vanish all by themselves if I ignore them.*

I'll pack up my stuff from the motel and move into one closer to Portage. That will take care of these... longings.

She opened her eyes.

Guthrie had leaned forward, his powerful arms resting on the wooden tabletop. "The motel is going to take a lot of cleaning and repairs, and the café will have to be rebuilt. I've invited your mom and dad and now you to stay here while Lila gets everything back in order."

What?

"Your parents said it was fine with them and didn't think you'd have any objection."

Objection? Oh, Guthrie, what am I going to do about you? Or, more importantly, about me? This just isn't a good time for either of us. Why didn't I realize how susceptible I'd be to a warmhearted guy like you?

Over two weeks later, Guthrie watched Hannah drive up and park her SUV on the muddy road near her parents' lot. He stood beyond the construction site and watched the crew from the factory-built-shell company work. A huge crane was poised over the foundation, and the workers were putting up the shell, wall by wall.

"Wow." Hannah walked up beside him. "The windows are in and everything."

He ignored his marked reaction to her. She smelled of vanilla and glowed with energy. If he didn't hold himself in check, he might just pull her into his arms and kiss her—right here in front of God and everybody. He couldn't keep Hannah out of his thoughts.

Each morning, he found himself lingering in the kitchen listening for her footsteps on the stairs. Then she'd sit down with him at the table where he'd eaten breakfast alone for years. She lit up the room with her teasing smile and friendly laughter.

That evening after the Twenty-One Plus Night party, he'd intended to kiss her. That is, he hadn't intended to, but he almost had. Nothing had gone the way he'd anticipated since then.

More and more, Lynda had been letting Billy hang around her and the kids. Everyone seemed to think that Billy was a new man. They might be right, but the fear of history repeating itself still had the power to make Guthrie nervous. Hannah had been right, too. He could do nothing to prevent his sister from letting Billy into her life and in the process make what might prove the second biggest mistake of her life.

All Hannah had said that night in the church kitchen made sense, but he still couldn't quite shake the feeling that Billy couldn't be trusted with the heavy responsibility of fatherhood. Billy might think he could, but he might bite off more than he could chew. Yet hard as it was, Guthrie had held his tongue.

And Hannah… He'd let himself get too close to her. Hannah Kirkland had irritated him more than once, but he'd liked her right away. Everyone did. But she had this way of sticking her nose into his business. She'd insisted on helping him with the church roof out of concern for her parents. She'd spoken to him about Billy fearlessly and honestly. Who could stay mad at a kind-hearted, dark-haired, lovely…

"Oh, this is so exciting! I wouldn't have believed it if I hadn't seen it with my own eyes." Hannah's voice sounded her wonder. "The shell really will be up in twelve hours."

"Maybe less." He kept his tone noncommittal. The crane creaked as it swung another wall into place. How could he help noticing that the woman beside him bubbled over with vitality and charm? "You're looking good today." He couldn't have stopped the words if he'd been struck dumb.

"Oh?" She blushed.

Why had he said that to her? Hannah Kirkland was a writer. She was on TV. She wouldn't be interested in him, a small-town carpenter, a farmer in deep debt. Besides, he'd given up on love long ago when…*she'd* left. Then his father had gotten sick. Billy had… He pushed away the unhappy memories. Today was a happy day. Finally, this summer, something good was happening.

"After you left this morning, I got two calls." She spoke to him, but her eyes never strayed from the activity yards in front of them.

"Oh?"

"First my sister Spring called to say she would be coming to visit. Would you mind if she bunked in with me a couple of nights?"

"That'll be fine."

"And the county fair chairwoman called to ask me to judge the pie competition at the county fair along with your great-aunts."

"Oh?"

"That's the news." She turned to him with a smile bright enough to light up Milwaukee.

He grabbed at the safe topic she'd offered him. "It's hard to believe it's time for the county fair. It always means the real end of summer."

"Yes, and fall always flies by. You've got all your hay in?"

He nodded. "Yeah, and that's a real blessing. I won't have to pay for feed for my cattle this winter. They'll be fat and ready to sell to dairies come spring without huge feed bills."

And though he hadn't believed it would happen, Billy had started giving Lynda money each week. It wasn't enough so she could quit work and stay home with the kids, but it was enough to pay the groceries and a few bills. Not having to help Lynda as much allowed Guthrie to start paying off his debts faster than he'd anticipated. Even though he'd argued against it, the Kirklands were pitching in for groceries and bills at the farm.

Then Billy had tried to give him a check to help pay off the debt for Hunter's birth. Though Guthrie had refused Billy's check, telling him to give it to Lynda, it had felt good this month when Guthrie had been able to write a healthy figure on the principal line of the bank mortgage form.

Hannah turned halfway from him. "I hope we're not crowding you at the farm. We can always move out."

"No, not at all."

"But you might need our rooms. Your mom says your brother called today."

"Brandon?" Guthrie couldn't remember the last time his brother had communicated with them.

"Yes, he's coming for a visit."

Guthrie snorted. "She must have heard him wrong. He never leaves San Francisco."

"No, I'm sure she said Brandon's trying to come in time for the county fair. And he wants to stay at the farm. I'll be happy to move out."

A spark ignited Guthrie's temper. "No. You're staying. He can get a room at a motel in Portage or bunk with Aunt Edith and Aunt Ida. They'll enjoy having him."

"But your mom said—"

"He'll stay in town. Brandon never had any use for the farm." *Is Deirdre coming with him?* Guthrie felt a little sick at the possibility.

Under cover of the worn county fair marquee, open on all four sides, Hannah stood between Ida and Edith. The sweet scent of fruit pies wafted all around them and blended with the smell of warm canvas in the late September afternoon breeze. "Ladies, it looks like we have our work cut out for us."

They were surrounded by long tables covered with row after row of golden pies—cherry, apple, blueberry, peach, blackberry, strawberry, rhubarb and more, many more. Outside, gray clouds layered the sky, promising rain.

"I hadn't thought there would be so many entries," Hannah murmured, feeling like a piece of pastry dough that had just been flattened by a heavy rolling pin.

"It will be quite a challenge," Ida agreed, sporting an old-fashioned full apron in pink-and-white gingham.

"But we know how to do it." Edith, wearing a matching apron, nodded.

"What do you suggest?" Hannah bent over and propped one elbow on the front table. Right now, tasting pies ranked dead last in what she wanted to do.

"We start by looking at each pie."

"Judging for appearance?" Hannah guessed.

"Of course, dear." Ida smiled primly. "A good-tasting pie rarely looks bad, at least in a contest, you know. The cook wouldn't bring anything less than the very best."

"After we look, then we taste." Edith finished with a knowing grin.

So Hannah began, but as she judged she watched the ebb and flow of familiar faces around the centrally located pie-judging area. Part of her mind watched for Spring to arrive. Her parents had promised to bring her directly to the fair when she arrived. The other part of her concentrated on pie appearance, pastry texture, filling flavor. She marked these on her scorecard, as did the aunts.

But Hannah had to admit there was one face she was watching for even more than Spring's—Guthrie's. She had to turn this Guthrie trend around. Between Billy's return, Mom's health and the wait to look for the adoption papers, there was a great deal at stake in their families. She had to get over Guthrie and fast.

After the pies had been judged by the visual criterion, Hannah's vigil for her sister ended. Flanked by their parents, Spring, wearing an ivory linen shift, stopped and goggled at all the pies. "You're not really going to taste all these pies, are you?"

"I'm so happy to see you, too." Hannah's mouth twisted into a wry grin. She stepped outside the judging area.

"Oh, I'm sorry, Hannah." Spring hugged her sister and whispered, "I saw the house. It won't be long and you'll be in."

"No problem." Hannah gave her sister a special smile of understanding.

After meeting the aunts, Spring and their parents wandered away with Martha, who had Amber and Jenna in hand, and Hannah returned to the rows of pies.

At long last, Hannah, Ida and Edith finished the tasting and bestowed the ribbons on the top three pies. Hannah collapsed onto a lawn chair beside the pie tent. Carnival music accompanied the sound of shots from the target game and the ping of quarters tossed at jars. The buttery smell of popcorn and the sweet smell of cotton candy wafted on the increasing breeze. Crowds soon clogged the fairground walkways. Lynda and Billy with Hunter stopped to chat. Hannah smiled at seeing the three of them enjoying the fair together.

"Daddy," Hunter insisted, "I want a corn dog!"

"Okay, okay." Billy ruffled Hunter's mop of blond hair. "We'll be right back, Mom."

"Just one," Lynda called after them. "He's already had cotton candy and a funnel cake!"

Hannah, certain she'd eaten the equivalent of two whole pies, felt a little queasy. "Please don't talk about food."

Lynda laughed. "Pie contest get to you?"

Hannah noticed that Guthrie's sister looked even prettier than she had when they'd met. An inner glow had begun to glimmer in her eyes and expression.

Spring, clutching a white bear almost half her size, returned with Garner and Ethel. "Look, Father pitched quarters and won me a bear!"

Hannah made herself pout. "I want a bear, too."

Dad laughed.

Guthrie made his way through the crowd. Stopping near them, he smiled at her.

Her heart did a flip-flop, but Hannah covered it with a friendly wave to him. "Why weren't you here earlier? We needed help judging those pies."

"I was judging rabbits for the 4-H kids."

Hannah introduced him to her sister.

"Nice to meet you, Spring." He nodded.

"Rabbits!" Spring exclaimed. "They're my favorite!"

"Me, too. I love the ones with the lop ears, so

unusual." Behind them, Ida cut a generous piece of blueberry pie, put it on a paper plate and handed it to Guthrie.

"Yes, dear, eat," Edith encouraged. "You look tired."

Guthrie chuckled, then bit into the blueberry pie.

"Let me guess." Hannah rested her index finger on the side of her chin. "Blueberry is your favorite."

A drop of the purple juice and a berry slid down his chin. Hannah nearly reached out to catch them with her fingertip. She gave herself a little shake.

"Lynda! Lynda!" Billy shoved his way to his wife, who had reached up to wipe her brother's chin. "Is Hunter with you?"

"No." Concern leaped onto Lynda's face.

"He was right with me. I reached up for our corn dogs. I turned around and he was gone."

Chapter Twelve

"Don't panic. We'll find your boy," Hannah's father said, his face stern. "Hannah, do you have your new cell phone?"

Still stunned, Hannah slid it out of her pocket.

"Call nine-one-one. I'm sure I saw a deputy around here. I want the county sheriff right now. I think the little guy has just got himself lost, but these days we can't take any chances."

As her father talked, Hannah punched the numbers in. Her hands trembled. Had Hunter become lost in the crowd or had he been snatched by a stranger? When a voice answered, she handed the phone to her father.

With few words, he told the dispatcher the problem and hung up. "Now, Guthrie and Bill, there are only two parking lots. Bill, you take the north lot. Guthrie, you take the west. Gather a few friends as you go. The

sheriff said to refuse to let anyone leave. His orders."
Guthrie and Bill raced off in different directions.

Dad turned to his wife, Hannah, Spring and Lynda.
"I'm going to go to the man in charge of the public
address system, so he can broadcast an alert for Hunter.
The four of you take different areas, search for Hunter
and spread the word." He gave Lynda a quick hug.
"Don't worry. God is with him and with us. We'll find
him. Now go."

Grateful to be able to help, Hannah hurried away, her
heart racing. Visions of forlorn faces of lost children on
posters and milk cartons filled her with icy terror. She
tried to reason with her fear. Children got confused in
crowds and wandered away all the time, but her urgency
to search for Hunter didn't wane. As she hurried along
examining every nook, she watched for familiar faces.
She saw Lila coming toward her. "Lila, Hunter's lost!
Have you seen him?"

"No—"

The public address system crackled to life. "Attention. Hunter Garrett, a four-year-old boy with blond
hair, has come up missing. He is wearing blue jeans and
a Packer T-shirt. If you see him, please bring him to the
central judge's station. Thank you."

Lila rushed to catch up with Hannah. "I'll help you.
Lynda must be frantic."

Hannah nodded, but concentrated on searching for
a little towheaded boy in a Packer T-shirt. Each minute,
each step made her heart thump harder. *Dear Lord,*

please help us find him. Comfort Lynda and Billy. Don't let anyone hurt Hunter.

The minutes roared passed. Everywhere people, strangers and friends, were calling, "Hunter! Hunter!" Two sheriff's cars drove into the fairground and blocked the exits. Hannah welcomed the blare of their sirens and their flashing red lights. No stranger would be able to get far.

The sky was turning dark and stormy. Hannah and Lila made it to the west entrance. A young deputy there was talking to Guthrie. Guthrie had his arms folded over his chest, his face drawn into somber lines. She waved. He nodded.

Hunter, where did you go?

Then Hannah heard calling in the distance, happy shouting. "They found the little boy!" "He's been found!" With Lila huffing beside her, she ran toward the voices.

Beaming, Aunt Ida and Aunt Edith waited several yards away from the corn dog stand. Hunter stood between them, their arms around his small trembling shoulders. The little boy clutched their skirts in his small fists.

With a shout of joy, Lynda rushed to him and swung him up in her arms. The crowd fell silent. Needing to be close, Hannah pushed her way forward.

"I'm sorry, Mommy!" Hunter sobbed. "I'm sorry. I didn't mean to get losted."

Billy and Guthrie came into view, running from opposite directions. The crowd parted to let them and the sheriff and a deputy through.

Billy cried out, "Thank God! Where was he?"

Weeping, Lynda reached out her free arm, and the two of them embraced each other with Hunter in the middle.

Guthrie halted a few paces back, though he looked like he wanted to snatch the child from their arms and hold him close.

Choked with emotion, Hannah made her way to Guthrie and took his arm. Emotions ran high, and she feared he might do or say something in the heat of the moment that would do harm. But he didn't pull against her. Instead, he closed his large hand over hers.

She tried to read his emotions, but she only had his profile to judge.

"Where were you, baby?" Lynda asked her son.

"I wanted...a corn dog." Hunter sniffed back tears.

"Yes?" Lynda prompted.

Hannah leaned her head against Guthrie's arm, suddenly feeling weak with relief.

"But then I saw a quarter under there." He pointed to a long, green-draped table across the way. "And I crawled over there. Then I saw a grasshopper and I wanted to catch him, but I couldn't. Then I came back out and I couldn't see Daddy and I got scared. So I hid under the table until my daddy came back to find me. I was scared some stranger would get me. I wanted my daddy."

Hannah blinked back tears. Happy endings were so rare.

Lynda and Billy hugged their son again.

"It's okay." Billy smoothed the little boy's hair. "We just wanted you to be safe."

Again, Hannah expected Guthrie to speak up. Again, he remained silent, watching. She squeezed Guthrie's arm reassuringly.

He returned the pressure.

Hannah smiled, Guthrie's silence bolstering her.

"Aunt Ida and Edith, how did you find him?" Lynda asked the beaming ladies.

"We just thought like a child," Ida replied.

"Absolutely. We know that strangers do abduct children nowadays." Edith frowned. "So the pastor had to call the sheriff and such—"

"But children do just wander away. Always have. I remember Guthrie doing it at this fair when he was about six." Ida glanced at her nephew. "We found him the same way. Looking where a child might hide."

"Well, no harm done." Hannah's father spoke. "Thank you, Sheriff. Sorry we called you out."

"No problem. You did just what you should. I was close by, and my two deputies were on-site and were able to close off the exits. If this had been an abduction, your quick action would have prevented him from getting away." He turned to the crowd. "Everyone, the excitement's over. It could rain any time, so let's have fun!"

Hoping no one had noticed her clinging to Guthrie, Hannah dropped her hold on his arm. People drifted away as the wind brought the rain.

Guthrie turned to her. "I'm beat. I'm heading home." His voice rasped with emotion.

"Me, too. Too much pie," Hannah agreed, tired, but with a heart full of thankfulness.

She didn't want Guthrie to be alone right now. Billy's losing Hunter might have rocked the new equilibrium of Guthrie trying to get along with his errant brother-in-law. Guthrie hadn't reacted with anger or recriminations, as she'd feared. She wanted to know why. "I'll leave my car for my parents. Can I have a ride home with you?"

He nodded and soon held the door open for her to climb into his truck. As he drove onto the highway, the rain, which had been holding off all day, finally began. A rhythmic pitter-patter over their heads gave Hannah a melancholy feeling. Guthrie appeared to drive on autopilot, not really aware of her presence.

Finally, she drew in a deep breath. "Thanks for not going ballistic over Hunter being lost."

"I wanted to."

She heard both the grudge and the honesty in his voice. "I know you did. That's why I'm thanking you for not making things worse than they were."

"Kids wander off."

"They do." She couldn't believe her ears. He wasn't blaming Billy!

"I could see that Billy was really terrified when he thought he'd lost Hunter." He spoke the words as if they'd been and still were a revelation to him.

"Yes, I'm glad you saw that." Inwardly, she rejoiced for Guthrie's change of heart. A major breakthrough.

She ventured on, choosing her words with care. "Billy is good with the kids. I think he's learning to be a father more each time he's with them. You have to remember he didn't have a father and he hasn't had the years of experience you've had with the kids."

Guthrie nodded, but distractedly, as though his mind was filled to the brim with conflicting thoughts.

She let him wrestle with switching his mind-set against his brother-in-law to acceptance that Billy had become a new man. She stared at the gray scene beyond the windshield. The steady rain infused her with a feeling that the two of them in the truck cab were cut off from the rest of the world. Maybe Guthrie had the same feeling.

Finally, he spoke up. "I saw how Lynda turned to Billy when Hunter came up missing. I think she's starting to have feelings for him again."

"I think she's learning to," Hannah replied haltingly. "Billy's not the only one who's changed, you know. I don't think Lynda is the same woman she was at seventeen when Billy married her."

"How do you mean that?"

"Well, life changes all of us." She propped her elbow by the passenger window and set her chin on her hand. "I've gone through something similar." She cleared her throat. "Until recently, I was engaged."

"You were?"

She nodded.

"Can you… Do you mind…?"

"No, I don't mind. I was engaged to Edward for three years. We attended the same college, and he gave me a ring our senior year."

Guthrie looked surprised as he drove into the yard between his house and the barn and parked. The rain thundered overhead. Neither of them moved to venture outside the truck.

"What happened?" he asked.

She felt a freedom blossoming inside her. She'd wanted to put her thinking about Edward into words for weeks. But in Petite, she hadn't had anyone she'd wanted to confide in—except this man. She hadn't realized that until right now. She wanted to tell Guthrie. She hoped he'd understand. "I don't think either of us was seeing clearly or had become our real selves, our adult selves, yet."

"What do you mean?"

"I wasn't really acting like myself." She looked into his face. "In fact, I didn't really know myself yet. I didn't realize it at the time. I was so caught up in wanting to be a pastor's wife like my mother that I'd assumed a persona that didn't fit me, and I agreed to marry a man I wasn't deeply in love with."

"You weren't in love with him?"

She shook her head. "Not deeply. Not till-death-do-us-part deep. I must have thought he was just like my father. You see, I wanted to marry someone good and wise like Dad."

"Your fiancé wasn't good and wise?"

"No, or maybe I shouldn't say that. But just because he wanted to be a pastor didn't mean he was just like my father. And it was wrong of me to expect him, anyone, to be. But it wasn't just Edward.

"*I've* changed so much since I finally faced the truth about how wrong my assumptions were. I think I was only a shadow of myself. Breaking out of a mousy self-image, coming here to Petite, taking on the challenge of working with you, I feel like a totally different woman." Speaking these words liberated her as if wind lifted her wings and she was flying.

Guthrie nodded. He tried to imagine Hannah's fiancé. What man would be willing to give up an interesting and warmhearted woman like Hannah?

"I think Edward realized something was wrong long before I did. I hung on until it was painfully obvious that it wasn't going to work out with us. Breaking the engagement hurt." She inhaled deeply and smiled at him. "Now I'm glad I broke it off. I just wish he'd said something earlier instead of letting it drag out for nearly three years."

"Maybe he didn't think it was right for a man to beg off."

Her eyes serious, she pursed her lips and nodded. "You're probably right. But then I discovered…"

"You don't have to tell me."

She twisted on the seat to face him and inched closer. "I want to…if you don't mind listening."

"I'd be honored." His throat thickened.

She stared at the window beyond Guthrie's head, then made eye contact with him. "Two months after I broke up with Edward, he married someone else."

"Two months?" He was incredulous. "He—he was…"

She nodded, obviously in pain. "He must have been seeing her. That's what hurts."

"It would."

"Even if Edward hadn't been dating her, he must have known that he had feelings for her, not me."

Guthrie couldn't speak. His throat had closed up. He reached over and pulled her to him. He wanted to comfort her. But the feeling of her softness in his arms went to his head. *Hannah, Hannah…*

He kissed her hair, fragrant with spices, then her eyebrows. Her eyes closed. He kissed her eyelids, first one, then the other. Petal soft. He rubbed her fine hair between his fingers. Such softness brought feelings, emotions bubbling up from deep inside him.

A warmth, healing and vital, flowed through him like a cleansing prayer. Bill and Lynda…it could work out. Maybe *he* might get a second chance, too. The words, "I love you" whispered through his mind. If he could be sure these words were true, would he be able to say them to this woman? Did he, had he fallen in love with Hannah?

Unsure of himself, Guthrie brushed his lips against hers. "Hannah, you make me believe anything is possible. You make me believe…."

Tilting her chin, Hannah smoothed his golden hair, then rested her hand on his cheek.

The gentle touch of her fingertips rushed through him like brushfire. "Hannah, you're a wonderful woman."

The words were spoken so softly that Hannah barely heard them. She was more aware of the bristly texture of Guthrie's jawline under her palm, his latent strength that made her feel safe and protected within his arms. Guthrie would never say "I love you" unless it were God's honest truth. He wouldn't fall in love with someone while another woman wore his diamond.

Hannah pressed her lips to Guthrie's. She wished she had the audacity to say those three words, "I love you," to him. Inside her head, they sounded so right. But if he didn't return her feelings, they could cost her this brand-new intimacy with this special man, this wonderful man. While gazing into his blue, blue eyes, she stroked his rough cheek, and sparks danced up her arm.

"I mean…Hannah, you're so special." He glanced down. "You've become a friend, more than a friend. Tonight when I could have caused trouble, you came close to me. Just your touch on my arm gave me the patience to see the bigger picture, give Billy another chance, give myself another chance."

His last phrase, barely audible, took her breath away. She drew closer still. "Guthrie, I—"

They paused, their faces only inches apart. Hannah remembered the sensation of his lips caressing hers. *Guthrie, kiss me again.*

The sound of a vehicle. Her parents drove up beside them in her SUV. Instinctively Hannah pulled away and waved to them. Disappointment swallowed her up as if she were entering a dark tunnel. She didn't know what she had made Guthrie believe, what second chance he referred to. But another moment alone and she could have found out!

Rain beat against the roof of her parents' nearly finished house. Hannah grunted with exertion as Guthrie hammered the final nail into the four-foot by eight-foot piece of wallboard they were holding in place.

"Well, that's the first bedroom done." Guthrie stepped back.

Hannah heaved a sigh and pulled off her work gloves. "Let's take a coffee break." She walked down the framed-in hallway to the kitchen with the speckled white counter they'd put in together.

Two days had passed since the evening they'd kissed. That evening, tensions between them over working together and over Billy and Lynda reconciling had ended. Since then, Guthrie had been quieter than usual.

This hadn't surprised her. Guthrie struck her as the kind of man who thought matters over very carefully before making a decision. She respected this, but she'd like a hint of what he was mulling over. Was he thinking of her as she was of him? Was he thinking of kissing her again?

Maybe a friendly cup of coffee would loosen his tongue. Hopeful, she drew out the glass coffeepot from the warmer and held it up in question.

"Sure. I'll have a cup. Heavy on—"

She took over with a grin. "Heavy on the cream—"

"And don't forget a teaspoon of sugar for you, not me," he finished for her.

She chuckled. "I think we've eaten too many breakfasts together." In fact, the opposite was true. She looked forward to their quiet times together at the breakfast table each morning. She even woke early to lengthen their time alone at the table while her parents slept late upstairs. She stirred his cup and handed it to him. "We no longer have any mystery left."

"That's not true. There's a lot I'd like to know about you."

About to take her first sip, she lifted her eyebrows. This sudden move into a more personal exchange heightened her awareness of him standing only a few feet away. "Like what?"

He slid onto a step stool. "Like what your plans are once this house is done."

Stumped, she leaned against the kitchen counter. How could she answer that question? She couldn't say the truth—*I'd like to stay with you at your house.* That might be what a twenty-first-century woman would say, but not this twenty-first century woman! She was looking for a lifelong mate. Was Guthrie? After all, they'd only shared a kiss—all right, two if you counted the one she'd surprised him with in the church attic.

Also she'd just broken a three-year engagement, and Guthrie was right in the midst of a family crisis. And they'd only known each other two months! Recent events had already proved she'd made a poor decision when she'd accepted Edward's ring. Guthrie attracted her, but there just hadn't been enough time to gauge where all this was leading. She gave Guthrie the only honest answer she could. "I haven't decided."

"I'd like you to stay."

Hannah's heart did a quick double beat. She licked her dry lips. "You would?"

"I can't imagine Petite without you."

"Thanks. It's begun to feel like home to me, too."

"I'm glad."

But Hannah needed to know if Guthrie had done more than just think about reconciling with Billy. She didn't want the angry Guthrie to come back. She took her courage in her hands. "Have you talked to Lynda about Billy?"

"Yes, we had a long talk last night. Billy really sounds like he's changed for the better." He rose and set his empty mug on the counter. "Let's see if we can get two more rooms done today."

Though surprised, she followed suit. She had no choice. So much for sharing. *Guthrie, next please talk to Billy. With that resolved, then maybe we can talk about us, if there is a possibility for us.*

* * *

At the end of the long, exhausting day and during a pause in the pouring rain, Guthrie helped Hannah into his truck and drove them home. He parked beside the barn.

An unfamiliar sedan was parked close to his back porch.

"Whose car is that?" she asked tiredly, tightening and flexing her stressed shoulder muscles trying to relax them.

A stranger stepped out the back door and under the shelter of the little porch roof and stood there, waiting for them. The handsome man was dark-haired, tall and slender, dressed in expensive-looking gray chinos and a black sport shirt.

Guthrie made a sound of surprise. Hannah glanced at him. What about this stranger had startled him?

Guthrie got out of the truck. Unmindful of the lazy rain, which still sprinkled down, he opened her door, then led her to the porch. Though he didn't seem to hurry, Hannah sensed a tension in him.

"Brandon." Guthrie's tone was a puzzle to Hannah. Was it a greeting, a question, a challenge? She couldn't tell.

"Guthrie." The man responded in kind.

The warm sprinkle of rain refreshed Hannah, but the unspoken tension between the two men puzzled her. Guthrie hadn't been pleased to hear his brother was coming, and he certainly didn't sound welcoming now. What was wrong?

She offered her hand.

Guthrie said belatedly, "Hannah, this is my brother, Brandon."

Brandon walked down the steps and shook her hand.

As she exchanged pleasantries with Brandon, she wondered about Guthrie's renewed quietness. She'd thought, over the afternoon, that he'd begun to loosen up again.

"Have you seen Lynda?" Hannah asked.

"No, but I'm looking forward to it and seeing the kids." Brandon looked at Guthrie. "Mom says Billy's back."

Guthrie nodded. "Yes, he's grown up a lot. He's great with the kids."

Hannah frowned at Guthrie's dead tone. *Something's dreadfully wrong here, Lord. What is it?*

"I'm glad." Brandon looked both uneasy and upset. "Which room do you want me to take?"

"I'm sorry," Guthrie replied. "I've already got Hannah and her parents living with me after a fire in town. Aunt Ida and Edith are expecting you to stay with them. I'll call them and tell them you're on your way in."

"No problem." Guthrie's brother reached inside the door, brought out a gray duffel and a suit bag and walked toward the sedan.

Hannah called after him, "I'm sorry. I could go to stay with the aunts."

"No, this is fine." With a wave, he got into his car and drove away.

She and Guthrie stayed where they were, then she rested a hand on his arm. "What is it?" she whispered.

He glanced at her. "Do you get the feeling everything's getting dumped here all at once? When Dad died, when we really needed him, Brandon couldn't be bothered. And now he's back. I don't get it."

Hannah leaned close to him, resting her head on his arm. "Oh, Guthrie, you dear man." First Billy, now Brandon.

"I don't know how to handle this. I feel like having it out with him, but what good would it do now? It wouldn't change anything."

Hannah listened sympathetically but detected more in Guthrie's attitude toward Brandon. There was something else, some other unsettled business between these two brothers. *God, why does Guthrie have to deal with this right now? He just got adjusted to Billy coming back. Now Brandon shows up. I know You always know best, but couldn't this have waited?*

People crowded around Hannah in the brightly lit church basement to celebrate the new roof and refurbished attic. A large sheet cake was being slowly but surely devoured not only by the church members but by the good people of Petite. The marble cake with white icing bore the pink frosting salutation, Thanks Guthrie and Hannah!

Hannah shifted her weight on her tired feet and tried to ignore her uneasiness. Guthrie sat across the room with Hunter on his lap and talked with Ted and Billy. While Guthrie and Billy appeared to be making progress toward reconciliation, the unmentioned friction between Guthrie and Brandon had increased over the past few days.

Whenever Guthrie and Brandon were together, Hannah noted others watching them, measuring them. Obviously, the town of Petite wasn't in the dark about the root of the distance between the two brothers. She wished someone would give her a hint. Though Guthrie put on a good face, she hurt for him, even though she knew the last thing he wanted was sympathy.

Standing at Hannah's side, Brandon and his mother sipped coffee with Lila. Martha ran her fingers through her damp hair. Everyone had been rained on as they rushed between car and church. "When will this rain stop? I'm so worried for the farmers. They need to be harvesting the corn and soybeans now. How will they ever get into these wet fields with their combines or get the corn dried out?"

"It's delaying the work on my café. I can tell you that," Lila added. "If it weren't for my insurance, I'd be sunk."

"I'm sorry to hear that, Lila," Brandon said. "I had been looking forward to stopping in the Cozy for a fried-egg sandwich."

"Well, you come over to my house and I'll fix you one." Lila patted his arm. "I wouldn't want to send you back to San Francisco without one!"

Brandon smiled.

But Hannah thought his smile looked brittle and his eyes forlorn. She sensed Brandon had come home for some specific reason. What was it?

"Hannah, if you and Guthrie hadn't gotten this roof done, who knows how much damage this rain would have caused." Lila looked at the ceiling as though assessing the destructive power of the rain beating against the basement windows.

Martha shook her head. "The ground was saturated already after the spring rains. Where will all this water go?"

Hannah had heard Martha's worry repeated over and over in the past week of solid rain. The Wisconsin River and its creeks were already full, and the subsoil was soaked. In the spring, flooding had been narrowly avoided, but now the threat had returned fourfold.

"There was no need to thank Guthrie and me. We were just glad to get the roof done." Hannah was becoming a little embarrassed. After all, she'd helped Guthrie with the roof for a selfish reason, to free him up to work on her parents' home.

"Looking at you, I can't believe you're a carpenter." Brandon gave her a quizzical look.

Hannah shrugged. *Brandon, I haven't figured you out yet myself.*

"Mom showed me the videotapes she had of you and my great-aunts," Brandon continued. "They are hilarious."

She smiled, but wearily. This type of comment was

also wearing on her. Yes, the taped cooking spots were amusing, but that didn't diminish the quality of the recipes or the spontaneity the two aunts added to them. Hannah was proud of the recipes and the aunts. Her agent had called a day ago to say that the dairy wanted to continue to sponsor the spots after the first three-month contract and were talking about doing a promotional brochure booklet with dairy recipes. If that came about, her agent thought that demos might be picked up by Minneapolis and Milwaukee TV stations, too.

"I'm very grateful to your aunts." Hannah raised her voice so others could hear. "They add sparkle and charm to the cooking demos. I am in *their* debt."

Martha nodded. "This town has always underestimated my husband's aunts. I'm so happy that these TV spots show what they can do." She looked at Brandon. "You'll be happy to know that Hannah insisted they be paid for their contribution to the project."

Brandon looked more surprised than happy. "That's wonderful." He gave Hannah another searching look.

Guthrie approached Hannah from behind. He touched her shoulder. "They want us to go up to the attic for a few pictures."

"All right," Hannah assented, "but these have to be the last. I'm not very enthusiastic about all this fuss."

Guthrie nodded to Lila and his mother but ignored Brandon.

"I think I'll come along," Brandon said with a note of challenge in his tone.

"Suit yourself." Guthrie led Hannah by the hand to the attic.

Once there, Hannah and Guthrie posed for the two ladies who kept the church scrapbook while Brandon looked on. Brandon's presence seemed to nettle Guthrie, whose expression became stormy. Then just the three of them, Guthrie, Hannah and Brandon, remained in the attic.

Gales of rain thrashed the roof. The intensity overhead matched the friction between the two brothers. Watching the conflict in their gazes and body language, Hannah feared this would be their big showdown. It seemed to her that they circled each other like wrestlers sizing each other up. She said a quick prayer for peace.

"So?" Brandon challenged Guthrie. "Go ahead. I know what you're thinking. Ask me."

Guthrie stared at his brother. "Where's Deirdre? Didn't she want to visit her family, too? You won't tell Mom why she didn't come with you. Her parents haven't invited you over for as much as a cup of coffee—"

"Deirdre left me."

Guthrie's expression changed to shock. "Why would she leave you? What did you do to her?"

Brandon gave a sound of disgust. "Me? She's the one who's filed for divorce. According to her, I'm not the man she thought I was when she married me. I wasn't rising fast enough for her. So she found a man with big bucks who was looking for a trophy wife. She decided his checkbook was just her size."

Guthrie took a step forward. "That can't be true. Dee would never do something like that. She loved you."

Hannah listened in stunned silence as the two brothers evidently forgot her presence.

Brandon waved his hand dismissively. "You never knew the real Deirdre. I didn't wake up and realize how selfish she was till Dad died."

"Just because Dee isn't here to defend herself, I won't let you get away with saying things against her—"

Hannah wished she could disappear.

Brandon interrupted, "I should have known better than to fall for Deirdre! She drove a wedge between us from the beginning. I came back from school out east and thought you two had just dated. Why didn't you tell me what the depths of your feelings were for her? You still haven't forgiven me for marrying your first love, but you don't know how lucky you are. Did it ever occur to you that the reason I couldn't help Lynda or you out was that Deirdre spent every penny I made before I even brought the check home? Do you know how I felt when Dee told me she was leaving me? You couldn't guess. After four years with her, I felt nothing but relief!" Brandon turned away and hustled down the steps.

Guthrie headed after him. Hannah was right behind Guthrie. At the bottom, Brandon headed to the party, but Guthrie turned to the door. Hannah followed him. One second outside and chill rain soaked Hannah to her skin. Guthrie hurried ahead of her. By the dim light of the high pole lamp, she ran after him, slipping and stumbling on the wet gravel. He reached his truck and wrenched open the door. Sprinting, she closed the gap in time to throw open the passenger door as he cranked the key in the ignition.

"I'm going home!" he shouted over the noise of the rain pounding on the truck's roof.

"I'm coming, too!" She clambered inside and slammed the door behind her.

He clenched the steering wheel. "Stay here. I'm not going to be good company."

"You shouldn't be alone now." Brandon's words about marrying Guthrie's first love must be true. The thought made Hannah heartsick.

"I'm going to be alone the rest of my life." He glared at her. "I might as well accept that fact."

"Not if I have anything to say about it." Her words startled her, but she wouldn't take them back. It didn't have to mean anything more than one friend helping another. Even though she wanted so much more from Guthrie. Pushing away her own reaction to Brandon's news, she matched Guthrie's stare. Rain dripped from her hair and slid down the back of her neck.

He gunned the motor and took off.

Chapter Thirteen

Hannah had to hold on to the handgrip over the door as he sped down the road and out of town. The late September wind had picked up, and the rain could only be termed a deluge. The wipers battled in vain. She didn't know how Guthrie managed to stay on the road. The only explanation was that he knew the road well enough to navigate without seeing it.

She wished she'd brought her purse and cell phone with her. She hoped her parents wouldn't worry about her. But they would want her to stay with Guthrie and help him get over the shock of hearing that Deirdre had left Brandon for another man. After the breakup with Edward, Hannah knew how he must be feeling.

Guthrie slowed at an intersection.

Before Hannah could gasp, a low black car came out of nowhere—right across their path.

The truck fishtailed. Guthrie wrestled the steering

wheel. He pumped the brakes. The truck skidded to a halt, sliding onto the muddy shoulder.

He jerked it into park. "Are you all right?"

"I'm fine." Hannah leaned her head back, the shock waves vibrating through her.

"Idiot!" He hit the wheel with both hands. "He could have killed someone!"

She nodded. *Us! He could have killed us! God, go with that driver and please keep him from hurting anyone, himself included.*

Guthrie threw open his door and climbed out.

Anxious to help, Hannah got out the passenger side, right into the muddy shoulder. Her sandals sunk into the mire up to her ankles.

Gripping the door, she hoisted herself onto the seat, composed herself, then lifted her feet outside into the shower. Within seconds, the mud had been rained off. She closed her door and crawled over to the other side and let herself out, her need to help Guthrie pushing her into the harsh elements. *God, guide Guthrie so he can see the truth about himself and his family. Help him to feel Your love for him.*

In the glow of the red rear lights, Guthrie was standing on the highway staring at his back passenger side wheel, buried in the muck up to the bottom of the wheel rim.

"Can you get it out?" she shouted, shivering, her wet clothes clinging to her in the lashing wind.

"Yeah! I'm just disgusted with myself for getting stuck."

That sounded more like the Guthrie she'd come to

know. Already his good humor and honesty were reasserting themselves. Thank Heaven! "It wasn't your fault! Anyone else wouldn't have been able to avoid a collision!"

He climbed up over the wheel well and into the truck bed. "Can you help?" He held a long wood plank over the side to her.

"Sure!" She accepted one, then another rough, wet plank and propped them against the side of the truck.

He climbed out and took one.

"What are you going to do?"

"I'll put these under the wheel, then drive onto them and out."

"Won't they just sink in the mud?" she asked. "I tried to get out the other side and sunk up to my ankles."

"It's all I've got!"

"Okay." She watched him work the planks under the mired wheel.

"Get in," he directed.

She hopped inside and slid across the seat. He climbed in and slowly gave the truck enough gas to ease them out of the mud. He parked on the road with his four-way flashers on, then retrieved his planks and threw them into the truck bed.

The rest of the way home he drove more carefully, and she started to relax in spite of her soaked clothing and concern for Guthrie. By the time they reached the farmhouse, she was shivering in earnest with the chill.

"You're going to catch a cold," he said gruffly.

"I'll be f-fine."

"I'm going to get you inside and into a hot shower."

She thought of arguing and then wondered why. This was the Guthrie she loved, the man who couldn't help caring for others. She grinned. "Sounds too good to be true."

He parked and hustled her through the unrelenting rain and in the back door. "Now run upstairs and shower. I'll put the kettle on for hot tea."

"Oh, please, I'd love some of that spiced cider your mom brought from the farmer's market, warmed up."

"I'll put it on now." He pushed her toward the staircase. "Take your time."

She paused. "I'll save you some hot water."

"Don't worry about me. I'm not cold. I'll just change into some dry clothes."

Hannah hurried through a steamy shower and into her new blue flannel pajamas and matching thick terrycloth robe and slippers.

"Cider's hot," Guthrie called from the kitchen. "Your parents called and said they'd be home soon."

She scurried down the steps and into the warm kitchen, redolent with the fragrance of apples and cinnamon. "Mmm. That smells delicious." She sat down and accepted the daisy mug with a cinnamon stick in it. She held the cup between her hands and touched it to her cheek, then her forehead, enjoying the warmth it radiated. Her kitten, Sunny, hopped on her lap and began kneading a spot on the thick terry cloth for himself. Hannah enjoyed petting the soft fur, the cat's purring soothing her frazzled nerves.

Guthrie sat across from her, still looking upset.

Dear man. "Why don't you tell me about it? A trouble shared is a trouble halved."

He hung his head. "What do I need to tell you? You heard it all. No secrets left."

Impulsively, she reached over and took his hand. Her palm tingled with the contact. Edward's touch never overwhelmed her like this. "I told you about my engagement."

"I don't have any engagement to tell you about."

"Brandon said—"

"My brother said a lot, too much."

His dour mood had lifted, but traces lingered. She hated the fact that a woman had come between the brothers. Whether Brandon's words had been true or not, they'd upset Guthrie. She didn't know what to say, how to go on. She closed her eyes, asking for inspiration, then looking up, she asked, "Don't you trust me, Guthrie?"

At this, he met her gaze. "Sure."

"We've become friends, and friends don't dodge the truth."

"I guess so." He nodded.

"Did Brandon tell the truth? Did you love the girl he married?"

He slipped his hand from hers. "Yes."

Bereft of his touch, she waited, letting this one word really sink in. She shivered at what it meant. Guthrie had loved Deirdre. It explained so much, why Guthrie hadn't married yet, why he hadn't been happy to see his brother come home for a visit. Guthrie's faithfulness was one of his most endearing traits, but it could also work against him. Did he still have feelings for Deirdre? He hadn't given Hannah any hint of it. Did she have a chance with this man?

Still stroking the silky kitten, she began slowly. "I thought I was in love with Edward. Maybe you thought you were in love with Deirdre. Perhaps if you saw her now, you'd think a lot differently."

"I can't believe what Brandon said. Deirdre loved him." He twisted halfway from her.

"But we all change. You're remembering a high school girl." She longed to rise and walk around the table. She wanted to cradle Guthrie's face in her two hands and stroke his thick hair. He was such a dear man. She'd never thought or felt this about Edward. Why hadn't she noticed it at the time?

She forced herself to concentrate on the words he needed to hear. "Even if Deirdre came back here, do you think she'd still be the same girl you knew?"

He shrugged and propped his elbows on his thighs. His chin rested on his fists. "I don't know what to tell you. Everything's happened all at once."

"I don't know how you feel about me now. But I thought the other evening after Hunter was found, you and I came close to… I think we could become more than friends, Guthrie. Or, at least, we have a chance to go in that direction." She paused, her heart speeding up with uneasiness. She had to be honest, but she couldn't take all the risks. Guthrie had to do his part.

He stared at the floor. "Dee and I dated on and off all through high school. She'd run hot, then cold, if you know what I mean." He glanced up.

Hannah nodded.

"After senior prom, I told her I loved her, but she didn't want to marry. She said she wasn't ready to settle down. I thought I'd just have to wait until she was ready."

Closing her eyes, Hannah imagined how Guthrie must have reasoned this out.

"Then I graduated from high school and Brandon came back after finishing law school. Mom and Dad had a party for us. The next thing I knew Dee and he were dating, then when he got a job offer in San Francisco, they eloped."

Hannah hated to be cynical, but everything Guthrie said made her believe Brandon's words at the church had been true.

"The only way I accepted Dee marrying Brandon was that she loved him more than she had cared for me. But now he tells me she didn't. How can I believe in love?"

Oh, Guthrie, you don't understand subterfuge, dishonesty or selfishness at all. Lord, give me the words, Your healing words.

Careful not to disturb the kitten napping on her lap, she took his hand. "You do believe in love. I don't think you realize what a loving man you are. You are a man filled with love for his family. That's love."

"That's not the kind of love I mean."

"Every kind of good love is related. Don't tell me you don't believe in love when I see the love you have in action."

He pulled his hand away and wouldn't meet her eyes.

"Guthrie, are you going to let all that you are, your strength of character, your kind heart, be turned inward, wasted? Or are you going to share it?"

He turned a somber gaze to her.

I love you, Guthrie! She imagined wrapping her arms around Guthrie and reveling in his warm, brawny embrace. "You helped your sister when she really needed it. Not just with money, but with time and affection for her children. You've forgiven the man who hurt her and your father during his last days on earth. You carry a load of debt for Lynda and her children, yet you didn't charge the church a penny for the labor to fix the roof. You are a wonderful man."

He pushed his fingers through his hair. "I'm just a regular guy."

She swallowed, gathering her courage. She had to shock him out of this blue funk. "You have to use the same honesty with Brandon that you used with Billy."

"What do you mean?"

"I mean when you saw how much Billy loved his kids, you began to give him a second chance." The kitten on her lap slept peacefully as she stroked its soft fur. The cat's blissful slumber contrasted with the wrenching emotion in Guthrie's voice. She centered herself in her love for Guthrie, her spirit of trust in God.

"How can I know if what Brandon has said is true?"

"Maybe that isn't what God's trying to get you to learn with Brandon."

"Well, what am I supposed to be learning?" Guthrie grumbled.

Hannah gathered her thoughts. "You changed toward Billy because you saw that he had changed, reformed. Maybe with Brandon, you need to show love to him whether he's right or not. God doesn't love us because we're good. He just loves us—no matter what."

Guthrie stilled, gazing into her eyes. "For while we were yet sinners, Christ died for us," he recited softly.

She nodded and replied with a companion verse. "We love Him because He first loved us."

He exhaled deeply. "I'll pray about it, but I'll need God's help to get over this…if I can get over this." He looked into her eyes. "Why do you put up with me, Hannah Kirkland?" He lifted her hand and kissed it.

Her heart thrummed in her ears.

"I'm sorry if I upset you tonight," Guthrie continued. "I wish we could go away somewhere and be together. There are so many things I've wanted to tell you, but here it's just one thing after another—"

The phone rang.

With a grimace, Guthrie picked up the receiver of the wall phone. "What? Don't worry. I'll come right in."

"What is it?" His expression had her worried.

"The creeks have overflowed their banks. My aunts need me."

Flood? She stood up, carefully letting the kitten jump down. "I'm coming with you."

"The river is expected to crest at Portage four feet above flood level in two days."

"What does that mean to Petite?" She imagined her parents' new house being washed away.

"The downtown near the bridge will be under water."

Lynda and the aunts' houses flooded! "Oh, no."

"The state is sending out sandbags. The Red Cross will be bringing in volunteers. I've got to get to town and start helping my family get ready."

"Wait for me. It'll only take me a minute to get into jeans and sweatshirt. Please write a note for my parents."

"I'm just going to my aunt's to move stuff from the basement to the attic. You don't—"

"*Please* wait for me." She raced for the stairs.

About three hours later, Hannah's hands quivered with exhaustion as she held a cup of decaf coffee.

"Guthrie, you and Hannah need to get some rest," Aunt Ida said as she poured cream into her own cup.

After hours of working silently beside Hannah and Guthrie, Brandon had refused coffee and had gone to bed.

Guthrie looked up. "We still need to move—"

"We're putting our foot down." Edith shook her

finger at him. "Now Ida is going to bunk in with me tonight. Hannah, you will take my bed—"

Hannah objected, "No, I—"

Ida wagged her finger at Hannah. "Don't argue. Guthrie can sleep on the couch in the parlor."

For the second time that night, Hannah found herself dressed for bed, this time in a borrowed lavender-flowered nightgown. Edith's room had been stripped of almost everything but the bed. Even the rose-patterned rug had been rolled up. Guthrie planned to store their beds and the sofa in Hannah's parents' unfinished home, which perched well above flood stage.

Bone-weary, Hannah sighed and lay down upon the bed. Moving furniture had been exhausting, but her earlier conversation with Guthrie about Brandon had taken its toll, too. The two brothers had worked side by side, but Brandon's bitter words had been too fresh for both of them to put aside. She'd seen them trying to cooperate, but the hurt was still there between them.

Fatigue weighed down her arms and legs. Her thoughts drifted. Dawn would come within a few short hours. Just as she closed her eyes, she heard Guthrie groan and collapse onto the sofa. So near and yet so far.

For a second, Hannah savored the memory of Guthrie's tender kisses. They had drawn her heart closer to him and evoked a longing for more. She took in a ragged breath.

Lord, help Guthrie learn to let the past go. Soften his heart toward his brother. I'm so tired…. Good night. I mean, amen.

* * *

Morning dawned, a rainy blustery morning. In her Packer sweatshirt and jeans from last night, Hannah stood in the aunts' kitchen talking on the phone to Lynda. Around her, the two aunts were cooking a substantial breakfast for them, scrambled eggs, bacon, pancakes. The delightful fragrances made Hannah's stomach do flip-flops of anticipation.

"What?" Hannah couldn't believe what Lynda had just said.

"Bill has to leave this morning for a court appearance in Oneida County," Lynda repeated. "I'm going with him."

"When will you be back?"

"He said we'll be back as soon as we can. He said it could take more than one day."

"How serious is it?"

"It's a misdemeanor left over from his past. He's hoping the judge will dismiss the charge in light of the changes he's made in his life. He has a lawyer hired and affidavits from his drug counselor and boss in Chicago, his boss here and your father."

"You said we. He's letting you go with him?"

"Yes, I pestered him till he finally gave in. Mom and the great-aunts will take care of the kids."

Hannah's heart sank. This development would hit Guthrie when he was already down. "Okay. I'll be praying for Billy."

"Don't worry, Hannah. I know Guthrie will be upset, but Bill couldn't put this off any longer."

Guthrie, followed by Brandon, entered the kitchen.

"Your sister wants to speak to you." Hannah handed him the phone.

"What is it, Lynda?" Guthrie asked gruffly.

Hannah sat at the table and gave him a tentative smile. This news on top of everything else gave new meaning to the phrase, "It never rains but it pours."

Guthrie listened with a worried look. "Do you have to go with him?" Pause. "Okay. We'll pray for you two." He hung up and sat across from her.

Brandon slid into the chair beside Hannah. "Good morning."

Hannah greeted him an uneasy smile.

"What's wrong?" Brandon glanced at her, then at his brother.

"More bad luck," Guthrie muttered. "Can't anything go right?"

"Now we'll have none of that at the breakfast table," Aunt Ida scolded from the stove where she was flipping pancakes. "A lot has gone right. We've got Hannah and her parents."

"And Bill's back," Edith added. "By the way, I think we should call him Bill now. He's grown up."

"That's right," Ida concurred. "And Brandon's home finally."

Guthrie's expression didn't lighten.

"Now cheer up, Guthrie," Ida urged.

Brandon nodded. "Yeah, you don't have any real problems. No one's divorcing you."

"Brandon, it wasn't right for you to take up with Deirdre right after she broke up with your brother." Ida shook her spatula at him.

"You wouldn't have liked it if he'd done that to you," Edith agreed. She was lifting bacon out of the cast iron frying pan onto paper toweling.

"And we knew that Deirdre only married you, Brandon, to get out of this town." Ida scooped the last of the griddle cakes onto a platter and brought them to the table.

Edith began cooking scrambled eggs. "The fact is she didn't love either of you."

"She's the kind of woman who never brings peace to a home, only strife." Ida poured everyone coffee and sat down.

The two men stared at their great-aunts, plainly not believing their ears.

Brandon recovered first. "I wish you'd told me all this nearly four years ago," he said with a sour twist to his mouth.

"Deirdre was what we used to call a siren. You wouldn't have listened to us four years ago." Edith put the platter of bacon and eggs on the table and sat down.

Ida nodded. "No, just like if we told Guthrie now that he'd better hold on to Hannah and not let her leave Petite, he wouldn't listen, either."

Hannah pursed her lips, but a giggle still slipped out of her mouth. Leave it to the aunts! "Thank you, ladies."

Guthrie started to speak, but was interrupted.

"Any time, dear." Ida patted Hannah's hand. "Edith, will you say the blessing?"

They all joined hands and Edith said, "Dear God, please give the young men and women who will be sandbagging today strength, good health and safety. Please give our nephews the faith and wisdom they need to end the strife in this family. Thank you, Lord, for everything, even this flooding. Amen."

The prayer touched Hannah's emotions. This was the prayer of the truly faithful, thanking God for everything, even the trials. She swallowed to keep back tears. Too little sleep and too much conflict were getting to her.

"Guthrie, don't frown so," Ida said gently. "Bill and Lynda will be back before we know it. And in the meantime you can concentrate on settling things with Brandon."

Hannah's eyes widened. The aunts' batteries were certainly charged today!

"I'm just supposed to forget my feelings?" Guthrie frowned. "I don't have any right to them, I suppose?"

"No, that's not what your aunt means," Hannah declared. "She just means life goes on. Bill deserted his family but has now changed. Your brother has discovered the truth about his wife and is going to have to go through a painful divorce—"

Ida cut in. "That's right, dear. Now, everyone, eat! Angry words upset digestion!"

Guthrie nodded. "I'll be fine. We've gotten through worse than this." He lifted his fork, but in spite of his brave words, his defeated expression hurt Hannah's heart. He looked like a man without hope. How could he entertain thoughts of a future they might share if he couldn't hope?

"Eat your breakfast, Guthrie." Aunt Ida frowned. "It will be a long hard day."

"Yes," Edith said, "after you finish moving Lynda's belongings up to the attic, you'll have a rough day or two of sandbagging. The state has started down by the bridge over the river by Lila's motel. The Red Cross is due by noon."

As if in response, the rain outside gushed harder. Hannah quivered at the thought of going back outside to be drenched again, but it couldn't be avoided. Whether Guthrie continued to reject the possibility of a happy ending for Brandon, Lynda or himself, the whole town of Petite faced a long hard fight to keep the water at bay.

Hannah closed her eyes for a moment. *Lord, Guthrie is a wonderful man, but please shake him out of this new slump, this dark valley we're in. Maybe it will never work out for us, but he needs help to accept Brandon back into his family. Please be with Bill and Lynda today as they try to put the past behind them once and for all. Soothe Brandon's broken heart. And lift Guthrie's spirits. Give him back his hope. I think I love him, Lord!*

Chapter Fourteen

Hannah had water in her boots and mud up her nose. In a line of about twenty-five volunteers, she and Guthrie worked side by side moving sandbags to reinforce the river levee. Guthrie handed her another soggy, sand-filled cloth bag. Her arms had the strength of overcooked spaghetti. Shivering in the cold rain, she nearly dropped it, but managed with a grunt to heft it on to the next person. Since morning light they'd lifted a mountain of bags to create a wall to protect Petite from the waters of the Wisconsin River, their only hope to keep Petite from flooding.

Without warning, Hannah's knees buckled. She sank down in the soupy mud that surrounded them. The steady rain and cold gusts beat against her hooded yellow rain slicker. Her heart raced, and she breathed rapidly as if she'd been running. *We still have more bags to put into place!*

"What's wrong?" Guthrie asked.

"I can't get up." She felt like a flattened toothpaste tube—all her stuff had been used up. She knew she should feel something about this. But a pervasive numbness tamped down everything except the sensations of being exhausted and cold to the bone.

A man wearing a Red Cross vest ran down the line tapping shoulders. "Come on. A group of students from Madison has come to relieve you. The Red Cross van has hot coffee and sandwiches. And there are blankets and cots at the church. You've done a great job! Now move out and make room for the fresh workers."

Catching her hands, Guthrie pulled Hannah to her feet. She leaned against him as he half-carried her up the levee. Without his support, she knew she would be crawling on her belly up the muddy incline.

"Guthrie!" a familiar voice called. "Hannah?"

Hannah looked up to find her sister right in front of her. "Doree!" Shock. Joy. She threw her arms around her sister's slender shoulders. "Why? What…"

"I came as soon as I heard the announcement on the TV asking for volunteers. How are Mom and Dad?"

Hannah found herself weeping.

Wearing a red vinyl poncho like a beacon in the gray scene, Doree put one hand on each side of Hannah's face. "Hannah, what's wrong! Did something happen to—"

"She's just overtired." Guthrie reclaimed Hannah so she could lean against him again. "We've been tossing around furniture and sandbags since breakfast."

"Mom and Dad are fine." Hannah tried to smile. "They're coordinating with the Red Cross at the church. I'm fine. If only this rain would stop."

"I've got to go now. Tell them I'll see them later." Doree walked backward, still talking. "I'll talk with you later!"

Hannah nodded as Guthrie led her away. She looked up and gave him a weak smile.

"Don't worry." Guthrie tucked her closer. "We're going to the Red Cross van. We'll pick up some food, then head for the church to sleep."

Soon he sat her in a chair in the warm church basement. A plate of sandwiches sat on her lap. She couldn't remember carrying them.

"Eat," Guthrie ordered.

She stared at the food, unable to pick up a sandwich. "I…can't."

"Here." He lifted a cup of coffee to her lips. "Careful. It's hot. Just sip it."

Strong hot coffee trickled inside her, warming as it went. "I'm so cold."

"That wind made us feel the chill more." He held a sandwich to her lips. "Eat."

She opened her mouth, bit and chewed. "I'll try to feed myself." She couldn't remember that chewing had ever been such hard work before. Her taste buds seemed to be out of order, too. She only felt the texture of bread on her tongue. She glanced at Guthrie. He looked as though eating had become a chore for him, also. "You need to eat, too."

"I don't need any encouragement." He devoured a sandwich in two bites and picked up another. With his other hand, he put her sandwich to her lips. "Come on. A few more bites and you'll get enough strength to finish your meal."

"Okay." She chewed and swallowed another bite. Tuna fish, the sandwich was tuna fish.

With a groan, Brandon collapsed onto the chair next to them. "Whew. My muscles are getting muscles."

She stared at him. Her tired brain reminded her Brandon and Guthrie were at odds, but she couldn't manage to act as a buffer between them right now. She needed to focus all her energy on taking her sandwich from Guthrie's hand and lifting it to her mouth.

"I'm surprised you've held up, big brother," Guthrie said in a calm voice, then devoured another sandwich.

Hannah concentrated on chewing. Guthrie was right. The food and coffee were bringing her back.

"I'm not the weakling you may think I am." Brandon swallowed half a sandwich. "I work out regularly. But I am tired."

"So am I," Guthrie said.

"Wow." Brandon's eyebrows shot up. "I'm surprised to hear you admit that."

"Don't fuss," Hannah mumbled. Finishing her sandwich and coffee, she handed the plate and cup to Brandon. The food had made her feel human again, but her exhaustion couldn't wait. "I can't sit up anymore. I've got to lie down."

Handing his plate to his brother, Guthrie jumped up and led her to cots that had been set up in the Sunday school rooms. She lay down on the first empty one and fell asleep instantly.

Guthrie gazed at her, warm emotions surging through him. Hannah. She'd worked beside him last night and all day, helping out the town she'd only lived in for a couple of months. She'd worked as hard as any of them. She'd become a part of them already. What a woman!

Bending over her, he pulled off her boots, which stuck out over the end of the cot, and opened her slicker. "Take a break, Hannah. You deserve it." The temptation to kiss her lured him. Her soft lips invited his touch, but he'd been such a jerk lately. What had gotten into him, grumbling at everyone? At Hannah. She'd talked to him straight, spoken the truth. His bruised heart felt a touch of warmth, healing.

"She's really something, you know that?" Brandon appeared at his elbow.

Guthrie kept his gaze on Hannah's face. "Yes, she's a real lady."

"Don't let her get away." Brandon turned.

Guthrie caught his brother's elbow. "I'm…I'm glad…."

Brandon glanced over his shoulder. "I'm glad I'm here this time, too. Will you give me another chance?"

Guthrie thought a second, picking out his words with care. "Our family always gives a second chance."

Brandon blinked back tears and walked away quickly.

Guthrie stared at Hannah. *Will you give me a second chance? I've let my family, my anger get in the way.* Would she give him the right to kiss her, to love her?

"Hannah! Hannah!"

Hannah opened her eyes and stared at the strange ceiling. *Where am I?*

"Hannah!"

Small hands tugged at her shoulder.

She glanced into Amber's face. "What is it?"

"Misty's not in the church. She's lost."

Hannah's mind tried to process the sentence. Couldn't.

"Our kitty's lost!" Jenna shouted from the other side of Hannah. "Help us!"

Hannah sat up. "When did you find that she was lost?"

Amber looked near tears. "We were playing with her, but she wanted to go outside—"

Jenna cut in. "Mommy told us not to go outside. But we didn't have a cat box."

Amber took over again. "So we let Misty outside. But she didn't come back!"

"Where's your mother?" Hannah stretched, trying to wake up her stiff and aching body. She slid her feet into her soggy rubber boots.

"She's outside helping put up the sandbags so the water doesn't get us," Jenna replied.

"But we don't want the water to get Misty, either." Amber's teary eyes were as round as dimes.

Hannah stood up, tugging her yellow slicker around her. If she didn't take care of this, the children would disturb someone else or try to find the cat themselves and probably get lost or worse. "Okay."

"You'll take us to find her?"

"No, you girls must stay here inside where it's warm and dry. Who's taking care of you?"

"The great-aunts." Amber took Hannah's hand.

"Take me to them."

Through the darkened church basement, where volunteers slept on cots and floor, the girls led her to the church kitchen. Both the aunts lay, curled up in blankets, sleeping on the benches on each side of the built-in table. In the low light, Hannah looked at the kitchen clock that read five forty-seven. Barely sunup. She sighed.

"Don't disturb your aunts. Come to the front door with me." The side entrance had been sandbagged shut, along with the whole foundation of the church, to keep water out. This precaution had been taken even though the church sat on a rise above most of Petite.

Upstairs, Hannah opened the double church doors. A gray dawn met her gaze. The chill rain poured down like a constant running faucet. The sound irritated her. Why couldn't it just stop?

"We'll come out with you," Jenna offered.

"No! Don't you dare step a foot outside. If you do, I'll come right back in." Hannah fastened her slicker and pulled a small flashlight from her pocket. "Now go sit by a window and watch me."

The little girls turned away, and Hannah closed the door firmly behind her. She walked down the rain-slick steps. Rain splashed into her face. Wind whistled through the leaves above, giving the wind a voice. Shouting echoed in the distance, farther up the shoreline. The crew had made progress building the barrier against the rising water. The flood crest should come in a few hours. Either the sandbags would hold the water at bay, or they wouldn't.

Hannah knew she'd have to return to the sandbagging after breakfast. The all-night crew would be ready to be replaced. Doree was out there in the shadowy predawn. Mom and Dad had probably gone to Guthrie's for a few hours of sleep. Her little kitty, Sunny, probably slept at the end of their bed.

"Misty. Misty," she called in a high, sweet cat-calling tone. "Here kitty, kitty." She stumbled through the muddy parking lot, filled with familiar and unfamiliar vehicles. She bent over, looking underneath them, thinking the cat might be hiding under one.

She dragged herself down one aisle of mud-splashed vehicles, then another until she came to the north edge of the lot. "Misty, here kitty."

"Me…eee…uuuu," a little feline voice pleaded. "Me…eee…uuuu."

Hannah looked up to see the drenched kitten halfway up an old oak tree at the edge of the church cemetery just beyond the parking lot. Some noise, some stray dog must have frightened the kitten into scampering high.

Well, the kitten hadn't gotten very far up, and the tree wasn't too high or hard to climb. She could rescue Misty. She waved at the church windows and pointed toward the cat. She wanted the girls to know she'd found their kitten.

She took hold of the lowest branch and tried to walk her feet up the gnarled trunk. Her feet slid down. She dropped her hold and shook off her boots and tried again in her socks. She needed to grip the tree with her feet. This time she made it and swung herself up and around to sit on the branch, which swayed with her weight. "Come on," she murmured to the tree, "I'm not that heavy."

Reaching up, she grasped the next branch and stood, then hoisted herself onto the branch where Misty crouched.

"Hold on, Misty." Hannah sat on the branch. "I'll get you." She continued to talk to the kitten to keep the little creature from being frightened into climbing higher. "Come here, Misty. Here, kitty, kitty."

Soaked to her skin and trembling with the cold, Misty mewled more plaintively than ever. The frightened kitten didn't budge.

"Oh, dear." Hannah sighed. She inched out on the branch slowly, slowly, then caught the kitten with the tips of her fingers and dragged it to her. The limb beneath them swayed. Cradling the kitten close to her, she made comforting sounds to Misty.

Ever so carefully, Hannah shoved herself in reverse until her back touched the trunk of the tree. Her heart pounded in her ears. Her weariness had sapped her reserve energy. She leaned against the trunk and hoped for a spurt of energy. And how could she get down one-handed?

"Hannah." Guthrie's unexpected voice came from below her. "Can you get down?"

"No, I don't think I can. I just have no energy, and the branches are so slippery. I'm afraid I'll drop the kitten." Her words tumbled out one on top of the other.

"Wait there. I'll get my truck."

Hannah couldn't figure out what the truck could do for a cat in a tree, but her mind was too fuzzy to think. Within minutes, she heard the truck park underneath her.

"Okay, Hannah, look at me."

She glanced down at Guthrie, who was standing in his truck bed right beneath her.

"Now lean forward, wrap one arm around the branch in front of you and hand Misty down to me."

Hannah obeyed. Her fingertips held the kitten about two feet above Guthrie's hands.

"Just drop her. I'll catch her."

She let go of the kitten and Guthrie caught it.

"Now wrap both arms around the branch and let your feet down. Then I'll be able to get hold of you."

Again she followed directions. Just as her hold on the limb slipped way, she found herself sliding into Guthrie's brawny arms. She tucked her chin against his neck and rested on his strength. *Safe.*

"Oh, Hannah," Guthrie murmured. "Only you would climb a tree in the middle of a deluge to rescue a kitten, even if you are exhausted and even if you didn't know how you could get down. You wonderful, crazy, hard-headed woman!" He hugged her.

"I've been an idiot getting mad and not paying you the attention I should. You're right—whatever happened to Bill and Lynda, what does that mean to us? So Deirdre didn't love me or my brother. What does this have to do with us? Have I ruined everything we could have between us, getting stuck in the past, holding onto the pain? I love you, Hannah. I see that now, and nothing will ever change it. You sweet, loving woman." He kissed her. Again. Again. "Hannah, my sweet Hannah."

Clinging to his shoulders, Hannah gave herself up to the bountiful sensations and deep emotions stirred by kissing Guthrie. *This man is the one, Lord! I see it, feel it so clearly now!* She couldn't stop kissing him. "I love you, too, you stubborn, irritating, wonderful man."

Rain flowed over their heads like a shower of blessing, a baptism of love. Hannah clung to Guthrie. His warmth joined with hers overcame the nip of the dawn. Holding him and being held by him struck Hannah as the most wonderful gift she'd ever received.

"Guthrie! Guthrie!" Aunt Ida scolded from the church doorway. "Bring Hannah and Misty in right now. You can finish kissing Hannah and proposing to her inside the church."

"Yes, you don't want your bride to catch her death of cold!" Edith admonished.

Guthrie looked at Hannah with a grin. "Will you?"

She gazed into his blue, blue eyes, knowing that this was his proposal, honest and direct, just like the man. "I will, with all my heart." On the outside, she was rain-soaked and bone tired. Inside, her heart glowed with her love for Guthrie and the knowledge that he loved her, too, with a down-to-earth, till-death-do-us-part love. *Praise God from whom all blessings flow!*

Hannah and Guthrie stopped to smile at each other. They'd finished painting the last wall of her parents' new home. Outside the bay window, the first lazy snowflakes of winter floated down.

Guthrie reached over and dabbed his paintbrush, wet with light blue paint, on her nose.

"Don't start," Hannah warned him, waving her brush provocatively.

His brush held high, he pulled her to him and kissed her.

Hannah savored the spiral of warmth that curled through her. "I love you," she whispered against his lips.

"I love you, too, blue nose." He tightened his embrace. "Are you sure we have to wait till May to get married?"

"Hey, watch that stuff!" Lynda called as she walked inside. "It's addictive!"

"Too late! We're already hooked." Hannah smiled,

but didn't leave Guthrie's luxurious embrace. With her free hand, she laid her brush across the paint can, and so did Guthrie.

"Just came to say goodbye," Bill said, entering after his wife. "I'm off to basic training."

Reluctantly abandoning her fiancé's arms, Hannah went over and hugged Bill. "We'll miss you."

"But you're doing the right thing." Smiling, Guthrie shook Bill's hand.

Hannah rejoiced at the sight.

Bill's court date, which had taken him away during the flooding, had ended in a dismissal of all charges. With his slate clean, Bill had enlisted in the army, and his future with Lynda and the children was plotted out.

After basic training, his family would accompany him for four years of military duty, after which Bill intended to enroll in college full-time for a career in counseling. Hannah always felt a little teary when she thought of Bill and Lynda's reunion. And the mountain of sandbags they'd put up had protected Petite. The future looked bright for the small town. Praise God, everything had turned out well.

"This house is going to be just lovely." Lynda looked around with admiration.

Guthrie nodded. "Just needs the carpet to be laid, then we put up the last trim."

"And my parents will be in before Christmas." Hannah returned to Guthrie's side. When they were in a room together, she couldn't bear to be away from him. She was beginning to plumb the meaning of "the two shall become one." To her, holding Guthrie's hand had become essential, akin to breathing.

"This is going to be the best holiday season for the Thomas family in years." Lynda beamed. "Bill and I are back together even if we'll be apart for Christmas Day itself. Getting back together was something I never even thought I'd *want* to be possible."

"But I feel bad for Brandon. Deirdre is going on with the divorce," Bill said somberly.

"But he's regained his family," Hannah said with a bright smile. Before Brandon had flown back to San Francisco, he and Guthrie had reconciled. Brandon had decided to make a completely fresh start and relocate from San Francisco to Chicago. Guthrie was going down to Chicago to meet Brandon and help him get settled. "He'll be moved to Illinois by December, and we'll be home in Petite for Christmas."

"Mom's thrilled." Lynda's smile brought a glow to her expression.

"My sisters will both be here, too." Hannah beamed with happiness.

His arm around Hannah's shoulders, Guthrie leaned his cheek against her hair, breathing in her sweet spicy fragrance. Warm joy flowed through him. *Thank you, God.* He gazed at Hannah, then Lynda and Bill. "We've been blessed."

Epilogue

Her bedside clock told Hannah it was after midnight. The house had been quiet for over an hour. Feeling like a criminal, Hannah crept out of her room and down the hall to her father's office. Her parents and she had moved into their new house the second week of December, three days ago. Spring and Doree were due to spend the Christmas holiday in Petite. Hannah wanted to get the search for the birth certificate over before the hectic days of the holiday began.

She eased open the office door and silently closed it without latching it, afraid the click would sound like a gunshot in the silent house. She hadn't wanted to go against her mother's wishes or invade her parent's privacy, but she'd agreed because, with her mother's diagnosis, it was a good idea to discover her mother's natural parents. She couldn't chicken out now.

She went directly to the tall gray filing cabinet,

which she knew held the family records. She slid the top drawer open, then switched on the desk lamp. Fingering through the drawer, she located a file headed Birth Certificates, Passports and Social Security Cards.

She paged through it, glancing at her birth certificate and her sisters', her father's, then her mother's. She gazed at the document in disbelief.

The door to the office opened behind her. "Hannah? Is there anything wrong?"

Her father's voice made her gasp. She stared at him, dumbfounded.

"I heard you get up and come into my office. What's the matter?"

Caught in the act. Hannah's guilt made her face flushed and hot. "Hi."

"Why are you looking through the family files?"

Her pulse racing, she couldn't lie to her father. "I needed to see Mother's birth certificate."

"Why?"

Had she blown it completely? "Is Mother awake, too?"

"No, she's still asleep. Why did you need her birth certificate?"

Hannah cleared her throat and straightened. "Spring, Doree and I, decided we needed to find Mother's natural family."

Her father studied her for a few long breathless moments. "Does this have something to do with your mother's leukemia?"

"Yes." Hannah heaved a sigh of relief. "We want to

find her family in case we need to contact them for a bone marrow transplant in the future."

"Your mother told you girls she didn't want to do that."

Hannah nodded, wishing her two sisters were there to take some of the heat. She needed Spring's quiet eloquence and Doree's brash confidence. "We want to do this for our own peace of mind. If Mother's leukemia comes back, we want to have the information ready if she should change her mind. We wouldn't say anything unless she decided she wanted to know. We just want to be prepared."

Again, her father stared at her, searching her face for answers. "I can understand that, but you won't find any information on her birth certificate."

Praying he would know the reason, Hannah handed him the document. "I see that. It doesn't say anything about Mom being adopted! Why doesn't it?"

He took the paper. "Adoption was much different in the 1940s. When an adoption took place, a new birth certificate was issued with the adoptive parents listed, not the birth parents."

Hannah's hope fizzled and died. "Then how do we find out who the birth parents were?"

Dad pursed his lips in the way that told Hannah he was holding something back.

His expression gave her hope. "Do you know something about Mom's birth?"

He frowned.

"Dad, please tell me." She stepped closer and touched his arm. "We just want to help."

"I'm certain your motives are pure, but I don't like to go against your mother's wishes. She has always maintained that she didn't want or need to know about her natural parents."

He put a comforting arm around Hannah. "You don't understand, but it used to be a disgrace to have a child out of wedlock. Your mother doesn't want to bring back painful memories to her parents. And there's a good chance they might not even still be alive, you know."

"If you know something, Dad, please tell me." She leaned her head against his chin.

"I do have some information." He paused. "Your grandmother gave it to me on her deathbed. I've never even told Ethel about it. Her adoptive mother told me not to mention it unless Ethel wanted to know about her birth."

Please tell me, Daddy. Mom needs to have the information. "Dad, we're doing this for Mom."

"I know, dear, but I can't just give the information to you because you want it, not when it violates your mother's wishes. That's not how your mother and I run our marriage. To go against her, I need to pray for guidance in this. I'll have to take some time before I can give you an answer."

Hannah knew better than to argue. If her father said he was going to pray about something, he prayed. She and her sisters would just have to wait and pray that her father would be moved to give them the information they needed to be prepared to help their mother. At least, he hadn't given her a flat no. *Oh, Lord, is what we want to do right? Are we on the right track? If we are, please let our father give us the information we need.*

* * * * *

Dear Reader,

I don't need to tell you how important family is. I hope you were touched by Guthrie, a man who loved and supported his abandoned sister and her fatherless children. To forgive people who've hurt us is hard enough, but to forgive those who've wounded those we love sometimes feels impossible.

God sent Hannah to help Guthrie forgive his prodigal brother-in-law and then his own brother. Only after Guthrie had shed the painful past through forgiveness was he free to gain Hannah's love.

This novel was the story of Hannah's love. The next story is about her older sister, Spring, and an exciting man from her past. Over both stories, though, hangs the question of their mother's past. Will the sisters find the grandparents they seek?

Lyn Cote

FINALLY FOUND

In all your ways acknowledge Him,
and He shall direct your paths.
—*Proverbs* 3:6

Thanks to Roxanne Rustand,
my award-winning critique partner.
I'm honored to call you friend.
And to my sister, Carole.
Thanks for being a great sister.

Acknowledgments

Thanks to Doris Rangel
for information on the *quinceañería*.
And special thanks to Priscilla Kissinger,
aka Priscilla Oilveras, for help with my fledgling
Spanish.
¡Gracias!

Prologue

"God Rest Ye Merry, Gentlemen" played softly in the background. Everything around Spring Kirkland harmonized to create a holiday scene worthy of gracing any Christmas card. The windows of her parents' new home were fogged with moisture from the warmth from gingerbread baking in the kitchen. But nothing in this holiday setting distracted Spring from the hidden purpose for her trip home.

Her sister, Hannah, wearing a red-and-green apron, flipped on the oven light and leaned over, peering through the glass oven door. "These gingerbread cookies are just about golden around the edges." Without glancing over her shoulder, she added, "Doree, keep your fingers out of that frosting."

Pulling her finger back from where it had been poised over the bowl of white butter cream, Doree exclaimed, "You're no fun! I was only going to steal a taste."

Though Spring's nerves moved her to start pacing, her sisters' sparring amused her. Dark-haired Hannah, the professional cook and food writer, was in her element: the kitchen. Blond Doree, their younger sister, still in college, was enjoying her role as family tease.

The three of them had been left alone in their parents' brand-new house in Petite Portage, Wisconsin, to bake cookies for the Christmas Eve service at church in two days. Ever since Spring had arrived last night, one unspoken question had been hanging over them. With their parents out of the house, the time finally had come to ask *the question*. She cleared her throat.

The timer on the stove buzzed. Hannah set about lifting the sheets of cookies out of the oven. The fragrance of gingerbread filled the air.

Spring started again. "Hannah, you said you had some news for us about—"

Someone knocked on the door. Spring went to answer it. "Oh, hi, Guthrie." Holding in her frustration, she stepped back to let him in.

"Guthrie!" Hannah flew to the kitchen doorway, still holding the spatula in one hand and wearing a Christmas oven mitt on the other.

"Mmm." Guthrie made a sound of approval. "Sure smells good in here." He drew Hannah close for a quick hello kiss.

Hannah giggled and kissed him back.

Folding her arms in front of her, Spring felt torn. She couldn't help beaming at them. Hannah had certainly found her match in Guthrie Thomas, the carpenter who'd built her parents' home. But why did he have to stop by right now? They only had until their parents returned to discuss this!

"Guthrie, I'm amazed at the creative excuses you come up with to see Hannah." Doree smirked from the other end of the kitchen where she leaned against the doorjamb. "What explanation are you using this time?"

Guthrie chuckled. "No excuse. Just dropped in to greet your sister, Spring."

"Then, say hi to her," Doree instructed dryly with a motion of her hand. "You haven't even looked at her—"

"All in good time," Hannah murmured, then she moved aside to let Guthrie take a few steps forward.

Guthrie held out his hand to Spring.

She gripped it. "Oh, you're cold."

"Yeah, the temperature is dropping, all right. Glad you're here, Spring. Hope you enjoy your first Christmas in Petite."

"I'm sure I will."

She'd liked Guthrie, her sister's fiancé, from the very first time she'd met him, but she wanted to get to the topic topmost in her mind. She glanced at Doree and saw the same anxiousness reflected there.

Guthrie turned his attention back to Hannah. "I have to go do some chores at the farm, then I'll be back to take the three of you out to the tree farm to get your family tree."

Hannah kissed him lightly on the cheek. "Thanks. I

just have two more balls of dough to roll out and bake. We can finish frosting them afterward."

Guthrie kissed her cheek, then left with a wave. Spring closed the door behind him, shivering in the cold draft.

"You two have got it bad," Doree taunted cheerfully.

Hannah smiled and walked toward the oven. "You can start frosting and decorating the first batch now. It should be cool enough."

Spring halted near them. If she didn't ask the question quick, someone else might interrupt. "Hannah, tell us what you found on Mother's birth certificate."

Hannah continued placing raw cut-out cookies one by one onto a baking sheet. "What I *didn't* find was what was really important."

"Then, what didn't you find?" Sitting at the table, Doree started frosting the first cookie.

"Mom's birth certificate had been altered to show only the adoptive, not the natural, parents." Hannah glanced up.

"You mean you didn't find out anything?" Doree demanded.

Spring's spirits dropped, and she slumped onto a kitchen chair. Their mother's life might depend on this information. "You mean we've hit a dead end already?"

"In a way, yes. In a way, no." Hannah slid another two sheets into the oven and set the timer. "This would be so much easier if we didn't have to keep it from Mother."

"Don't be irritating." Using red rope licorice and Red Hots, Doree began carefully crafting a face on her gingerbread boy.

Spring's worry had turned to dread. She had to know the truth. She made herself pick up a cookie to frost. "Just tell us."

Hannah sighed. "A few days after we'd settled in here, one night late, I went into Dad's office and opened the file that holds all the family records."

"Yes," Doree prompted, and bit off the head of the first gingerbread boy she'd decorated.

Hannah frowned at her. "But after I found the birth certificate, Dad walked in!"

"Oh, no." Spring put down the cookie she was frosting.

"What did you tell him?" Doree demanded.

"The truth, of course. He caught me red-handed."

"What did he say?" Spring asked. All the sweetness in the air was beginning to cloy in her throat.

"After I told him I was looking for Mom's natural parents and why," Hannah went on, "he explained why the natural parents' names weren't on the birth certificate. Then he said he did have some information that our grandmother gave him on her deathbed about Mother's birth."

"He did!" This surprised Spring. She popped up again, unable to sit still.

"So what was the information?" Doree insisted.

"He said that he couldn't violate Mother's wishes—"

"Oh." Doree groaned.

Hannah continued. "Unless he prayed about it and felt that it was right to go against Mother's—"

The outside door opened, letting in a rush of cold air.

Spring, pacing the floor, spun around. "Father!"

"I thought so." Her father took off his gloves and unwound his navy-blue scarf. "It smells delicious in here."

Going against Mother and Father wasn't something Spring had decided to do lightly. And now, with her father's unexpected return, she felt as though she'd been found with her hand in the cookie jar. "What did you think, Father?"

"I thought you three would be talking about your mother, so I came back—"

"Where'd you leave Mom?" Doree asked.

Father, the local pastor, sat down at the table with them. "I asked her to type something for me at the church office. I have to go back in a few minutes, then we'll head to Portage for her blood checkup." He picked up an unfrosted cookie and took a bite.

"Dad, have you changed your mind?" Hannah set down the dough she'd been flouring to roll out.

Dad nodded, then finished swallowing his first bit of gingerbread. He reached for Spring's hand and drew her to the chair beside him.

"Don't keep us guessing! What do you know, Dad?" Doree persisted.

"First, dear Doree, I want you to know I've decided to tell you all the information I have." He waited till all eyes had turned to him. "Your grandmother Gloria, who adopted your mother, wanted me to have the information about Ethel's birth mother because she said Ethel someday might want or need to know about her birth."

Hannah nodded while Doree bit her lower lip.

Spring's anxiety surged inside her. Mother's leukemia was in remission now, but would it last? If it hadn't been for this disease, they wouldn't have to delve into the past. They wouldn't need to find possible bone marrow donors for her.

Father went on. "Your grandmother told me two facts about your mother's birth. She told me that her natural mother died from complications of the birth and that her name was Connie Wilson."

Shock zinged through Spring. "Connie Wilson?"

Everyone turned to look at her.

Father asked, "Is that name familiar to you?"

With surprise shimmering through her, Spring sat up straighter. "Yes, I know who Connie Wilson was."

Chapter One

The semi-truck's air brakes screamed in protest, and the huge cab bounced as it slowed to miss Great-Aunt Geneva's 1985 gold-toned Cadillac. Spring's heart stopped, then surged into an inner cacophony.

Without turning a hair, Aunt Geneva completed her illegal left turn across two lanes of bumper-to-bumper traffic.

"All these tourists! The northern 'sunbirds' have arrived for the winter." Aunt Geneva shook her tinted blond-over-gray head. Wearing a purple linen suit with her customary double shoulder pads, Aunty sat at the wheel like the captain of a cabin cruiser. "The traffic around here gets worse and worse all the time. And half of them never learned how to drive in the first place."

Spring's heart still thumped sickeningly. *Dear Lord, get us to the country club alive. I should have insisted on driving*. Out her window, the turquoise-blue waters of the Gulf of Mexico beckoned Spring in vain. The soft, warm breeze flowed in through the car window and over her face. As she kept an eye on the six lanes of traffic on Highway 19, she ran her fingers through her long hair, trying to keep the wind from tangling it.

"I'm just so thrilled that you've come to visit!" Aunt Geneva repeated for the umpteenth time, taking her eyes off the road to smile at Spring.

"You're making me feel guilty," Spring murmured nervously, eyeing the intimidating cement truck traveling beside her. "I come every year."

"But only for a week in February! This year I have you for three whole months in Gulfview! It will be just like having you at the university again." Aunty sounded her horn, swerved into the left lane, then cut in front of a bus.

Desperately holding onto her composure, Spring nodded. "I'm looking forward to it, too." She swallowed to moisten her dry mouth. "January, February and March in Milwaukee can sometimes be so…grim."

"I know, my dear, I spent many dreary years there."

"But Milwaukee's a fun town, and I'm near my parents—" Spring squeaked, "Red light!"

Aunty obligingly squealed to a halt.

Flying forward against her seat belt, then back against the seat, Spring hoped she hadn't suffered whiplash.

"Well, you were with them for Christmas. I loved the

pictures you brought of Ethel's new house. At last, she has the house she's always deserved."

Spring wondered had she applied enough deodorant this morning? The warmth of the day and her aunt's fearless driving style was putting hers to the test!

"Now, don't get me wrong. Your father is a wonderful man, but Ethel hasn't always had everything just as I would have wanted it for her. The clergy don't bring in the bucks."

"At least, none they can spend in this world," Spring pointed out gently. Why hadn't she offered to drive? How could she have forgotten her aunt's kamikaze driving style?

"Exactly so." Aunt Geneva nodded. "But she does have you three girls, and you mean the world to her."

Thinking of her sisters made Spring recall her mother and the leukemia. Spring's worry swelled within her. Would she and her sisters really be able to discover their mother's biological parents?

Even before her father had mentioned Connie Wilson during her Christmas at her parents' home, Spring had planned to spend time in Florida with Great-Aunt Geneva. Spring had taken a leave of absence from the Milwaukee Botanical Gardens to come to Florida for a few months to help Aunt Geneva, now in her late eighties, make the move to a retirement home.

The name, Connie Wilson, had rung a bell in Spring's mind—a moment during a visit to Aunt

Geneva years ago. Had her memory been correct? Would Aunt Geneva have more clues for them?

"Penny for your thoughts, dear."

Spring couldn't bring herself to ask this most pressing question so early in the trip. Getting information about Connie Wilson might take some finesse. Something from the past warned Spring that this was true.

Piloting her massive sedan around a broad corner to a quieter local street, Aunt Geneva left the crush of traffic behind. Before Florida had boomed in the late eighties, her aunt's adventurous driving style hadn't been so dangerous. But now…

Breathing a sigh of relief, Spring recognized Bougainvillea Avenue, which would take them to her aunt's longtime country club. "Is the retirement home near Golden Sands?"

"No, no, dear, I have a little surprise for you. We have to stop for a brief meeting here first. Then we'll go on to tour the retirement home. Though, since you've come, I already feel twenty years younger."

Spring didn't return a comment on this "little surprise" of her aunt's. She was different from her sisters. Doree would have made some outrageous quip. And before Hannah had ever left the house, she would have asked for an itemized itinerary, but Spring just relaxed against the velour seat. Aunt Geneva always had a plan and she always got her way! Why fight it?

Aunty's car surged up the long drive to the venerable

country club past bountiful azalea bushes, decorated with blossoms in every shade of pink imaginable, lining the way. Seagulls squawked overhead and the scent of the salty Gulf of Mexico spiced the air. Spring closed her eyes, savoring the moment. *Thank you, Lord, for bringing us safely here.*

The car jerked to a halt. A uniformed valet stepped out from under the canopied entrance. "*Señora* Dorfman, good afternoon. A lovely day."

The young Hispanic man, no doubt a college student still on break from school, helped her aunt out of the deep cushiony seat, then drove the car away to park it in the covered lot.

Aunty marched away with military straightness and purpose. Aunty had served in the WACs, the Women's Army Corps, in the Second World War and her gait still showed this.

Spring hurried to keep up with her, as they entered the low, rambling club. Only one-story high, painted white with graceful verandas on all sides, Golden Sands had been established before 1940 and still retained its southern charm. Palm trees and red hibiscus basked in the sun. Florida "tacky" had never been permitted within its gates.

Spring wondered what the surprise was and what meeting they would be attending. Aunty had served on every committee here at one time or another. But safely out of the car now and walking into the familiar building lulled Spring into a lush, dreamlike contentment. Two of Aunty's many friends waved to them from a round table on the veranda. Aunty steered Spring to meet them.

"We thought we'd meet out here, dahlings," Eleanor in her floral-print rayon dress said, smiling. Though Eleanor had lived in Florida for more than thirty years, she still retained a touch of a New York accent.

"Yes, we're so happy the weather decided to behave for your visit, hon." Verna Rae, born and raised in Tampa, had a soft southern burr to her voice.

"You look lovely in that shade of pink, Spring. Like a princess." Eleanor squeezed Spring's hand in greeting.

"You're prettier than ever, but we've got to help you get your tan started, honey. You're so pale." Looking over her half-glasses for reading, a gold chain dangling over both ears, Verna Rae examined Spring from head to toe.

After greeting both the ladies with affectionate kisses, Spring sat down with her back to the club, so she could view the vast green golf course beyond the veranda. "You ladies know I've always been pale."

"When we were girls, we would have killed for such creamy skin like yours, dahling." Eleanor nodded. "But after the war, everybody started wanting a tan. Now they say skin cancer. Always wear sunblock, and they talk numbers. My granddaughter won't let her little one out without number thirty. That's what she tells me the doctor told her. Do you wear number thirty, too?"

Spring smiled. "Yes, otherwise I burn."

"Well, maybe you ought to lower that number and get

a little color, honey. I've had a tan for forty years and no skin cancer. I like a healthy glow on a young girl like you." Against the white cotton duck of her slacks and short-sleeved top, Verna Rae's skin resembled tanned leather.

Spring would have died before commenting on this, so she just smiled. "I'm sure I'll pick up some color while I'm here. That Florida sun won't let me get away untouched." *I'll get my usual million tiny golden freckles!* "Are we all here, then?"

"We have one more member coming—" Eleanor said.

"Yes, we thought we'd like the man's point of view." Verna Rae gave a decisive nod of her head.

A man's point of view? "On what?" Spring asked.

"On the April Garden Show, of course. Didn't I tell you?" Aunty looked honestly surprised.

But her cat in the cream expression was reflected in the other two ladies' faces. Spring didn't like the sound of this. Was this the surprise, then, having her at the garden show meeting? Or was the other shoe about to drop?

"Do you still have one each year?" She didn't want to organize a garden show! That's what she did all the time at the Milwaukee Botanical Gardens—plan different types of shows, exhibits, always new ideas to draw in people and contributions to the gardens. *I'm on vacation!* She felt like fleeing to the nearest exit.

"Oh!" Aunty exclaimed, looking over Spring's head. "Here's our last member. Good morning, Dr. Da Palma."

"Good morning to you, Mrs. Dorfman," a voice, deep and rich, replied.

Spring instantly recognized that once-familiar voice and froze where she sat. *It can't be.*

A tanned hand pulled out the chair beside her and a long, lean man in a light tan suit sat down.

The hair on the back of her neck prickled. Slowly she lifted her eyes to his face.

It was him. Even though she hadn't seen him for years, she'd recognize Marco Da Palma's classically handsome face anywhere. Why are you here, Marco? Their eyes met and shock after shock lapped through her.

"Why…" He stared at her. "Spring Kirkland?"

Nodding like a puppet, she held out her nerveless hand. "Marco, how…how good to see you."

Aunty beamed at them. "I thought you two had attended university together."

"Yes, I had the pleasure of taking a few under-graduate classes with your niece, Mrs. Dorfman." Marco smiled.

In Marco's presence, Aunty, Eleanor and Verna Rae perked up visibly, while Spring willed herself to remain and look calm. Did her panic show on her face? Meeting him again like this!

"Are you down for your yearly visit?" Marco asked.

Spring gave a little start. How did Marco know she visited Aunt Geneva every February? She hadn't seen him since graduation. "No…this year I'm here for a longer visit." Stilling her inner tremors she drew herself up straighter. "My aunt wants my help to move into a retirement home."

"A retirement home?" Marco studied Aunt Geneva for a moment. "You hadn't mentioned that to me during your recent checkup."

Check-up? Spring tried to make sense of this remark.

Aunty fiddled with the many lavish rings on her fingers. "I thought it might be advisable to look into the possibility...at my age, you know."

Verna Rae and Eleanor both looked away, suddenly vitally interested in a group of retired men at the golf course tee nearest them.

Spring tried to guess what was going on among the three older ladies, but Marco's presence was playing havoc with her mind.

Marco said, "Don't forget to come in for your blood-pressure check, Mrs. Dorfman."

Spring frowned. "I didn't know you were my aunt's physician, Marco."

"I am." He nodded his head at each of the three older ladies around the table. "I took over most of Dr. Johnson's practice when he retired two years ago."

"And we're so happy you did," Eleanor crooned. "It's such a nice thing. To go to someone who we saw grow up right before our eyes. I'd hate to have to tell a stranger all about my ailments."

"That's right, hon," Verna Rae agreed. "Marco has been part of this club since he was a groundskeeper's assistant in the summers. What were you when you started? Fourteen?"

Marco nodded.

Spring thought it was a stiff nod. Now that Marco was a doctor, did he prefer not to remember the years he spent working at Golden Sands? He'd always struck her as a proud man. She hoped the ladies hadn't pierced him with their well-intentioned words. Evidently, as a successful Golden Sands scholarship student, he'd been offered a membership after graduation.

She took a deep breath, pushing away all the memories that seeing Marco had evoked. "Perhaps we should get the meeting started? I'm sure Marco is a busy man."

"Well, so was Jack and you know what happened to him?" Eleanor said in a teasing tone.

"Jack?" Spring couldn't think what the lady was alluding to.

"The Jack who did all work and no play." Eleanor waggled a finger at them. "A very dull boy was Jack."

The meeting went downhill from there—in Spring's opinion. The day of the garden show had been set for the second Saturday in April. The three ladies brought out the notes kept by last year's committee.

Beside her, Marco appeared interested—but was it pretense? She felt for him. She didn't doubt for a moment that he'd been "guilted" into coming. Marco had been one of the many students who'd benefited from Golden Sands scholarships and employment. He was the kind of man to repay debts, even if they included garden club meetings.

She'd frozen into a polite pose and couldn't even make small talk. The points of the discussion slipped past her. All she was aware of was the clean line of Marco's profile and the citrus fragrance of his aftershave.

"Spring, dahling," Eleanor prompted. "Aren't you feeling well? You haven't said two words."

Her already warm face blazed. "I'm sorry. I don't seem able to concentrate. Maybe it's the change from winter to summer. I just can't get my thoughts together."

Eleanor gave her a knowing wink.

"I think we've done enough today," Verna Rae said smoothly, folding up the file from last year's event. "We'll meet again next week. Same time. Same place."

"I'll try to attend," Marco said as he rose. "But I think I will be on call for the hospital that day. If an emergency comes up…" He shrugged, then turned to go.

"Why don't you walk me and my niece to the door?" Aunt Geneva stood up.

Spring cringed at this ploy. *I can get there by myself!* But she couldn't demur. It would be too impolite.

"My pleasure." Marco helped Spring out of her chair. His hand brushed her bare arm, and she tingled with the contact.

"We are going to drop by that retirement home on Azalea Drive." Aunty marched toward the entrance, with Marco and Spring on her right.

"I've heard good things about that retirement home." Marco glanced at Spring.

Marco's nearness tightening her throat, Spring concentrated on putting one foot in front of the other.

"Yes, yes. It's supposed to be lovely." Aunt Geneva lifted her chin.

At the entrance, Marco waited with them for the valet to bring out the car. When it arrived, Spring tried to get a turn at the wheel herself. Her aunt insisted she knew the way to the retirement home and ended up behind the wheel again. He held back a smile, knowing full well why Spring wanted to drive. Mrs. Dorfman's Wild West driving was notorious around the club. Spring must have nerves of steel.

Spring Kirkland. More lovely than ever. He began to think over the possibilities. Maybe she would be of some help.

Chapter Two

"Now this is one of our deluxe suites." The tall elegant man with silver at his temples smiled as he ushered Aunty and Spring through the door.

Spring hung back and let her aunt take the lead. The sitting room stretched in front of them, done in shades of ivory and sea-foam green with touches of polished brass. A sliding glass door at one end overlooked a garden where seniors sat chatting and some playing cards around shaded tables.

Spring turned her gaze back to her aunt. Her nerves still quivered from seeing Marco again.

"Ah," Aunty murmured as she scanned the room.

"Of course, you can redecorate to your own taste. This is the only one I have to show you now. We keep pretty full."

Spring frowned. Why had her aunt and friends decided to drag Marco into garden show meetings, of all things? Had they been matchmaking or just trying to liven up the meetings?

Aunty nodded to the man, then walked through another door into the bedroom with its adjoining bath.

A dreadful thought occurred to Spring. Could Marco possibly have thought *she'd* asked for him to be included on the committee for her sake? She cringed inside.

The gentleman followed Aunt Geneva, pointing out the bed that adjusted like a hospital bed for comfort, then pointed to grip bars added for safety in the bath.

Spring brushed aside her preoccupation with Marco and what he thought of the meeting, or of seeing her again. What could she do about it now? She'd just have to make certain she remained outwardly composed. Marco had shown nothing but politeness at seeing her again. She would follow his lead, no matter how his presence affected her.

The gentleman trailed Aunty back out into the sitting room again. "Do you have any more questions?"

"No, I went over your literature before, at home."

Forcing her mind back to the present, Spring tried to gauge her aunt's reaction to the retirement suite, but Aunty was giving no clear indication of what she was thinking. Aunty said the right things and looked like a prospective tenant, but...

The gentleman cleared his throat. "I don't want to seem forward, but we don't have vacancies very often. If you're interested, let us know as soon as you make a decision. I have two more couples looking at this suite today."

Aunty nodded. "I will. Thank you for your time." The tour came to its natural end, and Spring walked beside Aunt Geneva to the front, where Aunty had parked her car in the shade of a live oak.

Wondering why the tour had struck her as not quite right, Spring asked again to take the driver's seat.

"You still don't like my driving, do you," Aunty replied with a wry smile.

"Let's say, I'm not quite as adventurous at the wheel as you are. Besides, I enjoy driving a cabin cruiser through town."

Chuckling at this familiar answer, Aunt Geneva sighed as she eased into the passenger seat. She handed over the key. "You're a good girl, Spring."

"You're a good aunt." Spring looked over and glimpsed a strange expression on her aunt's face. "Are you feeling all right?"

"Of course, I am. That doesn't mean I don't have aches and pains. You can't live to almost ninety without those. More's the pity."

Spring felt guilty. She'd been so busy thinking about Mother and about Marco that she'd been ignoring her great-aunt's dilemma. The prospect of leaving her home of more than thirty years must be painful. "Why are you thinking of moving into a retirement community or residence? Do you feel the house is too much for you to handle now?"

Aunty avoided her gaze. "I don't know. I just thought I should look around and see what is available. You're the closest thing I have to a daughter. I don't have any family here in Florida and I've seen other retirees wait too long to make a graceful move to a retirement community. I'm trying to decide if now is the right time for me to move or should I wait."

"I see." Spring had disappointed her aunt by not settling in the Sunshine State after college. It had been a difficult decision to make, since Aunt Geneva had paid for Spring's childhood operations to correct a clubfoot, then later for college—even the money to pledge a sorority.

But at graduation, she'd gotten an offer from the prestigious Milwaukee Botanical Gardens while her sister, Doree, had still been a school girl at home in Milwaukee. After being away for four years, Spring had wanted to spend time with Doree before she left their parents' nest.

"Why don't we stop at Joan's and see if she has anything that will catch your eye?" Aunty suggested.

Spring wanted to decline. She had more than enough clothing in her closet at home, but Aunty loved to take her shopping. Buying beautiful outfits for Spring had constituted one of Aunt Geneva's greatest pleasures since Spring was six.

Her asthma had been bad that winter, and her parents had sent her to Aunt Geneva's house for a winter of sun and convalescence. Having no children of her own to spoil, Aunt Geneva had showered Spring with gifts and was still delighted to do so.

Spring grinned. "Sounds like fun to me."

Aunty's face broke into a broad smile. "Wonderful!"

Soon Spring parked in front of a trendy strip mall in an exclusive section of town. As they strolled into the boutique, Joan, the owner, greeted them. "My two favorite customers! You're here for a long visit, Spring?"

Shopping with Aunty always summoned up childhood memories of the lovely clothes Aunty had sent to Spring so generously. In turn, Hannah had accepted the hand-me-downs without complaint. But of course Doree had flatly refused to touch them! If Doree were here now, she'd certainly be angry that Spring hadn't immediately broached the subject of their mother's biological family. But the right time just hadn't presented itself.

Before long, Spring walked out of the dressing room in a rose silk sheath. Aunty sat in a split-bamboo chair near the three-way mirror. With her back to it, Spring posed gracefully. "What do you think, Aunty?"

Aunt Geneva studied her. "Turn."

Spring obeyed in a practiced motion.

"What do you think?" Aunty asked her.

I wish I didn't have a mission to carry out. I wish I could just relax and enjoy myself. But Spring, centered in front of the mirror, examined herself critically from all angles. "It fits well."

"Do you like it?" Aunty asked.

"Not enough to buy it." Spring had been so certain that she'd heard the name Connie Wilson from her aunt's lips.

But maybe she was wrong. She'd only been about twelve when she'd come upon that photograph of Aunt Geneva, her only sister, Gloria, and their childhood friend. Had the friend's name really been Connie Wilson?

The process continued. Spring finally tried on a three-piece peach linen ensemble. In front of the mirror, she announced, "I can't resist."

"Your gold herringbone chains and bracelet would be just the thing for it," Aunty agreed with a dazzling smile.

Spring nodded and Joan beamed in satisfaction. Spring walked out with the outfit carefully folded in gold tissue paper and tucked into a long gold-and-white box, tied with gold curling ribbon.

"That's just the kind of outfit you need for that University of Florida alumni cruise." Without argument this time, Aunty eased herself into the passenger seat.

Spring wondered if the morning had tired Aunty. "I had that in mind when I selected it. It's going to be fun, seeing all my college friends again." Would Marco be going, too? *Where had that thought come from?*

"I wonder if Dr. Da Palma will be going on the cruise, too."

"I don't know." Having Aunty put her thoughts into words shook Spring. She was going to have to be very careful around Aunty and her friends. Why did older women take it as their duty to try to match everyone into pairs?

"You'll have to ask him at the next meeting. A cruise

is just what he needs. He's an excellent doctor, but he doesn't seem to have any life apart from his practice. He should be looking for a wife."

Spring acted as though this didn't matter to her at all. "That's just like him. I mean, that was how he was in college." And she'd had to accept it then.

Evidently he hadn't changed.

"Marco, you're not paying attention." His petite mother nudged him. "Are you done eating?"

From his seat at the round table in the dinette just off the kitchen, he glanced up. "Sorry, Mama. Just a long day." He could hardly admit to himself that he'd been remembering how elegant Spring Kirkland had looked at the garden show meeting.

"Well, I'm glad you stopped here for dinner or you'd probably have skipped another meal."

"Believe me, when I get hungry, I eat." Marco finished the last bit of the spicy casserole. He wiped his mouth with his paper napkin and pushed his plate and silverware aside. "Okay, Paloma, get out that calculus and we'll get it done."

"Don't call me that name!" His teenage half-sister twisted her face in a heartfelt grimace.

"It's your name, *little dove*." Marco teased her with the translation of her Spanish name, one that had been in her father's family for generations.

"I'm just Maria, okay?" She ducked around the corner, then returned with her book and notebook. His sister had taken a recent dislike to the family name her father had insisted she have, and she'd announced she would be called by her middle name, Maria.

"Why don't you want to be distinctive? There are millions of Maria's, but very few Paloma's." Two weeks ago, Paloma had decided to change her name. So far she'd had very little luck in changing her family's mind. Had someone at school teased her about her name? If she kept this up, he'd have to delve deeper and see what was bothering her.

Their mother shook her head at them and left with Marco's dishes in her hands. Paloma wiped the table with a napkin, then spread her textbook and notebook in front of her brother. "I'm having trouble with these four problems."

For the next twenty minutes, Marco and his sister went over her assignment. Then the back door opened and shut. "I'm home!" The cheerful voice of his stepfather, Santos, boomed in the kitchen. His mother's laughter greeted her husband.

Marco and Paloma looked up, as Santos walked into the dinette. "Marco, *hola,* did you have a good day?"

Marco nodded, glancing at the barrel-chested man who had married his mother when Marco was fourteen.

"I see our girl needs more help with her math." Santos, a plumber, rolled up the sleeves of his khaki work shirt to wash for his late supper.

"We're just finishing up." Marco looked at his sister. "You've got that now?"

"Sure. At least, for today. I just hope it sticks for the test." Paloma made a face.

"Your brother has set you a good example. No going out with friends this weekend if that test score isn't good." Santos shook his finger at her.

Paloma frowned. "I know."

Wishing Santos wouldn't always wave Marco's success in his little sister's face, Marco rose and lifted his sports jacket from the back of his chair. "I think it's time I went home."

"You don't have to run off like that," Santos objected.

"I've got some patient notes to look over and early rounds at the hospital."

"You need to learn to relax a little now, son. You have earned the right to enjoy yourself."

"Medicine is a twenty-four hours a day, seven days a week kind of job."

"Then, you doctors need a better union," Santos joked.

Marco nodded politely to his stepfather and walked out to his car. As he drove away, his mother stood at the kitchen window, waving goodbye.

Loneliness snaked through him. Santos was a good man. His mother was happy, and Paloma was a treasure. But he'd never felt at home in that house. His family really had ended with his father's death, and nothing could change that. Or, at least, nothing ever had.

Then Spring Kirkland's lovely face flickered in his memory, as it often had in the days since he'd seen her again—after all the years apart. He'd meant to call her to ask for her help, but every time he stood with the receiver in his hand, he ended up putting it down without calling. What would he say?

"Spring?" Hannah's voice came over the phone line.

Trying to suppress her nervousness, Spring settled back in the chair beside her bed, but she couldn't stop herself from accusing. "Hi, you didn't call me when you said you would."

"I'm sorry. I've been really busy. Deadline frenzy with my new cookbook." Hannah sounded stressed.

"Did you find out about Mother's latest blood work?" Spring asked.

"I was going to call you last night, but I forgot you're an hour earlier than we are—"

"What did the test reveal?" Spring interrupted.

"It wasn't as good as the doctor had hoped, but he said not to worry."

Easy for him to say. Hannah's worried. I'm worried. "Is Father upset?"

"He says he'll just continue to pray."

Of course, prayer is what we all are doing, but why don't I feel comforted? Spring tried to think what to say. "How's Guthrie?"

"Wonderful."

Spring couldn't think of anything more to say and guessed that her sister felt the same. The dread over their mother's health had silenced their usual chatter.

Spring started, "I'll call soon—"

"Have you asked Aunt—"

"I will."

"All right. Good night."

"Good night." Spring put down the receiver. *No more waiting for the right time. Tomorrow I ask Aunt Geneva about Connie Wilson.*

Suppressing a yawn from lack of sleep, Spring stood on the patio outside her aunt's sweeping Florida room, the all-season porch that spanned the rear of the house. Beyond the patio, palm trees stood like sentinels above her aunt's lush garden, and beyond the fence, the azure Gulf. Spring took up her box of well-used pastels and contemplated the blank paper on her easel. She hadn't had time to draw for nearly six months. She didn't really feel like it now, but she'd decided this would take them out of the house, away from her aunt's housekeeper, Matilde. Whatever was said, she wanted to keep the secrets surrounding her mother's birth private.

"You make such a picture standing there." Aunt Geneva sat in the shade of the roof with her knitting in her lap.

Spring glanced down at her white shorts and pale yellow shirt—nothing special. Once again, she tried to come up with a way of introducing the subject of her mother's natural parents. Her mind was a blank.

"What should I sketch today? Something I can see or something inside my mind?"

"Suit yourself, dear." Her aunt's needles clicked,

weaving pale pink baby yarn together into a knit cap for a newborn at the nearby hospital.

Spring stood there, wondering which to do. Worry over her mother's illness and her own timidity about asking Aunty "the question" capped any creative energy she possessed. In default mode, she selected blue and began to stroke a fine layer of blue chalk over the top half of the paper on the easel. *Just say it!* "Aunty, you know about Mother's illness…."

"Yes, dear, I've been so thankful for her remission. What would your father do without her? Ethel has always been the practical one. I wonder if your father has ever realized how lucky he's been in having a wife like Ethel."

"I'm sure he has—"

"Well, he better, that's all I can say."

Spring glanced over her shoulder at Aunty. How could she just ask—out of the blue like this? Taking a deep breath, she began the foundation for the big question. "You know, before she went into remission, the doctor said that she might need a bone marrow donor. All three of us girls were tested, but none of us was a match."

"Uh-huh." Aunty appeared to be counting stitches.

Spring gazed skyward, gathering momentum. "That was a great worry to us. I mean, what if Mother had reached the point where she needed a donor and none of us could help her?"

"I see." The needles started clicking again. "But that didn't happen."

"But it might have. It might happen in the future."

"But Ethel is in remission!"

The moment had come. No more beating around the bush. "Aunty, my sisters and I want, need—"

"*Señora* Dorfman, Paloma has come." Plump Matilde, with her salt-and-pepper gray hair in a bun, ambled out through the Florida room to the patio, her arthritis slowing her. A pretty girl who had long black hair and wore blue jeans and a red T-shirt trailed behind her.

Spring paused and turned. Matilde had been her aunt's housekeeper for the past thirty years. She'd spoiled Spring right along with her aunt. But right now, when she'd just worked up the courage to ask her aunt THE question— she wished Matilde anywhere pleasant but here.

"Excellent." Aunt Geneva smiled. "Hello, Paloma. So you're going to start helping Matilde out on the weekends?"

"Yes, ma'am." The young girl looked up shyly.

Aunt Geneva motioned toward Spring. "This is my niece, Spring."

"What a pretty name." The girl glanced at Spring, then seemed to freeze, gazing at her.

Spring hated it when people stared, but she merely returned the girl's regard. The Hispanic girl's face was lovely, fresh, her expression so winsome. "I'd love to paint you." The words popped out of Spring's mouth.

"Oh! I…" The girl blushed.

I've embarrassed her. Spring had forgotten how sensitive teenage girls could be.

"Oh, that would be wonderful." Matilde clapped her hands. "Her *quinceañería* is in just a few months, the end of April. It would be a wonderful gift for her parents!"

"What's a quinceañería?" Spring asked.

"It's her fifteenth birthday, a special occasion in a girl's life. The custom comes from Mexico, where her father was born. I went to school with her father, Santos."

"But I'm here to work," Paloma said quietly, looking from one to the other of the three ladies.

"Well, you can sit for me briefly in between your chores," Spring suggested.

"Excellent!" Aunt Geneva beamed.

"Bueno," Matilde agreed.

"Come sit here in this chair," Spring instructed as she pulled a wicker chair into place. The sun would come over the girl's shoulder and cast interesting shadows over her face.

The front door chimes rang out. "I'll go get that." Matilde hurried away, favoring her bad knee.

Spring arranged the ill-at-ease girl in the wicker chair. "With the garden behind you, this is going to be lovely."

"But I'm in work clothes. I—"

"Today I'll just begin. I just need to look at you and study your face and form. When we get to the clothing, you can bring something else to pose in." Spring lifted the girl's chin to the right and left, trying to decide which was her best side.

"Señora, it's the doctor." Matilde stood aside at the doorway.

At these mundane words, Spring spun around. *Marco! Here?*

Marco walked in, carrying a small black bag.

The sight of him in a crisp dark suit sent a sharp zigzag of excitement through Spring. All the years away from him melted away.

Marco began in an all-business tone—unaware of Spring and oblivious of her marked reaction to him. "Mrs. Dorfman, you didn't come for your blood-pressure check—" He broke off, staring at his sister. "Paloma, what are you doing here?"

Aunty and Matilde turned to look at him.

Matilde recovered first. "Marco, your sister is going to start helping me on the weekends. I need another pair of hands on Saturday. And now Spring wants to draw her portrait for her *quinceañería*. A present to thank your parents!"

"Paloma, when did your father decide you needed to start working?" Marco demanded, glaring at her.

Marco's tone bothered Spring. He was overreacting. *What's going on?*

Paloma rose hesitantly. "I…I want to start saving for college. Matilde had mentioned that she'd be needing help…I…" The girl's voice died away.

Marco scowled.

Knowing Marco from years ago, Spring realized he was humiliated to have his sister working as domestic help. Marco's overly sensitive pride had been all too evident years ago and that had not changed.

"So, Doctor, you've chased me down," Aunty rallied. "I was planning on coming over early next week. Anyone would think I was at death's door—"

"I'm your doctor and I told you I wanted to monitor your blood pressure closely through this month. Now please take off your jacket and I'll get this done. I'm on my way to the hospital to check on some patients."

His sharp tone surprised Spring. *Please, Marco, don't be so upset.* Then an unwelcome thought intruded. What was so wrong with Aunty's blood pressure that Marco would come to the house?

Aunt Geneva followed his instructions, and he put the black cuff on her arm. Though unsettled by this development, Spring tried to act naturally. She motioned to Paloma to sit back down, then contemplated which color to use next.

The young girl looked uncomfortable and kept glancing at her brother. Spring smiled at her, trying to put her at her ease while she strove to ignore her own keen awareness of Marco.

"Well, how did I do?" Aunty asked tartly, when Marco finished.

Spring was silently asking the same question.

"You're still higher than I want you to be. I don't want to increase your blood-pressure medicine until I'm forced to. Have you started exercising, as you promised me?"

Aunt Geneva sighed. "No, I've been so busy—"

"Make time." Marco packed up his blood-pressure

kit. "I expect to see you walking regularly and losing a few pounds."

"Yes, Doctor." Aunty grimaced.

Spring frowned. Was this what had prompted her aunt to think about retirement homes? She had to find out if her aunt's health really was declining, even if it meant putting herself in the path of Marco's unconscious yet risky charm.

"I'll be going now." Marco glanced at Spring.

She tried to read his expression but couldn't. "I'll walk you to your car. Paloma, why don't you go ahead and help Matilde, and when you're done come back to me."

Spring didn't give anyone a chance to object. She walked swiftly toward the house with Marco in her wake.

Outside, in front of her aunt's sprawling ranch, walking toward Marco's car, she asked, "Is my aunt's health something I should be concerned about?" She lowered her gaze to limit Marco's effect on her.

"I can't be specific, but let me tell you that I'm glad you're here. She needs someone who can get her to take better care of herself."

Spring worried her lower lip. "Is it her age?"

"Age is a factor, yes."

"She's always been so healthy, I think it's difficult for her—" *and for me* "—to accept the fact that she is finally feeling the effects of being nearly ninety."

"No doubt, that's correct. Now, make sure she comes to me twice next week."

"To save us a trip, could you check her blood

pressure after the next garden show meeting?" Spring chanced a glance at him—suddenly glad that he was her aunt's doctor.

Marco pursed his lips. "I'm glad you brought that up. I need your help."

Spring lifted one eyebrow. "With what?"

Chapter Three

With Spring's lovely blue eyes gazing up at him so seriously, Marco felt as tongue-tied as a young boy. Why hadn't the years toughened him so that this beautiful, unattainable woman would no longer have the power to make him want to pull her close for a stolen kiss?

Spring Kirkland, I thought I'd completely forgotten you.

But his heart had played him for a fool again. He still wanted her. He still couldn't have her.

She touched his arm. Even through the double layer of fabric, shirt and jacket, her touch shocked him. He swallowed to moisten his dry mouth so he could answer her.

"What is it, Marco? You look so worried."

Get a grip, man. "I'm just...busy. When Dr. Johnson sold me his practice so reasonably, it was a great stroke of luck—"

"Don't you mean a blessing?" She let her hand drop

to her side as she leaned gracefully against the car. Her long, slender legs stretched out in front of him.

He couldn't take his eyes off her. Didn't she realize what an enticing picture she made? Why hadn't some successful Anglo man married her by now? He hung onto the thread of their conversation. "A blessing, yes. But taking on a full practice right away brought huge responsibilities with it."

She folded her slim arms in front of her. The sunlight glinted off the diamond tennis bracelet she wore.

He steeled himself against her allure. "I joined Golden Sands so I could contribute to the club's scholarship program, which had been a godsend to me. But I've never really used the membership. I've been hoping you could help me."

She nodded, encouraging him.

"I'm not the country-club type and I don't have time to waste on garden show meetings. I've been wanting to ask you for days—can you think of a polite way of getting me out of them?"

"I see. You want me to help you resign from the committee?" She pursed her lips. "You're wasting your time?"

"It's not that I'm ungrateful for all that Golden Sands did for me. Without working there and without the club's generous scholarships, as a fatherless immigrant from the Dominican Republic, I wouldn't have been able to finish college without a crushing load of debt, but…" He pushed one hand through his hair, hating to voice so much of his history of need. "I just think my time would be better spent doing what my education prepared me to do—medicine."

Her long, golden hair flowing over her shoulders and veiling her face, she looked down at the asphalt drive. "You were upset to see your sister working with Matilde?"

The question, so off the subject, threw him. "What?"

"You don't want your sister to work for my aunt." She glanced up at him, her lovely face so intense.

He tried to read her expression but couldn't. How had she known how embarrassed he'd been? "I just don't think it's necessary for her to work right now." The words sounded stiff even to his own ears.

"I think you have some seriously wrong ideas about my family." She tossed her hair back from her face.

Her totally unexpected words, along with her undeniable attractiveness, left him in confusion. He clung to the topic at hand. "What has that got to do with what we're talking about?"

"A great deal." She pushed away from the car. "I'll let you get back to your *busy* practice."

Unable to stop himself, he turned as he watched her saunter away. He'd obviously had no effect on her! "Will you help me?"

"I'll consider what you've told me."

He couldn't make himself move until he'd followed her with his gaze all the way into the sprawling white house. When she shut the double doors behind her, her spell over him was finally broken, and he slid into his car and drove away.

Something had happened between him and Spring just now, but what? Why had she spoken of his sister? And what did she mean *he* had seriously wrong ideas?

"Aunty?" Spring tapped on her aunt's bedroom door that night.

"Come in, dear."

Spring stepped inside and closed the door behind her. Ever since Marco had visited early in the day, she had turned over and over in her mind what he'd said to her, along with what she still needed to ask her aunt— plus her own turbulent feelings about both. Right now, though, she'd decided to concentrate on the question she'd been sent by her sisters to ask. That was the most important.

Dressed for bed in a flowing lavender caftan, Aunt Geneva reclined on her chaise longue by the window, knitting another bootie. "What is it, dear? You look worried."

In her pale pink pajamas, Spring perched on the chair near her aunt. "There's something I need to ask you. You may not want to give me the information, but I hope— we all hope—you will."

Aunty's eyebrows rose above her reading glasses. "This sounds very serious."

"It is." Spring gripped the arms of her chair.

Aunty removed her glasses and set them, along with her knitting, on the small table beside her. "Does it have to do with Marco?"

"Marco?" The thought startled Spring. "This has nothing to do with Marco. Aunty, I—"

"Why aren't you married yet?"

Spring gawked at her aunt. "Marriage isn't the subject I wanted to talk to you about—"

"Well, this is the conversation I've intended to have with you for a long time now. You are always so distant and cool around men. You never flirt or use your beauty in any way I can detect. You just don't seem to know how to attract a man. Why not?" Her aunt stared at her.

Spring tried not to react to her aunt's bald words, but they echoed too closely the things her sisters had been telling her for years. That awful sinking feeling slid through her. No one understood the pressures she'd faced.

"Aunty—"

"You're beautiful!" Aunty flung her hands wide. "I should be fighting like a lioness to protect you. Men should be following you around like lovesick puppies—"

"Stop!" Spring pressed her hands to her warming face. Tears threatened to overflow. "I don't want men around me…acting like lovesick puppies or…vulgar idiots!" Unwelcome images and words from the past crowded Spring's mind, especially that night on campus that Marco had come to her rescue. She willed herself to block out the unpleasant sensations these memories carried with them. Goose bumps crawled up her arms.

"Dear, sweet child." Swinging her legs over the side of her chaise longue, Aunty sat up and clasped her hands around Spring's small wrists. "Tell me what has upset you. Please."

Slowly Spring lowered her hands, but she averted her face.

Aunt Geneva let her own hands drop to her lap. "Tell me. Be honest."

Spring drew in a shuddering breath. "I don't like *that...kind* of attention from men." She shivered. "I don't like it when they get close to me and...say things to me when they don't think anyone else can hear."

"You mean...sexual comments?"

"Sometimes...vulgar insinuations." Spring's face blazed as she recalled some of these, still vivid in her memory. "They act like I'm not a real person...like I'm just a face, a body...."

"You poor dear." Aunty frowned. "Those kind of comments would wound someone like you, someone shy, especially someone raised like you were in a parsonage."

"What was wrong with the way I was raised? Mother and Father are wonderful parents!"

Aunty clenched her hands. "They are, but they never told you how beautiful you are or prepared you for the power beauty brings with it. They didn't warn you of the special demands of being so lovely—"

"You're not making any sense!" Spring hated this! She'd come in to ask about Connie Wilson, not to discuss her "beauty"!

"We should have had this conversation years ago! I

don't know why I didn't recognize this in you before. Now I can see how it all fits together."

"What are you talking about?" *None of this fits together!*

Aunty leaned against the arm of her chaise. "You're kind of young to remember Marilyn Monroe, aren't you."

"You mean the movie star in the fifties?" Shaken, Spring couldn't understand where her aunt was heading with this.

"Yes, she was a beautiful young woman, but men never saw anything but her beautiful face and figure. She died young and all alone. A very sad story."

"What does that have to do with me?" Spring's temples started throbbing.

"Your parents being good Christians raised you to judge people not by their appearance, but by their value to God." Aunty gave her a knowing look.

"Of course, they did." *They taught me what was right.*

Aunty shook her head ruefully. "But most people judge by appearance only. Ethel and Garner should have taught you how to handle the extra attention you'd receive as a beauty, how to put men—rude men—in their place."

"You can learn that?" Spring stared at her aunt.

Aunty nodded. "If only I had realized, I could have helped you. Why didn't you say how much you were hurting?"

"I didn't think...I didn't know..."

"Sweetheart, we've got to do something about this.

I can't make you less sensitive, but I can help you come out of this shell you've built around yourself." Aunty took both Spring's hands in hers. "We can't let this spoil your life. You are the sweetest, kindest girl in the world, and we're going to get you over this, so you can find your one true love!"

My one true love. Longing swelled inside Spring. Her expression must have given her away.

"You are in love!"

"No, I—"

"Who is he?"

"Aunty—"

"Is it Marco?"

The rapid-fire questions overwhelmed Spring. Before she could stop herself, she nodded.

"Oh, but that's wonderful! Marco needs a woman like you in his life! He's just going to waste! You two would make a wonderful pair."

"Aunt Geneva, no!" Spring gasped, trying to rein in her aunt. "Marco isn't interested in me. He might be dating someone else—"

"No, I don't think he is, but we'll check with Matilde. How fortunate you two are both on the garden show committee."

"You didn't get him on the committee just because you knew I would be here—?"

"No." Aunt Geneva shrugged and made an apologetic moue. "We insisted he join us mainly because the man has no social life."

"Coming to garden show meetings would give him a social life?" The sweet foolishness of this plan released some of the tension Spring had been feeling.

"Of course not, but we decided it would get him to the country club, and we would see what developed from there."

"Marco says he's too busy. He wants to get off—"

Aunt Geneva shook her head adamantly. "Not a chance. Marco has got to start having a life, not just a career."

Spring sighed. She felt beaten and shaken, as though she had just run through a hailstorm. She still hadn't posed the big question she'd come in to ask Aunt Geneva. But she couldn't make herself bring up another emotionally charged topic now. She rose and kissed her aunt's soft cheek.

When she reached the door, her aunt's voice stopped her. "What did you come here to ask me?"

Spring shook her head, too weary now to take up the task of asking her aunt about Connie Wilson.

"Now, don't you worry, dear. Tomorrow we'll begin bringing you out of your shell and into Marco's much-too-serious life. Dr. Da Palma won't know what hit him!"

Dazed, Spring walked out, feeling like a condemned woman. The possibilities for embarrassment to both her and Marco loomed over her. Aunt Geneva and friends were capable of anything! *Don't worry, she says. Don't worry?*

* * *

The next morning, Spring and Aunty decided to have their breakfast in the airy patio off the kitchen. Warm sunshine, the rhythmic sound of the waves, and the call of gulls made an idyllic setting.

Still in her pink pajamas, Spring sighed, then rolled the tangy, fresh-squeezed ruby-red grapefruit juice over her tongue. "Thank you. I've dreamed about your breakfasts, Matilde."

"Matilde," Aunt Geneva in pink curlers and matching robe ordered, "sit down. We need to talk to you."

Spring prayed, *Please, Lord, don't let her—*

"My niece is interested in Marco."

Plump Matilde sat down, then bounced in her chair. "*Bueno, bueno.* Marco's mother will be thrilled—"

"Don't!" Spring held up her hand the way a crossing guard would. This was exactly what she'd dreaded! "Don't tell *anyone*, especially Marco's mother! Please!"

"Oh, *querida,* don't worry." Matilde patted her arm. "I meant only that his mother will be thrilled when you and Marco are engaged—"

"He isn't even interested in me!" Spring exclaimed.

"*Yet,*" Aunt Geneva pronounced. "Now, Matilde, I wanted to speak with you to make certain Marco has no romantic interest in anyone else."

"No, no, he's always working. Before he was always studying. His mother invites pretty girls to the house. She hints. But he's always too busy. She wants grandchildren—"

Spring bent and rested her forehead in her hand. "You're getting carried away." These women were transforming her college crush on Marco into future grandchildren!

One on each side of Spring, Aunt Geneva and Matilde patted her shoulders.

"Don't worry, Spring," Aunty replied. "You just need a little coaching."

Spring cringed. She'd have to think of something to keep this from spoiling her friendship with Marco and making fools of both of them.

Aunty again turned to her smiling housekeeper. "You remember how quiet and unspoiled our Spring has always been. Well, she needs to overcome her natural shyness."

Relieved that her aunt hadn't mentioned her humiliating experiences with men, Spring gazed at the two older women, praying this conversation would end as soon as possible.

Matilde nodded, her double chin quivering. "Yes, I remember. And Marco, ever since his father died, has stayed so serious. Working, saving, studying. He needs you in his life, Spring."

Matilde's words touched Spring's heart. Marco didn't need her. But if what Matilde said was true, Marco certainly needed to make a change. He did take life too seriously. He had overreacted to his sister helping Matilde. He didn't even want to take time to cater to three older ladies for a few meetings.

She would do what she could to help. If the ladies wanted to think she was "flirting" with him, well, it would provide them something fun to do, too. But she'd have to explain matters to Marco. She didn't believe in manipulating a man, and Marco had always been too proud, too intelligent to be "molded," anyway. But a life without fun wasn't healthy for Marco.

The next week Marco, this time in a black suit, white shirt and black tie, towered over Spring sitting on the country club veranda. Her nerves thrummed inside her, but she kept her polite smile in place.

"Good afternoon."

Aunty, Eleanor and Verna Rae echoed her, beaming at him from their seats around the same table they'd occupied last week.

Her pulse speeding up, Spring noted the way the lines around Marco's mouth tightened even as he smiled. *Please relax, Marco.* He sat down beside her. Waves of tension radiated from him. *Why are you wound so tightly, Marco? What is it deep inside you that makes you try so hard?* She worked hard to reveal only a reserved mask. Marco, so close, drew her attention and awakened her senses to everything about him. The scent of his lime aftershave, his long slender fingers, the way his ebony hair glistened in the sunlight.

"Today we have to go over our list of sponsors," Verna Rae began, intruding on Spring's musing.

"What do your sponsors contribute?" Spring asked, fighting the effect of Marco's nearness.

The three ladies turned their attention to her. Eleanor replied, "Our sponsors contribute money for advertising, dahling, and for the prizes we give the winners."

Spring nodded. This kind of meeting was second nature to her. She held onto the familiar in spite of Marco's presence. "How many entries were there last year?"

Eleanor glanced at her notes. "Fifty-three."

"That many?" Spring gave a nod of approval. "Who were last year's sponsors?"

The meeting droned on.

Ring-ring, ring-ring. Marco reached for the cell phone at his belt.

At the sound, Spring felt her neck muscles tighten. The three other women paused to gaze at him with worried pouts.

After a brief phone exchange, he rose, looking relieved instead of concerned. "I've been called to the hospital. One of my patients has been brought in. My apologies." Then he looked pointedly at Spring. "Would you walk me to my car? I'd like to ask you a favor."

Feeling conspicuous, Spring stood up, wondering if the plan she'd come up with would fit the bill....

With a polite nod to the ladies at the table, he ushered her down the central hallway. His sleeve brushed against her bare arm. She tingled.

"Did you think of a way for me to get out of the committee gracefully?" He spoke close to her ear.

His warm breath against her skin sent pleasurable chills up her nape. Spring stepped outside into the dazzling sunshine. Gathering her courage, she said, "Why don't you take me to dinner tonight?"

"Dinner?" Marco looked puzzled. "What has dinner got to do with anything?"

"We need to go away somewhere and talk." *And my aunt and Matilde will think I'm coming out of my shell, so they won't humiliate us by "helping."*

Confusion in his expression gave way to understanding. "I see! When would you like me to pick you up?"

"Seven." *I don't think you do see, but...*

"Excellent." He slid behind the wheel of his car. "I really appreciate your helping with this. Thanks."

Trying to suppress an unexpected elation, Spring watched him drive down the boulevard lined with rosy azaleas. She realized she was playing with fire: spending time with Marco could endanger her concealment of her secret feelings for him. *You're going to learn how to have some fun, Marco—and fast—so this risky strategy I'm following ends before disaster occurs.*

But a smile played around the corners of her mouth as she walked back to the ladies on the veranda.

Three pairs of curious eyes gazed at her.

"Well?" Aunty prompted.

A grin Spring couldn't stop lifted the corners of her mouth. "He's picking me up for dinner at seven tonight."

"Hot dog!" Eleanor squealed. The three octogenarians performed an impromptu high-five times three.

Spring felt a little giddy. She sank down onto the chair. *It isn't a real date,* she reminded herself. But her heart refused to listen to her silly common sense. Dinner at seven with Marco!

Chapter Four

"I just know you've messed up." Doree's strident voice accosted Spring. She had picked up the beige front hall phone.

Spring frowned. "And hello to you, too. No, I haven't asked Aunt Geneva yet—"

"Why not?" Doree shouted.

"Doree, I won't let you abuse me over the phone. You think everything is easy about this, but it isn't." *Grow up, Doree.* "Asking about Mother's family is not easy."

Doree groaned. "You don't have all year. You only took a three-month leave of absence."

Did Doree really think she was delaying everything on purpose? "I am quite aware of the amount of time I have. I'll call you in a few days."

"Well, you had better!" Doree scolded and hung up.

How could her sister think Mother's health didn't matter to her? For a few seconds, the urge to redial her younger sister and tell her to back off swept through Spring mightily, but she resisted it. Doree was very young and naturally brash. But Doree wasn't the one asking the question. So far, all Doree had done was crack the whip over her two sisters. Maybe Doree would feel differently if the shoe were on the other foot. *Dear Lord, help me ask soon.*

"Are you wearing those shoes?" Aunty asked in a disapproving tone, coming up the hall behind Spring.

Spring looked down at the bone low-heeled pumps she wore. "Yes, are they smudged on the back or something?" She turned one heel to glance at it.

"You need a higher heel. Come to my room."

High heels? Spring trailed after her aunt. "I don't like to wear high heels. They're uncomfortable—"

"Men love women in high heels." Aunty nudged Spring in front of her into the bedroom, then led her to the huge walk-in closet. "It's fortunate we wear the same shoe size."

Spring tried to think of a way to avoid her aunt's assistance. Aunty's shoes fit Spring in size, but not in age bracket. And did she really "fit" high heels? Spring doubted this.

"Let's pull out a few pairs I've saved." Aunty deftly pulled open a drawer from the back of her closet.

Looking over her aunt's shoulder, Spring glimpsed rows and rows of high heels in every color of the spectrum. Had Aunty saved every pair she'd ever owned? "I don't remember seeing you wear any of these."

"These are my favorites from the past. See this pair—my wedding shoes." Aunty displayed a pair of white silk pumps obviously made when Franklin Delano Roosevelt still slept in the White House.

Her wedding shoes! Spring reached for them. "Oh, Aunty! I—"

"No time for nostalgia now. Marco will arrive at any time. Here, try these—" Aunty put away her wedding shoes and brought out a pair of gold-colored sling-backs with three-inch heels.

Gaudy was the word that leaped to Spring's mind. "I don't think I've ever worn—"

"Try them." Aunty pushed them into her hands.

Feeling like some bizarre Cinderella, Spring obediently kicked off her comfortable pumps and slipped on the heels. Her feet looked like they belonged to someone else.

"Now walk up and down the room in front of my wall mirror," Aunty ordered.

Spring wanted to refuse, but stiffened her resolve. She did want Marco to see her as more than just an "old college acquaintance" this evening. Maybe golden slippers would jar him into reassessing her. Without glancing at the mirror, she walked back and forth across the large room. The height of the heels made her feel wobbly. They shortened her stride, too. In spite of these reactions, Spring tried to walk naturally.

Aunt Geneva studied her. "Ivory is a good color for you. I like that sundress. It's a little long, but it skims your figure nicely."

Spring didn't know what to say to this, so she gave no reply. Aunty had taught her all about fashion, but she'd never mentioned how to attract men with one's style.

"I think that jacket has to come off, though."

Spring paused. "I thought it might be a little cool this evening."

"Then, carry it over your arm. And if you need it, be sure to ask Marco to put it around you. It's just the kind of intimate gesture that you should use to snag his interest."

Spring closed her eyes, wondering if she was still in her right mind. *I don't do things like this.* But she obediently removed the matching linen jacket and laid it across her arm.

"Look at yourself as you walk."

Spring glanced up and gave her aunt a quizzical look. "What?"

"You need more sway to take full advantage of the high-heel effect," Aunty explained as she motioned with her hands.

"What's the high-heel effect?" Spring stared at her.

"Look in the mirror."

Spring obeyed. "What am I looking for?"

Aunty rolled her eyes in mock dismay. "Don't you see how it makes your legs look longer and how it tips you just a bit forward?"

Drawing close, Spring studied herself in the wall mirror, turned sideways. She did appear a bit different. "You're right. I never knew!"

Aunty shook her head and muttered something Spring couldn't understand. "Dear, I wouldn't ask you to make these little changes, but you're trying to attract a man who ignores women, ignores a woman like *you*! You have to shake him out of this, this…fog he's in!" Aunty stepped back and scanned her niece.

Spring pursed her lips. "This just doesn't feel like me…."

"It's just a side of you we haven't let out before."

Sighing, Spring decided to let the changes Aunty had made stand. Marco seemed a true challenge for her to tackle with her first attempt at being… approachable.

"Anything else?" Spring propped one hand on her hip.

Drawing close, Aunty gave her a quick hug. "One more thing. Come over to my jewelry case."

Aunty's antique oak jewelry armoire stood three-feet high next to her vintage gilded vanity table. While Aunty sat, opening and closing drawers, she motioned Spring to settle on the adjacent chair. "Ah, this is just what we want." She held up a thin gold *Y* chain. "Dr. Da Palma needs a little direction, and this will keep his eyes on you." She slipped the gossamer chain over Spring's head and arranged it so that the two golden teardrop ends dangled above the sundress's *V* neckline.

Spring shivered as the chain settled onto her sensitive skin. *Oh, Lord, this just seems so artificial, so planned. I want Marco to notice me, just for me. Do I really need to make this effort? Is this just a silly crush I should have gotten over—*

Her aunt's musical doorbell rang.

Spring's heart leaped into her dry throat. She drew in a deep breath, then rose and picked up her jacket.

"This is it," Aunty murmured, beaming with anticipation. "I dare Dr. Da Palma to ignore you tonight!"

Spring nodded, feeling a bit queasy. But she didn't give in to the weakness. She marched down the hall toward the door.

"Slow down, dear!" Aunty urged in an undertone.

Spring slowed and tried to walk more femininely, or in a way Aunt Geneva would think looked more feminine. *I feel like a mannequin in a department store! This just isn't me, Lord!*

As Matilde opened the door for Marco, she beamed at Spring.

Spring looked up and caught Marco's expression. Framed by the doorway, wearing a dark suit, he looked handsome, but as uncomfortable as she felt.

A rush of excitement caught her by surprise. At last, she was going out with Marco. Never mind that she'd had to do the asking. To gain control, she inhaled, then said in a friendly tone, "Good evening, Marco. You're right on time."

"I have early rounds at seven tomorrow morning," he said with a straight face.

Matilde exhaled loudly, then scolded, "This is not the time to talk of work! You pick up a lovely *señorita* and you already tell her you will not take her out for long?" She finished with a tart-sounding Spanish phrase.

Marco looked pained.

Matilde made him feel silly, just as her aunt was exasperating her.

Better get a move on! Picking up her handbag from the hall table, Spring stepped over the threshold past Marco. "Don't wait up for me, Aunty." *Where had that come from? An old movie?*

She walked on, trying to remember to walk like… what? A movie star? Fashion model?

Marco hurried after her.

She reached his car first but waited for him. She tensed as he drew near.

"Is there something wrong with your lower back?" Marco opened the car door for her. "You're walking a little differently than usual."

Spring groaned inside but gave him a bright smile. "New shoes."

"Maybe you should exchange them for ones with a different heel. Those don't look very comfortable." He slid into the car next to her.

Good grief. Was Marco even impervious to the "high-heel effect"? "I'll keep that in mind. Where are we going?"

"I don't know." He started the car and drove down the drive. "Where would you like to go?"

Marco's lime aftershave filled the small space of the front seat. Spring's mind went blank. "Anywhere is fine."

"All right."

She tried to think of another topic, but nothing came

to mind. Fortunately, Marco drove without asking further questions.

Ten minutes later, he led her into a modest Greek restaurant near the downtown section by the hospital. A middle-aged waitress with a thick accent seated them and handed them menus.

Spring held the menu and gazed around her at the unprepossessing restaurant—a counter, tables, booths and nondescript carpet and neutral colors. For *this,* she had scrutinized her whole Florida wardrobe and suffered three-inch heels?

"We can go somewhere else, if you like." Glancing over his menu at her, Marco looked unsure of himself.

"No, this is fine. Do you eat here often?"

"It's near the hospital."

"I see." Her flattened tone must have nicked him.

"I'm sorry it's not very special, but I know the food is good here," he said, sounding defensive.

"You misunderstood me. I love Greek food. I just thought..." How could she fault him? She'd forced him to take her out. But he'd brought her to the restaurant he ate at frequently because it was near the hospital and had good food. This proved true every worry Aunt Geneva and Matilde had. The man had no clue about dating! Even if Matilde hadn't already told them, Spring knew now that Marco didn't date much. He didn't even have a regular "date" place or two ready when needed.

"I thought of taking you to the country club, but then people might have thought we were actually dating."

Stung, Spring demanded, "Would that have ruined your reputation or mine?"

"What?" Marco eyed her with suspicion.

Spring bit her lower lip. The man was impossible. She'd seen an English comedy where the husband and wife were arguing in the kitchen and the wife had begun throwing the carrots she was peeling at the husband. Now Spring knew just how the woman had felt!

She eyed the basket of hard rolls on the table, but decided against tossing any at Marco. He'd probably have her rushed to the psych ward at the hospital across the way.

The morose waitress returned. Spring ordered the moussaka and Marco ordered the gyros dinner. The waitress walked away, and Spring and Marco just stared at one another.

"Have you given any thought to how I can gracefully get out of the garden show committee?" Marco picked out a roll as though trying to do something to cover his uneasiness.

Stalling, Spring scanned the other couples eating at the tables around them. How could Marco have brought her here for a cozy dinner? Most appeared to be medical employees or lone people who might have relatives at the hospital. No doubt the food here ranked above the hospital cafeteria's. She supposed she should be grateful Marco hadn't taken her there!

To Spring's left, however, sat a young couple in a booth. She could tell they were on a date. She studied the girl's posture. She was leaning forward with her elbows on the table, closer to her young man. Spring frowned. She'd been raised to never put her elbows on the table. But she needed to learn how to appear…available.

Spring gingerly set one elbow on the table and leaned forward a little.

"Well?" Marco insisted. "Have you thought of an out for me?"

Spring looked into his mahogany-brown eyes and was snared. She couldn't look away. *Oh, Marco, notice me. I can't help noticing you.*

"Is something wrong?"

Startled back to the present, she gave him a bright, persuasive smile. "No! I have some…information for you." She leaned closer to him.

"You make it sound like it's something I don't want to hear."

The girl to Spring's left giggled and leaned farther forward on the tabletop. Spring quickly looked away. *I'm not a teenager!*

She settled back against her seat, letting her hands drop to her lap. "You must promise not to repeat this, because they meant well."

"Who meant well and about what?"

"My aunt and her two friends are concerned that you work too hard and don't take any time for fun."

Marco stared at her, his lips parted in surprise.

Well, she certainly had his attention now. She

imagined leaning across the table and touching his lips with her fingertips. That unquestionably would be a signal of her interest in him—but they were in a Greek restaurant, not on lovers' lane. *Lord, I'm no good at this. Show me how to let him know I'd like to find out if we could be more than old college acquaintances.*

The waitress intruded silently, setting in front of them their Greek salads, fragrant of herbed oil-and-vinegar dressing, and their tall glasses of iced tea with generous lemon wedges. Then she left them.

Marco picked up his fork, but merely held it in his hand. "Fun? Are you trying to tell me the garden show meetings are being held for *my* amusement?"

Spring sighed. The girl to her left traced the rim of her soft drink glass and flirted with her eyes. Spring copied the tracing movement, but didn't flirt. She didn't feel up to it now.

"Marco, the ladies have watched you grow up. They are very proud of your success, happy they were able to be of help to you. But their interest in you doesn't stop with your becoming their doctor." *Help me, Lord. Please don't let this sound lame.* "They want to see you happy and…having fun." She left out *happily married,* for obvious reasons.

He stared at her.

She traced the rim of her iced tea glass, then took a sip of lemon tea to moisten her dry mouth. The teenage girl gave a provocative giggle. *Who had taught her how to do that?*

"You have got to be kidding." He looked at her with desperate eyes.

"I'm not kidding."

"Are you sure this is...why I'm on that committee?" She nodded.

He put down his fork. "Why do they care?"

She glanced again into his dark eyes. She knew many men didn't easily comprehend human relationships. Father did, but his job had included counseling so he'd studied human psychology and listened to Mother.

"Because they are good people. They like you."

"But I worked as a caddie at the club. I washed dishes there. I was just a young immigrant boy who qualified for scholarships..."

She straightened. Did he believe that nonsense? Is that how he saw himself? "So you were a caddie. What does that matter? Don't you realize that most of the Golden Sands members are self-made men and women? They succeeded and they wanted you to succeed, too. What's so mysterious about that?"

His intense gaze made her face warm with a blush. "My aunt Geneva was the daughter of a carpenter. She and her husband served in World War II. After the war, her husband took the risk of becoming a contractor and made his money in the postwar building boom. Eleanor is the daughter of immigrants from Russia, and Verna Rae's family were farmers. None of them was born with a silver spoon in her mouth."

Marco turned this new idea over in his mind. The

people at the country club viewed him as...what? Something like a son, a protégé? Was that possible? "I always felt..." He looked to Spring. "I never thought of it that way before."

She nodded. A gold chain glimmered around her ivory neck. Something was different about Spring tonight. Her serenity didn't appear quite as complete as usual. Why wasn't a beautiful and elegant woman like her married by now?

"But what has that and the garden show meetings got to do with having fun?"

She smiled, though her mouth looked stiff, disapproving. "They want you to take time to enjoy your success." She folded her hands like a bridge over her salad. "Aunty says the older one gets, the more one treasures the *intangibles* of life. They won their success with hard work, but they know what success costs. I think the three ladies want you to learn earlier than their own husbands did that all of us should take time—"

"To smell the roses?" he finished for her, his tone terse.

Spring gazed back at him with a serious expression, then tensed, "Well, if you help with the garden show, you certainly will be in a position to do that." She took a bite of a tomato wedge, and eyed him while she chewed.

He squirmed under her regard. "So that means I can't just resign from the committee?"

She took another sip of iced tea. "I have an alternative to suggest."

Her every move was so graceful, it was hard for him to look away. "What?"

"You need to show that you're taking time to have some fun. What hobbies do you have?"

Forking up some of the salad, he considered her question. Spring's beauty distracted him. Swallowing, he shook his head. "No hobbies."

Spring made a face at him. "You caddied. Did you ever play golf?"

He shook his head. "No time."

She sighed loudly. "There's another matter I haven't mentioned, but which the ladies are also concerned about."

"About me?"

"Yes." She skewered a Kalamata olive and popped it into her mouth.

His mouth went dry. "I'm afraid to ask."

She lifted her eyebrows.

"All right." He cleared his throat. "I'll bite. What else am I neglecting?"

"You're not dating."

After dinner, Marco walked with Spring to the parking lot and opened her car door for her.

"It's a bit chilly. Help me with my jacket?" Looking over her shoulder, she handed it to him.

He took it and helped her slide her slender arms into the sleeves. When he pulled it up around her neck, she reached up to adjust the collar and her fingers brushed his. Warmth rushed through him.

She slid inside the car. "Thanks."

Reeling from his reaction to her, he nodded, then walked around and let himself into the driver's seat. All that Spring had said to him seemed to parade in his mind like announcements on one of those lighted marquees you saw on TV: *THE GOLDEN SANDS LADIES THINK YOU WORK TOO MUCH... THEY'VE WATCHED YOU GROW UP AND ARE PROUD OF YOU....THEY THINK YOU SHOULD BE DATING....*

The messages boggled his mind. Spring's nearness had breached his carefully tended defenses, sending disconcerting sensations through him.

"Will you think over my suggestion?" Spring asked.

He tried to focus on her words. "You mean, that I need a hobby?"

"Yes."

"Do you think it will get me off the committee?" He still had a hard time believing what she'd explained.

"If they see that you're having fun—"

"With you?" This suggestion was the most dangerous to his equilibrium. Spring affected him too much. He'd mapped out his life. A woman like her would never be within his reach.

"Well, is there someone else you'd prefer?" She glanced at him in the low light.

Someone else? Anyone else! He kept emotion out of his voice. "No, but no one would believe that you'd be interested in dating someone like me—"

"Someone like you," Spring snapped. "What's wrong with you?"

Her words stung him. "After all you said at dinner, if I didn't know you better, didn't know you are as truthful as the day is long, I'd think you were nuts!"

"If you think that I'm somehow beyond you, you *are* nuts. You seemed to have a really off-kilter way of looking at yourself, Golden Sands and me."

She said he was "nuts." Spring had always spoken so formally. He had to bring her to her senses. She had to face reality. "At the university, you pledged at one of the most exclusive sororities. You weren't on scholarship and working—"

"You've got it all wrong, Marco. My father is a pastor of a small church in Wisconsin. We aren't a wealthy family." Her words surged over him. "Aunt Geneva paid my way through college and insisted I pledge a sorority. She also helped both my sisters with their educations. But since I decided to go to school here, Aunt Geneva helped me more. I told you that you have some funny ideas about my family, about me."

"Maybe I do." *But I doubt it. Your father wouldn't welcome me, an Hispanic immigrant, with open arms. Just because I'm a doctor now doesn't change who I am and who you are. No matter what you say.* That point had been driven home to him on more than one occasion in college.

He pulled up to Mrs. Dorfman's front door.

Spring said in a stiff tone, "Don't get out. I'll see

myself to the door. You said you have an early morning."

She sounded *muy enojado*, very upset. Why? "Spring, I—"

With a wave to Marco, Spring walked to the door and into the house. The man was impossible! Dense! This plan would never work! One of her high heels pinched her toes, but she didn't slow. She closed the door behind her.

The house was only dimly lit, but this didn't fool her. She stifled her frustration. She couldn't dash Matilde's and Aunty's hopes. "Aunt Geneva?"

"We're in your aunt's room," Matilde called out. "Come. We've been waiting!"

Spring walked down the hallway toward the light. The sound from the TV suddenly cut off.

Matilde in a bright turquoise robe met her at the door. "Where did he take you?"

Exhausted from an evening of trying to be different, more desirable than usual, Spring walked past Matilde over to the chair beside Aunty's chaise longue. She collapsed onto it.

Aunty sat up. Her housekeeper hurried after her and perched on the end of the chaise.

Shrugging out of her jacket, Spring sighed. "He took me to a Greek restaurant near the hospital."

"Not to the country club?" Aunty raised her eyebrows.

"Not to the Riviera Restaurant on the Boulevard?" Matilde complained, crestfallen.

"I don't think he considered it a real date, so he just took me to a restaurant he was used to."

Matilde grimaced and shook her head. "The man is *loco*. A beautiful *señorita* like you, he takes to a plain restaurant!"

Aunty studied her intensely. "Do you think you made any progress with him?"

Spring sighed and slipped off the heels. "He's going to be a hard nut to crack. But I think I've got him thinking."

"Thinking? About what?" Matilde demanded.

"About there being more to life than work."

"Well—" Aunty drew in a long breath "—that's a start."

"I'll pray tonight for you, *querida*." Rising, Matilde patted Spring's cheek. "Marco isn't stupid, but you have much to teach him."

Spring nodded. When Matilde closed the door behind her, Spring looked to her great-aunt. "Are you too tired to talk?"

"What is it?"

Spring leaned back against the chair and closed her eyes for a moment, drained but keyed up. "I don't have the energy to pose this gracefully. I've been trying to ask you a very important question since I arrived here over a week ago. The right time never seems to come—"

"What is it?"

"Was your childhood friend, Connie Wilson, my mother's biological parent?"

Chapter Five

Aunt Geneva stared at Spring, openmouthed.

Her heart suddenly thudding, Spring waited for several moments, then she prompted, "Aunty, will you tell me?"

"What…why?" Aunty shook her head. "How?"

"My sisters and I are afraid that Mother might come out of remission—"

"But she's been fine! Why are you worrying?"

"She is now, but she's still tested every three months. Remission isn't the same as cured. Recurrence is always possible."

Aunty looked shocked, unhappy.

Spring reached for her aunt's hand. "We want to be prepared. Not one of us girls was a bone marrow match."

"I was tested, too." Aunty squeezed Spring's hand but looked down.

"Mother didn't tell us that you were tested."

"Of course I was."

Spring leaned closer. "And you didn't match, either?"

Her aunt shook her head as though in pain. "We're not blood relatives, after all. There was only the slimmest possibility of a match."

"Then, you know how helpless we felt." Releasing her aunt, Spring leaned back, feeling her own deep weariness. "We just can't let it drop. If at all possible, we want to locate Mother's natural parents—"

"No!"

"Why are you so adamant?" Spring observed her aunt closely for her reaction. "Why won't you tell me about Connie Wilson?"

Her aunt seemed stricken. "Who is Connie Wilson? Who gave you that name?"

"You did."

Aunty's mouth fell open again. "I never did."

Pursing her lips, Spring nodded. "You did. You showed me a photograph of you and grandmother and a friend—"

"When?" Aunty snapped. "I don't remember that."

Spring went on gently, "I remembered your friend's name, Connie Wilson."

"It's a very common name. I might have had a friend with that name." Aunty stared at her hands.

"But you acted very upset that you'd showed it to me. I couldn't figure out at the time why you were so quick to regret that I saw that photograph of the three of you."

"I don't remember it at all. Besides, who told you a Connie Wilson was Ethel's mother?"

"Your sister—my grandmother—told Father on her deathbed."

Aunty frowned and looked as though she was struggling against tears. "It's not what you think—and you're asking me about events that happened over fifty years ago."

"It doesn't matter how long ago Mother was born and adopted. My sisters and I have decided we must find her natural parents."

"I can't believe that Ethel has agreed to this—"

"She hasn't." Spring rested her head back against the chair.

"You're going against her wishes, behind her back?" Aunty turned pink with agitation.

Spring nodded. "My sisters and I can't stand the thought that she might need a donor and might die because none can be found in time."

"But even if you located— They might not agree to be tested."

"That's right, but at least we'll have done all we can do to help Mother. We won't contact them, just locate them. We'd be ready if her remission ends. Now will you tell me about Connie Wilson?"

Aunt Geneva shook her head. "I'm sorry, dear. You know how much I love your mother. I only had one sister. We were both childless, and she only adopted one child, your mother. There's much about this you don't know—and you're asking me to break a promise I made to my sister fifty years ago. I can't do so without a lot of thought and prayer."

"That's what Father said when we asked him for help, but surely you can understand how difficult this is for my sisters and me."

Spring waited, silently praying for God's will.

Aunty moved her hands in a nervous gesture, then touched her temple as though it pained her. "I'm very tired—"

Accepting this dismissal, Spring rose, kissed her aunt's lined cheek and paused. "Do you know how much I love you?"

With a wan smile, Aunty patted her face. "I love you, too, my dear. Now go to bed. It's been a long day and night."

Spring nodded, and dragged her tired body down the hall to her room. She undressed beside her bed, then donned her pink pajamas and slipped between the crisp sheets. The word *exhaustion* didn't come close to describing how tired she felt. Her body and mind ached with fatigue. She hated the shock she'd just given her dear aunt. *Lord, bless her, my family. Bless Marco and help me know what I'm to do about Mother and about loving him.*

As soon as Spring was fully awake the next morning, she dialed her bedside phone. When the ringing stopped and a familiar voice answered, she said impetuously,

"Hannah, I'm so glad I got you! I don't know what I would have done if you hadn't picked up."

"Spring, you sound upset."

"I am. Last night I asked Aunt Geneva about Connie Wilson—"

"What did she say?" Hannah's voice was eager.

"She bluffed her way through it."

"What do you mean?"

"I dropped the name Connie Wilson on her, and she tried to deny any knowledge without—"

"—actually denying it," Hannah finished. "What are your plans?"

"I'll wait her out. Keep praying."

"I will."

Spring needed help on another front: handling Doree. "And do me a favor. You remember how it feels to be on the front line—"

"I do. Don't worry. I'll relay this to Doree."

"And—"

"And I'll threaten her with dismemberment if she calls to bother you!"

Spring sighed. "I love you, sweet sister."

"Ditto."

"How's Guthrie?"

"I love him so much, my teeth ache!"

Spring laughed out loud and said goodbye. *Lucky Hannah!* She'd found her true love on a church roof.

Wearing a white dress with a *V* neck and puffed sleeves, Paloma sat in the wicker chair in Aunt Geneva's garden. Spring picked up her pastels and began to sketch Paloma's face and form.

"Your choice of dress is excellent," Spring murmured.

"I bought it for her." Matilde sat beside Aunt Geneva and behind Spring. Paloma had spent most of this Saturday helping Matilde clean cupboards in the kitchen and pantry. "I want this portrait to be a surprise for Santos and Anita."

"I'll do my very best," Spring promised. "I hope your parents will be pleased."

Paloma scowled. "Nothing pleases my father."

"Querida," Matilde soothed, "he just wants what's best for your future."

"I got a *B* on a math test, and he acts like it's the end of the world! I'm grounded for a whole week!"

That did seem a bit strong. On the paper, Spring outlined Paloma's shoulders and began carefully sketching in her arms. "The week will be over before you know it," Spring said encouragingly.

Matilde nodded. "You will do better on the next test, and everything will be fine."

Spring smiled at Paloma. "I need you to relax. I know this can be tiring, but you'll do fine."

The young girl relaxed her shoulders and lifted a subdued but smiling face to Spring.

"Perhaps your brother could talk to your father?" Aunt Geneva suggested.

"My half-brother never talks to my father. My father

talks, but Marco never says anything but *sí, no, gracias* and *de nada.*"

"Marco will come around someday," Matilde predicted placidly.

Marco is definitely a stubborn man, Spring agreed silently. *I wonder why he won't talk to his stepfather?*

Three days later, Marco looked as if he were close to being in a coma. On the Golden Sands veranda, the garden show committee was in the midst of its third meeting. Spring tried to look interested, or at least awake. How could she be so bored, yet keyed up at the same time?

Aunty asked, "Well, what is your decision?"

"I don't know," Eleanor exclaimed. "What do you think, Verna Rae?"

Spring couldn't even remember what they were trying to decide. Too many other thoughts kept popping up and distracting her.

Aunty had turned down another retirement home yesterday—the fourth one. *Doesn't Aunty want to move? Did she ask me down to help her or was it just a ruse to get me here for longer than one week? Does she need me more now that she is approaching ninety?* The thought wasn't a new one. She'd always known she'd move back when Aunty needed her. Had that time—?

"Maybe we should ask our male colleague?" Verna Rae drawled. "What do you think, Doctor? Should we take out an ad in the *Suncoaster?*"

Marco's eyes had glazed over. "What?"

Spring couldn't help him now. She'd offered him a way out, but evidently he preferred sitting here through another interminable meeting to trying the alternative. This fact did nothing for her ego. She had to be rock bottom on his list.

Discouraged, she slouched against the back of her chair. Had he counted on his phone rescuing him this time, too?

Trying to ignore Marco was maddening. Because of temperatures in the humid eighties, he'd shed his suit jacket and tie. Didn't the man own anything but suits? His white shirt, unbuttoned at the top, revealed a *V* of strong, tanned neck. The breeze sent tantalizing hints of his lime scent. How could he snare her notice without even trying—especially when she'd tried to catch his and failed miserably?

Spring realized her low spirits had come from so many things, including her mother's illness and her aunt's refusal to tell her about Connie Wilson. But how could she not take Marco's attendance at the garden show meeting as a sign that he'd rather do *anything* than spend time with her? This reflection lodged in her throat like a rock.

All three of the ladies gazed at Marco.

He stared back at them.

He doesn't have a clue. Spring bridled.

"Why don't we take a vote?" he suggested.

Spring wanted to unmask his inattention and ask, *On*

what, Marco? But she shouldn't embarrass him—even if he did find her unappealing.

The vote on buying the ad in the *Suncoaster* passed with unanimous approval, after Marco hesitantly raised his hand to make it so. And the meeting rumbled to an end.

As they all rose to depart, Marco cleared his throat. "Ladies, I'm sorry but I'm going to have to resign from the committee."

Spring held her breath. He'd refused her suggestions. What excuse would he give?

"I'm going to take Spring up on her offer to teach me how to play golf. I've been invited to participate in a March golf tournament, a fund-raiser for our hospital, and I need to prepare for it."

The three ladies beamed at him. Spring felt her lips part in surprise. She was just an amateur golfer herself! Still, a thrill shuddered through her. She tried to ignore it, but a smile lit her face and sparked a rosy glow deep inside her.

"Are you sure you haven't played golf before?" A few days later, Spring stood beside Marco at the club's driving range under a brilliant blue sky. She had dressed with care in white shorts and a blue, cotton-knit top. She had some concern about her appearance today, since Matilde had contributed her bit to Spring's new look. Saying Spring needed to do something more with her hair, Matilde had swept up one side of it with a tortoiseshell clip. A sheaf of blond hair rose over her ear and cascaded temptingly to her shoulder—at least, that's what Aunty had said. "You were a groundskeeper. You must know some golf."

"I know which club to use for which kind of shot. I know how to score. I know some other odds and ends."

His lack of enthusiasm could have been cut with a knife. Spring found this admission fit the peculiar attitude he had about himself and his relation to the country club that he'd revealed on their "date."

"But you never played?"

"I never had a set of clubs." He shrugged, looking away.

So he hadn't had clubs. And had he wanted to play, but feared jeering from the caddies?

Spring gazed at the green lawn in front of them. "Well, you do now—"

"Your aunt didn't need to give me her late husband's gear."

Spring swung her hair back over her shoulder. "It was just gathering dust. He was about your height, so we can use them to get started. You're just borrowing them until you have time to purchase your own—"

"I don't know that I intend to take this up—"

"My point exactly," she cut in. "Now, do you know how to take a proper stance when you address the ball?"

He said in a grim voice, "I know I have to stand in line with the hole and at right angles to the ball."

She ignored his tone and fidgeted with the gold

locket on her neck. When she realized what she was doing, she dropped her nervous hand to her side. "Good. Set your tee and let's see your stance." She stepped back. *You specified golf lessons and you're going to get golf lessons!*

Without comment, Marco bent to set his tee and ball. He selected the one wood from the bag and took his place beside the tee.

Spring eyed him critically, trying to ignore how handsome he looked in navy slacks and crisp white shirt with his cuffs rolled back—though it was not really golf garb. "Stand straight with your shoulders back, head up and arms at your sides."

Marco obeyed.

Her insides stuttered like a damaged CD, but she went on in a calm voice. "Keeping your back and legs straight, push your bottom out, bring your head over the ball."

Marco grunted but followed her instructions.

"Relax your knees." Giving Marco, a man who emanated intelligence and competence, simple directions struck Spring's funny bone. She suppressed a grin.

"Okay, what next?"

Spring had heard men sound happier when getting a parking ticket, but she said calmly, "Let your arms swing freely."

As instructed, he swung his arms—and grumbled more.

"You are now in address position. Now here's your club." She glimpsed an older man who stood a few feet away, watching them. Amusement lit his face. No doubt triggered by a *woman* trying to teach a *man* how to play golf.

Spring tried not to make eye contact with the stranger. She wasn't in the mood for any humorous comments about her teaching Marco. And this man looked like the kind of duffer who had a store of jokes he wished to share. Normally she'd indulge him, but Marco presented enough of a challenge to her patience already.

"Now let's see your grip." Spring motioned toward Marco.

He took the club and placed his hands around it, just so.

To view the grip from all angles, she bent and nudged his wrist slightly. She caught herself just before she slid her hand up the taut, smooth sinew of his arm. She turned her head and bumped noses with him. "Sorry." She blushed.

She cleared her throat. "Good. You must have learned the Vardon grip from watching others. It's the most successful—"

"Can I hit the ball now?" Marco asked in a voice that announced he was clutching the frayed ends of his patience.

Spring suppressed a sigh. She hadn't thought Marco would enjoy being taught by a woman. Marco was Latin, after all. Was this a token of his machismo?

"Go right ahead."

He swung and connected with the ball, which flew across the driving range.

"Not bad. You'll be ready for that golf fund-raiser before you know it." She glanced up at him, a thought occurring to her. "There really is a tournament, isn't there?"

He nodded. "I didn't enter it the past two years, didn't have time." He grimaced. "I can't believe we're here really doing this."

His complaint cut her. "What's the big deal?" Was passing an hour or two with her such torture? "So you spend a couple of hours a week swinging a club and walking in the sunshine—all to prepare for a good cause. Is that an unhealthy way to spend your time, Doctor?"

"No, but I have—"

"Yes, I know you're a *very busy man.*" She shook her head at him. "But even the busiest man needs regular relaxation and exercise. I'm sure you've said that to a patient or two, haven't you?"

His expression told her that she'd "got" him. Without showing any visible satisfaction, she continued, "Now let's try that again."

Ring-ring. Ring-ring. Marco reached for his cell phone. "Hello."

For one moment, Spring glanced at the white, puffy clouds overhead. Had Marco prearranged a call just to get away? But she watched Marco's face draw down into serious lines.

"Yes, I'll come right away. Of course." His tone was laced with concern.

She watched him close the phone.

"I'm sorry I have to leave."

She took a step closer.

"Something's come up. I have to go."

She scanned his face. "You're looking really upset."

"It's nothing." He turned away to slide the shaft of his wood back into the golf bag.

She frowned. Should she press him? If he didn't look so apprehensive, she might guess that he'd grab at any straw to shorten their lesson. But his anxiety felt real.

Her natural inclination was to accept his evasive explanation, but she was trying to break out of her shell and into this man's life. She stood straighter.

"You're not being frank with me. What is it?"

Chapter Six

Marco stared at Spring. The question didn't sound like her at all. "I don't have time—"

"Fine. Let's go."

Did she sound disappointed? Why? Then another thought hit him. "I forgot that I drove you here," he apologized.

"No problem. I'll call a cab."

Her long tawny legs distracting him, he tried to figure out what she really meant. She'd told him she wanted to know why he was leaving, then said she'd just call a cab.

"I should take you home."

"Taking a cab is not a problem."

But it was to him—and though he didn't understand why, he just couldn't leave Spring here. This irritated him. He lifted the golf bag to his shoulder. Careful not to glance at her, he reached for Spring's golf bag, a wheeled version, to push it to the car for her. "I need to stop at the high school first."

"Did something happen to your sister?"

"Why would you ask that?" he asked in a sharper tone than he'd intended.

"I'm sorry, I just thought she might be ill…"

Why did this have to happen now? He'd been handling being close to Spring. He'd kept his mind on golf, ignoring her golden beauty. Pausing for a moment, he ran one hand, then the other, through his dark hair.

"It is about my sister."

She gazed at him as though waiting for him to say more, but his concern made him mute.

"Maybe I could be of help?" She looked up at him.

He directed his gaze skyward, trying to achieve perspective. *I'm making a mountain out of a molehill. It's just a high school scrape.* "Okay. The school called my stepfather, but he couldn't leave work right now. He's dealing with an emergency plumbing job and can't get away. My mother can't be reached."

"Is Paloma ill?"

He frowned. *I wish.* "I have to go to school to talk to the vice-principal. She's been suspended—"

"Paloma? I can't believe it. She's such a sweet girl. Would you like me to come along?"

Thrown by her offer, he started walking toward the parking lot. He couldn't deny that what she'd suggested appealed to him. Paloma, in trouble at school? What could she possibly have done? "Would you…come along?"

"Of course, I will. Paloma must feel awful."

He snorted. "She's going to feel worse when my stepfather gets home." Maybe that's why he didn't feel comfortable going to get his sister. Paloma, now a teenager, had become a puzzle to him.

"We'd better get going," Spring urged. "Paloma needs us."

After a quick drive across town, Marco pushed open the heavy school door for Spring. Inside, the voice of a teacher explaining an algebraic equation drifted from the open door of a classroom. Marco hadn't been to the high school since he graduated. The dusty hallways lined with gray lockers brought back memories, feelings he'd totally forgotten. He hadn't liked them then; he didn't like remembering them now: uncertainty about himself, his ability to be good enough to achieve his goals and an edgy distance from those around him.

Each step gave him a bit more sympathy for his little sister. Did she have any of the same feelings? But she'd been born here. She'd never been a stranger in this country the way he had been.

A shrill bell stunned him, and a roar of voices and pounding of feet exploded in the hallway. The vice-principal's office loomed at the end of the hall. The crush of students bustled around them. Marco drew closer to Spring. He didn't like the way some of the teenage males were gawking at her. He ushered her to the door.

Inside the office, the secretary behind the counter sat at her desk, talking on the phone. A line of dejected students slouched on a row of rigid plastic chairs along the wall. Paloma looked out of place among them. She glanced up and froze.

Spring walked directly over to her and leaned down to murmur in her ear. Spring sparkled in the drab setting like a diamond on faded cloth. He'd had the same feeling when he'd taken her to dinner. His life didn't seem to have the proper "settings" for someone like Spring.

Waiting for the secretary to get off the phone, Marco controlled his frustration while wondering what Spring was saying to his sister. What had Paloma done to get herself suspended?

The secretary hung up and looked to him. "You are?"

"I'm Paloma's brother, Dr. Da Palma."

The secretary glanced over to his sister. "Doctor, please come into the office. The vice-principal will talk to you now."

Marco looked at Spring. She patted Paloma's shoulder, then left her to accompany him. He let her precede him inside.

The gray-haired vice-principal jumped up and came around his desk to shake Marco's and Spring's hands, then seated her in a chair in front of his desk.

Marco didn't like the way the other man's eyes lingered on Spring, especially her legs. Marco made the introductions and sat down.

"What has my sister done?"

The man's gaze still centered on Spring, he began, "She's never been in trouble—"

"I know that," Marco said. "What has she done?"

The vice-principal stared at him. "She talked back to a teacher rudely, but what earned her a suspension was refusing to come to my office when told to do so."

"That doesn't sound like Paloma." Spring leaned toward the desk, her golden hair falling forward on one side. "I know she was upset about a test grade. Did this happen in math class?"

Distracted by the picture Spring presented, Marco forced himself to follow the exchange.

"Yes, yes." The vice-principal nodded. "That sounds like it might be what motivated this incident, but—"

"Low test score or no, Paloma knows she's supposed to obey her teachers." Marco glared at him. The man was ogling Spring. One thing Marco did know about Spring: she didn't like men drooling over her.

As though he realized what Marco was thinking, the man drew himself up and faced Marco. "That's why she's been suspended for one day. She won't be allowed back in school until Friday."

"Will she be allowed to make up work she's missed?" Spring asked.

"Yes, of course."

"Anything else?" Marco stood, ending the meeting.

The vice-principal rose, too. "No. Thank you for coming down. Normally, I wouldn't send a student home with anyone but a parent, but Paloma's father has given permission for me to release Paloma to you."

Relieved to get Spring away, Marco nodded and led

her from the office. At the secretary's motion, Paloma jumped up and joined Spring and him.

After the three of them had stopped at Paloma's crowded locker to get her things, they walked out the school doors into the bright winter sunshine. Marco drew in fresh, chalk-free air.

"What a big deal," Paloma grumbled.

"Your father better never hear you say that!" Marco snapped. "You'll be grounded for the rest of your life."

"I will, anyway!" Paloma yanked open Marco's car door and heaved her heavy schoolbag into the back seat. "A one-day suspension! That teacher just has it in for me!"

Chagrined by his sister's tantrum, Marco opened his mouth, but before he could speak—

Spring opened her arms. "Come here, Paloma."

His sister hesitated, then let Spring enfold her. Paloma began to cry.

He observed Spring's strategy with some surprise. But the contrasting picture of the two of them, one fair and one dark, caught his attention. The urge to put his arms around both of them tugged at his control. He'd always thought Paloma pretty, but seeing her standing next to Spring made him realize how close his sister was to becoming a young woman. It also made him grateful to Spring. She seemed to know exactly what to say.

Spring held his sister and murmured words close to Paloma's ear that Marco couldn't hear. After a few moments, Spring brushed back the dark brown waves around his sister's face. "Now, no more angry words. You made a mistake. You'll make it right and it won't happen again."

"But you don't know my father—"

"Your father loves you and wants what is best for you." Spring placed one of her hands on each side of Paloma's face. "This too shall pass." She smiled. "That's my mother's old saying and it's a true one. Now slide into the back, and we'll drive you home."

Spring's words indebted Marco to her.

Though tears glistened on her face, Paloma obeyed, and Marco opened Spring's door so she could get into the passenger seat. He got in himself and drove away pondering the openhearted way Spring had reached out to Paloma. Evidently he'd made the right decision in bringing Spring along. Her gentle hug had certainly changed his sister's attitude. Personally, he'd felt more like shaking Paloma than hugging her.

His sister's suspension had caught him by surprise. He tried not to think how upset his stepfather would be. Santos wasn't a harsh man, but he was a strict father and he expected a lot from his only daughter.

Marco glanced sideways at Spring. Now he could take Spring back to her world, where she belonged. "I'll drop you at your aunt's home first."

"If that's what you want. I'm fine either way." She rested her slender arm along the open window. Fine freckles like gold dusted its length.

Why did he always have to notice things like that

about her? He turned right, heading for Highway 19, which would take them to Mrs. Dorfman's Gulf shore home. His cell phone rang.

He took it from his pocket, lifted it to his ear. "Hello." His mother's voice answered him. "Your car? Where are you, Mother?" With a sinking sensation, he listened to her tangled explanation. "The school—" Pause. "I'll come right away. No, I insist. The corner of Bayshore and Main."

"I'm sorry, Spring," he apologized, frustration stinging him. "I've got to—"

Spring cut in. "Your mother is waiting at the corner of Bayshore and Main. Did she have car trouble?"

He nodded.

"That's fine. I told you, I'm in no hurry." She lifted her blond hair from her neck. "The day's getting warm."

Ignoring as best he could the lovely pose she presented, he turned left at a green light and headed toward the older section of Gulfview, the one he'd left behind at fourteen when his mother had married Santos.

"I don't like her waiting alone down there—"

"Someone from the halfway house is probably with her," Paloma said. "They take good care of her, or Dad wouldn't let her go."

Marco didn't answer, but drove on. To have Spring beside him and not show his awareness of her was becoming an increasing trial. What a day! First his sister, now his mother's car problems—all the while, Spring beside him, forcing him to deal with the attraction to her he'd thought he conquered.

As soon as he picked up his mother, he'd drop Spring off and head to the hospital. He was glad he didn't have anything serious to deal with this afternoon. *I just need to call and check on Mr. Gardner.*

"Does your mother work at the halfway house?" With both hands, Spring pulled her abundant hair back into a ponytail.

Though aggravated with himself, Marco admired her slender, pale neck.

"Yeah, she volunteers there to teach the women how to sew their own clothes." Paloma obviously had found some bubble gum. Marco smelled the distinctive sweet aroma. A bubble popped behind him.

"What kind of halfway house is it?" Spring dropped her hair and shook her head, letting her fine golden hair settle around her shoulders.

"It's for recovering drug offenders," Marco said, hoping that would put an end to this line of conversation. Why did women always want to know all the details?

Spring said, "I've never been able to accomplish more than just mending. My mother and my sister Doree, though, sew beautifully."

He lifted an eyebrow. *Her mother sews? Why?* Spring always wore the very best—anyone could see that.

Paloma popped another bubble. "You've got a sister?"

"I have two sisters, Hannah and Doree," Spring replied.

"Those are great names. Where'd they get them?" Paloma asked.

"We were all named for women in my father's family."

"Gee, that's how I got stuck with my name."

"There's nothing wrong with your name," Marco said in a low voice.

Paloma began, "Oh, yeah—"

Spring cut in smoothly. "It was my mother's idea. She was fascinated by my father's family Bible that listed all the deaths and births for five generations. She never liked her name—"

"What's her name?" his sister interrupted.

"Ethel."

"That's worse than Paloma!"

Marco let out a slow breath. *All this about a name.*

Spring opened her purse and pulled out a tiny jar. "Paloma's a lovely name. It means 'dove,' doesn't it?"

"Yeah, but what's so great about being named for a bird?"

Spring dipped her little finger into the jar, then applied the finger to her soft-looking lips. "The dove is a special bird. When Christ was baptized by John, the Spirit of God came down from heaven in the form of a dove and it rested on Jesus. And when Noah wanted to know if the waters were receding, he sent out a dove to fly over the land. The dove is a symbol of God's presence. It's a beautiful name."

"Gee, nobody ever told me about it that way. My dad says there has been a Paloma in his family every generation since before America was a country."

Out of the corner of his eye, Marco noticed that whatever Spring had applied to them, her lips looked dewy, thoroughly kissable....

"How wonderful." Spring licked her lips, then pressed them together.

"What does Doree mean?" Paloma watched Spring as though memorizing her every move.

"It means 'golden one.'" Spring capped the tiny jar and slipped it back into her bag. "My other sister is Hannah, 'graceful one.' Both were named for great-grandmothers."

Marco had driven them to what people had twenty years ago called Spanish Town, before political correctness had come in vogue. It was the old downtown of the original city. In spite of urban renewal attempts, a few storefronts remained boarded up.

Spring pointed to a Mexican restaurant ahead. "That looks like a good place to eat."

"That's Mamacita's," Paloma enthused. "It's great! They have the best tacos in town."

Glancing over her shoulder, Spring grinned at the girl. "You sound hungry."

"I am. I missed lunch."

"Well, so did we." Spring touched Marco's arm.

He tightened his resistance to her, but she was sitting so near. She had been calm in the face of his sister's ill temper and now her slender form was so at ease next to him. She casually lifted her hair off her nape with a flip of her wrist. All too aware of her movement, he made himself stare at the road ahead. He was melting inside, and it wasn't because of the temperature.

Spring suggested, "After we pick up your mother, why don't we stop at Mamacita's for lunch?"

"Mamacita's?" Marco echoed. Mamacita's was a great restaurant, but he couldn't imagine Spring enjoying a meal there. He'd been ashamed he'd made the blunder of taking her to the Greek restaurant the other night. He should have thought of someplace special to take her. But he hadn't wanted her to think he assumed it was a date, and in the end, she'd probably concluded he didn't know that she deserved better. Men didn't take a beauty like Spring to just anyplace!

Spring grinned at him. "I'm definitely in the mood for Mexican today."

Her grin made him forget his irritation, but—

Paloma gave a hoot of agreement.

Fighting the effect of Spring's glowing face, Marco shook his head. "That isn't the kind of place you'd like to eat lunch."

"Why not?" Paloma demanded. "Mamacita's is great. They make their own tortillas and their *sopaipillas* are to die for!"

"Then, Mamacita's is *definitely* my kind of place." Spring angled herself on the seat so she faced him— turning her loveliness on him full force.

Marco shored up his resolve, but her effect on him couldn't be blunted.

At the start of the day, he'd been irritated even to

have to spend the morning learning to hit a little ball around to please the garden committee ladies. The brief golf lesson had been all the time in Spring's presence he'd been prepared to handle.

Suffering the temptingly beautiful woman beside him as the day progressed had become a test he didn't want to continue. And he certainly didn't want to involve her in his family problems. Irritation simmered in his stomach. Nothing was going as he'd planned!

He spotted his mother in the block ahead, right in front of the Hacienda Bakery. The wrecker was loading her red economy car onto a flatbed tow truck. Marco parked across the dingy street. "You two can stay—"

Paloma hopped out of the back seat and waved her arm in a sweeping arc. "Hey, Mom, we're here!" Spring smiled as she crossed the street with Paloma.

What is this—a party? Marco brought up the rear. He approached the heavy, bearded man in khaki work clothes. "What was the problem?"

The man shrugged. "Her car just decided to die here. You'll have to ask the mechanic for a diagnosis." The man was holding a clipboard and handed Marco's mother the yellow copy. "I'm ready to take off. Good timing."

Marco's mother thanked the man, who then slid into the cab of the Tomaso's Towing truck and drove away with a grinding of gears and a loud rumbling of the heavy-duty engine.

"Marco, I'm so sorry I had to call you." His mother

looked at Paloma, then her eyes slid to Spring. "And why aren't you in school, Paloma?"

Marco tried to recall if he had ever mentioned his knowing "Matilde's Spring" to his mother. He didn't want her to start matchmaking again. In the past two years, a series of pretty girls had "dropped in" while he was visiting his mother. He was sure they'd been invited.

"It may take some time to sort out." Spring offered her hand. "I'm Spring Kirkland."

Marco grimaced. He couldn't focus his mind. He should have thought to introduce them.

"You're Matilde's Spring? *Ay!* I feel like I know you. Matilde has talked about you since you were a little girl." His mother glanced from him to her, as though trying to read their minds. "Did you two meet at Golden Sands? I didn't know that you knew one another."

Spring smiled. "Marco and I went to the university at the same time. We had a few classes together. I met him again at the country club recently."

"You did?" His mother eyed him.

Marco nodded, hoping his mother wouldn't jump to conclusions. Spring was out of his league, and he knew it.

"Yes, now I'm giving Marco a few golf lessons." Spring chuckled.

"You are?" His mother goggled at him.

"Mom," Paloma interrupted, "Marco's taking us to Mamacita's for lunch."

Marco was steaming inside. He wanted Spring home and himself safely at the hospital checking on Mr. Gardner. "I didn't say that. I don't think Mother wants you rewarded for having been—"

"It's just lunch," Spring cut in with a bright smile. "We have to eat, Marco."

Why had Spring stopped him from telling his mother about Paloma's suspension?

Before Marco could make the three females realize that he would not take them to Mamacita's for a late lunch, the four of them were sitting down at a booth in the back.

"Oh, just smell all those lovely spices, cilantro, cumin, chili pepper. Mmm." Spring beamed. "Did you know my sister is a professional food writer?"

"Cool!" Paloma exclaimed. "What kind of food?"

"Everything. This is just the kind of place she loves. When she takes a road trip, she always stops at cafés like this and get recipes from the local cooks."

Marco sat stiff and uncomfortable. As the day progressed, he'd felt as though control had slipped through his fingers. Like coming to Mamacita's. He'd eaten at this little café so many times, but seeing Spring, so blond, so elegant, across from him made him feel… He couldn't explain it. It just didn't feel right.

"Hey, Marco," Lupe, Mamacita's daughter, greeted him, "long time no see."

He nodded to her.

"You finally bring a woman with you—but did you

have to bring along your mother and sister as *dueñas*." Lupe, a cute-enough brunette in tight jeans, chuckled at her own joke.

Paloma spoke up. "This is Spring Kirkland. Isn't that a great name?"

"Sure is. Hello, Spring, I'm Lupe. What do you want for lunch?"

"What should I order, Marco?" Spring looked to him.

Ignoring the disconcerting effect of her clear blue eyes on him, he shrugged. "Everything's good."

Lupe put one hand on her hip. "Don't sound so enthusiastic, silly man, *tonto*. Why don't you have the combo platter, Spring, since you haven't been here before."

"Fine." Spring handed Lupe her menu. "I'm unusually hungry today."

"The combo will take care of that!" Lupe quickly wrote down the other three orders and left to get their beverages.

"Now I want to know why Paloma is not in school." Mother looked across at her daughter sternly.

Paloma's face fell.

Marco opened his mouth to explain, but halted.

Shaking her head at him, Spring touched Paloma's shoulder. When his sister looked up, Spring nodded, encouraging her.

"Mom, I was suspended from school."

Mother gasped. "What will your father say?"

Paloma looked down at the tabletop.

"He'll say," a man's voice boomed from the doorway behind them, "why are you celebrating at Mamacita's!"

Marco closed his eyes. His stepfather. *The whole family, just what I needed.* Fitting Spring into his life wouldn't work. They were from two different worlds. Today proved that.

Nothing had gone as planned. In his mind, the hospital across town beckoned him like a haven. There he was in charge and completely safe from being tempted by a woman like Spring.

"How did you know we were here?" Mother asked.

"When I didn't find you where you said you were, I stopped at the halfway house. Someone saw you walking here." Santos grabbed a chair from an adjacent table and swung it to the booth. Focused on Paloma, he sat down, looking grim. "Now, daughter, what did you get in trouble for?"

Spring said, "Perhaps you'd like me to leave while you discuss this?"

Santos did a double take, then stood up hastily. "*Pardone.* I didn't see you there, miss."

"I'm—"

Paloma interrupted her. "This is Spring Kirkland, Matilde's Spring."

His face brightened. "Matilde is an old friend. It is an honor to meet you, *señorita.* Matilde has watched you grow up." He shook the hand Spring offered him.

"Spring came to school with Marco and picked me up, Dad," Paloma admitted, holding her chin high.

"I'm very sorry about being suspended. I just lost my cool."

Marco couldn't believe his ears. Where had his defiant sister gone?

"We will discuss this at home." Santos gave Paloma a stern look. "Now! The job I did this morning made me wish I was two men, and I'm hungry enough to eat for both of them."

"Good." Lupe laughed as she came up behind him, grinning. "I put in an order for the *Grande* platter you always order." The waitress set down soft drinks for all of them and moved on to another table.

"I thought this was going to be a dreadful day," his mother said. "Santos had that emergency call. My car broke down. And Paloma had to be picked up from school. But somehow everything looks better at Mamacita's."

"And I got to meet all of you, too," Spring added with a smile.

Marco kept a straight face. He didn't share his mother's sentiments.

After a leisurely lunch, Santos went on to another job, and Marco dropped his mother and sister off at home. He'd wanted to drop Spring at her door first, but his sister needed to be home in time for an after-school baby-sitting job.

He drove, keeping his eyes on the street. In a few moments, he'd have Spring at home and he'd be on his way to the hospital. He felt he was about to round third base and reach home plate at last.

"Well." Spring sighed with satisfaction. "I think we made a good start on golf, in spite of everything." She touched his arm. "Are you really that upset about Paloma getting into a scrape at school?"

His arm tingled at her touch as he tried to think of what to say. What did she want him to say?

"What's wrong? Tell me," she prompted softly.

He glanced into her eyes cautiously. "No. I don't think my sister will do it again."

"Then, what has upset you?"

"Upset?" He frowned.

"You've been on edge all day. What's wrong? Is there something, a patient, on your mind?"

Something on his mind! Spring's nearness for most of a day had worn down his defenses. He longed to lift her hair like spun gold and feel its softness on his fingertips. "Wrong?" he managed to mumble.

"You've been preoccupied. I…I don't know how to describe it exactly. You just haven't been fully with your family, with me today." She gazed at him as though trying to will him to speak.

He struggled against his awareness of her. She smelled of gardenias like the ones his mother grew in her backyard. The scent had taunted him all day. "I just have so much to do and today was wasted—"

"The day wasn't wasted. Your sister needed you and you were there to help her. You ate a meal with your family. I don't get to do that very often anymore, usually just on holidays. Your sister will soon be in college, then married and living in another city or state—before you know it. It was a good day, Marco."

He tried to process her words. "Spring, I—"

His cell phone rang.

Chapter Seven

Marco nearly pitched the phone out the open car window. Groaning inside, he flipped it open by his ear. "Yes!"

"Marco, it's Lupe. I'm here with Aunty, *Tía* Rosita. She is weak and nauseated. She looks awful!"

Tía should be fine. What's changed since the last time I checked on her? "Has she been taking her medication?"

"I asked her that, and she insists she has been taking it, but I know something is wrong. Will you come?"

No, I want to take Spring home! "Yes, I'll come right over." He snapped the phone shut, then dragged his eyes once more toward the dangerously lovely lady beside him. He'd thought his "ordeal" had been about to end. "I'm sorry. It's an emergency. I have to go straight—"

"Of course. Don't mind me. I don't have to be home at any special time."

Trying to shore up his defenses against the alluring Spring, he turned left at the next green light and headed straight back to the old neighborhood where they'd eaten lunch. Lupe had a level head and wouldn't call with a false alarm.

Spring pulled her own cell phone out of her purse. Today had shaped up better than she ever could have planned. Marco had been forced to let her into his life as more than a mere acquaintance. God's hand had been busy all day!

"Hello, Matilde, it's Spring. I won't be home until late. Marco has been called to an emergency and he doesn't have time to drop me home. If he has to stay long, I can always call a cab. Okay. Bye."

"I'll get you home. Don't worry."

Spring glanced at him. Between buildings, she glimpsed the mid-winter sun slipping toward the Gulf of Mexico. Gold and violet streaked the sky. She'd spent the day with Marco and it had been wonderful! If only she could guess what he was thinking…if he was thinking about her.

"You still do house calls? I thought that was a thing of the past."

"This is a special case." He concentrated on his driving through the tourist-clogged traffic, still trying to ignore the fragrance of gardenias that wafted from her.

"How so?"

"This is an old friend of the family." *Tía* had given him, as a ten-year-old, the job of running errands and had paid him with cookies. "*Tía* emigrated from Cuba in the sixties and retired last year at age sixty-five. For some reason, her paperwork has gotten misplaced or hung up on someone's desk in the Social Security system. She should be on medicare, but every time she applies, the computer—"

"Spits her out." Spring folded one lovely leg under her and angled herself toward him.

His self-discipline was getting a workout today! Training his eyes forward again, he nodded, a grim set to his jaw. "Yes, I think that describes it. I've written letters, made calls, submitted forms—"

"But every effort to get her benefits activated fails." She laid her slender arm along the top of the seat, her hand only inches from his shoulder.

"That sums it up." His words were curt.

Why? Was it the heavy traffic? Or was he irritated because he hadn't been able to drop her off and go back to the hospital? She had a feeling his whole life revolved around the hours he spent there. He'd even used a hospital benefit—a golf tournament—to justify taking time to learn golf.

Aunty, Eleanor and Verna Rae were right. Whether Marco and she "connected" romantically or not, he needed to get a life.

He clung doggedly to their conversation. "You sound like you have some experience with this type of government tangle. How?"

"I told you my father is a pastor. When he pastored

a large church in Milwaukee, something like this would pop up occasionally. One time, I remember he spent one solid day in the local Social Security Office trying to get a widow with two small children her survivor benefits." She raked her fingers through her glorious hair.

He clenched his jaw, resolved to get this emergency call over and end this exquisite torture. He turned his thoughts back to what she'd said about her father's efforts. "Did he succeed?"

"Not until he'd spent weeks following up on it— phone call after phone call. Fortunately, our church had some generous members who supported the woman until the benefits finally started."

With relief, he pulled into the alley behind the Hacienda Bakery. *Tía* needed him and he needed to get a time-out from being alone with Spring. "I think you should come in with me."

"I planned to." Spring got out of the car and followed him toward the back staircase.

The unappetizing smells in the alley from the Dumpster made him hurry up the outside wooden staircase behind Spring.

"I've eaten up your day with my family—and now this."

She grinned at him. "You forgot to complain about the time I wasted on your golf lesson."

He shook his head at her. It wasn't only him. Spring hadn't acted like herself all day.

On the top step, Lupe waited. "I apologize if I spoiled your plans. I didn't want to call you. In fact, *Tía* is really upset with me about it. But I came over to check on her before going home for the day, and she just looked *so bad*."

Spring smiled at Lupe. "No problem. We didn't have any definite plans." *That's for sure.*

Focusing on his purpose, Marco ushered them ahead of him into the flat above the bakery where *Tía* had worked for more than thirty-five years. The uncomfortably warm apartment was small and crowded with furniture. *Tía* never parted with anything. How would Spring handle this?

Marco heard *Tía* comforting her cat, Alejandro, and called out, "*Tía*, how do you feel?"

"*Terrible.*"

He grinned to himself. At least *Tía* hadn't lost her spicy tongue. A good sign. Walking into the tiny kitchen, he dropped his small medical bag on the kitchen table. *Tía* sat on a straight chair in a faded pink housedress. Round and full-cheeked, she *looked* like a woman who'd worked in a bakery most of her life.

He touched *Tía*'s forehead. *Warm, flushed and dry—not good.* He pinched the skin on her forehead.

"Don't do that," she scolded.

His pinch of her skin remained "tented" for several seconds before it sank back to normal. *Loss of skin elasticity.* He felt as if he were reading the textbook symptoms of uncontrolled diabetes. But Lupe had said *Tía* insisted she'd been taking her oral medications.

He dug into his bag, then put the blood-pressure cuff around her arm.

"You fuss so much, Marco. I'm just a little run down…"

He frowned as her voice trailed off. Her eyes wandered as if she couldn't focus. *Changes in the level of consciousness,* his mind went on, reciting the list of symptoms. He eyed the blood-pressure gauge: 105/70. *Bad.* He frowned. "*Tía,* have you been taking your pills regularly and testing yourself?"

"Of course, Marco. Who came with you?" The old woman looked past him to where Lupe and Spring stood side by side.

Had *Tía* just noticed Spring? That was a danger signal in itself. *Tía* never missed anything.

Marco unwrapped a sterile lancet and pricked *Tía's* middle finger to do a blood-glucose test. *Glucose running way too high. What had brought this on?* "Lupe, please get me her bottle of pills from the refrigerator."

Lupe handed him the amber plastic bottle of pills.

He studied the date and number of pills listed on the pharmacy label. Today was in the last week of February. The bottle should be almost empty. It was half full. He fumed. Didn't she understand how serious her diabetes was? He held the bottle in front of her face.

"You haven't been taking your pills."

"I have—"

Spring leaned closer. "Perhaps you've only been taking them every other day?"

After gazing at Spring for a moment, *Tía* nodded, looking ready to burst into tears.

Marco's patience cracked. "But you have to take them every day!"

Tía's face twisted with distress. "How can I, Marco? I need heart pills. I need diabetes pills. I have arthritis. I'm good for nothing, and medicare says *Tía* doesn't live here." The old woman jabbed her thumb at herself. "But here I am! So much for government officials. Some of them remind me of ones I left behind in Cuba forty years ago!"

Marco dropped his blood-pressure and blood-glucose kits back into his bag and snapped it shut. "*Tía*, I need to take you to the hospital."

"No, no." Her voice rose shrilly. "I can't pay—"

"If I wait any longer, we'll need to call an ambulance and that will cost even more money!" Marco declared in no uncertain terms.

"Maybe I just wait for the hearse to come for me." *Tía* folded her plump arms over her bulky middle. "Then I won't have to worry about how hard I worked for over thirty years, and now medicare—"

"*Tía*," Lupe began, "don't say—"

Spring stepped to *Tía*'s side and took her hand. "Please come now. You don't want to make the EMTs carry you out. Just think of those steep stairs. I wouldn't want to be carried on a stretcher down them. Do you?"

Tía studied Spring. She sighed. "No, I wouldn't like that."

Spring gently coaxed *Tía* onto her feet.

Tía glanced around. "Have you seen my cat?"

"No, do you want me to look for her?"

"He's a he-cat, Alejandro." *Tía* called the name, but no cat appeared.

"While Marco and I help you down the steps, perhaps Lupe could find Alejandro, turn off your lights and lock up."

"Sure," Lupe agreed.

Tía reached for an oversize black purse on the countertop. "That would be good. Lupe needs to get home and cook for her family."

"Then, we shouldn't keep her," Spring said.

Amazed, Marco listened as Spring charmed the stubborn old woman into agreeing with his orders. He'd never guessed at this side of Spring.

"Should we feed Alejandro?" Spring held *Tía*'s hand in both of hers, as the old woman lumbered through her apartment.

"No, I fed him just before Lupe came." Still, she scanned the room as though looking for something.

"And he has enough water for the evening?" Spring reached over and took down a sweater from a hook beside the door.

The old woman grunted. "*Gracias,* I was looking for that."

Lupe said, "Don't worry. I'll take care of everything."

"*Gracias,* Lupita." As the old woman leaned on Spring, she tottered the last few paces to the door.

Draping the sweater around *Tía*'s wide shoulders, Spring sent Marco a glance, and he hurried forward to open the door for them.

In a gentle voice, Marco cautioned, "Now, we don't have to rush down these steps. You set the pace and I'll follow it. Spring, would you please go down beside *Tía?* Then *Tía* can put one hand on my back, while you support her on one side."

They obeyed him. The three of them connected by their hands made a slow, halting, procession, step by step, down the rickety stairs. The wood creaked with the combined weight of Spring and *Tía* on the same step. Finally at the bottom, Marco unlocked the back seat door, and Spring helped *Tía* sit and swing her legs inside.

Tía heaved a loud sigh. "Marco, you've found yourself a sweet girl." Looking drained, she leaned her bulk back against the seat.

The old woman's words hit a nerve. But now wasn't the time to tell her that her assumption that Spring and he were a couple was wrong. Better for now to just to let her think what she wished.

His patient's deteriorating condition needed all his attention. He didn't like the lack of sweat on her brow.

"I'll sit in the back with her," Spring murmured. She followed him to the other side of the car and climbed in.

This accomplished, Marco drove down the length of the alley and onto busy Main Street. As he drove, he observed in the rearview mirror that Spring was taking *Tía*'s hand. He had never doubted that Spring was a good person, but he'd never imagined she could fit in with people so unlike her. It was a revelation to him.

She held *Tía*'s hand all the way to the hospital. He pulled up at the emergency doors and parked. Spring hopped out of the car without his assistance and met him at *Tía*'s door. With his arms under hers, he helped the old woman out of the back seat and into a wheelchair outside the door.

"Do you want me to help her inside while you park the car, or should I park the car?" Spring asked.

"My reserved space is just around the corner. I'll park and meet you inside." He walked briskly to the car and drove off.

By the time he entered the emergency doors, Spring had already piloted *Tía* to the counter and was speaking to two nurses. One held a clipboard and pen. The other gripped *Tía*'s wrist as she took a pulse.

He hurried to them. "Let's get this patient on an IV drip of 0.45 normal saline. Get me a current weight, and I'll have the insulin order for you in a second—"

The nurse with the clipboard said, "Of course, we'll treat her immediately. But she says she has no insurance or medicare. You know we have to put down some guarantor—"

Spring leaned close to the nurse and whispered just loud enough for the nurse and him to hear, "I'm sure my aunt, Geneva Dorfman, will take care of this."

"Oh." The nurse's eyes widened. "Of course, then."

The other nurse said, "Her pulse is weak and thready." She took the wheelchair over from Spring. "*Señora,* I need to weigh you, then start that IV."

"She looks like she's lost weight to me," Marco observed.

"I don't want to get weighed. I know I'm too heavy," *Tía* grumbled, as the nurse pushed her away in the wheelchair.

Spring turned to him. "Is there anything else I can do?"

He held her upper arms. She'd helped this emergency call go so smoothly. He didn't know how to thank her.

She put one hand on his and nodded. Her tender expression twisted something inside him, and a rush of emotion flowed through him. Suddenly, he wanted to kiss her. He turned abruptly away and went to his patient.

Over the next few minutes, Marco concentrated on treating and stabilizing *Tía* Rosita. Finally, he helped heft her onto a gurney, which would take her up to a room. He walked beside it toward the elevator.

"But, Marco, I don't have any money for this!" *Tía* complained once more.

"Don't worry." Spring trailed along on her other side. "We'll sort this all out in the morning."

The old woman's face crinkled up, ready to cry. "But—"

"*Tía,* you don't have a choice." He started to give her a good scare. "Neither of us wants the alternative. Let's just get you on your feet—"

Spring interrupted him. "Don't you think God is capable of providing for you?" She grasped *Tía*'s hand again. "You must trust in God about this. He loves you and He will see that you are taken care of."

The panic drained away from *Tía*'s expression. "I'm a forgetful old woman." She shook her head. "God has brought me through much."

Spring squeezed the gnarled hand. "Then, don't doubt Him now." She quoted, "'God is able to provide exceedingly beyond what we ask for.' Don't forget that. Now just rest and do what the nurses tell you to. I'll come and visit you in the morning, and tonight I will include you in my prayers."

Tía's face puckered with tears of gratitude. "God bless you, *señorita*."

Marco echoed this silently.

The orderly wheeled the gurney onto the elevator. Stepping inside, Marco took the last bit of room. "Spring, do you mind waiting here? I'll be right down to take you home."

"Of course. *Buenas noches, Tía*." Giving a warm smile, she waved.

About ten minutes later, after clarifying his instructions, Marco found Spring chatting to two nurses near the emergency doors. The nurses looked up at him with peculiar expressions and funny little smiles. What did that mean? Did they think it odd that someone like Spring would be hanging around with him?

Looking unconcerned, Spring rose and wished them

goodbye. With a polite nod to them, he escorted her to his car. "I'll take you home now." Taking her home had been his goal since late morning. Now he could do it, but why was his mood sliding to somber?

She glanced at her watch. "We missed dinner. Why don't we stop at the Greek restaurant again?"

Marco heaved a long breath. He had to get her home before he did something that would betray his interest in her. She'd been so caring, so wonderful today, his feelings for her had grown way beyond what was appropriate. "Don't take this the wrong way, but I'm just too stressed to sit in a restaurant."

His reply daunted Spring. She'd felt them drawing nearer to each other, and his words made her feel as if she'd been pushed away. Forcing herself not to slip back inside her shell, Spring considered how Doree or even Hannah would handle this. She stiffened her resolve and suggested, "Why don't we go to your place and order in?"

Entering Marco's town house, Spring looked around at the stark interior. *It's nearly empty!*

He must have read her mind because he explained, "I haven't had the time…or the inclination to decorate."

Her mother always said single men only "camp out" in a place. It took a woman to make a home. Spring said with a positive lilt, "You have a good amount of space to work with."

Scanning the layout of the first floor with its narrow entry hall, great room and small eat-in kitchen, she tried to imagine it with furniture. She walked to a lawn chair that sat facing out the sliding glass doors to the darkened backyard. "I should come over and place some pots of flowers around the patio for you. At least you'd have something cheerful to look at when you got home at night."

Marco didn't know how to reply. He'd never brought anyone to his apartment. How had she gotten him to bring her here? The answer came to him, but wasn't what he wanted to hear. After spending all day and into the evening with her, he'd been loath to take her home. Spring's cheerful presence exerted a power over him that had grown and strengthened, just as he had feared. Her sensitivity had been so helpful, so un-anticipated. She even made his forlorn town house look better, just standing in it. He no longer wanted to take her home.

"*Tía* will be all right, won't she?"

Grateful for this safe subject, he nodded. "She should be. She'll have to be in the hospital a few days, so I can get her blood-sugar levels stabilized. How did you guess she had been taking only one pill every other day."

Spring sighed. "It's the kind of thing people of her generation do. They don't understand how not taking medicine correctly will affect their medical condition, and they think they will save money. But in *Tía*'s situation, she had an understandable motive—her frustration over her medicare glitch."

She moved closer to the sliding glass doors, gazing out at the pools of light illuminating the path between the town houses. He couldn't take his eyes from her.

She glanced back at him and smiled. "But my father had to deal with older parishioners, some who had plenty of money and medicare, and they still couldn't bring themselves to spend the co-payment for their medication. Father explained to me that it wasn't just surviving the Depression."

"What is it, then?" he asked.

"The seniors of today were raised at a time when doctors had few effective drugs available. I mean, sixty years ago penicillin was just in its infancy. In our grandparents' youth, medicine was more of an art than a science. It's our generation that expects medical miracles and sues if we don't get them!"

"I'd never thought of it that way." And it was true. Her explanation made some frustrating conversations he'd had with older patients comprehensible.

She grinned at him. "I'm hungry. What should we order?"

Shouldn't he suggest they go to a decent restaurant, after all? It was so hard to figure out how to handle this newly discovered Spring. "What do you want?"

"I've been longing for pizza!" She spun around and faced him. "My aunt's only failing is that she doesn't like pizza. Again, ordering pizza wasn't an option when Aunty was growing up."

"Pizza, it is, then. How about Antonio's on Canal

Street?" He opened the *Yellow Pages.* "What do you like on your pizza?" This seemed a surreal conversation. Ordering pizza with Spring Kirkland in his unfurnished town house. What did she think of that?

"What do you prefer?"

"The works," he said firmly.

"Just the way I like it, too. " She lowered herself gracefully into one of the lawn chairs.

Sitting down on a nearby lawn chair, he handed her the phone and let her give the order. He felt himself grinning but couldn't stop himself.

When she was done, she smiled back at him.

He swallowed a huge, dry lump in his throat.

Spring ran her fingers lightly through her hair. "We've had quite a busy day."

To say the least! He wondered if her hair would feel as soft as he imagined. "I'm sorry to take up your—"

"I didn't mind. I needed a day away from Matilde and Aunty. I love them both, but having two mother hens clucking around me all day for several weeks…" She gave an exaggerated shrug.

"Well, you'll be going home soon, won't you?" The words clouded his mood and rang an alarm inside him. *Spring is only here on a visit. Get used to it.*

"I don't know." She frowned. "I know you're not supposed to give out information about patients." She glanced at him. "But I'm concerned for my aunt. How serious is her condition?"

Rising, he turned his gaze to the night, which had

closed in around them. "You're right. I can't tell you that unless she's given you medical power of attorney."

She nodded. "I won't press you, then."

"Why did you say your aunt would take care of *Tía*'s medical care?"

She looked surprised, as though he shouldn't have to ask this. "She's done that on and off over the years, both here and up north. Often, my father or mother would call her and she would send a check to our church benevolence fund, which would then pay for needed medical attention for some person without insurance."

"I never knew." Though he should have guessed. After all, the generosity of the members of Golden Sands had benefited him. It was a debt of honor he'd never be able to repay.

"Oh, Aunt Geneva has a big heart. You know she paid for all my operations."

"Operations?" This startled him, and he turned to her.

"Yes, I was born with a clubfoot." She motioned toward her trim ankles. "Aunty paid for all the operations so I could walk. I forget how many surgeries I had before I was five. But it took many years before I was able to walk into a hospital without experiencing real panic."

He tried to process this. He'd never thought of Spring as a person born with a serious handicap. It didn't fit her. "Your parents didn't have health insurance?"

"Of course, they had some, but my operations were so costly we had to have help. I told you that you didn't really understand my family. The fact Aunt Geneva is wealthy has nothing to do with the rest of us."

He took a step closer as he tried to adjust his thinking.

She moved toward him. "Then, just when I got done with all my operations, I came down with asthma. Since I have the type of asthma that is worse in cold weather, I spent several winters here with Aunt Geneva and Uncle Howie. Fortunately, I outgrew it, but that's why Aunt Geneva and I are so close. She has been a second grandmother to me. And, of course, Matilde is like an aunt to me."

Her nearness worked on him like mesmerism. "So your family isn't wealthy?"

She chuckled. "You're a slow learner, Doctor. Now do you understand the kind of family I came from? It probably isn't very much different from your family."

This he did not believe, but he didn't say so. The fragrance of gardenias drew him to her. She glowed like burnished copper in the low light. He couldn't stop himself. He took another step closer to her.

"Isn't there a free clinic here?"

Spring's out-of-the-blue question rendered him speechless.

"Is something wrong?" She leaned nearer.

"Why would you ask that?" He had trouble getting the words out.

"Because after what happened with *Tía* Rosita tonight, I think there should be one. Would you talk to some other doctors about starting one? Often if several health-care professionals band together in an area, they can get one off the ground. It has a positive effect on a community."

Her question had sliced his chest open and bared his heart. He could barely speak. "That's been my dream."

She stood right next to him. He stared at her rich golden-brown lashes. She was close enough to kiss. He tilted his head.

She gazed at him. "Really?"

The pizza delivery boy chose that moment to knock on the door. Marco turned, putting aside the chaos Spring's nearness and her innocent question had unleashed. A few minutes passed while the transaction— money exchanged for pizza and soft drinks—took place.

"Mmm. This smells delicious. I've been so hungry today! Usually I have very little appetite." Spring surprised him by carrying the pizza out onto the patio. "Bring out the chairs. Let's eat *al fresco.*"

Still bemused by her presence, he carried out the chairs, and they sat down in the dim light and popped open their soda cans. Spring lifted a huge slice of pizza loaded with everything on it, smiled at him, then took her first bite.

Entranced, he followed suit. The pizza woke his empty stomach with a jolt—just as Spring had charmed his stressful day. *Spring, you are more wonderful than I knew or ever guessed.* He couldn't say anything at first. He could only chew and gaze at the beautiful and sensitive woman in the shadows beside him.

She lowered her slice of pizza. "So tell me about your dream."

Chapter Eight

With the first tangy bite of pizza on his tongue, Marco froze. How could he answer her? He'd only shared this with his mother…and God.

"You don't have to tell me. I didn't mean to pry."

Her sensitive apology pulled the linchpin that had held back his voice. "When I got the chance to buy Dr. Johnson's practice, I realized that I would be in a position to be of service to my community sooner than if I'd had to slowly build my own practice."

She nodded. Marco let the balmy evening wrap itself around them. It was easy to imagine them far away from others on a twilight island. A very pleasant sensation. Her flaxen hair caught the lamplight and glowed like a halo. A dribble of tomato sauce decorated the corner of her mouth.

The sight made her more endearing than he'd

thought possible. He couldn't help himself. He reached over and dabbed it away with his napkin.

Grinning, she submitted. "Thanks. Go on. Please."

"Well, *Tía* Rosita is only one of many people who need short-term medical care—"

"People who slip between the cracks?"

Her encouragement urged him on. "Yes, people who've lost their jobs, people who've just immigrated, people whose paperwork gets lost by medicaid or medicare—"

"Exactly." She finished her slice. "What have you done so far?"

Sated by the tasty pizza, he wiped his face and hands. Her matter-of-fact attitude made it much easier to bring this subject so close to his heart out into the open. "I've been looking around for a site."

"In the old downtown?"

He glanced at her. "Right." How had she guessed that?

Nodding, she supplied the answer to his unspoken question. "Real estate's cheaper and the location's accessible to more prospective patients and public transportation."

Her incisive comments once more caught him by surprise. "That's true."

"Did you find a place?"

Her unexpected interest in his dream and her nearness made him vibrate inside like a plucked guitar string. He leaned forward in the low light, wanting to see the excitement on her face more clearly. "Yes, there's a vacant church on Van Buren."

She shook her head and rested her back against the chair. "I always hate to see a congregation move out of its building."

In the duskiness, her white shorts and her long pale legs reflected the scant light. She took on an ethereal quality, like a fairy princess. The effect made his mouth dry.

"They outgrew their facility."

"Then, they should have planted another church in another neighborhood and helped it get off the ground. Then this community would have two churches instead of one and one empty building." She shook her head in disapproval. "But parishioners move out of the original neighborhood. The neighborhood itself changes...."

The common excuse for moving away from people deemed "undesirable" hit him smack between the eyes. Jolted back to reality, he gave a harsh laugh. "Changes. You mean the residents become undesirable."

"Unfortunately, that's often the case." Spring sat up and leaned forward, too, her elbows resting on the plastic chair arms. "But it's often hard for people to look past surface differences—and if there's a language barrier, the gulf can be hard to bridge. And when property values drop, it brings crime."

He brushed these excuses aside. "Let's face it. There are just different kinds of people. New immigrants have always been shunned in America." He couldn't keep the bitterness from his voice.

Looking wounded, Spring bowed her head as though

praying. She looked up. "Some of what you say is true. But I think you're judging people by your preconceptions rather than by reality. You shouldn't give in to prejudice."

He gasped. He couldn't believe his ears. "Prejudice! Me?"

She nodded. "Perhaps you've been wounded in the past by some people who lack understanding and love for others."

"Sheesh. You *are* a pastor's daughter." How could she ignore all the people who looked down on anyone with darker skin or an accent?

She frowned. "What do you mean?"

Marco scowled. "I mean..." What did he mean? Could he tell her he thought her idealistic, completely unrealistic? How could he?

After a few weighty moments of heavy silence passed, Spring looked into his eyes. Laughter from a distant patio contrasted with her serious expression. "So how are you going to pay for the church?"

He broke eye contact. "I don't know. I've been trying to figure out how to come up with the down payment."

"Yourself?" She made it sound as if he'd said something ridiculous. "That doesn't make sense."

Almost offended by her sharp tone, he raised his eyebrows at her. "What do you mean?"

"You can't do a project like this all by yourself. Even if you could raise a down payment by yourself, how would you come up with the monthly payments or pay for improvements?"

She'd brought up the questions he'd most wanted to avoid. "I wasn't planning on doing it all by myself. I thought I might interest another doctor or two. I've been praying about that."

She leaned closer with a coaxing smile. "Then, it's time to step out and expect God to do wonders. Definitely, a few more doctors would help, but you need other—"

Marco shook his head. "I don't want to be one of those people who goes around with his hand out—"

She grimaced. "Then, you might as well put the idea away for many, many years. You may finally make enough money to do this all alone or with another doctor. But it could take twenty years or more."

"What do you suggest?"

Stretching her arms overhead as though tired, she smiled at him. "So glad you asked. You don't realize that you're talking to a professional fund-raiser."

She wasn't making sense. "You work at the Botanical Gardens!"

Lowering her arms, she pointed to herself. "I'm the community relations director. My job is to bring the public to the gardens, and that often includes raising money for different exhibits. I'm just the lady you were looking for."

"I don't see—"

She held up both hands, halting him. "That's because you don't have a plan."

"A plan?"

"Before you can go about raising money, you must

have a plan." She began ticking off on her fingers, one by one. "A plan that shows your goals, the good you intend to do, how much is needed and your methods to achieve the clinic."

He stared at her, speechless. How could he put this special, secret dream onto a chart for everyone to see?

She smiled back at him. "After you draw up your plan, you need to get in touch with prospective donors. It's quite easy, you see."

He didn't see. He regretted exposing his deep aspirations to her. How could he just open up to strangers the way she expected?

"Oh! I just had a wonderful idea. I know where we can start looking for contributors." Before he could stop her, she jumped up and hurried back inside. Returning within minutes, she was talking into her cell phone. "That's wonderful, Mimi. I can't wait. Great!" She hung up and clapped her hands. "We're in luck."

"Luck?"

"Yes, our university's annual spring alumni cruise has had a last-minute cancellation. There's a cabin open for you!"

Late, after his office hours the next afternoon, Marco walked into his mother's fragrant kitchen. *"Buenas tardes, Mama."*

She stood by the stove stirring a pot, the contents of which filled the air with the fragrance of chili pepper. "Marco, *hola*. What brings you by?"

He leaned against the worn countertop and tried to think of an answer. Spring Kirkland and her outrageous proposal popped up immediately. He couldn't believe he'd uncovered his dream to her. And now a cruise— she wanted him to reveal himself to people who'd shunned him in college. Never! Shaking his head, he glanced into the dinette.

"How's Paloma?"

"She's in her room studying until Santos comes home."

"Is that her penalty for being suspended?" Marco had been concerned about this, hoping Santos wouldn't pre- cipitate another crisis with a harsher punishment.

"She's grounded for another week—except for her Saturday job." She spooned up a bit of bean mixture, then blew on it to cool it before tasting.

The mention of the job tightened his nerves. "Why is Paloma working? If she needs help for college, I'll—"

"Son, Santos's business is doing well." She shook more salt into the pot. "We are well able to pay for her education."

"Then, why is she being sent out to work as a domestic?"

"Marco!" his mother scolded. "Work is good. What is the shame in helping Matilde by doing the heavier jobs? Matilde is nearly sixty now."

When he made no reply, she continued, "I'm sorry you had to work as hard as you did, but you chose to go into medicine. That's much more expensive than just a four-year degree. And Santos was just establishing his business. Otherwise, when you were in college, we'd have helped you more."

Marco felt his jaw clench. "My education wasn't Santos's responsibility."

His mother made a sound of irritation. "After all this time, you still haven't accepted Santos. Why? He's a good man. He cares about you."

Every word she said rang true, but he couldn't change his feelings. They'd solidified too many years ago. When he thought of his stepfather, his heart always felt laden, rock hard. "I have no argument with your husband. He's just not my father."

"He's your stepfather. Without him, I'd still be living in Spanish Town. He's always tried to make you feel a part of this family, but you always hold back. Why?"

His mother turned her heated gaze upon him, and he felt the full impact of her words. But he still couldn't put his response to his stepfather into words. Why did it matter to her? He'd never been rude or disobedient to her husband.

Marco pushed himself away from the counter. "I'll be off then."

"No!" She pointed her ladle at him. "I'm not letting you do that anymore—walk out when the conversation doesn't go the way you want it."

His lips parted in surprise, he stared at her.

"Now, you came here to talk to me about something

and you're not leaving until I hear what it is. And you're staying for dinner. No argument."

He lifted his eyes to the ceiling. First Spring. Now his mother. Thoroughly disgruntled with the women in his life, he considered leaving, anyway.

"I'm making rice, too," his mother coaxed.

Black beans and rice, his favorite. He grinned even though he didn't want to. Glancing at his mother, he took a deep breath. "Spring wants me to go on the alumni cruise with her next weekend."

His mother's mouth dropped open. "Marco!"

"You've given me my answer." He folded his arms. "It's ridiculous." He should feel relieved, but his mood only darkened more.

"A cruise. How wonderful!" His mother clasped both hands around the ladle handle. "At last, you're going to take time for yourself. And Spring—such a lovely girl and so sweet! She's wonderful!"

"This isn't what you think!" he cautioned, even as Spring's face came up vividly in his mind. "I was afraid you'd jump to the wrong conclusion." His frustration mounted. "I'm just not in her league—"

"Nonsense! You're a successful doctor with a fine practice, and I could see how her eyes lingered on you. She likes you. With just a little encouragement—"

His mother's reaction made him more than a little desperate. His heartbeat became magnified throughout his body. He couldn't let anyone know that he wanted Spring even though he was doomed to never attain her.

"No! Mother, I don't have time for romance, and Spring Kirkland isn't interested in me, never will be."

His mother pursed her lips and frowned at him. "Then, why did she invite you to go on the cruise with her?"

"It's not like that. This is business." *Just business.*

"What business?" She perched both hands on her hips.

"You know the church on Van Buren I've been looking at as a possible site for my clinic?"

"*Sí.*" She turned back to the pot and stirred it.

"Spring says that I need a plan for the free clinic and I need backers. She says I can get backers on the cruise. You know, from fellow alumni."

His mother looked impressed. "That girl has a head on her shoulders. She's not just a lovely face." She nodded decisively.

He'd tried not to think of Spring just in terms of her physical beauty. *She's so much more.*

"So when do you leave?" Mother smiled at him.

"What?"

"When's the cruise?"

"I haven't agreed to go." Marco backpedaled. "It would be a huge waste of time. And an alumni cruise…it's not my kind of thing."

"Why not? Alumni means people who graduated from the same school, doesn't it? So that means you'd belong. I think a cruise would be a good thing for you to try."

I never belonged. He tried again. "But I never went in for social stuff like that at school. Spring was in a sorority." He remembered grimly the faces, the names of a few guys she'd dated. None of them had been worthy of her. "She'll want to be with her friends. I'd just be in the way."

His mother turned to face him again. "Sometimes I could just shake you." The dripping ladle waved in front of his nose. "When are you going to realize you need to get away from that hospital!"

The sound of his stepfather's car pulling into the carport made them both turn to the outside window.

"I'll be going—"

"No, you won't!" Mother grabbed his arm and waggled her ladle at him again. "You're staying for dinner and you're going to carry on a conversation with your stepfather…or…or else!"

After enjoying black beans and rice and helping Paloma with her algebra, Marco went to the hospital. He strode up the comforting, familiar hallway; all the clinical scents and sounds soothed his ruffled nerves. He wanted to check on *Tía* Rosita before going home for the night. Her glucose level still concerned him. He needed to be sure she would be able to go home tomorrow as he'd promised.

Laughter came from *Tía*'s room. *Spring's laughter.* He froze just inside the door, shock waves radiating through him.

"Marco!" *Tía* exclaimed. "Your lady friend came to see how I am!"

Lovely in a stylish blue dress, Spring turned to him. Her gaze measured him.

His pulse throbbed in his ears. He could almost hear her asking, what had he decided? He'd have to say no and make it stick. What was dearest to him couldn't be put on display before people who wouldn't understand.

Walking directly to his patient, he pasted a smile on his face. He lifted *Tía* Rosita's chart and read the latest notes made by the nurse on duty. *Tía*'s blood-sugar numbers had stabilized. His smile became genuine.

"Everything looks excellent. You'll be home tomorrow."

"*Gracias,* Jesus." The old woman pressed her hands together.

Spring beamed. "Praise the Lord."

Tía patted Spring's hand. "This sweet girl has been telling me that you're going to go on a cruise—"

"I just said we might go on the cruise," Spring interrupted.

Marco cleared his throat, his stomach a simmering pot. He would put a stop to this right now. "I'm not going to be able to get away—"

"You must go!" *Tía* insisted. "You take no time for fun."

Marco had had enough. Didn't anybody understand? He hadn't chosen a "fun" career. People's lives depended on him. He couldn't just run off to have a good time!

Spring touched his arm, sensitizing him to her even more. "Marco, don't take *Tía* Rosita in the wrong way. You take good care of your patients. You help your sister." She smiled at him. It melted his aggravation. Did she know her power over him? "*Tía* just wants you to have a good time."

"That's right," the plump silver-haired grandmother agreed. "Now, Marco, you walk this pretty *señorita* to her car. I told her she shouldn't be out alone after dark. It's not safe."

The ploy smacked of matchmaking, but what could he say? He bid his patient good-night. As Spring strolled at his side to the elevator, he became aware of two things. First, every nurse turned to watch them; second, he had to fight the urge to take her hand.

Spring entered the elevator first. He followed, then faced their "audience." At his frown, all the nurses suddenly looked busy.

When the elevator doors closed, Spring looked down at herself. "Do I have a button open or a stain I didn't notice?"

He ground his teeth. "No, they just have never seen me with a woman before."

Obviously disconcerted, Spring stared at him while the elevator dropped level by level. "I'm sorry. I didn't come to embarrass you. I didn't know you were coming up this evening. I just wanted to visit—"

"It's all right. It's not your fault." He stifled his anger. If anyone was guiltless in this cosmic matchmaking, Spring was. She wasn't the kind of woman who pursued men.

The double doors opened. Spring stepped out. Walking beside her, breathing in her light floral perfume, he followed her to the exit. Their progress again elicited staff attention, not even faintly discreet.

Moments later, once more, they stood together beside her car in the dark, summer-like February evening.

Spring looked up at him. How she longed to rest her cheek against him and feel his arms close around her. But first she had to make that possible. Even as she fought her own reticence, she had to chip away his defenses, too. Now she had to shake him out of his rut and into her life, or at least try.

"Have you made your decision?"

"I don't—"

"Please." She halted him by grasping his forearm. Her stomach did a somersault at her own forwardness, but she continued, "I'm not asking you to marry me. I just want you to go on a cruise to see if we can manage to raise funds for a free clinic I know you want. Why are you hesitating? Is it me?"

Chapter Nine

The balmy night closed softly around them as it had on his patio. Spring's heart lodged in her throat while she awaited his reply. Pressing him about the cruise... Had she pushed him too hard? Would he withdraw completely, destroying her new, tenuous link to his life? Spending the day with his family, then the evening on his patio, had drawn her rampant emotions so much closer to the surface. She'd suppressed her feelings for this proud man for so long. She was playing with fire. She could win him or lose any chance with him at all. In spite of the warm breeze, she shivered with uncertainty.

"My hesitance has nothing to do with you."

His tone begrudged her every syllable.

Praying that her voice wouldn't shake, she went on. "I'm just trying to help. A free clinic would do so much for the downtown, help so many people."

He bowed his head as though praying or searching

for words. A dove in the live oak near the entrance cooed, unseen.

She waited, silently beseeching heaven. *God, please let him break out of his reserve. Help him see what needs to be done. Let me encourage him, not just because I want to work beside him, not just because I love him, but because together we might do Your work. You are the Great Healer. Please….*

"I think your offer of help is sincere and I do accept that I need backers if this project is going to get off the ground, but…" Again he measured out each word as if it were fine gold dust.

She went on praying. One car then another drove past, looking for parking places. A blaring siren shook the quiet as an ambulance careened up to the emergency doors.

Glancing toward the hospital, he sucked in breath. "I have never gone in for social occasions. You know that—"

"I didn't, either, until Aunt Geneva insisted I pledge a sorority." Did he still see her as so different from him? She wished she could take his broad shoulders into her hands and shake him out of all his preconceptions. The thought of holding Marco worked its way through her like the warm Gulf breeze that fluttered the short tendrils around her face. She pushed them back.

"Your aunt insisted? You mean, you didn't want to?"

She shook her head. In the face of all the complexity of human beings, he'd neatly labeled everyone and put them in the slots he'd created. Didn't he see how ridiculous that was? "No, I was petrified during Rush Week. I didn't want to join something that felt out of character for me, but I didn't want to disappoint Aunty, either. Anyway, I thought no sorority would want me. I was shocked when the Deltas pledged me."

He firmed his jaw as he gazed at her.

His classic profile, cast in shadows from the street lamps high above them, filled her with longing. Why couldn't this be simpler? Why couldn't she just say, "I think I love you"? *Someday I will.*

She swallowed to moisten her dry mouth. "A few of the girls were stuck on themselves. Every group has some of those. But after attending several of the functions, I realized that some were in the same situation I was. Their mothers or grandmothers had been Deltas, and they had been pushed to pledge, too. As soon as I found that out, I relaxed and started making friends."

He nodded.

She wished she could tell what he was thinking, but his handsome face resembled a portrait of a bold and determined *conquistador,* a man accustomed to conquering city after city. She hadn't chosen the easiest man to fall in love with. Taking a deep breath, she ventured into another sensitive point. "I've been thinking that you haven't attended any alumni activities, have you?"

He shook his head.

She pursed her lips. "You haven't seen how people

change. You shouldn't think of the other alumni as
college students anymore. Just as you have changed,
matured, so have the people you don't think you'll fit
in with. Things that might have mattered then, don't
now. We're all nearly a decade older than we were in
college."

"I hadn't thought of that." His reply sounded more
natural.

Her inner pressure eased a bit more. "I think you'll
be surprised at what a mellow group some of us have
become. I still keep in close touch with four Deltas. I
know their husbands, too. Some went to school with us.
Some didn't. They'll all be on the cruise, and I'm
looking forward to relaxing and having fun with them."

"Won't you regret having to do fund-raising, then?"
He stretched his lean body back against her aunt's car.

"I have become accustomed to it. And talking with
friends and acquaintances will make it easier. Maybe
you don't realize it, but you and I are *known* quantities.
Since we're all Florida U alumni, we'll have a common
connection with them or their spouses. We just have to
get the ball rolling, and our project will be a topic of
discussion during the tour."

Saying her plans out loud reassured her, and she
hoped it would do the same for Marco. *I'm not a silly
coed, Marco!* She scolded herself. *I can't help it if
you're the one who makes me feel so unsure.*

She continued, "I don't plan on doing any hard
selling, if you know what I mean. We'll just circulate

and, when an opportunity presents itself, you and I will introduce the topic of a free clinic. It will sell itself."

"Do you think so?" He stared at her.

She blushed warm under his scrutiny. "I wouldn't mislead you, Marco. And we need to let the alumni committee know you want that cabin they're holding for you, or it might go to someone else."

He took a big breath. "All right. If you think the clinic will sell itself, we have to try it."

Bottling up her joy, she suppressed the desire to fling her arms around his neck. She merely smiled and nodded. "You might even have a good time."

He grimaced. *That would take a miracle, Spring.*

When Spring walked in the door, Aunt Geneva and Matilde lay in wait for her. "*Tía* Rosita called," Matilde started first. "She said you were in her hospital room when Marco came."

With a gleam in her eyes, Aunty took up the thread. "She said you two left together."

Spring gave them a half frown, half smile. How did *Tía* and Matilde know each other? "You two are like the CIA. You have your contacts everywhere!"

"Tell us!" Matilde urged. "Did you persuade him?"

Spring nodded. "I have to call—"

Matilde began singing "La Cucaracha" and doing what must have been the rumba. Not to be outdone, Aunty joined in.

"You two!" Spring laughed, but she was caught in

crosscurrents of elation and anxiety. Would it be as easy as she'd led Marco to believe? Would he really feel more comfortable now than he had in college? Would she be able to help him raise money for the clinic? Would she and Marco have a chance to draw even closer while away from their everyday lives?

The phone rang.

Spring picked up the one in the hall. Her mother's voice took her by surprise. "H-hello," Spring stuttered.

"Did I startle you?" Mother asked.

"Yes." A worry niggled its way into Spring's mind. "Is everything all right?" She really meant, *Are you all right?*

"Everything's fine at this end. I just wanted to ask Aunt Geneva if she was up to another guest."

"You'll have to talk to her." Spring frowned. "Is Doree wanting to come down for spring break?"

"I don't know about that, but I do know *I* need a break from snow!"

Spring smiled then. She'd dreaded Doree popping up here, badgering her in person. She'd talk to Aunt Geneva about Connie Wilson again after the cruise. Maybe this time Aunty would give them something to go on. "I know what you mean. Here, I'll hand the phone to Aunty." She did so, after murmuring to her aunt that it was Mother.

Matilde nodded and rumba-ed away toward her room off the kitchen. With a grin, Spring walked down the long hallway to her own room. She wondered why Mother had decided to come for a visit. Was she feeling well or not? And would this make it harder or easier to get Aunt Geneva to open up about Mother's natural parents? When Spring thought about her mother's leukemia, the familiar ache tugged at her heart.

Marco couldn't believe what he was doing. He held the door open for Spring and followed her into Scott's Shop for Men. He'd never shopped anywhere but department stores at the mall. Why had he let his mother talk him into asking Spring for help choosing clothes for the cruise?

But he'd come home and found his mother going through his bedroom closet, exclaiming that he had almost nothing but suits. He'd given her a key to his town house just in case she ever needed it, but she'd never used it before!

After scolding him for not furnishing his town house aside from the bedroom, she'd proceeded to tell him that he had to go shopping before he went on the cruise. His resistance had been futile. Then she'd talked him into calling Spring and arranging a shopping "date" for the next day after his office hours. What was going on? He felt as if he'd been sucked under by a relentless undertow.

Still bemused a day later, he trailed after Spring over the luxurious maroon carpet between the neat racks of slacks and shirts. He noticed her slender spine. The subtle sway to her walk made it difficult for him to draw breath. A well-dressed silver-haired salesman greeted them.

Marco didn't appreciate the man's appreciative glance at Spring. *Behave yourself, abuelo.*

Spring informed the salesman, "We're going on a weekend cruise, and Marco needs swimming trunks, a few tank tops, matching shorts, a few sport shirts and slacks."

Disgruntled, Marco listened to Spring as though she were talking about someone else.

"What is the gentleman's size?" the salesman asked.

Spring turned to him.

Marco gave his sizes, and before he knew what was happening he was in the fitting room staring at the full-length mirror. *Why am I here? I never try on clothing in a store!* He contemplated walking out and telling Spring this, but decided doing so would only make more discussion necessary. And she wouldn't understand, anyway. *Just try them on and get this over with!*

Still wearing his white dress shirt from office hours, he pulled on the electric-blue spandex trunks Spring had picked out.

"How do those look?" she asked from her chair outside by the three-way mirror.

"Like swim trunks," he growled. *Ugly ones. I look ridiculous!*

She chuckled. "Come out."

Like a condemned man, he walked out to face her.

"Oh, I like those! Don't you?"

He shrugged. He could endure them, he supposed— if he didn't look down.

"If you don't like them, I could pick out a few more."

Anything but that! "No. These are just fine." He failed to keep the revulsion from his voice.

The salesman wandered away to help another customer. Spring stood up. Coming close to him, she murmured, "If you don't want to shop here, we can go somewhere else."

The sweet scent of gardenias floated from her, calling to him to take a step closer to her.

She gazed up into his eyes.

Her eyes. So blue. So serene. Filled with such innocent appeal. "Let's get it over with," he grumbled. "I just don't want to buy a bunch of clothes I'll never wear again."

"Don't you ever go swimming? Your town house complex has two pools."

"I've never had time—"

"Let's not go there." She waved her hand as if a mosquito had buzzed in her ear. "From now on, once a week in season, you're going to go swimming."

He only half followed her words. The way her golden hair curved around her oval face and down her back became his focus. "Why?"

"Because you don't want these trunks to go to waste." She giggled at him.

Her giggle released some tightness inside him, melted his resistance to her persuading. What was it about Spring that dissolved the willpower he'd honed over time? She made him forget what he was saying. She took him shopping. She'd talked him into going on a frivolous cruise, of all things!

Spring held her breath. She'd been afraid he was

about to bolt. The teasing she'd used to overcome his stiffness had always seemed to work for Doree. She'd seen her sister charm two and three males at a time with her insouciant comments. Would it work for her?

"You're the limit, you know that?" he said at last. "I hate these trunks. Get me some in navy blue, Miss Shopper."

Spring's spirits took flight. *It worked! Good old Doree!* "Yes, Mr. Shopper," she replied with a salute.

Before long, they'd agreed on a pair of navy blue (not spandex) trunks, two pairs of chinos—one mocha and one oatmeal, two coordinating knit shirts, two pair of denim shorts and two white tank tops. But shopping for a man as handsome and well-proportioned as Marco hadn't been difficult. He could make anything look good! Spring sighed with satisfaction.

"Anything else I'll need?" Marco asked with a half smile and a sardonic twist in his voice.

Remember Doree—keep it light; keep it sassy. "Just don't forget to pack your killer smile, Doctor."

Marco just stared at her.

She smiled back at him and hoped she could carry this off. Maybe she should call Doree for advice, inspiration? Two days to castoff!

Spring walked up the slanting gangway to the cruise ship. Her heart beat like the impatient waves lapping, slapping against the ship's hull. She hated feeling so nervous. Taking a deep breath, she tried to center herself in God's peace. Her mind recited, "Be anxious for nothing, but give thanks to the Lord in all things." *I am thankful. Lord, please take this frantic feeling from me.*

She dared a glance at Marco, who walked beside her. He looked intent and serious, hardly like a man about to leave for a three-day vacation! *But I probably look just as tense!* Another deep breath in and out.

Nudging him, she whispered, "This isn't a floating dentist office. Put a smile on that face."

He gave her a fierce look in return, then visibly relaxed his expression. "How's this?" he asked in an undertone.

"Much better." Though her stomach still did the flutter-kick against her ribs, she smiled in return. Appealing to God had already begun loosening her concern. If what she was doing wasn't in God's plan for Marco, her and the clinic, she'd find out soon enough. The old hymn "Trust and Obey" played in her mind: "Never fear, only trust and obey." The tension inside her began dissolving like sugar in water.

"Spring! Spring Kirkland!" a voice hailed her from above.

Shading her eyes, Spring scanned the ship's deck. At first, she couldn't make out any faces, then she recognized the person who was waving to her. A smile lifted her face, and happiness poured through her like warm sunbeams. "Mimi! Mimi! I see you! Hi!"

Mimi, a petite redhead, waved again, leaning over the railing. "Spring, I knew you'd be early! Come on! I've already got the ball rolling. Is that Marco with you?"

Spring bobbed her head yes and stepped up her pace. "Marco, do you remember Mimi Stacey?"

"No, I don't think so."

She dragged at his arm, hurrying him along. "She was my roommate my last two years at Florida. She married Jeff Handelan. Do you remember him?"

Her touch awakened a tingling along the length of his arm. Trying to ignore her effect on him, Marco kept up with her. What had she asked him? He frowned over the name. "He sounds familiar."

"He was on the football team for two years—"

"Oh."

The way he said "oh" irritated her. "He's not the stereotypical jock. He was on the honor roll all through college and has gone into corporate law. He's done quite well."

"Oh."

Stubborn man. But the joy of seeing Mimi again carried Spring along.

"What did she mean," Marco asked, "she's already got the ball rolling?"

"What do you think? Why are you here?" She shook her head at him as she topped the gangplank. A ship's photographer, dressed in crisp white, motioned them to pause. "I've already called everyone who might be helpful, and the clinic is already a topic."

Marco gawked at her.

The photographer snapped their photo.

Chapter Ten

As Spring and Marco in swimwear walked to the pool area on an upper deck, the hot Gulf sun beat down on her bare shoulders. The cloudless blue sky stretched above and the turquoise Gulf of Mexico rippled all around. White seagulls wheeled and squawked overhead. The ship had cast off early in the afternoon, and she was living her dream—she and Marco together.

Still, she trembled inside.

Marco continued his impersonation of a grumpy bear—a grumpy bear in new navy swim trunks. Why had her calling people and starting the talk about Marco's proposed free clinic upset him so? Did he intend to counter her every move, or would he cooperate?

She closed her eyes, again tapping into God's peace and asking for blessing. *Let me know Your will, God. If I'm supposed to be with Marco, let it become plain to both of us. If the free clinic is in Your plan, let us find*

contributors easily. I'm only human. I want what I want.
But Your will be done.

She drew in a deep breath. "There are a pair of lounge chairs." She headed toward the two, side by side by the pool.

Marco trailed after her like a robot, no expression, no comments. He could ruin everything! How could she shake him out of his dour mood?

She eased down onto one wooden lounge chair and Marco claimed the other. He let the back of it down slightly to recline, folded his arms and closed his eyes, as forbidding a pose as she could have imagined. Was he pouting or just oblivious to how to attract people in an engaging manner? Spring wanted to shake him!

Even if he didn't feel like giving her any attention, he had to look approachable, smile and talk to people. Doing his impression of Ebenezer Scrooge wouldn't win him any friends or contributors. She had to loosen him up and do it without anyone noticing. She'd never had to do anything like this before. How did one get a man to laugh? Her mind brought up the picture of her youngest sister surrounded by a circle of jovial young men. How would Doree handle this situation? That was easy. Doree always did the unexpected.

After a moment's consideration, Spring reached into her beach bag and pulled out her sunscreen lotion. She mustered her courage and brooked no cowardice. Still aghast at what she was about to do, she rose and perched on the edge of Marco's lounger, forcing him to make room for her.

His eyes flew open.

"I know you probably won't burn—" she kept her tone light "—but I will. Would you put sunscreen on my back, please?"

He stared at her as if she was speaking Swahili.

Her nerves jiggling like soft-set gelatin, she shoved the tube into his hand, lifted her long hair and turned her back to him. *Get with the program, Marco!*

She waited. Finally, he snapped open the tube and she felt his firm hand on her back. The lotion felt cool, but her already sun-warmed back heated up as if it were blushing. Could backs blush?

"Be sure to put a thick coat on or I'll burn," she murmured from under her hair, as though men applied lotion to her back every day. She tried to reel in her reaction to his touch, but the task proved hopeless. Marco's touch was lovely. "Put a good coat on my shoulders, too."

Marco paused, then followed her instructions.

"Hey! That looks like hard work. Need any help?"

Spring thought she recognized the man's voice. Still holding her hair over her face, she looked up sideways. Yes, it was unfortunately the person she had thought it was. "Marco's doing just fine, Pete. No need to help."

Pete grinned with mischief in his eyes. "You missed a spot. Is it, Marco?" Pete offered his hand.

Marco paused just long enough to make Spring worry. Would he make polite conversation or be brusque? But after rubbing the excess lotion onto his muscled thigh, Marco took Pete's hand and shook it. "Marco Da Palma."

"Peter Rasmussen, Class of '91."

"Class of '89," Marco responded.

"Yeah, I thought you looked familiar. About time Spring dragged someone along with her. You'd think she'd have better luck getting dates—*Oof!*"

Spring had stopped his teasing with a punch to his middle. "You're getting soft, Pete. Maybe a few laps in the pool will get you back into shape."

Pete raised both hands in mock surrender. "Touchy, touchy."

Spring straightened, letting her hair fall over one shoulder. Marco handed her the tube. She motioned Marco to turn his back to her.

He stared at her without moving.

Doree never took no for an answer, so Spring quickly turned his shoulders the way she wanted them and applied a quick coat to Marco's shoulders and the back of his neck, the areas that her father always sunburned.

As though still unsettled, Marco cleared his throat. "What line of work are you into now, Pete?"

Spring wiped the leftover cream on Marco's nose, then moved back to her own lounger, breathing a silent sigh of relief.

"I've moved back to Florida and have just opened a

law practice with another alumnus, Greg Fortney. Did you know him?"

"The name sounds familiar," Marco admitted.

"He graduated with your class." Pete called out, "Hey, Greg, come on over and meet Marco, the lucky man who came with Spring."

"Spring?" A tall lanky man stood up and walked over. "Not Spring Kirkland, the Snow Maiden?"

Spring hated the nickname she'd been given at college. But she tried hard to look as if she didn't care. Otherwise, Greg and Pete would tease her mercilessly.

Marco shook hands more firmly than he usually did with Greg. He'd heard Spring called this sobriquet, the Snow Maiden, at college. He hadn't liked it then. He liked it less now. But he took his cue from Spring. She was smiling at Greg, so Marco went along. *Just don't say anything else "cute," Greg.*

"What are you doing for a living, Marco?" Pete asked.

"I'm in private practice in Gulfview Shores."

"Law?" Greg asked.

"Family medicine."

For the next few minutes, Greg and Pete grilled him about med school and told a few law school stories. Marco tried to look interested, but so far they hadn't said anything he'd taken time off to board a ship to hear.

"Limbo break!" a feminine voice proclaimed.

Pete and Greg joined in the general shouting of approval. Before Marco could bow out, he'd been towed into line with most of the people who'd been lounging around the pool. He glanced around for an escape route.

"This will give us an appetite for dinner tonight!" Pete announced.

Spring turned back to Marco and murmured, "Would you rather not? It's always a lot of fun."

Her enchanting expression, a mixture of hope and doubt, made it impossible for him to refuse. He smiled for her benefit. "I don't think I've ever limboed before."

She chuckled. "I never last long, but watching the last few squeeze under is hilarious."

"Okay." He'd take his turn, fail, then just become an onlooker.

One of the cruise's social directors, a tall brunette in a yellow bikini and a dangerous-looking tan (hadn't anyone warned her about skin cancer?), stood by the stick that would be lowered inch by inch, and named the prizes for the person who could bend backward the lowest. The distinctive melody for the dance boomed out. Marco hadn't noticed the many speakers around the lounging area until then.

Pete started the chant. "Limbo! Limbo!" Soon it competed with the blasting, raucous music.

Lithe and graceful, Spring moved along in front of Marco. He had a hard time keeping his mind on the dance. He didn't want to stare at her. It would embarrass her. Fortunately, she'd chosen a discreet one-piece suit in a bold blue. If she'd selected one of the brief bikinis some of the other female alumni sported, he'd have been forced to feign seasickness and go back to his cabin.

Spring's turn came. The pole was at chin height, so she slipped under it easily. Marco followed her and made certain he didn't disturb the pole by accident. If he messed up too early, it would make him even more noticed.

Pete and Greg hot-dogged under the pole amid laughter. The bouncy melody played on as the line made another circuit, another, another. Bumping the pole off its supports, Spring laughed at herself, then clapped in time with the music.

Caught up in the rhythm and gaiety, Marco bent backward and eased himself under the pole. By now, the line of contenders had thinned to less than a dozen.

When the pole touched Marco's waist, he decided he could blunder now and disappear into the crowd. He bent backward and began inching under the pole—

"Hey, Snow Maiden," Greg called from behind Marco. "Bet I can outdo your boyfriend!"

Marco gritted his teeth. *Not on a bet, Greg!* The pole grazed his navel—

Pete catcalled, "You're gonna lose it, Marco boy!"

Marco bent back and shuffled his feet forward inch by inch…then he was on the other side! Cheers went up.

Marco's face blazed with exhilaration and the unaccustomed experience of being the recipient of applause.

Spring patted his arm in approval.

Marco suffered her touch—sweet agony.

She started another chant. "Marco! Marco!"

The limbo melody played on. One by one, the remaining dancers were eliminated. Finally, only Pete, Greg and Marco competed for the prize. Giving in to defeat, Pete leaped over the pole, which now came knee-high to him. Greg grunted and bent backward, moving forward. He nearly made it, but his incipient paunch did him in. The pole clattered to the ship's deck.

Marco faced the pole. Should he just quit and let the prize go to the last person who'd made it through? A glance at Spring's hopeful face routed this idea.

Everyone fell silent as he flexed his knees as low as he could, bent his shoulders back as far as they would go, then began to bounce forward on his feet. The pole passed over his knees, his thighs, his navel, his chest—then he faced his greatest obstacle, his chin. Closing his eyes, he extended his neck back as low as it could go. He bounced forward, the silence around him suffocating. The pole shaved his nose, then skimmed his forehead— He cleared it!

The result was bedlam.

He stood up, blinking.

"You did it! You won!" Spring threw her arms around his neck.

In a natural reflex, he wrapped his arms around her. A ship's photographer snapped a victory photo of them. Pete and Greg thumped him on the back, shouting their congratulations.

Marco could hardly breathe. The combination of

being the center of attention for the first time in his life and the sweet sensation of Spring in his arms swept away any conscious reactions.

"This is going to be fun!" Mimi shrilled in Marco's ear, or just below his ear. The four of them—Mimi and her husband, John, Spring and him—had just disembarked from the cruise ship onto the wharf of an island stop. The tropical sun blazed down on them, glinting off anything chrome or metal.

Spring's old college roommate, Mimi, didn't even come to Marco's shoulder. Her bubbly personality had irritated him at first when John and Mimi had joined them for dinner the night before. But Mimi had proved a delightful companion, funny and sweet. John appeared to stand back and enjoy his wife's easy charm. Marco had felt accepted and drawn into the good company in a way he'd never before experienced. He tried to analyze it but couldn't.

Now he gave Mimi a smile, then glanced to Spring. Her face glowed with her excitement as they put distance between themselves and the ship.

"I want to find something totally outrageous for my sister Doree's birthday," she said.

"Is she still in Madison at the university?" Mimi tugged at John's hand.

"Yes, she's a sophomore." Spring pulled at Marco's hand, too.

"What's the hurry?" Marco asked, enjoying the

vacation-happy Spring beside him. "We've got the whole morning."

"It might take all morning to find something outrageous enough for my sister!"

Marco felt a twinge of conscience. He really didn't know much about Spring's family—just that her father was a pastor and they weren't rich. "Do you have any other siblings?" he murmured for her ears only.

She gave him a startled look. "Just Hannah, the food writer."

He grimaced. "Now I remember. You were telling Paloma about her on the way to Mamacita's."

She gave him a dazzling smile. "You remember that?"

He nodded, feeling guilty he'd made her remind him.

"Maybe you should find something for Paloma?" Spring suggested with an uncertain expression.

"You're right. She'd love something from here." *Why didn't I think of that?* Spring's constant thoughtfulness touched him. What a gentle heart she had.

He glanced around at the island thoroughfare they had just started down. Tropical shades of peach, pink, turquoise, tan and yellow decorated the tourist street on the island. Venders roamed along the street hawking their wares—straw hats, colorful stuffed animals, parrots, fresh flowers in bunches. Little open-air shops touted postcards, huge fun sunglasses, dried starfish and sea horses, and seashells.

"Will you help me find something for Paloma?"

"Of course."

When Spring took his hand, it seemed natural. Being away from their family and the town where he practiced medicine had stripped him of his reticence. He felt like a different man from the one who spent his days walking hospital hallways. Spring had been right to insist he come.

A break once in a while could be more than beneficial. Now her soft hand in his filled him with a wonder he could hardly process. *I'm holding hands with Spring and we're on a tropical island.*

After browsing in a series of crowded tourist shops, Marco chose a colorful toy parrot for Paloma, then dropped back behind the ladies with John, as their foursome went from store to store.

John, at his side, gave him a friendly grin. "Hope you're wearing comfortable shoes."

Marco lifted an eyebrow.

"We may end up walking up and down every street on this island. Mimi never stops shopping *till she drops.*" John gave his wife a loving glance.

Daunted by this remark, Marco looked down the long street of shops.

Glancing around, John halted when he saw Mimi go into yet another one. "How about we stay out here and have something to drink and wait for the ladies?" John motioned toward an open-air café on the opposite side of the dusty street.

"Sure." After calling their intentions to Spring and Mimi, Marco followed John to a table shaded by a woven canopy. They ordered chilled mineral water and sat back. The cadence of happy voices, reggae music in the distance, the brilliance of the sunshine—all combined to make a tranquil setting.

Marco sucked in a long cooling draught. He couldn't remember feeling so relaxed. "I hadn't expected to enjoy myself." The words slipped out before he took time to consider each syllable the way he usually did. What would John think?

"Yeah, there's nothing like a cruise with old and new friends." He lifted his bottle to Marco. "I wouldn't take the time to do this kind of stuff, but Mimi always keeps tabs on what's going on and when I need a vacation."

"You're lucky." And Marco meant it.

John chuckled. "And you're the envy of half the guys on the cruise. I can't believe Spring still isn't married."

Marco stiffened, but he could read no ulterior message in John's face, his easy smile. "Spring is a very special lady."

"You'll get no argument from me." John swallowed the rest of his water and motioned for another. "I hear you're trying to raise funds for a free clinic."

Marco searched John's expression and began tentatively. "Yes, I'd like to be able to offer emergency and short-term care for people who don't have medical coverage, for whatever reason."

"Mimi says you've got a site chosen?"

Instead of tensing up as he had when Spring had first discussed his asking for contributions, the words, the plans flowed from Marco. John sounded interested and asked intelligent questions. One, then two, then three other guys from the cruise, including Pete and Greg, stopped by and joined in the discussion.

Marco absorbed the camaraderie, something he'd rarely experienced before. He seldom attended the hospital's social functions. Why was he accepted now, when he hadn't been in college?

He looked up to find Spring standing just outside the café watching him. Everyone seemed to accept Spring and him as a couple. The fact had astounded him at first, but the idea was becoming more agreeable hour by hour. He waved.

She smiled.

Tenderness for her flowed warm inside him. *Spring, is it possible? Do I have a chance with you?*

The ice sculptures glistened in the low light of the ship's large dining room. Spring sat at an oblong table beside Marco. The dinner buffet—succulent prime rib, Cornish hen, duck, lobster and King crab—had been sumptuous, as usual. She'd eaten more on this cruise than she had ever eaten before! The waist of her pale pink evening gown circled her a bit tighter than it had last year.

Tonight was the last night of the cruise. The thought saddened her. Would the special closeness she and Marco had shared here disappear when they returned to Gulfview Shores?

The cruise had been all she'd hoped for and more. Marco had relaxed and he'd begun to behave differently—as if he had finally noticed that she was a woman. Did she have a chance with Marco, after all this time? Tomorrow morning when she stepped down from the gangplank, would she turn back into a disenchanted Cinderella?

The live band struck up another romantic ballad. John took Mimi by the hand and led her to the dance floor. Soon every other couple at their table had moved onto the dance floor or to other tables to chat.

Marco looked to her. "Would you like to dance?"

"You dance?"

He grinned. "Paloma taught me for a hospital benefit."

Unable to trust her voice at the thought of being held in Marco's strong arms, she nodded.

He took her hand and led her through the maze of tables to join the other couples. Then he faced her, and his hand settled on the small of her back.

Thrilled at this dream-come-true intimacy, she rested one hand on his broad shoulder and clasped his hand in the other. In the dim light, she focused on his dark intense eyes and the feel of being so near the man she loved. She closed her eyes then and let herself revel in his embrace.

Marco felt as though his heart were being drawn from his chest. Her fragrance of gardenias, the low lighting, the mellow music, the soft form in his arms intoxicated him more powerfully than any wine he could have sipped. *Spring Kirkland in my arms.* The melody carried him on, dreamlike.

He thought of Spring's gentle care of *Tía* Rosita, her sympathy toward Paloma in the vice-principal's office, her enthusiasm for his free clinic. Most men only noticed the lovely package Spring came in, but her kind, generous heart had proved even more exceptional.

The dance ended.

Spring gazed up at him, her eyes glowing with tenderness.

For him? What could she see in him?

"Let's go outside and walk the deck in the moonlight," she murmured.

He nodded, unable to speak.

She took his arm.

Brushing past other couples, he piloted her through the crowded room, then out onto the deck. The warm night breeze caressed his face. He led her away to a quiet spot. A phrase came to his mind so inadequate to the moment, but he voiced it anyway. "It's a beautiful night."

His low, husky voice made prickles run up Spring's arms.

"I hate to see the cruise end." She moved closer to him.

"I feel the same way."

Bliss romped inside her. She'd never thought she'd hear him say those words. Could he be changing? "We didn't find any backers—"

He pressed his hand to her lips, stopping her words. "We tried. We did our best. Let's just enjoy our last night on board."

She nodded, holding back happy tears. Marco didn't even sound like the same man who'd called the cruise a "waste of time."

Marco didn't feel like himself at all. The blond lady in the pink evening gown beside him shimmered in the moonlight like molten Black Hills gold—irresistible. He took a step closer.

She leaned forward.

He bent his head.

She lifted her face.

His lips touched hers. *Spring…*

"Hey! Marco!" Pete's now familiar voice rocketed through Marco. His hands balled into fists. He turned to face Pete.

Pete grinned at him. "Sorry to interrupt, old man. But I think we need to talk. Greg and I want to back that clinic of yours."

Chapter Eleven

Had it all happened? Marco still felt a little light-headed. Lavender twilight hugged the Gulf as he opened the door of his car to let Spring into the front passenger seat.

When she glanced up, he nearly lost himself in the shadowed blue of her lovely eyes. *Qué bella es.*

Spring sighed. "I'm glad you're driving me home. I still feel a little unsteady—the ship and so much happening…."

He understood the hesitance in her voice. He was experiencing the same kind of disorientation. He'd come home a different man. How could so much occur in three short—change that to very *long*—days? He'd gone on the cruise just to get everyone off his back. He hadn't expected it to be so…what? He tried to process all that had happened, all that had shifted, changed.

Chaotic inside, he settled himself beside Spring and backed his car out of the parking space. "Do you think they were serious?"

"Yes. Pete can be irritating, always the clown, but evidently he has a serious side. I can't believe he would tell you something he didn't mean to do."

"I guess you're right. I just never imagined…" He shrugged his shoulders. *I never imagined just how much I wanted to be close to you.*

Spring turned to him with a smile. "Never ask God for something and expect nothing."

Her glowing face warmed his blood. Still, he couldn't just let her statement stand. "But prayers aren't always answered."

"Yes, they are. People only want a firm 'yes'— usually by way of an eye-opening miracle. They think that's God's one and only way of answering prayer. But God answers prayers in many ways and He gives *every* prayer one of three possible answers."

"And what are these three?"

"They are Yes, No, Wait. We humans prefer yes and tend to dislike the negative and patience answers."

"I must be accustomed to the latter two. I'm stunned. I admit it. I never expected to find donors, not big ones. And certainly not Pete and Greg." When Pete had interrupted his near kissing of Spring, Marco had wanted to deck him. The raw anger he'd felt came back. But it gave way to wonder. *Spring, you were ready to let me kiss you.*

She grinned, as though reading his mind. "'Be careful what you pray for, you might get it' is another favorite saying of my mother's."

He snorted. "She's got something there."

Spring swirled toward him on the car seat. "Aren't you happy? Isn't this wonderful? Pete and Greg will give you the whole down payment for the church—"

"*If* I can get nonprofit status." There was always at least one more hurdle to jump, in his life.

She waved this objection away with one hand. "They even said they'd draw up the nonprofit status papers for you to sign. Why would the state of Florida deny a free clinic nonprofit status?"

"I don't know, but I never take any challenge for granted." His voice roughened. One's own hard work was the only thing one could count on.

"I have faith in Pete and Greg, in the state of Florida, in God and in *you,* Marco Da Palma." She faced forward again.

Don't turn away. "I didn't mean to offend you."

"You didn't. I just get the feeling that you don't know how to trust God in every situation."

Did Spring have that kind of faith? "Do you?" he asked.

"It depends," she replied. "I try to. I think my parents do. It isn't easy. I usually want to stick an oar in and help God. That's what Aunt Geneva always says."

He gave a sardonic grin. "I believe that."

The sweet woman beside him giggled.

He threaded his way through the darkened streets of

Gulfview to her aunt's house. As he drove through the quieter residential streets, he watched emotion play over Spring's expressive face. *Do you want to be close to me too, Spring? Is that possible?*

Too soon he turned down her street. The early March sun had just dipped below the horizon casting its last golden rays, when he pulled up to her house. He helped her out, then carried her two bags to the door.

"It's been a long day."

"Yes, that engine problem slowed down our trip back to port, but I enjoyed the extra hours on deck. See?" She held out her arm toward him. "I'm almost golden."

Golden. Precious. Radiant. These words describing Spring wended through his mind. He wished for the music of the night before, so he could hold her in his arms again. He took her soft hand, hating to be parted.

She looked up at him expectantly.

"Spring, I…the cruise…everything." He struggled for words. "Our weekend was great. And I didn't expect it to be anything like it turned out."

She grinned at him. "I know. You made that clear. But I saw you mellow."

Her smile turned his heart inside out. Tugging on her hand, he pulled her into his arms.

A little gasp of surprise escaped her.

He waited. Would she pull away?

She leaned into his embrace.

Exultant, he tightened his grasp on her. "Spring, you're so lovely, so good…I…" He kissed her.

"Marco," she murmured against his lips as she twined her arms around his neck.

Marco immersed himself in the sensations Spring's kiss released within him. Strength surged through him and possessiveness made him draw her more tightly to him.

Spring lost the feeling of separateness between Marco and herself. His warm skin under her lips and his strong arms banded around her. She clung to him, not trusting her own strength.

At last, the delicious, thrilling kiss ended.

She stared up at him, dazed. She breathed out his name. "Marco."

"Mi querida," he whispered against her cheek.

She didn't know the exact translation of his words, but she loved the way he said it with such emotion, such restrained passion. She smiled up at him.

He loosened his hold on her, bit by bit, as though bringing them both gently back to earth. "I should be going. It's late," he apologized, then released her completely.

She immediately folded her arms in front of her, bereft. "I know. Good night."

"Buenas noches, Señorita." He touched her cheek, then moved away.

Waving, she watched him walk back to his car. She didn't go in until his car drove out of sight. Then turning, she opened the door.

"That was so romantic!" Matilde exclaimed, her hands clasped together.

"Oh, Spring, darling," Aunty declared, "the cruise must have been a success! He kissed you!"

"You two have got to stop spying on me!" Spring protested. Chagrin cut through her, fiery heat burning her cheeks. Even in her anger, though, she realized their spying came from affection.

The two older women had the honesty to blush.

"We didn't mean anything bad," Matilde rushed to assure her.

"Of course not," Aunty agreed, and bowed her head contritely for a moment.

Spring shook her head at them. She didn't begrudge them the joy of seeing what they'd hoped for, but knowing that she and Marco hadn't been truly alone in that special moment did cause some of its power to evaporate.

"We'll never do it again—" Aunty began.

"We never thought he would kiss you." Matilde sighed. "And such a kiss, too. My heart melts when I remember…" Matilde's voice stopped and she blushed a deeper rosy pink.

"I remember, too," Aunty said. "A rumble seat. His name was Floyd, but I thought he was the nearest thing to Rudolph Valentino I'd ever see." She sighed, then grimaced. "My jaw keeps aching. I was just to the dentist before you came, Spring. Ooh. I'm falling apart daily." Aunty pressed her hand to her jaw.

"Your jaw, your arm. Do you want me to get your liniment?" Matilde asked with obvious concern.

"No, I'll be fine." But her aunt's expression belied her short words.

Matilde shook her finger at Aunty. "You worked too hard today in the garden—"

"Stop scolding, Matilde." Aunty grimaced. "A couple of aspirin and I'll be fine. Now go to bed."

Shaking her head at their bickering, Spring picked up her handbag and rolled her wheeled suitcase down the hallway. "Come on. I'll tell you what happened on the cruise."

"Did Marco have luck getting backers?" Matilde called after her.

"Yes, he—"

"No, don't tell me! I want to be able to hear all about it from his mother. You two go ahead. I'm sleepy. *Buenas noches!*"

"Don't tell her Marco kissed me!" Spring begged her.

"No, no, I won't!" Matilde promised.

Spring and Aunty waved good-night to Matilde and walked into Spring's room. Aunty went straight to the bedside chair as though the short walk had drained her. Uneasy, Spring sank down on the bed.

"So Marco found contributors?" Aunty rubbed her arm.

Spring began watching her aunt closely, but replied, "Yes, two alumni who just opened their own law practice north of here in Sarasota. They just won a big case and wanted to tithe their earnings."

"Wonderful!"

"Yes, it's enough for the down payment on the church…. Aunty, is your arm troubling you?"

"Yes, Matilde is right. I must have done too much gardening this afternoon, though I didn't think I did any more than usual—"

Spring leaned over and took one of her aunt's hands in hers. What she saw sent her reeling. "Aunty! Your fingernails are turning blue."

Aunt Geneva glanced down. "So they are. How peculiar."

Spring reached for the phone and dialed, her pulse racing with alarm.

"Who are you calling?"

"Marco's cell phone number." Now she wished he'd stayed and come in with her.

"Why?"

"Because…" She held up her hand when the phone was picked up. "Marco, my aunt's jaw is aching. Her arm is giving her pain and her fingernails are turning blue. Should I be concern— Yes, okay. I will. Thanks." She hung up and dialed again, sick with apprehension.

"What's the matter?" Aunt Geneva asked, sitting forward.

"He said to call 911." She kept her tone neutral. "He thinks you're close to a heart attack."

"But—"

"Hello, this is Spring Kirkland at 677 Mimosa Lane. My aunt, Mrs. Geneva Dorfman, needs an ambulance.

Her doctor told me to call. She may be near cardiac arrest. Yes. Thank you." Spring hung up the phone.

"I'm not having a heart attack! I just strained my arm." Her aunt's face crumbled. "I…oh, oh, my chest…I…"

"Don't try to talk." Again, Spring kept panic out of her tone. "They'll be here right away. Don't worry." She ran to the door, opened it and called, "Matilde! Matilde!"

Spring held her aunt's limp hand in the brightly lit emergency room cubicle. Just outside the door, Matilde sat, her eyes closed, her lips moving in prayer. As Spring had driven them to the hospital following the ambulance, she had feared the housekeeper would have a heart attack herself.

At the hospital, after complaining about a feeling of heavy weight on her chest, Aunty lost consciousness. Now her aunt's mouth and nose were covered with an oxygen mask, and an IV had been inserted in one arm. She looked pale, sickly pale. Her fingernails were much bluer than when Spring first had examined them at home.

Marco, please come. Marco! Dear Lord, please take care of Aunty, please take care. Her mind alternated between these two pleas. Spring fiercely held tears at bay.

A doctor, a stranger to Spring, hovered around Aunt Geneva. "How long had your aunt been experiencing arm pain?"

"She didn't say. I'd just come home from a weekend away—"

Marco strode into the room. "Dr. Hansen!"

Spring's heart lurched in her chest. She rose from her chair but retained her aunt's hands.

"Dr. Da Palma, Mrs. Dorfman is your patient?"

"Yes, what have you done?"

Dr. Hansen handed him the chart. "The usual. I've had blood drawn, started an ECG, and ordered a *stat* chest X ray."

Spring heard the words, but didn't really understand them. She watched Marco's face, trying to read it.

Marco nodded and thanked the doctor. He turned to Spring. "I'm glad you called me. When did your aunt lose consciousness?"

"Just after we arrived here," Spring replied.

A nurse came for Dr. Hansen. He excused himself and left with her.

Spring let go of her aunt's hand and took a step forward. Marco came to her and wrapped his arms around her. She melted against him, seeking his strength. Just last week she'd never have sought his embrace so naturally. What a difference three days had made.

"Is she going to be all right?"

"For now." He kissed her forehead. "Dr. Hansen and the EMTs appear to have her stabilized, and the right tests have been ordered."

The touch of his lips fortified her, even as she glanced back at her aunt.

Matilde stood up and came to the doorway. "Marco, why is she unconscious?"

He turned his head toward her. "A heart malfunctioning can be painful. She may have fainted because of that. Or lack of oxygen in the blood. She's being given morphine, which would take away the pain but make her groggy. She's definitely in distress, but she's here in the hospital. She'll get the best care possible."

Spring rested her head on his chest, so comforting, so strong. She spoke words straight from her heart. "I'm so glad you're here."

He tucked her closer to him. "I'm glad you were there. You picked up on the symptoms of impending heart failure exactly. How did you know?"

"My father has had a few bouts with arrhythmia."

Marco tightened his hold on her.

"Isn't there anything else we can do?" She glanced into his deep brown eyes.

"No, *mi querida*, we'll watch her closely and make decisions about what is to be done. I'm going to call the staff's heart specialist. He'll read the tests, and we'll consult together."

A man in a lab coat entered the room. "I'm here to do Mrs. Dorfman's chest X ray."

Marco nodded, then led Spring from the room.

She glanced back at Aunty. The electrodes applied to Aunty's chest, the oxygen monitor on her index finger, the IV in her arm—everything made her aunt look so strange, so alone, so ill. Spring swallowed tears. *Dear Lord, help the staff here do what is best for my aunt. I love her so.*

* * *

About an hour later, a nurse moved Aunt Geneva upstairs to the cardiac intensive care unit, and Spring followed her. Aunty woke for a moment but was too weak to speak. Spring pressed her aunt's hand in both of hers. "You'll be all right, Aunty. Marco is here and everything is going as it should."

Her aunt nodded slightly, then closed her eyes.

Marco drew Spring from the room with him. "You'll be allowed in only fifteen minutes every hour. We'll go sit in the lounge area on this floor."

Spring objected. "You have to work in the morning. You might have to assist in surgery for Aunty. You need your rest."

"I'll be fine."

When she tried to object further, he pressed his hand to her lips. She conceded.

He led Matilde and her to a comfortable lounge area just down the hall. He helped Matilde settle into an arm chair. "Try to rest."

Matilde wiped tears from her eyes. "She's such a good woman." She clutched Marco's arm.

"She's getting the best care available and she's a strong woman." Marco covered Matilde's hand with his.

"You are right. She came through a war. She survived losing the man she loved twenty years ago." Matilde took a deep breath. "I will pray and have faith."

Marco nodded and patted Matilde's shoulder. He

motioned Spring to sit on a cushy sofa, then sat down beside her.

His presence made all the difference to her. Marco wouldn't let Aunty receive anything but the best treatment. She gave him a tremulous smile.

She noticed a beige phone on the table beside her, with printed instructions on how to dial an outside local line. More prayers could only help. She opened her purse and pulled out her phone calling card, picked up the receiver and dialed.

"Mother, it's Spring. I called for prayer support. Aunty's in intensive care...."

Chapter Twelve

Stiff, Spring sat up and stretched. Instantly, concern for her aunt balled tight in her stomach, making her feel nauseated. She hadn't left the hospital all night. Aunt Geneva had slept fitfully, but had finally stabilized. Still in cardiac intensive care, she was far from well.

Slumped back in the corner of the armchair, Matilde looked up, groggy. "What's happening?"

Spring glanced at her watch and stood up carefully, unsure of her legs after a night of on-and-off sleeping, sitting up and pacing. With both hands, she tried to brush the wrinkles from her skirt. "Marco and the heart specialist are to meet at seven this morning to make a decision about Aunty and heart surgery. It's about that now."

Matilde pushed herself up, stretching, too. "Oh, I need a cup of coffee—"

"*Hola!*" Anita bustled off the elevator toward them.

"I'm so glad you called me, Matilde. As soon as I made breakfast for Santos and Paloma, I came right over. You should go home and get some rest." Anita gathered Spring into her arms for an affectionate hug, much to Spring's surprise.

Spring breathed in the mingled fragrances of Anita's sweet perfume and fresh bacon—homey aromas, so welcome in this clinical setting. "I didn't know Matilde had called you."

"You were napping. I called about an hour ago. I know Santos always rises early."

Spring didn't know what to say. She'd never expected Marco's mother to come.

"I know we've just met," Anita said. "But I feel like I know you and your aunt from all Matilde has told us about you over the years."

"It's very thoughtful of you."

"Señora Dorfman is a good woman, and you're Paloma and Marco's friend." Anita smiled.

Spring's mind a jumble of thoughts, she urged Anita to sit down beside her, then filled her in on her aunt's night and what was going to be done for Aunty this morning.

Marco strode up the hall toward them.

Rising, Spring met him and held out her hands. She craved his reassuring touch.

He gripped them and pulled her a step closer. "I discussed your aunt with Dr. Carlson, the heart specialist on staff."

Spring nodded, unable to think of anything to say.

ECGs, ICUs, and IVs weren't a part of her everyday life. His nearness bolstered her. She longed to tell him so, but couldn't with his mother looking on.

Marco glanced past Spring. "Mother, you're here."

"*Sí,* Matilde called me. I thought Spring could use some more support."

Anita looked as though she were challenging Marco in some way Spring couldn't understand.

But Marco only nodded again, then turned back to Spring. "Dr. Carlson has ordered immediate surgery for your aunt. A double bypass."

Spring's knees weakened. She slipped back down to the sofa. "Then Aunty's condition is as serious as I feared."

Marco didn't let go of her hands. He sat down beside her. "Carlson is the best. I'm going to scrub to assist him. The good news is that your aunt's heart hasn't had previous damage and the bypass will bring her back to health."

"It's all happening so suddenly…." Spring's voice faltered.

Matilde began crying again.

"We're very lucky. Dr. Carlson had planned to take off today so he has time to do her surgery."

Spring pursed her lips. "I know you'll do what's best."

Then he surprised her by kissing her forehead. What would his mother think?

He stood. "Matilde, would you please take Spring down to the cafeteria and make sure she eats a good breakfast?"

Spring turned pink at his proprietary tone. Did he hear how he sounded? "No, I couldn't—"

Matilde cut in. *"Claro que sí."* She took one of Spring's hands. "Help me, Anita. This girl eats like a bird."

Marco let Spring's other hand drop, then leaned forward to kiss her. This time lightly on her lips. "Go. You need to eat."

His kiss ran through her like warm maple syrup, sweet and delicious, in spite of his mother's presence. Spring gazed into his eyes, reading his concern there. She nodded.

"Take your time eating breakfast. The surgery will take hours."

She watched him march away, longing to urge him to stay.

Anita excused herself to run a quick errand for Paloma, but promised to meet them in the surgical waiting area.

Downstairs, wandering down the cafeteria line, Spring selected tea and dry toast. Following behind, Matilde added fresh fruit and a bowl of oatmeal to Spring's tray.

A little queasy from lack of sleep, Spring frowned and tried to put both bowls back.

"No! You must eat to keep up your strength!" Matilde objected.

"I won't be able to eat—"

"You will." Matilde's chin rose stubbornly.

"But—"

The housekeeper sighed. "Eat what you can, *hija mia*. You don't need to eat all of everything, just a bit of each. Toast and tea will not give you the strength you need now."

Spring nodded but felt too nervous to eat. The appetite she'd acquired on the cruise had vanished, leaving her hollow.

She paid for her breakfast, and Matilde followed her to a table near the wall of windows overlooking the hospital garden. Pink azaleas festooned borders of white petunias in the bright sunshine. She bowed her head to give thanks. When she looked up, she still had no appetite.

The words she'd been holding in all night came rushing out. "I feel so guilty."

"Why?"

"I should have noticed Aunty wasn't feeling well." Spring felt her throat thicken with emotion. "I shouldn't have gone away—"

"No!" Matilde shook her head vigorously. "She was thrilled for you. Marco and you going on that cruise made her so happy."

Unable to speak, Spring forked a chunk of cantaloupe into her mouth. The fresh, cool fruit woke her taste buds and made her stomach clamor for more.

"Marco kissed you last night and this morning," Matilde murmured with a knowing smile. "What happened on the cruise?"

Spring paused with her fork poised over the fruit. What a question. How could she put all that had occurred into words to be said over breakfast. "Marco was able to get donors for his free clinic."

"Wonderful, but what happened between you two?"

Spring speared a fresh, ripe strawberry. "I don't know. We're closer but we haven't talked."

"*Ay!*" Matilde struck her forehead. "You will give me a heart attack, too. You two need someone to teach you how to fall in love!"

On her way into surgery, Aunt Geneva clutched Spring's hands in hers, communicating her anxiety.

"You'll be all right, Aunty," Spring murmured. "Dr. Carlson is the best in Florida and Marco will be with him. You won't be in surgery so very long."

"Spring, I've been thinking." Aunty's eyes looked frightened and distracted. "I should have told you about your mother's natural parents. If I should die today…no one else knows the truth!"

"You can tell me after you're out of surgery." Spring said it with a hopeful smile, though she felt the drag of worry around her heart. *Oh, Lord, please protect my dear aunt.*

Aunty had been given something to relax her, but obviously it hadn't lessened her anxiety. Her eyes filled with tears. "But, Spring, I—"

The orderly apologized, but pushed the gurney the last few feet to the pre-operating room door.

Spring waved to her aunt and blew a kiss. She watched until her aunt was out of sight, then her tears let down like a sudden storm. Feeling unreasonably guilty for ever asking about her mother's adoption, she turned and made her way to the surgical waiting room.

"Spring!" Anita welcomed her with open arms. "*Pobrecita,* you poor child."

"I love her so much," Spring said, her words mangled by a sudden rush of weeping.

"She will be fine," Anita comforted her. "Matilde and I will stay with you until she is out of surgery and we know she is safe."

"We're here, too, Spring." Verna Rae came in with Eleanor at her side, just behind Anita.

Verna Rae continued. "Hon, our churches are all prayin' for your aunt."

"She's a strong one, that Geneva," Eleanor added. "Don't count her out, dahling. She's got a lot of years left in her!"

Fresh tears spilled from Spring's eyes, but gratitude curved her face into a reluctant smile. "I'm so glad Aunty has such good friends."

"And such a good doctor!" Eleanor finished for her. "Matilde introduced us to Dr. Da Palma's mother here. She's a sweetheart, too—"

"So you have nothing to worry about, honey." Verna Rae patted Spring's arm.

Spring nodded. "Thank you. I'm better now." She sat down, and each lady found a comfortable spot near her in the corner of the surgical waiting area. Her spirits had risen.

God, be there and watch over Aunt Geneva. I love her so. And bless the doctors who are operating. Be with Marco as he assists. I love him, Lord—even if I can't bring myself to say the words to him.

"Spring." A soft, deep voice murmured her name. "Spring."

Chills up her spine woke her completely. She looked up into Marco's dark eyes. "Marco." Warmth swirled through her. She stretched in the chair beside her aunt's bed in the cardiac wing.

He whispered, "You should go home and get some sleep in your own bed. You've been here most of the past two days. Dr. Carlson is not concerned about your aunt's recovery at all. You can't do anything for her, can you."

"I wish I could do something. I'd feel better, then." Marco's low voice awoke her mind, body and heart—his tender concern for her, a priceless gift in a frantic time. Disheveled, she felt disoriented, as though she'd been tossed in a blanket several times, then dropped on her head. She glanced to her aunt, who lay sound asleep in her bed nearby.

"I was here when she told you to go home and rest," Marco coaxed, leaning close.

Spring laid her hand against his stubbled cheek. The contact sent a charge up her numb arm. "It's late. Why are you still here?"

He exhaled deeply. "I had a few emergencies at the

office, then I was called back here for some more. Now I'm going to head home for a shower and some real sleep."

"Sounds good."

"Up." He tugged her hands, pulling her onto her feet. "Your aunt told you to go home. I'm going to take you there."

His strength beckoned her. Her mood lightened. "I love it when you bully me." Her emotions bubbled up. She felt giddy—from fatigue, from relief over the successful surgery?

"You are overtired. Now come." He led her from her aunt's room.

Feeling light as fresh soap bubbles, Spring let him lead her. "You'll have to call me a cab—"

"I'll drive you home."

"My aunt's house is out of your way."

"No one but me will be driving you home," he informed her in a fierce voice.

His tone set off a ringing of joy inside her. She giggled. "You're so masterful, Marco."

He gave her a disgruntled look, but towed her closer to him.

She reveled in his nearness, his tender care. Soon fresh Gulf air flowed over Spring's face. The night was still new and she could hear the sounds of traffic on the nearby highway. She let Marco lead her to his car, tuck her inside and drive her away.

All that had happened over the past week had pulled

her away from everyday life. Her restless emotions lay just beneath the surface, ready to leap up at any cause. She laid her head back against the seat. "You have a wonderful family. Anita and Santos have been so kind."

"*Gracias*. My mother felt you needed someone, some family with you."

His words comforted her. "That's just what it felt like. I can see now why you are such a good man."

"I'm just a man—"

"Your mother said you were already fourteen when she married Santos, so the credit must go to your father. He must have made a lasting impression on you," Spring probed gently. Would Marco open up and tell her more about his personal life?

Marco's throat tightened. "My father was the best."

She stroked his arm, wanting, needing to make contact with him. "I'm so sorry you lost him. He would be very proud of you. How did you lose him? Was it an illness?"

"No." His voice sounded, felt hoarse. "He was killed in a car accident on Highway 19."

"I'm so sorry."

Marco couldn't stop himself. Words he'd never said to anyone else slipped through his lips. "I was with him in the car. A drunk driver hit us head-on. I was safely in the back seat. My father died before the ambulance came. I felt so helpless…. That's when I decided to be a doctor. I never wanted to be helpless again—when someone I loved needed me."

She slid closer to him, wrapped her arms around his right arm and nestled her face into his starched cotton shirt. "How awful for you. I know how that feels."

"You do?"

She rubbed her face against his shirt as she nodded. "My mother was diagnosed with leukemia three years ago."

"I didn't know!" He kissed her hair. "How is she? What are they doing for her?"

She pressed herself closer to him. "She's in remission now, has been for over eighteen months, but it was so scary. We were so afraid that we might lose her."

He covered her hand with his. "I'm so glad to hear that she is doing well."

She touched her cheek to his hand. "We, my sisters and father and I, still worry. What if the leukemia comes back?"

He spoke with urgency. "There are many treatments. We have so many new ways to treat leukemia—bone marrow transplants—"

"My sisters and I weren't matches."

"How about other family members?" Concern resonated in his voice.

She shook her head. "Mother was adopted, and we don't know anything about her birth family connections."

"That's tough." Marco thought about his only having his mother here in Florida. The rest of his relatives had stayed in Santo Domingo. He'd thought he had so little in common with Spring, but perhaps he'd been wrong.

So conscious of the lovely woman pressed close to him, Marco stopped in front of her aunt's home. He turned to Spring. She came into his arms so naturally that it took his breath away.

He forced back all the negative cautions that percolated up from his mind. *I want to kiss her. She wants my kiss. We're not so different!*

She lifted her face to him.

He kissed her, then stroked the golden strands of hair away from her pale, lucent face. *I love you, Spring. Te amo. Where will my feelings take us? Could you love me, too?*

Three days later, Spring sat beside her aunt's hospital bed and smiled. "You look stronger today."

"I feel like a crushed lettuce leaf."

Spring chuckled and enjoyed the light feeling it gave her. The past five days had been overloaded with worry, heart-wringing prayer and lack of sleep. But, at last, she felt hopeful.

Aunt Geneva stared into Spring's eyes as though she had something important on her mind.

Spring didn't look away. She thought she knew what her aunt wanted to discuss. "Are you going to tell me about mother now?"

Aunty nodded.

Though excited to be this close to the truth, Spring hesitated. "Are you certain you're up to this? I don't want you to overdo."

"I'm strong enough to talk. I've prayed about this every waking hour since I knew I was to go into surgery. You shocked me so when you asked me—out of the blue—about Ethel's parents. I've suppressed what I knew for so many years. I've thought more than once in the past ten years that maybe Ethel should be told."

Aunty paused to sigh. "Times have changed. Adoption used to be so hush-hush. Children were never even told they'd been adopted! Fortunately, your grandmother didn't do that! When Ethel was twelve, Gloria told her that she'd been adopted, but that Gloria and Tom couldn't love her any more than her natural mother did. Which was the truth. Gloria and I and both our husbands adored Ethel from the very first time we saw her."

"When was that?" Spring asked softly. How had her mother felt when she'd learned about her adoption?

"It's a sad story. Ethel's mother was Connie Wilson, a dear girl who grew up just across the street from your grandmother and me. She was a bit younger than me and a bit older than Gloria." Aunty's face took on a faraway expression. "So many years ago. So sad that Connie…left us so soon."

This thought had already occurred to Spring. "Connie died young?"

Aunty nodded. "It was wartime, you know, World War II. Connie went to work in a munitions factory in Milwaukee. She met a sailor from Great Lakes Naval Base near Waukegan, Illinois. He'd taken the North

Shore train to Milwaukee. They fell in love at first sight." A tear trickled down her aunt's soft, wrinkled cheek.

Sorry to have brought pain to Aunt Geneva, Spring handed her a soft tissue from a box on her bedside tray. "They never married?"

Aunty dabbed her eyes. "Connie had an engagement ring and she was so happy. But it was 1945, no time to be in love. He shipped out and was killed in action."

The long-ago story still had the power to stir Spring to pity. *Poor Connie.*

"But my mother was born."

"Yes, I believe that he intended to marry Connie. In fact, he wanted to marry Connie before he left, but her parents persuaded her not to marry until he came home. He wasn't good enough for them!" Aunty's voice became fierce. "They shouldn't have meddled. They let Bill go off to war. Then Connie came up pregnant, and they didn't want anyone to know. But Connie told me and Gloria."

Aunty's face started to pick up color again as her agitation mounted. "Her parents should have kept her home with them! People in town knew what kind of girl Connie was! Everyone knew she and Bill were engaged, and in wartime these things happen. But they hushed everything up and sent their only daughter away to an aunt's to have the baby."

"I'm sure they did what they thought was best." *But I could never do that!*

Aunty pursed her lips. "I've always believed that Connie wouldn't have died if she'd been at home when she had her baby. Who knew what kind of doctor she had, what kind of care!"

Spring couldn't think of any reply to this, so she returned to the reason she'd disturbed the past. "Did Connie have any brothers and sisters?"

"Only one brother. He died in the Battle of the Bulge." Aunty drew a long breath. "Such sad times to remember." She wiped away new tears.

Spring touched her aunt's arm. "What was Mother's father's name?"

"Bill Smith. But it's a dead end, Spring. He died when his ship was attacked in the Pacific. So you see, there isn't anyone—"

"Maybe he had brothers or sisters," Spring offered.

"He might have. It was so long ago, I've forgotten…if I ever knew that to start with. I can't give you much to work with to find out if he had any other family."

Aunty reached for Spring's hand. "But I wanted you to know. Your mother may want to know someday, and I might not be here to tell her the story." Aunty tried to smile. "Connie had a first cousin in Oconomowoc, too, but she may be dead or long gone by now. I only remember her first name, Mary Beth."

The sad story tugged at her heart, and Spring rose and kissed her aunt's cheek. "Thank you for telling me. We might never find any blood relatives and we might never need them. Mother's leukemia may never come back."

Aunty fussed with her blanket. "I just hope I've done right to tell you."

"Aunt Geneva, as you've said, times have changed. This should have been revealed years ago."

"You're probably right, dear. Connie wanted Gloria to take her baby. She knew Gloria had just married Tom and that they'd take good care of her."

"Connie's parents didn't want their only grand-child?"

Aunty pursed her lips. "Our mother always said they were too concerned about what people would say. Their loss. Ethel was welcomed into our family with open arms."

"Did Grandmother choose the name Ethel?"

"No, Connie named her."

"I wonder why she chose that name."

"I don't know. I'm sorry, dear, but I'm tired now."

"I'm sure you are. Close your eyes. I'm going down to the cafeteria and get something to eat."

"You do that, dear. I'm afraid you've lost weight again."

Spring grinned. "Not a bit. I gained weight on the cruise, and Matilde has had me under surveillance. I have not gone hungry!"

"Soon I want to hear all about the cruise!"

"Soon," Spring promised. She walked out into the hallway.

What would her sisters, Hannah and Doree, have to say about this? Was there any chance of finding blood relatives? The story didn't seem to give them much in the way of leads.

Is that Your answer, Lord? Are we to leave this all in Your hands and quit meddling, too?

"All right. Are we all on the line?" Spring asked over the phone, sitting on her bed at Aunt Geneva's house later that evening.

"I'm here," Hannah replied.

"Me, too!" Doree exclaimed. "So what's the deal? Did Aunt Geneva give you the scoop?"

Spring sighed. "Aunty is much better this evening. Thank you for asking."

"Of course she is!" Doree declared. "Mom called me last night and told me that—"

Hannah interrupted, "I think Spring is trying to teach you how to begin a phone conversation. Certainly *someone* needs to do that. Aunty just had serious surgery after having had a heart attack—you should ask about her health first, not just start gabbing."

Doree huffed into the phone, but said nothing.

Spring cleared her throat. "Aunt Geneva has told me the full story of our mother's natural parents."

"Wow!" Doree exclaimed. "I can't believe you finally got her to tell."

Spring talked over Doree's voice. Tonight, Doree's flippant attitude irritated Spring like a fingernail scraping against a chalkboard. "Aunt Geneva decided we should know, in case mother ever needed or wanted to know. Aunt Geneva says she is the only living person who knows what happened."

"Does that mean that mother's natural father is deceased, too?" Hannah asked.

"I'm afraid so." Spring sighed again.

"When did he die?" Doree continued her interrogation. "Did he marry and have other children?"

Spring drew on her waning emotional reserves. *What are you getting at, Doree?* "He died when his ship was attacked in the Pacific in World War II."

Doree enquired, "Did anyone attend his funeral?"

Spring frowned. "I doubt anyone from Mother's hometown. He and our grandmother's friend, Connie Wilson, were engaged but not married. I think he might have gone down with his ship. Would they even have held a funeral service?"

"What was his name?" Doree pressed.

"Bill Smith." Spring couldn't keep the exhaustion out of her voice. *Stop it, Doree.*

"Bill Smith? That's an awfully common name," Doree commented.

"What of it?" Hannah countered.

"Well," Doree demanded, "so many Bill Smiths died in World War II, but maybe not our Bill Smith."

Chapter Thirteen

"What do you mean by that?" Spring asked, frustrated.

"I mean that it's not over until I find *the* Bill Smith who was or is our grandfather," Doree insisted. "Mistakes in reporting men who died in action have happened in every war."

"Do you really think that's possible?" Hannah asked, sounding uncertain.

"I'm not giving up until every avenue is exhausted. This is too crucial to Mom's health not to try," Doree said. "Spring, give me all the details you can remember about our grandfather."

Spring thought back over her aunt's words. "He was stationed at the Great Lakes Naval Base near Waukegan, Illinois. Connie and he met in Milwaukee, where she was working at a defense factory. His ship was attacked in the Pacific in 1945."

"That's all you've got?" Doree didn't sound peeved, merely thorough. "I'm going to use the Internet for this search. You'd be surprised the kinds of government records that are open to the public and only a click away."

"Sounds like you know what you're doing," Spring conceded.

"If you get a chance—when it wouldn't upset her—you might ask Aunt Geneva if she knew what state or town he was from." Doree's concerned, businesslike tone surprised Spring. Maybe their baby sister was maturing.

"I will." Spring lay back on the bed, too exhausted to sit up. The cruise, Aunt's heart attack, everything!

"Spring?" Hannah's soft voice coaxed. "I know you're probably really tired, but my wedding plans are proceeding on schedule. When Mom comes to Florida, she's going to take your measurements for your maid-of-honor dress. I've chosen peach chiffon for the bridesmaids. It should look really good on you and Doree."

Hannah's June wedding. Spring had shoved it to the back of her mind, along with the fact that Mother would arrive in a few days. Now she tried to infuse her voice with some enthusiasm. "Peach will be lovely. I suppose you weren't able to dissuade Mother from sewing the bridesmaids' dresses?"

Hannah sighed with deep feeling. "It was a losing battle. She really wanted to do them, especially when I wouldn't let her sew my wedding gown."

"She's still making the veil, isn't she?" Doree put her

oar in the conversation. "Her veils are always so elegant. And I hope you're not doing something *precious* for bridesmaid dresses. I don't want to have to bury the dress when I'm done."

"You're insufferable," Hannah shot back. "For a crack like that, I should add lace and ruffles to yours!"

"I have a headache," Spring announced, too worn down to take any more sisterly banter.

"We'll let you go," Hannah hurried to say. "I'm sure you've been under a lot of stress. But I'm so glad you were there when Aunt Geneva needed you. Tell her I'm counting on her to recover and come to my wedding."

"I'll tell her." Spring rolled toward the phone's cradle on the bedside table.

Doree piped up, "When will you be back in Wisconsin?"

This stopped Spring in the act of hanging up. Should she tell them? She hadn't let anyone know of her intentions. "I don't know—"

"But isn't your leave of absence up in a few more weeks?" Hannah asked.

She decided to test out the reactions to her decision. "I'm thinking of staying here—but don't say anything yet."

"For good?" Doree exclaimed. "Does this have something to do with that guy who went on that cruise—?"

"On that note, good night, dear sisters. I love you." Spring hung up and closed her eyes. Hannah's wedding,

Aunt Geneva's illness, Mother's coming, the Golden Sands April Garden Show, Marco's free clinic, Paloma's portrait—her mind was crowded with such a multitude of things to do, but all she wanted to think about, to savor, was the vivid memory of Marco's heart-stopping kisses.

Her phone rang. She picked it up, hoping Doree hadn't thought of any more questions. "Hello?"

"Spring?" Marco's rich voice asked.

She sat up, her pulse speeding up. "Marco?"

"I'm sorry to call you so late, but I thought you'd like to know—"

"Is something wrong with my aunt?" *No, Lord, please.*

"No, it's about the clinic. Pete called and said he and Greg filed the application for nonprofit status for the Gulfview Free Clinic today." The pride in his voice was palpable.

"That's wonderful."

"Pete says it will only take a week or two to be approved." His voice sounded hesitant, shy.

Why? Was it because of how their relationship was changing? "This is exciting." She forced enthusiasm into her voice, wishing they were speaking face-to-face. *Ah, yés.*

"It is." He paused. "When we have a chance, we need to celebrate."

"Yes," she managed to reply. Her heart was so full, she couldn't get any power from her diaphragm to speak more.

"I'll bid you *buenas noches,* then." His voice caressed her.

"Good night." Spring hung up the phone once more. Closing her eyes, she imagined Marco beside her, holding her. At the thought, sensations—warmth and chills—alternately cascaded through her. *Dear Lord, if Marco is the one for me, please tell me how to let him know I love him.*

Then another wonderful idea for the free clinic popped into her mind. Would it work?

At the sight of the airport minivan, Spring flung open her aunt's front door. "Mother!" She rushed out and threw her arms around her mother.

Ethel, in the navy-blue traveling suit Spring knew so well, stopped in the midst of giving the shuttle driver a tip and returned the hug. Then she turned back to the driver and thanked him. He looked at the tip, carried her bags to the door and left smiling.

Spring experienced crosscurrents of joy at seeing her mother. She worried, however, that she might accidentally let the facts of the search for her natural grandfather slip. Blocking these from her mind, she picked up the heaviest suitcase and ushered her mother inside. "I would have been happy to pick you up at the airport."

"No, I'm used to the shuttle and I only had to wait about fifteen minutes for it. How are you, dear? How's Aunty?"

"I'm fine!" Aunt Geneva called from her new recliner out in the Florida room at the back of her house. "Put the bags in your room, then come out here. Matilde has made fresh iced tea with lemon for us, and cucumber-and-dill sandwiches."

Soon the four of them relaxed in the long, breezy room overlooking the garden. March rains had brought every leaf to a brilliant green and every bloom to a vivid pink, red or white. The shimmering turquoise Gulf framed the garden still life.

"This is the life." Mother sighed. "I just left two feet of snow in Wisconsin."

"I told you years ago that you and Garner should move to Florida," Aunty said in an I-told-you-so tone.

Mother smiled. "We love Wisconsin. But I did need a break this year. You know I would have come down sooner, but Spring said I should wait until you were home. You're looking good. How are you feeling?"

"Like a new woman, or, at least, I will when I'm completely recovered."

"Well, I hope that's in time for Hannah's wedding."

"I wouldn't miss it! And we may have another wedding in the near future," Aunty said with a nod toward Spring.

Spring blushed. *I should have expected this!*

Mother glanced at Spring. "Is it that young man you persuaded to go on the cruise?"

"Sí!" Matilde answered for her. "Marco Da Palma, the stepson of a dear friend of mine."

Paloma in blue jeans and red T-shirt walked in. "Matilde, I finished mopping the kitchen and all the bathrooms. What do you want me to do next?"

"Come and have a glass of iced tea," Aunty invited. "This is Spring's mother, Ethel Kirkland."

"Good morning, Mrs. Kirkland." Paloma smiled, then pointed to herself. "I'm Marco's little sister."

Mother returned the smile and greeted Paloma.

"Matilde, if Paloma has finished her chores, I'd like to get some more work done on her portrait," Spring said. "I've been so busy. But it's so close, I need to get it done."

"Of course!" Matilde got up. "Paloma, drink your tea, while I help Spring set up her easel. We only have a few Saturdays to go!"

Mother chuckled. "I see nothing has changed at your house, Aunty. Never a dull moment!"

On the Golden Sands veranda overlooking the green golf course, Spring sat back and sighed with contentment. She was about to initiate the plan she'd thought of to help Marco's clinic. At first, she'd dreaded being on the April Garden Show committee, but now she thought she detected the hand of God. The garden show would be the perfect vehicle for the plan that had unfolded in Spring's mind. She smiled at Aunt Geneva, Verna Rae and Eleanor, who ranged around the table.

"Ladies, I have a change in plans for this show I need to discuss with you three. I think this garden show is just what the doctor ordered…."

Spring watched Marco, tall and lithe, as he took a practice swing on the first tee. Another week had passed, bringing them closer to each other and to the April Garden Show. What would Marco think of what she'd set in motion?

Marco swung, connected with the ball and sent it flying over the fairway toward the green.

"Excellent!" Spring beamed at him.

He stood with his hands on his hips, watching the arc of his ball. "Not bad for a beginner."

She chuckled. "You're a natural and I hate you."

He grinned back at her.

She'd noticed Marco doing this more and more often. The dreadfully serious Dr. Da Palma was doing a vanishing act right before her eyes. "So golf isn't as bad as you thought?"

"It's addictive—and you knew that, didn't you," he said in a falsely accusatory tone.

She twirled the ends of an imaginary handlebar mustache. "Ha, ha, ha. It's all a part of my dark stratagem to make you have fun! I've got you in my clutches now, Doctor."

His sizzling smile to this silliness made her legs weak. She inhaled deeply, gathering her paper-thin resistance to this handsome man's potent charm.

His cell phone rang.

Spring tried not to look peeved, but they had yet to finish a golf lesson without at least one interruption.

Scowling, Marco pulled it out of his pocket and opened it. "Dr. Da Palma speaking."

Warm sunshine on her face, Spring closed her eyes

and breathed in the salty Gulf air. The day couldn't be more perfect—if only Marco wouldn't be called away.

"Really!"

Spring hadn't ever heard Marco sound so excited. She opened her eyes wider and took a step closer.

"That's great! I can't believe it went through so easily. How can I thank you? Great. Sure. Thanks again." He snapped the phone shut.

She took another step closer.

"That was Pete—"

She gave a little hop of anticipation. "The non-profit—"

"Status has been granted!" He threw his arms around her. "It's going to start—what I've dreamed of! And I owe it all to you!"

Breathless, she returned his embrace. "Not to me. I just got you started. God's blessing is written all over this. Pete and Greg just picked up the ball."

"I can't believe it!" He swung her up into his arms and kissed her.

Spring's breath caught in her throat. *Marco, I love you. When will I have the courage to tell you? And what will you say when I do?*

"Welcome! *Bienvenido a nuestro fiesta!* Welcome to our fiesta!" Anita greeted them in the driveway of her home.

Arriving at the fiesta to celebrate the clinic's achieving nonprofit status, Spring had dropped off her passengers and parked farther down the crowded block, then walked over. Now with her aunt, mother, Verna Rae and Eleanor at her side, she glanced around. The men had congregated in the front yard, sitting on the steps and grass. Santos waved cheerfully. She waved back as she scanned the male faces around Santos. No Marco.

After Spring introduced her mother, Verna Rae and Eleanor, Anita led them up the drive to the canopy in the backyard.

"*Por favor,* help yourselves to the food and drink. I'll find some chairs for you over in the shade."

"We're so thrilled for Marco!" Aunty announced. "You have a wonderful son! We think the world of him."

"*Gracias.*" Anita blushed. "The members of Golden Sands all did so much for Marco. I can't thank you enough for helping my son with his education."

"It was our pleasure," Eleanor said. "We love to see worthy students achieve their ambitions."

Verna Rae nodded vigorously. "It's the American dream, and we like to do our part to see it keeps happening."

The backyard overflowed with women and children. Spring waved hello to Paloma, who was surrounded by her young friends. *Tía* Rosita and Lupe from Mamacita's were pushing two little girls on the swing set. They waved to Spring. The happy scene reminded her of a church picnic. She glanced around discreetly for Marco.

"Hello." He appeared at her elbow. "I'm so glad all of you could come."

All the ladies with Spring fluttered around Marco, congratulating him. Spring couldn't control her face, which insisted on breaking into a ridiculously wide smile. Mother stood apart until the rush died down.

"Marco, I'd like you to meet my mother," Spring said. Mother held out her hand, and Marco shook it. Spring tried to look nonchalant, but she could tell by the assessing look her mother gave Marco that Aunty had divulged even more about Spring's interest in him. Fortunately, her mother wasn't the type to make mortifying comments.

"Hey! Spring!" Pete, wearing a University of Florida T-shirt and cutoffs, bounded over.

Spring smiled at him but mentally crossed her fingers. What would unpredictable Pete say?

"Brought plenty of chaperones, I see!" Pete announced to the world at large. "Good idea! Marco's quite the Don Juan!"

She could always count on Pete to be excruciatingly tactless. "Does anyone have a gag I could borrow?" she said wryly.

"Hey! I just call 'em like I see 'em," Pete announced.

She glanced at Marco to see his reaction. He didn't look like he'd even noticed Pete's teasing. His warm regard, centered on her, brought a blush that worked an intense path throughout her body.

She imagined Marco's reaction to the surprise she was busy working on. He'd be so happy. They'd celebrate with another fiesta!

* * *

Spring trailed the elderly real estate agent and Marco inside the empty downtown church, just a stone's throw away from Mamacita's and the Hacienda Bakery. It must have been empty well over a year. Broken windows had been boarded up and cobwebs fluttered from the high ceiling in the breeze from the open front doors. In the neglected sanctuary, the stained-glass window behind the pulpit still translated sunshine into brilliant blue, gold and red beams of light, cast over the dusty interior.

"Well, you've seen it all, then," the rotund real estate agent said. "Any other questions?"

"I don't think so." Marco's eye roved over the large room. "I'll stop at the bank and get the financing and paperwork started."

"Okay. I'll be going, then. Are you and the lady staying?"

Marco looked to Spring. "We'll look around just a bit longer."

"Then, be sure to lock up."

Marco and the man shook hands. When the realtor had departed, Marco ambled over to Spring and sat down beside her on an old wooden pew. Seeking connection with her, he slid his arm around her shoulder. For many minutes, they sat in silence. Did Spring feel the way he did about being here?

"It's very satisfying, isn't it," she said, answering his unspoken question.

"It's a start," he admitted. He stroked Spring's arm with the hand that secured her to him. "I'm glad you agreed to come with me."

She looked up at him. "I was so happy you asked me to join you! This location is perfect. A good-size parking lot. The bus stop right on the corner. And there's room for expansion in the open area at the rear."

He drew in a deep breath. So much had happened in the past few months—ever since Spring had come back into his life. "I think I'll send the garden show committee ladies roses."

"Roses?" She gave him an arch look. Had someone let her surprise slip out ahead of time? "Why?"

"Because if they hadn't guilted me onto the committee, you wouldn't have come back into my life."

Spring lost her breath for a moment, then she inhaled deeply. "I feel the same way."

"You do?" Marco looked as if he couldn't believe it.

"Yes." She nodded, then decided to let actions speak louder than words. She kissed him.

He turned her in his embrace and gathered her closer. He kissed her.

She closed her eyes, concentrating all of her senses on the touch of his lips on hers and the delicious rush of pleasure his caress brought her. "Marco," she whispered against his mouth, "I love you."

Her own words shocked her. But she couldn't mistake Marco's actions. He wasn't a man to kiss a woman whom he didn't—

"I've loved you since the first time I saw you in Professor Warnock's freshman biology class," he murmured.

Her breath caught in her throat again.

He kissed her.

"Why didn't you let me know?" she asked, dazed at hearing his declaration of love.

He shrugged. "How could I? You were so beautiful, so aloof, so blond! And I had no time or money for dating."

She nestled her face in the curve of his neck. "We were both too young, I guess. That was my very first college class. I was so nervous that day, I felt sick."

He chuckled against her ear, a lovely sensation to her. "Every guy in the room had a hard time keeping his eyes on the prof. They were all sneaking peeks at you."

She shook her head. "I didn't—don't—like it when men do that."

He nodded. "It made you shy, didn't it?"

She looked up at him. "You understand that?"

"Yes, you never liked men hanging all over you, and then that night…" He let his voice fade.

She appreciated his tact. He was bringing up one of the worst nights of her life. She snuggled closer to him. "I've never forgotten how you rescued me that night."

"And I regret I didn't get to break that guy's nose. That's what I wanted to do! I still think you should have reported him to the university. He was a pig." Marco's handsome face darkened with anger.

His strong reaction after all these years—was it an indication of how he felt about her?

That dreadful night, she'd gone out with a blind date. It had started as a double date, but the other couple had wanted to neck. Uncomfortable with this turn of events, Spring had asked her date to walk her back to her dorm. On the way, he pulled her off the lighted path into the bushes. He'd made it clear he wanted more than necking. Frightened, she'd run away from him—straight into Marco, who'd been walking home from the library. Marco had sent her "date" on his way and walked her back to her dorm himself.

"I'd have liked to give him a black eye along with the broken nose, but I didn't think you wanted to make a big deal out of it."

"You did just what you should have." She sighed. "That all seems a million years ago."

"And I feel like a different man since you came into my life again. And the cruise—it opened my eyes to how much I was still carrying the past around with me."

"What do you mean?"

"You were right. I was still thinking of myself as different from everyone because of being an Hispanic immigrant and having to pay for school by working and…charity."

"Scholarships," she corrected him. "You shouldn't have let that bother you. A lot of students—"

He pressed his finger to her lips, then kissed her right, then her left, eyebrow. "I'm seeing things clearly now. Yes, I faced discrimination when I was younger.

But I've been holding onto it in a way that…was keeping me from life…from you."

She lost her breath again. She inhaled, trying to reel in her rampant reactions. "Let's leave the past *in the past.*"

"I plan to…focus on the future." He ran his fingers into her hair, lifting it and watching it fall. "I achieved my goal to become a doctor. Now my objective to provide free medical services can begin. It will take years, but I don't mind."

She nearly voiced her good news for him then, but squelched it. The work wasn't finished yet. She'd wait until the right time, then surprise him. She traced the bow of his sculpted lips.

In response, he outlined the line of her ivory cheek with his forefinger. "When do you have to go back to Wisconsin?"

She thrilled at his touch. "I don't. I've resigned my position. I'm staying in Florida."

His eyes widened with surprise. "You are? You want to move here? I hadn't…I'd hoped…."

"Aunty needs me, and I just couldn't bear to go back—"

He cut off her words with another kiss.

She didn't mind at all. The future, their future looked so bright. And the best was yet to come. The garden show was just around the corner. She still had a lot of work to do before then, but she'd accomplished her goal for Marco, the man she loved and who loved her.

She whispered, "You'll be coming to the garden show, won't you?"

"Do you want me to?" Grinning, he nudged her nose with his.

"Yes, I think it would mean a lot to Verna Rae, Eleanor and Aunty." *And me. And you.*

"I'll be there, then."

Chapter Fourteen

The phone in Aunty's front hall jingled. "I'll get it," Spring called out, and picked up the beige receiver. "Hello."

"Spring! You'll never guess!" Doree shouted, "I found him! I found our grandfather! I just talked to him on the phone!"

Spring's mouth opened but no words came out.

"Did you hear me?"

"You talked to our grandfather?" Spring swallowed with difficulty. "He's alive?"

"Alive and kicking!" Doree crowed. "He retired to Long Beach, California."

"How did you find him, Doree?" Spring's mind raced. "I can hardly believe what you're saying."

"Believe it! I just started by finding out all the Bill or William Smith's who'd served in the Navy in World War II, trained at Great Lakes and were reported dead or wounded in the Pacific in 1945. You'd be amazed at the information I found."

Spring tried to put the brakes on Doree's runaway enthusiasm. "How do you know he's Mother's biological father?"

"Because I asked him."

"You asked him!" *No, Doree, no!* "We all agreed not to contact Mother's natural family unless we had to—"

"I didn't ask him about Mother. But after all the hours of research, I had to call him. I was just going to act like I was doing research on World War II veterans who'd been mistakenly reported lost in action, but he was so nice. I ended up asking him if he'd known a woman named Connie Wilson."

"Doree, you didn't!" They should have known not to leave an issue so delicate up to Doree. "How could you?"

"Well, I could and I did. And he said yes he'd been engaged to a Connie Wilson in Milwaukee in 1945, but that she'd died while he was away at sea. He even said that after he'd recovered from being wounded, he went to her hometown. But her parents wouldn't speak to him, except to tell him Connie was dead and that they didn't want to have anything to do with him."

"He did?" The cruelty of her great-grandparents withholding the truth about their daughter and her child from the man she loved made her chest tighten as though they'd pierced her own heart. "Why didn't they tell him the truth? That he had a daughter?"

"I don't know. But he said it took him nearly ten years to get over losing her. He didn't marry again until 1956. And get this, sis, he's got three grown children."

"Mother has half brothers and sisters!" This was more than she'd ever expected!

"Yes." Doree sounded smug. "Three other possible donors, if Mom should need them."

"Praise God. This is almost too much to take in all at once."

"That's why I didn't tell him that I was his natural granddaughter. I didn't want to give him a heart attack."

A movement in Spring's peripheral vision made her pause. *Oh, no!* "Mother?"

Looking dazed, Mother walked out from the doorway to the living room. "What have you girls done?"

Spring tightened her grip on the receiver. "Doree, Mother's here in the hallway."

"Oh, no!" Doree moaned into Spring's ear.

Taking a deep breath, Spring turned to face her mother. "Doree, Hannah and I have been trying to locate your natural parents—"

"You know I told you I didn't want you to do that!" Mother's voice quavered.

Spring had never seen her mother this pale, or shaking the way she was. "Mother, here, sit down." Spring pulled out the chair from the phone table.

Mother sat down, but in spite of her wan face her expression turned stormy. "Why did you go against—"

"We had to. If one of us had matched as a bone marrow donor, we wouldn't have pursued this."

"But—"

"But what if your remission ended. We couldn't take the chance."

Looking somber, Aunt Geneva walked out of another doorway. "I overheard you, too. I think we all ought to sit down and talk this over calmly. Tell Doree we'll call her back in a bit."

Spring obeyed her aunt, grateful for backup.

Frighteningly white now, Mother looked up. "You knew about this, Aunty?"

"Yes, and it's all for the best—if Bill did indeed survive. Don't you realize that he loved your mother and would have wanted you?"

Mother began to weep.

Aunty looked to Spring. "Let's all go out in the Florida room. It's time for all the old secrets and pain to come out into the light of truth."

An hour and a full box of blue tissues later, the tragic love story of her natural parents had been revealed to Mother.

Holding the receiver again with Doree on the line, Spring watched her mother wipe her eyes.

"I wish this…had been explained…to me years ago," Mother said haltingly. "I always thought that my natural parents didn't want me." She inhaled deeply, her tears drying. "That's why I was so adamant about not trying to locate them. I didn't want to be rejected twice."

"Oh, Ethel," Aunt Geneva lamented, "if I or your mother Gloria had known, we would have told you. Your natural parents loved one another and would have been married—if only Connie's parents had kept their noses out of things."

"Let me talk to Doree again." Mother reached out her hand for the phone. "Doree, call Mr. Smith back, tell him about what happened to…my mother, his sweetheart, and ask him if he'd like to meet me. If he truly loved my mother, I'll take the chance."

"Wow, Mom. I will." Doree hung up.

"Time will tell." Aunty sighed. "Now I'm ready for some lunch. I feel like I've just chopped a pile of wood. And I've never lifted an ax in my life!"

Though still teary, Mom chuckled at this.

Spring felt her spirits lift again. Only the tiniest doubt remained that Grandfather Smith would refuse to talk to Mother. *Oh, Lord, after years of misunderstanding and pain, please let this be a time of happy reunion!*

The April Garden Show judging had nearly ended. The airy Golden Sands Country Club, open to the public for the day, teemed and hummed with well-dressed residents and tourists in shorts and T-shirts, examining the colorful prize plants. In one area, an extensive variety of blooming orchids had been judged, while in another, tea roses of every shade were displayed. The main corridor was devoted to an educational display of Bird of Paradise. Area nurseries and greenhouses had set up sample garden displays on the lawn. The show had broken all past attendance records.

In the midst of stellar success, Spring's only problem was that Marco still hadn't shown up. And it was almost time!

"What's keeping him?" Aunt Geneva in a purple dress with gold buttons fretted for the tenth time.

"I don't know."

Eleanor appeared at Spring's elbow, her floral-print chiffon skirt swishing about her. "That Marco, where is he?"

"I don't know." Spring couldn't hold back the nerves eating at her stomach. "He promised me faithfully that he'd be here."

"Well," Verna Rae crowded closer to Eleanor, "if he isn't here, we'll just have to go on without him."

Spring worried her lower lip. *No, Marco, not another emergency call from the hospital.* "That's the head judge signaling to me. They're ready to hand out the prize ribbons."

"No stopping now," Aunty said in bracing tones. "We'll just have to proceed—Marco or no Marco."

Spring nodded, her optimism drooping by the second. She and the other three garden show committee members walked to the front of the large ballroom, which was filling with attendees taking their seats to see the prizes bestowed on winners and take part in the second part of the gala.

One last time, Spring turned back to the entrance. Marco strode in and paused, looking around. She stood on tiptoe and waved at him. *He's here! He won't miss it!*

She wondered if the happiness she concealed would burst out of bounds before the time came to reveal the joyful news for Marco. It was only minutes now!

Marco wended his way through the crowd toward her. Dressed in a black suit with a white shirt and silver tie, he was more devastatingly striking than she'd ever thought him before. His mere glance turned her into sweet, melted joy. *Marco, my love.*

Spring saw the transformation in him, which had come in the past few weeks. Smiling, he stopped to greet Golden Sands members and other friends, shaking hands and nodding toward her, the picture of easy but dignified charm. *My cup runneth over, Lord. Aunty's health is improving. I'm staying in Florida, and Marco and I have a future, a wonderful future ahead of us. Thank You, Lord. It's almost too many blessings to believe. I accept them with a grateful heart.*

Marco reached her and put his arm around her shoulder as though they'd been a couple for a thousand years. A glow like tropical sunshine coursed through her.

Happiness and thankfulness clogged Spring's throat. *This wonderful man loves me!* She tried to tell him everything with her smile. *Marco, I love you.*

She and Marco sank down side by side in the front row. He knit his long, tanned fingers with hers. This simple act made her heart hum with a silent ecstatic melody. Aunt Geneva went to the podium, and for the next fifteen minutes, prizes in various categories were awarded to beaming winners. When this had been wrapped up, Aunty signaled to Spring.

Shaking inside but exultant, Spring stood up and made her way to the podium. Love expanding within her, she let herself send a special glance to Marco. His eyebrows were lifted in question. She sent him a tremulous smile, then cleared her throat.

"As you know, the Golden Sands April Garden Show is in its thirty-fifth year. This year the Golden Sands board approved an addition to the program which we hope will become a part of this yearly event."

Spring drew in a deep breath. "As you probably noticed, a silent auction has been in progress all during today's show. Many generous Golden Sands members, local merchants and contestants have donated goods, services and prize-worthy plants to be auctioned off to benefit a new community project initiated by Dr. Marco Da Palma—the Gulfview Free Clinic."

Looking at Marco, she noted that he'd frozen in his chair. Well, she'd wanted to surprise him and she certainly had!

"While the grand total of the money generated by today's silent auction is being calculated, I'd like to thank several community leaders who instantly took to this idea and have already made sizable pledges. Would those people please come forward now?"

She stole a peek at Marco's face. She couldn't decipher his expression. What was he thinking?

She continued. "First, I'd like to mention that Peter Rasmussen and Gregory Fortney have donated the money for the down payment for the clinic's site, the former Faith Community Church on Main Street. They couldn't be here today, but send their best. Now—" she motioned toward a fashionable couple in their forties who stepped up to meet her "—this couple is Mr. and Mrs. Grady Jones. They have volunteered to pay the first year's monthly mortgage for the clinic."

Applause broke out. The Joneses said a few words, then stepped back. Next, Spring introduced the three different contracting firms who had offered to update the clinic's plumbing, electrical and handicapped accessibility, gratis. Applause greeted each announced donation.

Spring glanced at Marco. His face was devoid of any reaction. *What's wrong, Marco?*

A Golden Sands board member approached the podium and handed her a sheet of yellow paper. Seeing the total, she beamed. "Today's silent auction has netted the Gulfview Free Clinic 9,352.00 in cash."

The audience exploded into reverberating applause. A few men stomped their feet and whistled. Spring felt tears fill her eyes. *Thank you, Lord. You have moved people to such generosity, it takes my breath away.*

Marco looked like he'd stopped breathing, too. Should she have warned him or given him a hint?

Sitting beside Marco's mother, stepfather and sister,

Matilde and *Tía* Rosita rose. They both marched forward like women with a mission. Spring stepped back and let them have the microphone.

"I'm Matilde Ramirez and this is *Tía* Rosita. We don't have a lot of money, but we are going to make sure—with help from other women in the downtown community—that this will be the cleanest clinic in Florida!"

More applause.

But Marco sat, blank-faced and immobile.

Spring tried to think what to say, to do. What was Marco thinking?

In the back of the ballroom, a man stood up. Spring thought she recognized him and motioned toward him to speak. He raised his strong voice. "I'm Dr. Edward Clary. I'm the head of staff at Gulfview General and I work with Dr. Da Palma. I hadn't heard of these plans, but I'm certain that many of the doctors and nurses of Gulfview will be willing to donate time at the clinic—"

The room exploded with excitement. Many people stood to applaud. Soon the whole roomful was on its feet. The chant of "Speech, speech" began.

Spring eyed Marco. Would he come to the podium? Mother, who sat beside him, pushed him to his feet. He walked to the front as though his joints had stiffened. Abashed and uncertain, Spring stepped aside so he could speak into the microphone.

Marco looked out over the sea of happy faces and felt like slamming his fist into the podium. He took a steadying breath, spooling in his rage. *I have to get through this.*

"Ladies and gentlemen," he began, feeling his way carefully toward the proper words, not the ones he stuffed down inside, unsaid. "I had no idea—" *that's for sure* "—that today's garden show…would hold so many surprises. I'm stunned." *That's the truth.* "But Spring Kirkland appears to be full of surprises." *Shocks is more like it.* There was laughter.

"This clinic…which will provide free medical care for those who have insufficient insurance, no insurance or don't qualify for any government assistance, is vitally necessary in our community." Speaking about the clinic steadied him. He unclenched his right fist.

"To those of you who have donated items for auction, thank you. To those who have pledged time and money, I'm deeply indebted to you…." This grated his already raw nerves. *But I never wanted to be.*

Stifling his anger, he motioned for the new applause to quiet. "Thank you all, especially Spring Kirkland, whom I'm sure is responsible for all this." The unkindest cut of all. *How could you, Spring? How could you?*

The next afternoon, Spring stood, fretting in the parking lot of the Golden Sands golf course. The blue sky overhead, the tantalizing warm breeze, the gorgeous day counted for nothing. She consulted her watch again. Marco was twenty-two minutes late for their golf date. *He isn't coming.* The words echoed like a death knell inside her.

Something had gone dreadfully, dreadfully wrong

yesterday afternoon at the garden show. Somehow everything fresh and sparkling between Marco and her had disappeared in a flash. After the announcements of all the support for the free clinic, she'd stood beside him, accepting congratulations. But it had been like standing beside a glacier. *What is it, Lord? What did I do to anger him?*

With a feeling of fatalism, she flipped open her cell phone and dialed his apartment. No answer. She punched in his office number. No answer. She shrank from calling the hospital. As a last resort before giving up, she dialed his mother's number. "Hello, Anita, this is Spring. I'm trying to locate Marco. We had a golf date today."

"Oh, Spring, he just called me about something. He's at the church."

Did she detect worry in Anita's voice? "The church for the free clinic?"

"*Sí.* Do you have his cell phone number?" Anita asked.

Spring said yes, thanked her and hung up. She stared out across the green to the rippling blue Gulf beyond. *Lord, I feel like running home, crying my eyes out and hiding in my room for the next month. But that's the old Spring. I've come too far to go back. I won't lose the man I love a second time. But You're going to have to go with me and give me the words to say—because I haven't got a clue what's wrong!*

Spring parked her aunt's car in the littered parking lot on the west side of the white stucco church, then walked to its side entrance. Her heart pounded in her ears, louder with each step. What would she say? What would Marco say? Closing her eyes, she said one more prayer for guidance, then she opened the door and walked in. Immediately, she heard the *swish* of a broom and knew she'd probably find Marco at the handle end of it.

With flagging steps, she entered the sanctuary. Head down, Marco was sweeping the refuse in front of the pulpit into a neat pile. His posture telegraphed his despondent mood to her. *What is it, Marco?*

"Hello," she called, and paused by the last row of wooden pews. She remembered how they'd sat side by side here, sharing how much in love they were, such a short time ago.

Marco looked up. No smile welcomed her.

"We had a golf date." Her voice quavered in the empty, high-ceilinged room.

"Golf?" He sounded as if he didn't recognize the word.

"You know, the game where you hit the little ball into a cup?" She attempted a smile but it faded under his sober attention.

"I'm sorry. I guess I forgot."

His tone chilled her. Marco never forgot. A tremor of naked fear arced through her.

He made a sound of disgust, then rested both wrists atop the broom handle. "I didn't forget. I just didn't feel like golf today. I meant to call you. I just didn't…get to the phone."

She fought to remain calm. "Marco, I—"

"I'm sorry I made you track me down." He cut her off in a flat voice.

The sharp look he gave her made her freeze inside. Who was this cold-eyed stranger? It couldn't be her Marco.

"I—I see," she stuttered, tears only a breath away. "Well, I'll let you get back to work." Her brightly spoken words tripped over her tongue. "We can set up another date."

He nodded as if she'd just said, "Let's discuss that at the next funeral."

Before tears could overtake her, she turned and ran outside. She sprinted to her car.

Inside, a gale of weeping broke over her. Her head bowed, she sobbed into her hands. Mental photographs of moments spent with Marco flashed in a parade in her mind—Marco frowning over a golf shot, Marco doing the limbo, Marco in the moonlight...

Finally the tempest passed, leaving her weak and shaky. She prayed for calm and waited for it. Finally, still distraught, she started her car. She had to get home, home to Mother.

She found her mother in her aunt's garden. Without a word, but with tears flowing, she walked into her mother's arms. *This is what it feels like to have a broken heart. Oh, God, it hurts so bad. What has happened?*

Mother held her close and murmured soft words to

her, just as she had when Spring was a child. Slowly, Spring's tears ebbed.

"It's Marco, isn't it," Mother murmured beside Spring's ear.

Spring nodded, too exhausted emotionally to speak.

"I could see how he changed at the garden show. You don't have a clue why, do you?"

Shaking her head no, Spring caught her breath. "I thought he loved me."

"He does, dear. But without meaning to, yesterday you triggered something inside him. I don't know him so I don't have a clue what it might be."

"I didn't just imagine it?" Spring straightened and accepted the tissue her mother handed her.

"No, dear, I saw it, too."

"What do I do?" A stray sob shook Spring, then made her hiccup.

"Have you asked the Lord for his help?"

"Yes." *What else could I do?*

"Then, you've done all you can do. Just keep praying to God and loving Marco. Marco is an honest man, a man of integrity. When he sorts everything out, he'll come to his senses and tell you what's happened."

Spring closed her eyes, praying her mother was right, and that it wouldn't take another decade for Marco to come back to her.

Letting an hour pass after Spring's call, Anita decided she must take action. Fortunately, Paloma was at a friend's house. Santos had been called away by someone's plumbing emergency. She had the house to herself—the perfect time. She called Marco's cell phone number.

Marco answered.

She noted his dull voice. *No es un hombre feliz.* Not a happy man.

She tested her guess. "Is Spring still there?"

"No, she just stopped for a moment. I forgot our golf date."

Anita wasn't pleased to be proved right.

"Marco, I need you here pronto. It's an emergency."

"Mama—"

She hung up on him. And sat back to wait.

In exactly twenty-one minutes, Marco's car surged up her driveway. She rose, poured a fresh cup of black coffee for each of them.

He bounded in the kitchen door. "What's wrong?"

She turned to face him. *"You're wrong."* She handed him the coffee mug. "Sit down. It's time we had a talk."

He stared at her. "What?"

"Sit down, *por favor,*" she ordered.

Marco slid into the chair across from her at the scarred kitchen table that Santos had been nagging her to replace.

"Will you please tell me—"

"You hurt that sweet girl. She loves you, and you sent her away, didn't you."

"I don't know—"

"She loves you." She traced one of the grooves in the wooden tabletop. "Do you have any idea how rare true, real love is in this world?"

He stared at her. "Are you going to tell me what this is all about?"

"*Sí.* I watched the change in you at the garden show. Spring spent hours, days, weeks getting all the funds together so that you could have your clinic up and started by the end of this year, not ten years from now. And that's what's killing you, isn't it."

Her son glared at her.

She lifted her chin to him. "You wanted to work for years and do it *all by yourself,* didn't you?"

Her question had shocked him. She saw it on his face. "We should have had this talk years ago."

"What do you mean by that?"

Anita bit her lower lip. "It's always been difficult for us to speak of your father's death."

"Then, don't." He looked away, as he always did.

"We must. The time has come for you to let go of the past."

"I'm not holding onto the past."

She ignored his denial. "When your father died, something deep inside you altered. You had been a normal, happy child before that night. From that day, you became quiet and so focused on becoming a doctor."

"What is wrong with that? I had to be focused or…"

Seeking warmth, she placed both hands around the

hot mug. "I know. You would never have reached your goals unless you had drawn out the best that was in you. We were poor. I knew you'd have to fight for your place in the world, so I said nothing. I never tried to speak to you about this. But after you completed your training and bought your practice, I hoped that you would begin to take time to have a life. I have worried and worried over you the past two years."

He looked startled. "You never said a word."

"Would words have helped? I hoped some young woman would snare your heart. I even stooped to bringing some to your attention, something I'd vowed never to do."

He made a sound of disgust and wouldn't meet her gaze.

"Then this year, Spring came into your life. I knew right away that she was special and that you had feelings for her. You changed before my eyes. I thank God for her. Now you are not going to let your pride and pain destroy your life and hers. I refuse to let this happen."

"Destroy my life? You're not making sense."

"*You* are not making sense. Did you want a free clinic in that church or didn't you?" She challenged him with her eyes.

Marco fumed in silence. *This is none of your business.*

"Answer me."

"Yes, I wanted the free clinic—"

"But you wanted to do it all on your own. *Qué tonto!* What a silly man. How many years would it have taken you to raise the funds for it?"

"Not that long." He evaded his mother's penetrating eyes.

"Years! It would have taken years on your own. Should the sick people have to wait that long? To serve your pride!"

Stung, he snapped, "That's not true."

"That is how it looks to me. Tell me how it looks to you." She stared at him.

Anger roiled in the pit of his stomach. Words, phrases spun in his mind. His mother's accusation echoed in his heart. Pride? Was it really pride? Or something else?

"Why are you so angry at me now, at Spring?" she demanded. "You are angry because she stepped into your dream and made it come true, when you were too proud to ask. You wanted to spend years struggling to do this alone. You would deny others the joy of helping you accomplish a fine goal. Pride is the only answer I can think of. She hurt your pride because she did it quicker and easier than you could have alone. Tell me I'm wrong and make me believe it."

He wanted to tell her she was wrong, but he had no words. He couldn't lie. He had been so angry, he hadn't been able to think straight—not yet. Was his mother right?

"And I hate to say this to you, *mi hijo,* but it is the worst kind of pride. Putting your own accomplishment ahead of the well-being of others is wrong."

He couldn't reply. How could he make her understand? *It isn't just pride. The clinic was my task, my penance....*

"You're not God. He can do things in his way and use whom He chooses. Now, confess your pride to God, then get down on your knees and thank Him for bringing you a wonderful woman like Spring who loves you with her whole heart. She is a blessing from heaven." His mother got up and walked from the room.

His mother's words had gouged him like a sharp chisel. Each word had hit its target—his pride. Should *Tía* Rosita and others continue to go without health care because of him? Marco sat stunned by his mother's truth.

But something else tugged at him. He thought back over that painful night when his father died. For so many years he'd blocked the wrenching memories. His mother had said that he'd changed from that night, and she'd been right. What had he felt during the accident?

All the raw emotions, details—he let them rip through him. The odor of gasoline, the smell of burnt rubber, a blaring faraway siren, his own tears choking him. His father, gasping for breath, had held Marco's small trembling hand in his large rough palm and had left him. Horror had twisted inside him, squeezing him, leaving him breathless, crushed. Padre, *don't leave me.*

What had he felt that night? Had it been pride? No, he'd felt useless, filled with regret, remorse, guilt.

Marco rubbed his forehead and bowed his head. He didn't pray often away from church—but was this a mistake, too? Was it another token of his self-sufficient pride?

"I'm sorry, God. I forgot that I am just dust. I see my

pride and I'm ashamed. Please forgive me. But now I know guilt played a part in this also."

Still aching from his foray into the past, he remained with his head bowed for a long time as he pondered the years since his father's death. He'd driven himself from accomplishment to accomplishment. Guilt had been the whip that spurred him on. But in the achieving of goals, he'd depended on himself alone and no one else.

In his guilt, he'd let no one in. No man is an island, but he'd been a proud aloof island, and pride comes before a fall. Yesterday he'd fallen—he'd turned away from Spring, the beautiful and loving woman he'd fallen for at first sight. *How can I ever make it up to her? Will she give me a second chance?*

Chapter Fifteen

Marco drove directly to Spring. He bounded to her aunt's door and knocked.

Matilde opened the door. Glaring, she folded her hands across her ample waist. "You."

Her accusatory tone matched his self-recriminations. He drew in a deep breath. "I need to talk to Spring."

"You need to get down on your knees and kiss her hand."

"I intend to."

Matilde stepped back. "Then, you can come in. Spring! Marco is here for you."

A few moments later, Spring hung back at the other end of the hall. Her red-rimmed eyes belied her calm face. He noted her aunt standing behind her.

"Spring, will you go for a walk on the beach with me?"

She hesitated.

"You can go," Matilde said. "He's gonna apologize."

"He'd better apologize," Aunt Geneva added.

Marco held out his hand, and Spring came to him, but with downcast eyes. Her crestfallen look sliced him like a scalpel. Trying to think of the right words, he led her out the door. They followed the path through the gate down to the beach. The sun had passed its zenith. The beach was deserted except for an old woman and a little girl with copper curls who danced barefoot in the shallow surf. Sea foam puffed on the sand and diminutive crabs sidled away from their footsteps.

"Spring, I…" His voice faltered. "I apologize for acting like a jerk, an ungrateful jerk."

"Why?" Her voice was muffled against the sound of the waves. "What were you so angry about at the garden show? You wanted the clinic. Now you have it."

Marco plunged on. "But don't you see, I wanted it *my way.* I wanted to do it all by myself. I would have bumbled around for years trying to fund the clinic. I wouldn't have had a life, just a mission, a selfish one— even though it might have looked selfless. I didn't want your help. I didn't even want God's."

"Why?"

He struggled with himself, then decided to let go, tell her the unvarnished truth. "Do you remember when I told you about my father's death?"

She nodded but still wouldn't meet his eyes.

He halted and reached for her. After lifting her chin, he took her slender shoulders in both his hands. He'd look her in the eye—even though it pained him to speak of this. "I told you that watching my father die made me want to be a doctor. But more than that happened that night. Somehow I've felt responsible for my father's death…because I couldn't save him. I know it's not realistic—"

"But feelings are like that." Spring spoke in a shy voice as though they'd never spoken of love.

Like we're strangers, no! Don't shut me out, Spring! "I drove myself to be a doctor. Then, when I'd achieved that goal, I found another goal to sacrifice myself to."

"You mean, the clinic?"

"*Sí.* If I wasn't flogging myself toward another altruistic goal, I was failing."

"Just as you'd failed your father?"

She understands! He swallowed with difficulty. "*Sí.*"

"What does that mean to us? Is there an 'us'?" she asked, now looking into his eyes.

"I certainly hope so. Can you forgive me? I was wrong—"

She stopped his words with a kiss.

He wrapped his arms around her and put everything he had into his response.

A child's excited voice shrilled in the quiet. "Gramma, look! They're kissing. That man and lady are *kissing!*" The little girl giggled.

Spring started to giggle against his lips.

He felt her whole body shake with mirth. Pulling away an inch, he shouted, "Yes, I'm kissing her! And I'm proposing!" He slipped down onto one knee in the wet sand and claimed her hand. "Spring Kirkland, will you be my wife—even if I am a stubborn and proud man?"

She threw her head back and laughed out loud.

"Yes, Marco, I'll be your wife!" she shouted, then tugged him to stand up.

The little girl shrieked with glee, "Gramma, he was on his knee and now she's laughing!"

He swept Spring to him and kissed her with abandon. The sun golden on his back, the splash and ebb of the waves, the little girl's laughter, Spring's warm, soft form and his own joy—all flowing upward through him like a geyser. He'd never forget this moment for the rest of his life. *I'll never be alone again, Lord! I thank You— a thousand times, gracias!*

"Hi, Spring, this is—"

"Doree," Spring cut in.

"How's Mom?"

"Fine." Spring was afraid to ask the question uppermost in her mind. Her heart started beating faster.

"I'm here, too." Hannah's voice came over the line.

Spring had been planning to call Hannah herself, but it was ominous to have her sisters set up a conference call without warning her. "What's happened? Tell me."

"We have wonderful news!" Doree squealed. "Our grandfather and his three children are going to come to Hannah's wedding!"

"What?"

Hannah took over. "Doree called and explained

who she was and everything that had happened to Connie Wilson."

Doree burst in with her news. "He said that after he was wounded, he was laid up for a long time. He said he wanted to be well and able to support Connie before he returned to her. When he visited her parents, they told him she'd died, but he never knew anything about Connie having a baby—"

Hannah interrupted, "He said if he'd known, he would have taken Mother and raised her himself!"

Gladness for the present and sorrow over the past made it hard for Spring to speak, but she forced the words out. "Wait. Mother is the one who needs to hear this." She called for Mother and handed her the phone. "Doree has news for you."

Paloma's *quinceañería,* her fifteenth birthday party, was in full swing. A band played salsa music on a platform in the backyard. Children in their Sunday best danced around the adults on the driveway. A long table with nachos, enchiladas, frijoles, along with black beans, rice and plantains had been set up. On the grill, fragrant hamburgers, hot dogs and lime-basted chicken sizzled. Ladies in lawn chairs bordered the backyard fence. Out on the front porch and steps, the men congregated, laughing and joking.

At a picnic table, Marco sat at Spring's side holding her hand, which was adorned by a tasteful diamond engagement ring.

His mother and Spring's were admiring for the thousandth time the pastel portrait of Paloma that Spring had finished just a day before the party.

"I didn't know that Spring was an artist," his mother said, "but she did a fine job with our Paloma."

"She has a good eye," Mother admitted with modesty.

"I will treasure this always." His mother wiped her eyes.

"This is a thrilling time for both of you!" Aunt Geneva said. "A double June wedding for Hannah and Guthrie—"

"And for Spring and Marco!" his mother added with a smile.

"And I'm going to meet my father and my three half brothers and sister." Ethel dabbed her eyes, too. "You and Santos must stay with us, along with Aunty. We have plenty of room!"

"We would be honored." His mother's smile became mischievous. "Anyway, who knows? Next year we might be *abuelas*—grandmothers!"

Epilogue

The biggest predicament at Hannah's and Spring's double June wedding had brought a lot of different opinions—until a solution finally dawned on everyone.

Having a double wedding had sounded so efficient. After waiting for over a decade, Spring and Marco couldn't bear to spend a whole year making their own wedding plans. Hannah and Guthrie had made all their wedding plans and had been thrilled to share the day with Spring and Marco.

Now Hannah and Spring, dressed in their white gowns and the veils their mother had made them, waited in the Petite church vestibule. Spring couldn't hold back a few tears of joy.

"Stop that," Doree scolded. "If you start, we'll all be lost.

Hannah nodded. "For once, she's right."

Doree made a face at them.

The prelude music paused, then started again, signaling the procession to begin.

At Hannah's word, little Amber and Jenna, Guthrie's nieces—one blond, one brunette—wearing matching peach-colored dresses, started down the aisle scattering rose petals. Their younger brother, Hunter, paraded behind them, proudly holding up the white satin pillow to which two sets of wedding bands were tied.

When the three children reached the front, they went to sit beside their grandmother Martha and great-aunts Ida and Edith. Practical Hannah had decided children needed to be "anchored," not left to their own devices behind the two wedding couples.

Then Paloma, looking shy but very pretty in the peach gown originally meant for Spring, started down the aisle. From the groom's side of the church, Anita, Santos and *Tía* Rosita all beamed at her. Aunt Geneva and Matilde, sitting on the bride's side, dabbed their eyes and smiled encouragingly, too.

At the front of the church, Paloma took her place across from Pete Rasmussen, who'd flown up for the wedding. Exuberant Pete becoming Marco's closest friend ranked as another miracle on this day of wonders.

Lynda, Guthrie's sister, took her turn down the aisle. She stopped across from her husband, Bill. She and Bill had remarried in a private ceremony and were just back for a visit from the army base where they lived.

Always unpredictable Doree, the maid of honor, paraded down the aisle as though it were all a play in which she was performing. She faced Brandon, the best man, Guthrie's older brother.

Then came the solution to the dilemma of this unusual wedding—with their father as the officiating minister, Bill Smith was to give the brides away. Now Bill Smith gave an arm to both the brides, his two newly discovered granddaughters, and led them to the altar.

Though Spring's joy on the occasion of her own and her sister's wedding filled her to overflowing, it didn't compare to the exultation of seeing her mother sitting beside her half brothers and half sister as they watched Bill walk Spring and Hannah down the aisle. Spring bit back tears.

At the front of the church, blond Guthrie and dark Marco, both handsome in black tuxes for the occasion, waited for their respective brides. Between them, the brides' father, Garner, waited to read the wedding service.

Garner began. "Dearly beloved, we are gathered here…"

Standing just a step away from Marco, Spring waited for the moment that would make her mother supremely happy.

Father asked the important question: "Who gives these brides to these grooms?"

Tall and silver-haired, Bill declared proudly, "I give these brides—though I've only known them a day." As his eyes filled with tears, he looked over at his newly found daughter. "Ethel, I know Connie is smiling down on us from heaven today. Your name tells me that Connie still loved me. You see, Ethel was my mother's name. Connie named you Ethel as a sign, so I'd know you were my own dear child.

"How I wish I could have held you in my arms as a baby and walked you down the aisle when you married Garner. But by the grace of God, I'm here today, and we'll make up for the time we've lost—if He gives me a few more years. Praise God, my children and I have a whole new family to love."

* * * * *

Dear Reader,

I hope you enjoyed the romance of Spring and Marco. Marco made the mistake many make. He substituted doing good for trusting in God. Marco had plans to help others, but he wanted to do it all by himself. Pride and guilt can be powerful but destructive motivations. He was fortunate to have a wise and caring mother!

I hope you were touched by the happy endings for Spring and her sister, Hannah, but especially the reunion of their mother with her natural father. What a beautiful day!

God bless you with His bountiful love and blessings!

Lyn Cote

Love Inspired

For private investigator Wade Sutton, Dry Creek holds too many memories— and none of them fond. Yet he can't say no when the sheriff asks him to watch over a woman who might be in danger. Getting to know lovely Jasmine Hunter just might give Wade a good reason to call Dry Creek home once more….

Look for

Silent Night in Dry Creek

by
Janet Tronstad

*Available October
wherever books are sold.*

www.SteepleHill.com

Steeple
Hill®

LI87553

Love Inspired®

HEARTWARMING INSPIRATIONAL ROMANCE

Get more of the heartwarming inspirational romance stories that you love and cherish, beginning in July with SIX NEW titles, available every month from the Love Inspired® line.

Also look for our other
Love Inspired® genres, including:

Love Inspired® Suspense:
Enjoy four contemporary tales of intrigue and romance every month.

Love Inspired® Historical:
Travel to a different time with two powerful and engaging stories of romance, adventure and faith every month.

Available every month wherever books are sold,
including most bookstores, supermarkets,
drugstores and discount stores.

www.SteepleHill.com

When widowed rancher
Rory Branagan and his
young sons find
Goldie Rios sleeping on
their sofa, they are tempted
to let the disoriented
car-accident victim stay.
When her family heirloom
locket goes missing, they
help her search the farm.
Soon they discover the
perfect holiday gift—a
family that feels just right.

Look for

The Perfect Gift

by

Lenora Worth

*Available October
wherever books are sold.*

www.SteepleHill.com

Steeple
Hill®

LI87555

REQUEST YOUR FREE BOOKS!

2 FREE INSPIRATIONAL NOVELS
PLUS 2
FREE
MYSTERY GIFTS

Love Inspired®

YES! Please send me 2 FREE Love Inspired® novels and my 2 FREE mystery gifts (gifts are worth about $10). After receiving them, if I don't wish to receive any more books, I can return the shipping statement marked "cancel". If I don't cancel, I will receive 4 brand-new novels every month and be billed just $4.24 per book in the U.S. or $4.74 per book in Canada. That's a savings of over 20% off the cover price. It's quite a bargain! Shipping and handling is just 50¢ per book.* I understand that accepting the 2 free books and gifts places me under no obligation to buy anything. I can always return a shipment and cancel at any time. Even if I never buy another book, the two free books and gifts are mine to keep forever.

113 IDN EYK2   313 IDN EYLE

Name	(PLEASE PRINT)	
Address		Apt. #
City	State/Prov.	Zip/Postal Code

Signature (if under 18, a parent or guardian must sign)

Mail to Steeple Hill Reader Service:
IN U.S.A.: P.O. Box 1867, Buffalo, NY 14240-1867
IN CANADA: P.O. Box 609, Fort Erie, Ontario L2A 5X3

Not valid to current subscribers of Love Inspired books.

Want to try two free books from another series?
Call 1-800-873-8635 or visit www.morefreebooks.com

* Terms and prices subject to change without notice. Prices do not include applicable taxes. Sales tax applicable in N.Y. Canadian residents will be charged applicable provincial taxes and GST. Offer not valid in Quebec. This offer is limited to one order per household. All orders subject to approval. Credit or debit balances in a customer's account(s) may be offset by any other outstanding balance owed by or to the customer. Please allow 4 to 6 weeks for delivery. Offer available while quantities last.

Your Privacy: Steeple Hill Books is committed to protecting your privacy. Our Privacy Policy is available online at www.SteepleHill.com or upon request from the Reader Service. From time to time we make our lists of customers available to reputable third parties who may have a product or service of interest to you. If you would prefer we not share your name and address, please check here. ☐

LIREG09

Love Inspired.
HISTORICAL
INSPIRATIONAL HISTORICAL ROMANCE

After years of caring for others, Nola Burns is ready to live her own dream of running a Nantucket tearoom. And it will take more than charm for dashing entrepreneur Harrison Starbuck to buy her out. All Harry offers is a business proposition. So why should it bother him when Nola starts receiving threatening notes? As the threats escalate, he realizes he wants to keep her safe…forever.

Look for

An Unexpected Suitor

by

ANNA SCHMIDT

Available October wherever books are sold.

www.SteepleHill.com

Steeple
Hill®

placeholder